STORM CURSED

PATRICIA BRIGGS

ACE
New York

ACE
Published by Berkley
An imprint of Penguin Random House LLC
penguinrandomhouse.com

ISBN: 9780425281307

Ace hardcover edition / May 2019
Ace mass-market edition / January 2020

Printed in the United States of America
5 7 9 10 8 6

Cover art by Daniel Dos Santos
Cover design by Judith Lagerman

To the next generation:

Genevieve, Dylan, and Wren.
With faith and trust and fairy dust—
I wish you all your own happy thoughts
that you might fly.

ACKNOWLEDGMENTS

No book is written in a vacuum, and this one is no exception. All the faults, mistakes, and annoying things are my fault, but the following people have done their best to make this a good book: (in alphabetical order) Linda Campbell, Michelle Kasper, Ann Peters (aka Sparky), Kaye Roberson, Amy J. Schneider, and Anne Sowards.

Part of the fun of writing is going out and making new friends. This book owes much to Sheriff Jim Raymond and the rest of the good people at the Franklin County Sheriff's Office who kindly allowed Sparky and me to tour their office. In particular, Commander Rick Rochleau, who patiently answered lots and lots of questions and gave me insight into how the sheriff's office might interact with a pack of werewolves. He got himself permanently on my people-I-call-when-I-don't-know-what-I'm-doing list.

And, of course, Susann and Michael Bock have once again given Zee his magic (and his German). I am so glad that Michael decided to e-mail me about my bad German all those years ago.

Thank you, my friends.

One by one,
Two by two,
The Hardesty witches
Are traveling through.
With a storm of curses,
They call from their tomes;
They will drink your blood
And dine on your bones.

—CHILDREN'S JUMP ROPE RHYME,
OVERHEARD IN 1934
IN RHEA SPRINGS, TENNESSEE

1

~~~

"SO WHAT DID *YOU* DO, MARY JO?" CALLED BEN IN his crisp British accent.

Mary Jo shut her car door and started toward us and toward the mountainous metal barn that Ben and I waited beside. She gave Ben a quelling frown, and waited to speak until she had come up to us.

She asked, "What do you mean, what did I do?"

It was a little chilly, made more so by a brisk wind that blew a bit of hair I'd failed to secure in my braid into my eyes. The Tri-Cities don't cool off at night with quite the thoroughness that the Montana mountains I'd grown up with did, but night usually still kills the heat of day.

Ben bounced a little on his toes—a sign that he was ready and eager for violence. I could sense that his attention, like mine, was mostly on the barn, even though his eyes were on Mary Jo. "I killed Mercy three times in a single session of Pirate's Booty the night before last. I think that's why she woke me up to come out hunting tonight." He glanced at me and raised an eyebrow in an open invitation to address the situation.

Okay, that's not *exactly* what he said. As usual he spiced his language with profanity, but unless he spouted something truly amazing I mostly edited it out.

"You passed up the opportunity to gain a hundred Spanish doubloons in order to kill me that last time," I told him, unable, even days later, to keep the indignation out of my voice. In the fierce high-seas computer-generated battles the werewolf pack delighted in, a hundred Spanish doubloons was a treasure trove of opportunity for more or better weapons, supplies, and ship repairs. Only a homicidal maniac would give up a hundred doubloons to kill someone.

Ben gave me a wicked grin, an expression mostly empty of the bitter edge all of his expressions had once contained. "I was merely staying in character. Sodding Bart enjoys killing more than money, love. That's why his kill score is third on the board, just behind Captain Wolf and Lady Mockingbird."

Captain Wolf Larsen, stolen from the titular character of Jack London's *The Sea-Wolf*, is the nom de guerre of my mate and the pack Alpha. Lady Mockingbird, who was up by fifteen kills on everybody, teaches high school chemistry in her alter ego as Auriele Zao. She is a scary, scary woman. I've been told her high school students think so, too.

Ben's gaze, swinging back to Mary Jo, paused on the dark maw that gaped in the front of the huge metal barn, the only building within a mile of where we stood.

It was either very late at night or very early in the morning, depending on which side of sleep you were on. Dawn wasn't yet a possibility, but the waxing moon was strong in the night sky. The entrance to the barn was big enough to drive a pair of school buses through at the same time, and at least some of the ambient light should have made its way into the interior of the barn.

Ben considered the barn for a second or two, then turned a sharp grin on Mary Jo. "Mercy just confirmed why I'm here. What did you do to win the crappy job lottery?"

"Hey," I said, "before you all feel too sorry for yourselves, remember I'm out here, too."

"That's because you're in charge," Mary Jo said, her voice distracted, her eyes on the barn. "Bosses need to jump in the outhouse with the grunts occasionally. It's good for morale."

Mary Jo wore a T-shirt that read *Firefighters Like It HOT*, the last word written in red and gold flames. The shirt was loose like the sleep pants she wore, but her clothes didn't disguise her muscular warrior's body.

She looked away from the barn, turning her attention to Ben. "Maybe I owe this . . . *opportunity* to the way I treated her before Adam put his foot down." She tilted her head toward me, a gesture that, like Ben's raised eyebrow, asked for my input. She didn't meet my eyes as she once would have.

I was growing resigned to the way the pack dealt with me since my mate had declared me off-limits to anything but the utmost of respect on pain of death. By consensus, they mostly deferred to me, as if *I* were a wolf dominant to them.

It felt wrong and awkward, and it made the back of my neck itch. What did it say about me, I wondered, that I was more comfortable with all the snide comments and personal attacks than with gracious subservience?

"Wrong," I told her.

I pointed at Ben. "Killing me instead of getting rich is bad. Consider yourself punished."

I looked back at Mary Jo. "Ben is a simple problem with a simple solution. You are a stickier mess and this is not punishment. Or not really punishment. *This*"—I waved around us at the early-morning landscape—"is so you quit apologizing about the past for something you meant whole-heartedly at the time. And would do again under the same circumstances. Your apology is suspect—and annoying."

Ben made an amused sound, sounding relaxed and happy—but he was bouncing on the balls of his feet again. "That sounds about right, Mary Jo. If she were really getting back at you for all the trouble you caused her—it might land you on the List of Mercy's Epic Revenge. Like the Blue Dye Solution or the Chocolate Easter Bunny Incident. Getting called out at the butt-crack of dawn doesn't make the grade."

"So all I have to do is quit apologizing and you'll stop calling me out at three in the morning to chase goblins or hunt down whatever that freak thing we killed last week was?" she asked skeptically.

"I can't promise that," I told her. Mary Jo was one of the few wolves I could count on not to increase the drama or violence of a situation. "But it will . . ." Must be truthful. I gave her a rueful shrug. "It *might* mean I stop calling you first."

"Epic," she said with a wry glance at Ben. "Epic it is. I think I will probably quit apologizing." Then she said, "I suppose I'll find some other way to irritate you."

Hah! I'd been right—her apologies *had* been suspect. I had always liked Mary Jo—even if the reverse was not true.

She looked at the barn again and sighed heavily. "Have you spotted the goblin in there?"

She didn't bother trying to be quiet—none of us had been. Our prey could hear at least as well as any of us. If he was in there, he'd have heard us drive up. I was still learning about the goblins and what they could do, but I did know that much.

"No," I said.

"Do you think he's still in there?" she asked.

"He's still in there," I said. I held out my arm so they could see the hair rise as I moved it closer to the barn. "If he weren't, there wouldn't be so much magic surrounding it."

Mary Jo grunted. "Is it my imagination, or is it too dark in the barn?"

"I think I remember this," said Ben thoughtfully, peering into the barn. His clear British accent had the weird effect of making everything he said sound a little more intelligent than it really was, an effect that he conscientiously—I was convinced—canceled by adding the kinds of words responsible for whole generations of people who knew what soap tasted like. "You know—the whole seeing-fuck-all-in-the-dark thing?"

"I never was human," I told him. "I've always been able to see pretty well in the dark." After I said it, I had a thought.

There was a faint chance that the goblin's magic was affecting our eyesight rather than just spreading an illusion of darkness over the interior of the barn. I looked away from the barn to make sure my eyes were functioning as they should.

There was nothing but open fields around us, a couple of old wooden posts set into the ground as if they had once been part of a fence, and in the distance, a few miles away, I could see the new neighborhood of McMansion farmettes that I'd passed driving here.

Mesa, where we all now stood, was a little town of about five hundred people that was in real danger of being swallowed in the outward creep of Pasco's ever-growing population. It is flatter than most of the area around the Tri-Cities, with an economy primarily based in growing dryland wheat, hay, and cattle.

The town name is pronounced *Meesa*, not *Maysa*—which, even after all the years I've lived in the Tri-Cities, still strikes me as wrong. With so many Hispanic people living here, you'd think we would be capable of pronouncing a Spanish word correctly instead of borrowing from the ridiculous dialogue of a *Star Wars* character, right? But *Meesa* it is.

"Cain's hairy titties," muttered Ben, joining me in my observation of the rural setting. "What hermit was so misguided in life that he was hanging around this peopleless landscape at the bell end of the night and happened to see a freaking goblin disappear into a hay barn? And for that matter, goblins are city denizens like me. What the shagging hell is it doing out here?"

"No one living was here when it came," I told him in a sinister voice.

He gave me a look.

In a confidential whisper I said, "I talk to dead people."

He scowled at me. I wasn't lying but he knew me well enough to know that I was pulling his leg. He stared up at the barn with narrowed eyes. He snorted.

"Bollocks, Mercy. There's cameras here."

I don't think he actually saw them—I hadn't spotted any

yet. But Ben was a computer nerd; when in doubt, his brain focused on electronics.

"A surveillance system connected to the owner's iPhone," I confirmed, dropping my dramatic pose. "Apparently there was a party involving underage participants and several kegs of alcohol that ended up with a mess and several thousand dollars of damage. Thus the cameras and a motion sensor were installed. They made the farmer happy by interfering in two underage keggers, and tonight they alerted the owner of the barn that he had an uninvited guest. He called me."

"And you called us," said Mary Jo dryly. "Thank you for that."

I grinned at her and gave her my best John Wayne impression. "It's a dirty job, ma'am, but someone has to do it."

"Where's Adam?" asked Ben suddenly. "He wouldn't send you out alone after a goblin, not even a half-arsed, hay-shagging knob who doesn't know any better than to keep to the city like a civilized goblin should."

Like me, the whole pack had been learning about goblins, and gaining a new respect for them.

I shrugged. "He wasn't home when the call came. Top secret meetings. I left a message on his voice mail."

"A meeting at this hour?" asked Mary Jo.

"Goes with his job," I told her.

Adam, my mate, was not only the Alpha of our local werewolf pack, but he owned a security firm with two bases of operation that mostly did hush-hush government contracts. Meetings that went overnight were unusual—but not unheard-of. The past month there had been seven of them.

He couldn't tell me anything about the meetings—and that bothered him more than it bothered me. I didn't need to know who or what he was securing for whom. I knew my husband. He would never do anything he considered immoral, and that was good enough for me. Danger was a given—but he was military trained and a werewolf. He was as capable of protecting himself as anyone I knew.

Yes, I was scared anyway. But he was scared about some of the things I got involved in, too. We'd both gone into this relationship, this marriage, with our eyes wide open.

As long as he didn't *want* to keep secrets from me, I could deal with it when he had to.

"Ben had a good question," Mary Jo told me. "Why is a goblin hiding out in a barn in Mesa?"

"Running from justice," I said. "Probably. Do you remember all the headlines last week about the monster that killed that police officer out in Long Beach, California?"

"Goblin," said Ben thoughtfully. "I remember. His face was plastered all over the news. Are we sure this is that goblin?"

I pulled out my cell phone and showed him the snapshot of the goblin's face that the farmer's camera had caught. The area around the front of the barn had been pretty well lit before the goblin destroyed the security light.

There had been a camera when the goblin killed the cop, too. That video, grainy and indistinct, had been played over and over again on the news. The actual killing had been off-screen, but the goblin's face and inhumanity had been unmistakable.

Mary Jo peered around Ben and I tilted the screen to her.

"Not a pretty face," she observed. "What about glamour, though?"

Glamour was the magic the fae used to alter their appearance.

"Why would a fae want to look like someone who killed a member of law enforcement?" I asked. "That would be unholy dumb. It seems more reasonable to assume that this one is one of the goblins whose glamour isn't as effortless, so when he doesn't actively need to blend in, he resumes his normal appearance."

The farmer who'd called me an hour or so ago had been apologetic. His son worked in the Franklin County Sheriff's Office, and that was the law enforcement office he should have called.

"But I figure this creature didn't seem to have had much trouble killing that policeman down in California, and my son is working tonight," he'd said. "I thought I'd call you first and see if you might consider Mesa a part of the territory your pack protects." He paused. "If you come out, I'll have some explaining to do, but I expect that's better than attending my son's funeral."

I'd decided then and there, without consulting my husband, that we did consider Mesa a part of our territory. If I continued this trend, I was going to make us responsible for half the state.

But humans had very little chance against a goblin. I wasn't about to sit by while people were thrown into a situation they weren't equipped for when I was able to handle it safely. *Mostly* safely. Probably safely.

My eyes caught a movement in the cavernous darkness. Maybe if I changed to coyote I'd see better. Coyote eyes are good at seeing moving things in the dark. But I can't talk while I'm a coyote, so I couldn't relay intelligence to my allies. Taking the goblin on as a coyote would be even stupider than sending the human Franklin County Sheriff's deputies after it. The farmer had been right; a normal human stood no better chance than a coyote did against a goblin. Goblins might be considered among the less powerful of the fae . . . but that didn't mean they were weak.

I patted the steel and silver weapon that hung at my hip for reassurance.

The first game of ISTDPB4 (Instant Spoils: The Dread Pirate's Booty Four) that the pack had played right after we'd gotten back from Europe I had, totally uncharacteristically, won. Usually I was among the first to go—due to my special high-value target status as She Who Makes Treats as Soon as She Dies. But everyone had been treating me like a weakling after I got myself kidnapped by vampires. Irritated, I'd used dirty tricks to take out the usual winners and fought the rest to the bitter end.

Ben maintained that I'd won because they were all trying to coddle me. Honey said I was better at deviousness after being held by Bonarata, the vampire Machiavellian ruler of Europe. Po-tay-to, po-tah-to—both equally true. Adam said, with a sly smile, that the only reason anyone else ever won was because I didn't usually try too hard, but this time I'd had something to prove. Ahem. It is only right and proper that one's mate regards one with rosy glasses. Regardless, the next game, normalcy returned and they obliterated me in two rounds.

However, in honor of the occasion of my only win in three months, the pack formally presented me with a prize. Normally winners get fun things like foil-covered chocolate coins or kid-sized eye patches. Once, at the end of a four-game winning spree, Auriele had received a Lego pirate ship complete with plastic Jolly Roger.

But I earned a cutlass, the real thing, steel-bladed and silver-hilted. As a bonus, I got a whole bunch of werewolves who fancied themselves experts, eager to teach me how to defend myself so that no stupid vampires would ever be able to kidnap me again.

I didn't tell them that Excalibur herself would not have saved me from Bonarata. It is difficult to defend yourself when you are unconscious. Instead, I settled in and learned because *next* time I might have a chance to fight. My pack was thoroughly spooked at how easily the vampires had stolen me away—and I could feel their tension decrease as my skill with the cutlass increased. That made me work even harder.

I had some experience with a katana, which helped more than I'd expected. Most of the wolves who tried to teach me were no better than I was once you made allowances for the advantages of speed and strength that being a werewolf bestowed. They still made good sparring partners. But a couple of wolves really knew how to use a blade. The best of those were our lone submissive wolf, Zack, and the one-legged Sherwood Post.

I carried the cutlass wherever I went. It made me feel better, and it made the pack feel better. I'd expected to have trouble with the police, but it seemed to make them feel

better, too. Apparently if our pack was going to be protecting the humans in our territory from the fae, my carrying a
sword made us look more like we were capable of doing
our job. After the troll-bridge incident, we pack members
had achieved brothers-in-arms status with most of the law
enforcement types.

So I was armed with the cutlass and my favorite carry
gun, but my growing respect for the capabilities of goblin-
kind left me with no illusions about my ability to take down
a goblin. I was, when it came right down to it, not that much
better off against the supernaturally gifted than a run-of-
the-mill human was. Coyotes are not huge and powerful
predators. Which was why Mary Jo and Ben, my werewolf
minions, were with me.

"What are we going to do? Stand out here until the goblin gives up and runs out screaming, driven desperate by
boredom?" asked Mary Jo after a bit.

I listened for sarcasm and didn't hear any. That didn't
mean she didn't feel it—just that she was being careful. My
mate had been very clear when he put the fear of God into
the whole pack concerning me. I bit back a growl.

"We," I told them, "are waiting for backup." I looked at
the sky worriedly. I had just opened my garage for business
again two days ago, so I couldn't afford to be late. "I hope,
anyway."

"Who else annoyed you enough to call?" Ben asked.

"He didn't annoy me," I told him, "but I figured that we
might need an expert, so I contacted Larry."

"The goblin king," Mary Jo said, a little awe in her
voice. It might have been horror rather than awe, but I took
the optimistic view. "You called the *king of the goblins* in
the middle of the night. What did *he* do to you?"

Larry had moved to the Tri-Cities a couple of years ago
because, he said, matters were getting interesting here.
Common lore said that goblins ran from trouble, but you
couldn't prove it by Larry. I wasn't really sure if he was the
ruler of all the goblins or just the ones in the Tri-Cities—he
tended to be vague about specifics in the way of most of

the more powerful fae I'd dealt with. The only thing that Larry had said in my hearing about his rank was that goblins didn't use the term "king."

"Fucking goblin problem," said Ben good-humoredly before I could answer Mary Jo. "Who else should she have called, the elephant-shagging king of the expletive-deleted goblins?" That last sentence was about four words longer and he didn't actually say "expletive-deleted."

"To be fair," Larry answered mildly from just on the far side of my car, "I was still up. I tend to be nocturnal."

I hadn't heard a vehicle drive up, nor had I seen or heard where he'd come from. I'd have felt stupid for not being more alert, but Ben and Mary Jo both subtly stiffened because Larry had taken them by surprise, too. None of us were crippled with mere human senses. He shouldn't have been able to approach us without *someone* detecting him.

With the darkness hiding the unreal color of his eyes and with gloves on his hands, he could easily have passed for human. I couldn't tell if he was actively trying or if it was just an effect of the night.

He wore his medium-brown hair in a cut that even I recognized as expensive. His jeans looked too tight for hand-to-hand fighting except that they stretched easily as he moved. His shirt was a black tee that fit like a second skin.

He stopped on his brisk journey to close the distance between us as he passed my car, an old Jetta that had been well-used before the twenty-first century dawned. It was my chosen replacement for my obliterated Rabbit and it had proved to be a challenging project, one I was nowhere near completing.

Larry examined the Jetta mutely for a moment, then said, "Are you sure this is legal to drive?"

"All the lights work," I told him.

My Vanagon, which was otherwise in showroom condition despite its age, had a coolant leak somewhere. With a radiator in the front and the engine in the rear of the fifteen-foot-long van, finding a leak that was probably a pinhole was a long and frustrating process. Adam had taken the new SUV that had replaced the SUV the vampires had smooshed with a semi. That had left only the Jetta to take me goblin hunting.

I'd had to jury-rig the left rear turn signal with wires that ran out the trunk to the light, which was held on with zip ties. Then I'd crossed my fingers and headed out.

I was hopeful it would make it home as well. In case it didn't, I'd thrown my mobile tool kit into the backseat—or rather into the space where the backseat would someday be.

"Princess," said Larry doubtfully, "I think you have your work cut out for you. This car looks older than Zee." But his eyes had released my car and traveled to the barn. When he moved, he didn't hesitate, walking past me and the werewolves and into the doorway of the barn, where he stopped.

"Hey, you!" he called, standing on the edge between night-dark and lightless dark. The white toes of his New Balance tennis shoes were cut off from my vision as thoroughly as if they had been taken off with an axe.

Larry waited, his body intent, but no one answered him. He said something else—this time in a language with tongue clicks and a couple of odd sounds I'm not sure a human mouth could make. He wasn't particularly loud, but whatever he said was effective.

"No!" shouted a squeaky male voice from inside the barn. "Sanctuary. I claim sanctuary from this wondrous and glorious city said to be safe for fae and foe alike. Grant this me, dear my lord. An it is granted, I will happily emerge into thy keeping, great one."

I didn't know how old goblins got. I didn't know if they were one of the immortal or nearly immortal fae. I'd given back the only trustworthy book that recorded what the different kinds of fae were like before I'd known exactly how much I was going to need that knowledge.

I'd gotten the impression that the goblins were one of the shorter-lived races of the fae, but there was something about the way the voice in the darkness put together sentences and ideas that indicated that my memory or my interpretation might have been wrong. It was possible that "shorter-lived" meant something different to the fae woman who had written the book than it did to me. Or maybe our fugitive spent too much time at summer Shakespeare festivals.

Larry turned his body to me without taking his gaze away from the interior of the barn. "Do you know what he is running from?"

"Last week a goblin killed a police officer in California. The video of the incident was all over the news," I began, but paused when Larry glanced my way for a hair's breadth. Long enough for me to see the odd expression on his face.

"And people say humans don't have magic," he muttered, once again facing our fugitive. He made a circling gesture with one hand. "Never mind. Go on."

"He has a pretty distinctive scar," I told him, gesturing at the scar on my own right cheek. "His is a lot bigger. A goblin with that scar killed the police officer in LA who was trying to arrest him. The police have a manhunt"—I cleared my throat and corrected myself—"a goblinhunt aimed at him."

Larry muttered something to himself in that other language. Then he called out, "Apparently you have an affinity for getting caught on camera. Careless of you to allow a *mindless human device* to record you doing murder. And you let it catch you murdering a *knight* of the human law, no less."

He emphasized some of the words oddly, leading me to suspect that there were several deadly insults buried in Larry's comments. I knew that getting caught was very poorly thought of in the goblin culture—but I hadn't known that getting caught by technology was viewed as even worse. I found it reassuring that, apparently, even to the goblins, killing a police officer was a bad thing.

"No, no—I killed none," our prey squeaked. "No child of humankind died at my causing, great one. No. No murderer I. I killed nary a one. Not knight nor even child. Not a wee boy with blinky shoes. Not me. I would never so defy the Gray Lords, great one. No more would I ever defy thy commands."

That gave me pause.

As a matter of course, werewolves don't lie because most werewolves can tell if someone is lying. I was raised by werewolves, and although I am not one, apparently a coyote can tell if someone is lying, too. I only lie when I think I can get away with it.

But the fae don't lie because they cannot lie. They can twist the truth until it is a Gordian knot, but they cannot lie.

Still, that goblin's words seemed oddly specific for someone who hadn't killed a policeman or, apparently, a child with blinky shoes. But he wasn't guilty because he said so. Maybe, I thought, he'd been a witness. But his words sounded like a lie to me. Not even a good lie.

Both the werewolves relaxed, a subtle softening of their stances. He wasn't guilty because he said so. And unlike human criminals, that was actually a true thing, no matter how much it sounded like a lie.

Mary Jo turned to me. "Do we need to offer this goblin sanctuary? If the humans are going after him just because he is a goblin . . . isn't that what our claiming dominion over the Tri-Cities is all about?"

"No, love," Ben said in a mock-sorrowful tone designed—as Mary Jo's had not been—to carry to the goblin hidden in the barn. "Not our thing at all. We keep people safe—but sanctuary is a whole different level of stupid."

I was still trying to figure out how the goblin was being so specific if he had not killed the police officer and, apparently, a child. Goblins have glamour. Maybe another goblin—or one of the fae—had been trying to frame this one?

Larry's mouth twisted in a grimace. "At least tell me that you didn't get caught *on camera* killing the child," he said in a resigned voice.

I frowned at Larry. First, because he sounded as if getting caught on camera had been worse than killing the child. But mostly I frowned at him because he sounded as if he knew that the goblin was guilty. But the goblin couldn't lie.

"No, not I," said the voice inside the barn earnestly. "I killed not the wee boy with his two sweet blue eyes. Eyes like a robin's egg so round and innocent and tasty they were. Nor killed I the fierce-voiced police officer who came to stop me."

Mary Jo and Ben looked as perplexed as I felt.

"I am *innocent*," wailed the goblin in the barn. "Innocent and they will harm me if you do not protect me from the humans."

"The fae are part of the bargain we made," I said slowly. Did we owe the goblin sanctuary? I might have to go read the whole stupid document we'd signed again. At this rate, I'd have it memorized by Christmas.

"And goblins *are* fae," said Mary Jo. Larry snorted. Mary Jo continued, "At least insomuch that they have glamour and they are forced to tell the truth." But her voice was hesitant.

"We are a part of that ancient bargain, yes," agreed Larry, frowning at the barn. "If the powers that be hear us lie, a terrible and mortal fate comes to us, as to all fae. Those greater in power may fight off their fate for a time, but for the lesser fae, like goblins, we die the moment a lie, knowingly spoken, leaves our lips."

"That means we do need to protect him," said Mary Jo without enthusiasm. She looked at me and then away, careful not to express in any other way that she held me responsible for the pickle the pack was in. But then she straightened her shoulders, lifted her chin, and said, firmly, with an undertone of satisfaction I don't think she intended me to hear, "We protect the innocent."

She wasn't the only wolf who was finding . . . solace in their new role as heroes, which had replaced their old role of being monsters. The whole demeanor of our pack had been lightening up since my rash declaration on the Cable Bridge.

The *old* Cable Bridge. The new Cable Bridge was a year out, at least. Engineers were having trouble trusting the site after one of the Gray Lords of the fae had opened up the earth there and let it swallow the old bridge. The fae had offered to build another bridge, but so far the city planners were smart enough not to take them up on that offer. I think it was the no-steel part that bothered them, but I was pretty sure taking gifts from the fae would have been the bigger problem.

Ben sighed—he had obviously been looking forward to a fight. "It's not what we signed on for—but I guess it's what we have to do, since he's innocent."

Ben hadn't noticed exactly what Larry had said, not the way I had. Maybe I was paranoid, or maybe I'd just been spending too much time with the fae lately.

"I be innocent," said the fugitive goblin, sounding as though he was approaching the opening of the barn. His voice was fervent as he repeated, "I be innocent."

Larry rubbed his face, looked at me, and sighed, a sound more heartfelt than Ben's had been. "I am about to reveal something . . . Mercy, this cannot get back to the fae."

"The not-goblin fae," I clarified.

He nodded. "Yes, those folk."

"Okay," I told him. "We don't owe it to the other fae to give them goblin secrets."

"Swear to it," he said seriously. "This goes beyond me. This is for the safety of me and mine. Swear you will tell no one what I do here."

"No, great one," said the voice in the barn, his voice low and solemn. "No. Betraying our secrets is not worth my unworthy death, no it isn't. I should leave, a small and unimportant child, I. My fate is not worth betraying a great secret to such as these."

"*Silence!*" roared Larry in a very un-Larry-like voice. "Thou hast caused enough trouble for our kind. Thou hast no voice in what I choose to do."

"Everything I know," I warned him, "Adam knows. Everything Adam knows Bran knows."

Larry nodded. "Yes, yes, of course. Such is the way of mates. And Bran Cornick, too. The Marrok keeps secrets that make this seem small—unless, I suppose, you are a goblin."

"I will tell no one else," I told him. I looked at Ben and Mary Jo.

"I swear to keep this secret," Mary Jo said.

Ben said, "If it's not something that will harm people I care about, I will keep your secret."

Larry looked at us, all three of us, and sighed. "There was a day when I'd have bound you to silence and you would not have been able to speak, you know."

Yes, I thought, too much time with the fae. Or maybe just Larry. "There was a day when" didn't really mean he'd lost that power, though I knew that many fae held a lot less power than they once had. I thought about keeping my observation to myself. But if we were to share secrets, it would be best to establish an honesty baseline.

"I suspect you could do that on this day, too," I told him, and the look on his face told me that it was true—and that he was pleased I had caught him.

"So why don't you?" I asked him.

He shook his head. "I am a romantic and an optimist, Mercy Hauptman. I think that my relationship with you and yours, right here and right now, might be the reason my people survive the next hundred years. If I betrayed your trust—the trust that led you to call me to deal with one of my own—if I betrayed that trust, then I would wipe away any chance of real friendship between us, yes?"

"Yes," growled Ben, not waiting for me.

"Good enough," Larry said. "So I will trust that you three will understand the gravity of what I show you—that you will understand the consequences to my people and to your people, as well as all the humans on this planet, if the fae know what a very few of my people can do. And I trust you will tell no one except for Adam, and that he will tell only Bran Cornick, who will tell no one." He sighed again. "Unless he thinks it will benefit the werewolves. Ah, well."

He turned to the barn and spat out magic in a series of vocalizations that had nothing to do with language—and everything to do with communicating with the ground I stood on and the air I breathed. The noise he made hurt my ears, pleased my eyes with flashes of brilliant lights that were somehow still sound, and made my muscles turn to water.

Magic and I have a complicated relationship, but this was a new reaction.

I sat down on the ground so that I didn't fall. Ben—who was apparently not affected at all—knelt beside me. "Mercy?"

I shook my head, my attention on the barn where the unnatural shadows receded into normal darkness. Maybe a human would not have been able to tell the difference, but I could.

Larry dusted his hands together and said, in a voice I hardly recognized as his, because I'd never heard him sound so threatening, "Now, you rotting piece of putrid meat, *now* tell these good people how you didn't kill that police officer, how you didn't kill the wee boy with blinky shoes. Let the Powers take you and save us all some effort."

I let Ben help me back to my feet.

"But they sparkled like stars," said the voice in the barn, markedly smaller than it had been before. "How could I not dine upon that, great one? How could I let a human, *a human*, take me captive? How could I suffer that he touch me, who was once first of thirty?"

"He lied," said Ben softly. "He is a goblin, is fae, is bound by your contract—and still he was able to lie."

Larry nodded. "He hid behind a veil of magic so as not to trigger the curse of the bargain we made—that magic is a version of glamour that the other fae do not have. Yet. A secret that we have held . . ." He sighed and shook his head. "Forever. Until this driveling fool, so stupid he could not avoid a camera, tried to take advantage of my allies."

I was silent because I was too busy putting this together with something I'd heard. There had been a fae who had betrayed a bargain she had made with Bran a few years ago. He had trusted her to keep the peace when representatives of the European werewolves had come to Seattle to be told that the Marrok intended to clue the humans in that there were werewolves in the world. She had lied to him. It had always bothered me that that fae could lie—even though Bran said she'd paid for those lies in the end.

I wondered if that fae, the one from Seattle, had known

the goblin's secrets or had invented her own. If one fae could lie . . .

"Much better that they, too, believe that they cannot," murmured Larry to me, though I don't think I said anything out loud.

"So why now?" asked Mary Jo suspiciously. "That . . ." She hastily changed the word she was going to use. "That goblin in there is right. He isn't worth giving up a secret this big."

Larry shook his head. "We are an odd bunch, we goblins," he told her. "So little power compared to the rest of the fae. And yet some of us have gifts they would envy if they knew. I? I can sometimes sense important events in time." He looked at me. "I think that it is going to be important that you know that this goblin could lie to you. I don't know why or when. I don't know that it will be important to me. But I do think that your trust in me, Mercy, in my people, might be the saving of us all. And if I give you my people's most closely guarded secret, I believe you will remember that."

I blinked at him.

He flashed me a smile full of teeth and then looked at the wolves. "Want to join me in the hunt?"

"Absolutely," said Ben with an eager breath.

"That's what we're here for," agreed Mary Jo. She sounded more resigned than excited, but I could feel her intensity.

Larry glanced at me.

"I know," I said, resigned. "I'm not up to his weight. How about I guard the door in case you let him get by you."

"We won't let him get by us," said Mary Jo, stung.

Ben grunted. "Now you've screwed the pooch," he told her. "Never tempt fate."

No one felt like waiting around for the ten or fifteen minutes it would take for the werewolves to change, so all of them were in human form when they entered the barn. I could see them moving in a cautious triangle until darkness obscured them from my sight.

I unsheathed my cutlass and listened to the doomed goblin scream my name. There were some downsides to being called Mercy. First, I was really tired of that Shakespeare monologue. Everyone I'd ever dated, not excepting Adam, quoted it to me at some point. Did they think I'd never heard it before? Second, it sometimes left me standing in the dark, listening to someone being killed while they cried out to me.

For Mercy.

This one deserved what was about to happen to him, but I still tried to tune out the noises in the barn.

"She said, she promised I could come here for safety," cried the goblin frantically before it shrieked—a noise that ceased in the middle of a crescendo. "She promised."

She who? I thought.

I didn't have time to wonder about it because his words were followed by a wave of magic that weakened my knees. The ground rumbled and shook as chaff and dust billowed out of the barn. Four-foot-by-eight-foot bales of hay crowded out of the entrance to the barn like some giant child's blocks knocked over by a careless blow. The ground vibrated under my feet as they continued to fall for a few seconds more.

I didn't think even a thousand-pound bale would kill a werewolf—and I hadn't felt the hit from the pack bonds that would tell me if someone was dead or (less reliably) badly injured. But those bales had been stacked pretty high.

I started toward the barn but stopped when the fugitive goblin emerged from the barn, crawling over a bale. He wasn't running but moving silently, his attention behind him. He was taller than Larry, his build nearly human, but his bare feet were oddly formed—more like a dog's feet than a human's, with long toes unshielded by sock or shoe. If he was using glamour, he wasn't using it to try to look human despite the sweatpants he wore.

I took the cutlass in my left hand and drew my Sig with my right. The practical part of me knew that I should just shoot, but shooting someone in the back who had not (yet) tried to hurt me seemed wrong.

I could hear Ben now, swearing a blue streak in between

coughs. He didn't sound hurt—just angry. A small part of me listened for Mary Jo or Larry, but the rest of me was focused on the goblin.

This goblin killed a child, I reminded myself grimly, raising my arm.

I don't know if I would have shot him in the back or not because he turned his head and noticed me, spinning gracefully around to face me.

He hesitated and I shot him twice in the body and once in the head. The body shots made him flinch but there were no wounds in his chest where I shot him. Maybe I should have brought the .44 Magnum—but then I couldn't have shot one-handed with any degree of accuracy. The third bullet, aimed at his forehead, bounced off some sort of invisible shield and zinged off on a different trajectory.

He dropped his head a little, like a bull getting ready to charge, and laughed. "Little coyote. I was the first of thirty. Do you think you and your toy can stop—"

I shot him again. Twice. The first hit him just left of the center of his chest instead of bouncing off, so whatever magic he'd worked required effort rather than being an impenetrable shield he could keep up forever. But the second shot that should have hit him in the same place missed him entirely.

He didn't dodge the bullet. Bullets are very fast. He was just faster than I was. Between the time it took me to reacquire the target and pull the trigger, he'd moved out of the path of my aim and charged at me.

I dropped my gun—not by choice—rolled out of the way, and tried to nail him with the cutlass at the same time. I succeeded at the first two, but my left hand is not as quick as my right. He had no trouble sliding away from my blade, even putting in an unnecessary somersault in the air and landing on his feet like a performer in Cirque du Soleil.

It might have given him the opportunity to show off, but my cutlass swipe did keep him far enough away from me that I could roll back to my feet.

I have speed. It is my best superpower. I am as quick as

the werewolves, probably as fast as the vampires. I was not as fast as that goblin was. It was a good thing, then, that I didn't have to defeat him. All I had to do was keep him from escaping until the others emerged from the barn.

Unhappily for me, from the sounds I was hearing from the barn, it might take a while for my compatriots to fight their way free of the hay. Mary Jo and Larry were alive, I'd heard their voices, so that was something.

The goblin smiled at me. "Ah, it has teeth, does it?" He displayed his own, sharper and greener than human teeth. "That's fine. I like a bite or two with my dinner."

The hairs on the back of my neck stood up as he made a little throwing gesture toward me. Magic, I thought, though I couldn't tell what it had done. I couldn't afford to worry about it either, because, smiling broadly, he whipped out a long copper knife, maybe two-thirds the length of my cutlass, and struck.

I met his blade—his attack had been ludicrously forth-right and slow, especially given the speed he'd already demonstrated. Almost, I thought, as though whatever magic he'd thrown at me should have taken care of the need to pay attention to my blade.

Steel bit into the copper as I absorbed the interesting and surprising news that, for once, my weird semi-immunity to magic seemed to have (finally) worked on something that was really trying to hurt me.

The impact of the blades made him hiss in what sounded like surprise. But he didn't hesitate, changing his trajectory and his weapon in midattack. He opened his mouth and lunged for my throat with his big, sharp teeth.

Not for nothing had I endured a month of pirate-loving, self-styled-expert werewolves determined that I would wield the blade as well as any aspirant to Anne Bonny's title of Pirate Queen ever had.

I freed my blade from the weak final throes of his knife attack and backhanded him with the cross guard in the same motion. Sadly, the cross guard was silver (because werewolves) and not iron like the blade. Cold iron, even in the form of steel, would have gotten his attention.

My blow knocked him back, but he grabbed me by the shoulder and knee and took me down to the ground.

Down to the ground is bad when you are dealing with humans. When dealing with creatures of preternatural strength, it is deadly. I managed, somehow, to bring up the cutlass between us without cutting myself. The flat side of it pressed against me from hip to opposite shoulder. Which meant it did the same thing to him in reverse.

Iron is a problem for most fae to one degree or another, but it varies. The goblin screeched, a sound that made my ears ring, and the smell of scorched flesh abruptly hit my nose.

I was hopeful for a moment, but there was no flash fire. All the blade did was singe him a bit.

My martial arts instructor, my human one, recommends against going for a man's testicles under most circumstances, despite the advice of movies and novels. Most men over the age of puberty have a lifetime of protecting that area, so it is difficult to get a clean shot. And if you don't nail the man hard enough to incapacitate him, all you've done is really tick him off.

The same thing, evidently, is true of goblins and steel.

"Thou wilst die," he growled at me, pinning me with one arm and lifting the battered knife he still held with the other. Expecting, as most reasonable homicidal goblins would, that since I was not strong enough to break free, I would have to just lie there and die.

Hah.

I shifted to coyote and, while he struggled to parse what had just happened, I wiggled out of his hold, leaving my clothing behind but not my weapon. A little foolishly (I was told later), I snagged the cutlass in my teeth as I ran.

I grabbed it by the hilt. No one outside of those cheesy old movies or computer games would really grab the blade itself unless they were very, very certain that the blade was a dull movie prop.

I dashed to the barn, putting a hay bale to my back. Then I regained my human form and, naked, took the cutlass in my right hand and faced the goblin. He'd regained his feet while I'd run. He snarled something uncomplimentary and bounded toward me, the battered copper blade raised high.

I raised my blade to a guard position—and then Larry jumped over my head and landed light-footed on the ground about six feet in front of me. Which put him directly in the path of the charging goblin. He had no weapon that I could see.

"Mine," Larry said in a voice so power-laden it could have belonged to the Marrok.

Before the other goblin could do more than slow his charge, his scarred face blank with horror, Larry reached out, grabbed the goblin by shoulder and leg—a move very like what the goblin had used on me, but even more effective. And brutal. The goblin king used the other's forward momentum to swing him high—and jerk his shoulders and legs in the opposite direction than they go.

It was a move requiring skill and strength that I wasn't sure any of the werewolves could have duplicated. In one move, Larry broke the other goblin's back and dislocated his hip with a twin pop that sounded like a pair of guns going off.

He dropped the goblin on the ground and let him writhe for a moment. Then, with a snake-quick movement, he stopped the screaming by breaking the downed goblin's neck.

"Well, fuck," said Ben from on top of the hay bale behind me. "Larry, you wanker, stealing all the fun."

I twisted to look. Mary Jo and Ben were both standing on top of the bale that Larry had jumped from. Mary Jo had a cut on her ribs and blood on one hip, though the wound it had come from had already healed over.

A slice on Ben's cheekbone was fading, but his shirt flapped loosely from the top of his shoulder to the bottom seam. There was a piece of muscle missing from his pectoral. The skin had settled over the top of the injury, but I knew that it would take a few days for the muscle to fill in.

I turned my attention back to the most dangerous of us here.

Larry was, as far as I could see, unharmed.

"So that's done," Larry told me cheerfully, as if he hadn't just brutally killed someone, shedding that aura of power he'd gathered so easily it was disconcerting. Bran, the Marrok, could do that, too.

Larry stared down at the body a moment, frowned, then pulled a long-bladed bronze knife from somewhere on his person. He grabbed the goblin by his hair and sliced the head off the body. It seemed like overkill. Maybe, I thought, Larry needed to make sure that the other goblin was dead.

The knife must have been extra sharp because he looked like he didn't make any more effort than someone cutting up a watermelon. He dropped the head on the ground, cleaned off his knife, then pointed it at the head.

To me he said, "Take that to your human law enforcement. Tell them that the goblin king showed up and brought justice for their lost child and the guardian who gave his life so valiantly. Tell them I regret that I could not do more than ensure that this one will do no more harm."

"I thought you didn't call yourself the goblin king," I said.

He shrugged and sheathed his knife through an opening in his pant leg—it looked like a dangerous way to sheathe something that sharp. "Good publicity is good publicity. It was recently pointed out to me that I am what I am; it doesn't matter what title someone outside our community tapes to my forehead, eh? The goblin king is something humans know about."

"You are coming out to the public, then, mate?" Ben asked.

Larry grinned—and it looked right except for the seriousness of his eyes. "We are already out to the public, *dude*." The stronger than normal emphasis on the "dude" made me think it was an answer to Ben's "mate." "But, yes. We are going to do some publicity work for ourselves here. Make ourselves a Power with allies—and then we are not so likely to end up food for the Gray Lords. Speaking of food . . ."

Unconcerned by the gore, he picked the body up, sans head, and slung it over his shoulder. The dislocated leg flopped, and the broken back made the body move oddly.

"I'd leave you the body, too," he told me, "but I'd have to explain to the missus that I went hunting and didn't bring back food for the family. The head should be enough to ID him."

He glanced again at the disembodied head, a shadow of regret on his face. I wondered if he had known the other goblin, or if he was just regretting the necessity of killing one of his own.

He looked up and saw that I was watching, then muttered, "The eyes are the best part."

I stared at him.

He saluted me with his serious-eyed grin, took a step back, and disappeared—gone from sight and sound.

Ben said, "Huh." After a moment, when the scent of the goblin king faded into nothing, he said, "Well, sod off, then, and bon appétit."

"He might have been joking," I said without conviction. I liked Larry, but that didn't mean I understood him.

2

~~~

GRUESOME AS IT WAS, I HAD TO ADMIT THE HEAD was easier to pack into the Jetta than a whole body would have been, especially since there was no upholstery or carpet in the space where (hopefully) someday a backseat would reside.

I wrapped the head in the blue tarp that I'd been using to keep the interior of the Jetta dry (the seal on one of the windows and the trunk was gone). I'd throw the tarp away as soon as I got rid of the head. Tarps are cheap.

I managed to handle the gruesome object without dousing myself in blood. My clothing had actually fared pretty well under the circumstances. There was a rip in the shoulder of my shirt—and it was possible that had happened in the fight and not when I'd changed to coyote. But my underpants were undamaged, except for the dirt I'd had to shake out. I'd even found both of my socks and shoes.

With the head stowed away, I settled into the driver's seat of the Jetta and mentally crossed my fingers. When it started on the first try, I was a bit surprised.

I muttered, "So far, so good." I tend to talk to cars—not

only when I drive them, but when I work on them. I don't know that it helps, but it sure doesn't hurt.

Before I could put the car in gear, the passenger door opened and Mary Jo plopped into the seat beside me.

"Who do you suppose he was talking about?" Mary Jo said as she looked around for the seat belt. She tipped her head back to show she meant the dead goblin when she said "he" rather than any of the other choices.

"There isn't a seat belt on the passenger side yet," I told her. "And which of them was talking about who? And don't you have your own car to drive?"

She quit fussing and settled in. "Ben's going to arrange for someone to pick it up. Ben's allergic to law enforcement, so I got elected to accompany you. And as far as the 'which of them was talking about who' . . . first, it should be 'about whom.' Second, didn't you notice that the goblin was nattering on about someone, a 'she' who told him he should come here? That we'd give him protection from the humans?"

"Oh, those whos," I said. Let Mary Jo try to figure out if it should be those "whoms" or "whos"—though for the record, I was pretty sure I was right this time. "I'd ask our passenger, but he's not talking."

I thought about the rest of what she'd said—and the way she'd settled into my car as if she had no intention of getting back out.

I said, "I don't need company. Thank you for the thought, but, as I said, there is no seat belt for your seat yet. I would rather not drive up to the sheriff's office with someone sitting illegally in my car that—if examined by a stickler—might not be legal to drive."

I must not have gotten quite the right amount of unfelt gratitude in my voice because she laughed. "Look. *Adam* will not be happy if we let you go by yourself."

She brought out the Alpha card, and we both knew she was right. If I made her get out—and I wasn't sure I could do that—I could very well be getting her into trouble.

But it was my job to protect the pack, not theirs to protect me. "I thought you were still flying under the radar about being a werewolf," I said. "Won't some of the people at the sheriff's know you in your firefighting identity?"

Just because some of the werewolves were out didn't mean that all of them were. For instance, Auriele aka Lady Mockingbird was a teacher, and we weren't sure just how well the school district would take knowing she changed into a werewolf. Her husband, Darryl, Adam's second, had been outed when fighting that troll on the Cable Bridge. He worked for a think tank with all sorts of government secrets for which he needed clearance. He'd run into a few bumps on that—though he'd gotten through.

Mary Jo shrugged. "I told my department and everyone in it after the troll incident." Her body language was casual, but I could smell her contentment. "They took it better than I expected, actually." She grinned a little self-consciously, a more open expression than any I'd seen from her since Adam and I had become a committed couple. "They quit giving me crap about being a weak woman. Now they're trying to figure out just how quick and strong I am."

Hazing? I wondered. But she didn't seem unhappy about it so I let it go.

"Okay," I told her. "Just remember, if we get pulled over because you don't have a seat belt on, you are an adult and so the ticket belongs to you."

She snorted. "I think that's only when there is a seat belt to wear."

She might have been right. I guessed that if a police car pulled me over, they might be more concerned with the disembodied head than whether Mary Jo was wearing a seat belt. I'd given her an out, reminded her what she risked—that was all I was responsible for.

I put the Jetta in gear—the clutch was stiff so it took a little effort. We puttered off the field and onto the bumpy dirt road: a werewolf, a coyote shapeshifter, and a goblin's head.

I called Tad. No Bluetooth in the Jetta so I had to break

the law to do that, too. Seat belt and cell phone—in for a penny, in for a pound.

"Mercy?" he said, sounding groggy. "What's up?"

"I'm delivering a goblin's head to the sheriff's office. I don't think they'll be worried about me getting out in time to make it to work this morning."

Tad grunted. "Anyone I know?"

I had to stop and wait before turning onto a better class of graveled road because there was a line of cars speeding past. You know you're in a hotbed of agriculture when there is a traffic jam at four in the morning on a gravel road. They were trying to beat the heat that was supposed to be over a hundred degrees by midafternoon.

"I don't know who you know," I told him grumpily. I hated being late to work. The traffic didn't make me happier, either. "He killed a policeman and a child, and he's dead now."

Tad snorted. "Jeez. Grouchy much? No worries, Mercy. I can handle it until you get in. You need to hire someone else to answer phones, though, if you need me to keep twisting a wrench."

"Let's get through a couple of months first," I told him. "I hate to hire someone if we're not making enough to pay ourselves."

"Optimist," accused Tad, and then he disconnected.

Traffic finally allowed me to continue our journey. Eventually we made it to a paved road that was much less busy. I breathed a sigh of relief because the shocks on the car had not been a priority for me before now. "I wonder what he meant when he said he was the first of thirty."

"Who?" Mary Jo asked.

I'd been talking to myself—which probably was rude, so I didn't admit that to Mary Jo. Instead I tilted my head toward our backseat (if there had been a seat) passenger. "Him. He bragged about being the first of thirty. Maybe 'a first of thirty.'"

"The goblins were soldiers, right? In the various fae wars. Maybe they divided themselves up into groups of thirty."

She said it as if it were common knowledge. I'd never heard it before and I'd had a book written about the fae by the fae. I started to ask her about that, but she kept talking.

"Or," she said, wiggling in her seat, "maybe there were once thirty tribes of goblins and he was chief. He's dead now, so it hardly matters. Mercy, you need to do something about this seat. It sucks."

I frowned at her. "This is a Wolfsburg Edition. That's an original leather seat."

"It's broken," she said. "It tilts to the outside. I'd be more interested in who sent him here."

"She," I muttered, wondering if I could fix the seat or if I was going to have to get a new one. It looked like it was pristine, but Mary Jo was the first person I'd had sit in it. Hopefully it was just a bad weld. "The goblin said 'she.'"

"I don't like it when troublesome fae get *sent* to our territory," Mary Jo grumped, wiggling until her seat made a *thump-thump* sound. "It makes me wonder who else they may have sent."

"And why," I agreed. "If you keep moving that seat, it might give up altogether and you'll be sitting with our other passenger in the back." She snorted, but quit wiggling. Thoughtfully I continued, "At least it was a 'she.'"

She lifted an eyebrow.

"That means it wasn't Coyote. Anyone other than Coyote I can deal with."

She hissed like a scalded cat—and I didn't think she had even met Coyote. "You know better than to tempt the fates like that. There are thousands of things and people out there that are worse than Coyote." No, she had *never* met Coyote. "Knock on wood," she demanded.

I grinned, because she really sounded panicked. "Feeling superstitious, werewolf?"

She turned so that she could sneer at me—and her seat broke loose, tipping her abruptly toward the door. She smacked her head into the window.

"Looks like you took care of knocking on wood," I observed serenely. "I don't think it was that important, but hey . . ."

She growled at me.

I patted the cracked dashboard and murmured to the car, "I think we are going to be good friends."

THE TARP HAD BEEN OLD, AND APPARENTLY IT HAD a few places that weren't leakproof.

It might be a trick getting into the sheriff's office with it dripping blood. The Franklin County Sheriff's Office was located in the heart of downtown Pasco in the county courthouse complex, and even though it was still very early, there were a few people out and about.

I looked at the little building that served as the secure entrance into the complex and realized it was closed.

I don't know why that thought was the nickel in the gumball machine that made my common sense start working. But it finally occurred to me, as I gripped the top of the Jetta's door so I could lean down and examine the tarp a little more closely, that I might be in trouble.

I have never had difficulty understanding the rules of living as a human. Nor had I had difficulty understanding the rules the werewolves who had raised me lived by—or the supernatural community as a whole. Granted, I did a better job of living by human rules, but I'd been older when I started—and I didn't have Bran Cornick, the überking of the werewolves, trying to shove the rules down my throat.

What I understood for the first time, contemplating that bloody tarp, was that I seldom had to deal with both sets of rules at the same time. It had made sense, by werewolf rules, that the renegade goblin should die. Even if we had apprehended him, I don't think any jail would have held him for long. And what he would have done to the population of prisoners in the meantime didn't bear thinking on.

There was no doubt of his guilt. He had confessed, eventually and sideways, to killing a child as well as killing the police officer. Justice had been unholy swift, maybe, but it had been his king who had carried out the sentence. All a little medieval, but that was the way of the fae and of were-wolves.

It had made sense, from a werewolf perspective, to take the head back to the police because they had jurisdiction over the crime the goblin had committed. Werewolves were all about order and authority. Moreover, the goblin king, who was de facto responsible for the miscreant goblin because they were the same species, had told me to do it. He had the right and the *authority* to determine that since the goblin had sinned against the humans, the humans should have the evidence that justice had been served, to wit, the head.

Larry meant to use the dead goblin as a political gambit, a statement of power combined with a declaration that he was on the side of justice, if not the law. That he considered the murder of humans to be wrong. And all of that was well and good.

But now I was standing near the heart of human justice—the courthouse. And from that human perspective . . . I frowned at the bloody tarp. Nothing of what I'd done made sense from a human perspective. Killing someone was a crime, even if the one you killed deserved it.

I may not have killed the goblin—but . . . I wasn't sure I could prove it. I'd bet a million bucks that Larry the goblin king would not be recognizable on the video feed from the barn. In fact, as I considered it, I was pretty sure that the cameras would have quit working the moment he was aware of them. It had been pretty dark about then—it was still pretty dark. If he had shown up at all, then he would have been little more than a shadowy figure.

Only the four of us—Larry, Ben, Mary Jo, and I—knew that it hadn't been I who'd killed the goblin. No one could prove it *was*, either . . . but oddly I didn't trust human justice as much as I trusted the werewolves. Justice is easier when the judge, jury, and executioner can tell if the accused tells a lie.

"Are you making friends with him?" growled Mary Jo

from the sidewalk. "He's probably not going to be a good conversationalist."

"I'm trying to figure out how I end up at work this morning," I told her. "Instead of in jail."

Because I had done everything wrong. I should have called the sheriff's office from the barn. I'd have liked to believe that the goblin king had magicked me into following orders. But I had just been caught up in what was right and proper on the magical side and forgotten that human law enforcement wasn't going to think highly of this.

She grunted. Then she squinted at the head a moment herself.

"Well, damn," she said in the voice of someone who has suddenly realized something. "Look what a stupid thing you did."

I looked at her and raised an eyebrow.

She lifted her hands, palms up. "You're the boss here, Mercy. I assumed you knew what you were doing."

I gave her a look and she broke down and laughed.

"I know," she said. "Me, too. He's just got that kingly thing going. And maybe I was distracted trying to figure out if he is actually going to go cannibal or if he's going to take the body back for some sort of ritual funeral or something. And . . . well, I guess I just don't get fussed about dead people . . . dead anything, anymore. I forgot that our human counterparts aren't going to feel the same way."

She looked around and sighed. She pulled out her phone and pressed some numbers on it.

"What?" a groggy and grumpy voice said. Then, irritably, "I'm off today, Carter, not late again. Go screw yourself."

"This is Mary Jo," she told him. "I need your official help."

There was a three-beat pause.

"Mary Jo," he said, sounding much more awake—but his voice was raw. "We're done, you said. No more. Well, done is done." And he disconnected.

"Ex-boyfriend," Mary Jo told me. "Renny's a good guy,

but he started to get too serious. I don't do serious with the humans. Doesn't seem fair." She tried to sound hard and did a fair to middling job of it, so I guessed it had hurt her, too.

She pressed the numbers again.

"Go away," he said.

"*Official*, Renny. I'm standing outside your place of work with Mercy Hauptman. We have a dead goblin's head in the backseat of her car. We'd like to donate it to the coroner's office through official channels. Since the head was made bodiless in Mesa, I kind of figured that might be up your alley."

He disconnected.

Mary Jo gave her phone a look, started to press numbers again, but then her phone rang.

"Goblin head?" Renny said. "Did you say a goblin *head*?"

"I did," she responded.

There was a long pause.

When he spoke again, his voice was all business. "If you are in the front parking lot, drive around the block to the back gate of the employee parking lot and wait for me. It'll take me five to dress and another five to get there. I'm calling this in—so if you are screwing with me, I'll see your supervisor." And he clicked off without giving Mary Jo a chance to say anything.

"Give him a severed goblin head, and he forgets all about how mad and hurt he is." There was a little tightness around her eyes that I tried not to see, because Mary Jo didn't want me to see her pain. So instead I paid attention to the sarcasm in her voice when she said, "*Obviously*, it was true love on his part."

MARY JO'S EX, DEPUTY ALEXANDER "RENNY" REN-ton, turned out to be a fit man somewhere near my own age (midthirties) and a few inches over six feet tall. He had a good blank face, which he used as he gave the contents of the back section of my Jetta a thorough visual examination.

Then he turned to study Mary Jo. His blank face intensified until it became broody.

"A werewolf, huh?" he said finally.

She tilted her head at him in mild inquiry. The expression on her face caused him to laugh ruefully.

"Of course I know," he told her. "Why else would you be escorting the Alpha's wife around at too-early o'clock in the morning? Besides, your people talked to my people because we share information between the sheriff's office and the fire department like that."

She smiled at his wry tone. "You mean someone started bragging that the fire department has a werewolf and the sheriff's office doesn't?"

"Maybe," he said, nodding. "Do I have anything to worry about?"

"Oh," she said, her face suddenly concerned. "Oh, whoops. Um, have you been getting a little hairier than usual? Have to shave a little more often? I've heard that it starts that way for the guys."

"Cut it out, Mary Jo," I growled. "Be nice to the helpful deputy." I looked at Renny. "It's not easy to get Changed to a werewolf. I guarantee you that you'll be in no doubt about it if ever it happens to you."

"Good to know," he said. He looked at Mary Jo and shook his head.

"Do we have the right to remain silent?" Mary Jo asked.

"You aren't under arrest," he said with a quelling look. "Not yet, anyway. As long as you didn't kill him, you probably won't be. But Captain Allen is coming in and asked me not to start anything until he gets here. This would have been a lot easier for you if you had called us in the first place. Before there was a dead goblin whose head is in the back of the car. You know better, Mary Jo; why didn't you call us in?"

She looked pointedly at me.

"The farmer didn't want to be responsible for getting people killed," I explained. "I agreed with him. Goblins are outside your ability to deal with."

Renny's eyes got cold, and he studied me for a moment.

"All due respect, ma'am, you don't know what we are capable of dealing with."

"All due respect, Renny," said Mary Jo, "I have a pretty freaking good idea of your capabilities. And I think Mr. Traegar's decision to bring us in first was the correct one. *We* don't really know what we're dealing with when it comes to the fae—there is no way that the sheriff's office would. We had two werewolves, Mercy, and the goblin king out there—and if it weren't for the goblin king, we'd have failed to bring him in ourselves."

He gave her a look. "I am going to ignore—just for a minute—how much my geek side is loving that apparently there is a goblin king in the world. And that he is—again apparently—here in the Tri-Cities. Even knowing that David Bowie is gone, I am giddy about this." He said all that in a very dry, professional tone.

I was starting to really like this guy.

"What I am not ignoring is the name of your farmer," he continued. "Mary Jo, did *Keith Traegar* really call in the werewolves to keep his son from fighting goblins? Traegar, who has anti-fae, anti-werewolf, and Bright Future signs all over his property?"

I had noticed the signs, actually.

Mary Jo laughed. "I thought you might enjoy that."

Deputy Renton paused, then looked up at the sky, brightening now with true dawn. When he looked back at Mary Jo, he was grinning with pure, unadulterated joy. "I am so going to rub Jack Traegar's nose in this for a very, very long time. His daddy called in the werewolves before he called his own son."

He took in a deep breath, regrouped, and rubbed his hands together. "Where were we?" It seemed to be a rhetorical question because he answered it before anyone else said anything. "Ah, yes. The bloody head."

He ducked down to take a look into the back of the Jetta again. "What we need, ladies, is a garbage sack. I will leave the body part in question with an official representative of the fire department and go find one. Wait here."

And he trotted off to the dark building, whistling lightly under his breath.

"I like him," I said at the same time Mary Jo said—in affectionate tones—"Weirdo."

We looked at each other—and she broke first. "Okay," she said. "Maybe I'll see if he's willing to give us another try. Anyone who is excited about the prospect of a goblin head might be able to deal with a girlfriend who is a werewolf."

"Always a good sign when they don't run screaming," I agreed.

She tilted her head at me. "Maybe if you hadn't decided to become Adam's mate, I might like you."

"Maybe if you weren't such a backstabby puppy, I might like you, too," I told her.

"Backstabby puppy?" Her voice rang with indignation. Then she grinned. "That shoe might fit." She sobered. "I wanted someone human for him."

"Him" was Adam, my mate.

"No coyotes allowed," I murmured.

Mary Jo's expression hardened. "He deserves someone who will take care of him, who doesn't bring him more trouble."

I raised my eyebrows. I'd thought we'd gone through all of this.

She waved a hand, her tough face giving way to sadness.

"He needs a Christy," she told me honestly. "Someone worthy of him."

Christy was Adam's first wife. She was a cold, self-involved, manipulative bitch and I hated her. And I couldn't express my opinion about why I hated her without causing a civil war in Adam's pack, most of whom were her willing slaves.

"Why on earth would you want to do that to him?" I heard myself say. "Wasn't once enough?"

Her mouth opened and then closed.

"She encouraged him to hate what he is," I told her hotly. "Werewolf and man, both. Even back at the beginning, when I first met them, met *him*, when I still disliked him for being the control-freaky dominant that he is—even then I just wanted to smack her when she would look at him with big eyes and say, 'You're scaring me, Adam.'" I knew I'd done a passable imitation of Christy's voice from Mary Jo's widening eyes. "Do you know how long it took me to get him to express even mild anger after she left him?" He still occasionally waited for me to wince or back away from him when he was in a temper.

And I had exposed his pain to Mary Jo, who had no right to it.

That bit of shame finally put a guard back on my tongue. I ran my hands over my face a couple of times. "And I don't know where that came from. He's been divorced for a long time and she is, finally, in Eugene again, moved to her own damned town, and it is almost far enough away." I'd really hoped that she'd find the man of her dreams in the Bahamas. The Bahamas were a lot farther away than Eugene. "Mary Jo, do you hate Adam so much you'd wish another Christy on him?"

Mary Jo's mouth curled up. "Tell me how you really feel about her, Mercy."

I growled at her and her smile grew, then faded back. "I'd forgotten that," she said. "Forgotten how she'd cringe from him. From all of us." Before I could read the expression on her face, her eyes went to the building and I knew Renny had returned.

"Showtime," I said.

———

AFTER LEADING US UP A SET OF STAIRS AND through a couple of locked doors, long hallways, and the main office, Renny brought us into a room that I presumed to be a conference room—because that was what the sign next to the door read. It was bigger than I expected, big enough for six or eight people to sit around the table comfortably.

He'd dealt with the head himself, loading it, tarp and all,

into the big black garbage bag. It had dripped more than a little. I felt a twinge of Lady Macbeth—"who would have thought the old man to have had so much blood in him?" The upside was that the mess made my decision as to whether to get new carpet throughout the car pretty easy.

He put the head on the table, steadying it when it rocked a little. He hadn't looked at the head itself—I didn't blame him. I didn't want to see it again.

"Properly," he told us, "you should have called the coroner in and this wouldn't be a problem at all." He glanced at Mary Jo. "You should know that much about procedures."

She shrugged and gave him a nod. "I do, and you're right. It's just that La—the goblin king told us what to do. It didn't occur to me that we might have made smarter choices until just before I called you."

I still didn't think Larry had done anything magical to influence me. Maybe I was fooling myself, but I thought I'd have noticed if he'd tried anything like that. But given that Mary Jo had done the same thing I'd done—maybe if the king of the goblins tells you to do something, you do it. Something like the way an Alpha wolf can make people, even people not in his pack, follow his command. I'd say "his or her command," but so far as I knew, there were no female Alpha werewolves.

Renny was frowning at Mary Jo. "Having never seen a goblin king, I'll take your word for that. I'll give that explanation a toss at the captain and see if it floats with him, too."

He looked around. "Take a seat. Anything substantial you've got to say should wait for the captain. Can I get you something to drink?"

While we waited for his captain, I called Adam and told his voice mail everything that had happened, beginning with the fact that we were all safe and Mary Jo and I were sitting in the sheriff's office with the goblin's head.

I got a call as I was finishing up the message and wasn't quite agile enough with the phone to pick up the call. But the Benton County Sheriff's Office called me back.

I listened for a few minutes, then told them where I was

and handed the phone to Mary Jo's Renny. He got about sixty seconds into the call before an expression very close to ecstasy crossed his face.

"Could you repeat that?" he said. "No, I'm not laughing at you. I heard you just fine. I only want to hear it one more time because I'm pretty sure that I'll never hear exactly those words together ever again."

WE LEFT RENNY STILL WAITING FOR HIS CAPTAIN with the goblin head. I assured him that I didn't want the tarp back.

Driving out to meet the Benton County Sheriff's officer, I looked at the sunny sky and sighed. I called Tad again.

"You are going to be late because why?" asked Tad blearily. Then he sounded more alert. "Didn't we already have this conversation? Or did I have a nightmare? It was about a dead goblin, right?"

I sighed and said, "It was about a goblin. Now it's about zombie miniature goats. Or miniature goat zombies. Nigerian dwarf goats. Twenty of them running free all around Benton City, apparently."

"Miniature zombie goats," murmured Mary Jo. "I think that sounds the cutest. I can see the newspaper headlines now."

"Are they dead?" Tad asked.

"That's what 'zombie' means," said Mary Jo loudly, to make sure Tad heard her. "But we're on our way to kill them again."

There was a little pause. Tad said, "Zombie miniature goats. Roaming the countryside. Doing what zombie goats do . . . whatever that is. I think there might be a song in that. Or a movie that is only supposed to be good if you are high on something psychedelic. Okay, Mercy, I'll see you around lunchtime. Good luck with your mini goat zombies."

"Thank you," I said with dignity. "I don't know about lunch, it depends on how long it takes us to find all of the goats."

"Do you need help?" he asked.

"Always." I sighed. "But it is too late for me. You just stood there watching when I went out on that bridge and started blabbing about the Tri-Cities being our territory to guard, when any idiot could have seen that I needed you to shove a gag in my mouth."

He laughed and hung up. The jerk.

THE OUTSKIRTS OF BENTON CITY, ANOTHER OF the little satellite towns that surrounded the Tri-Cities, were filled with small-acreage farms sprinkled amid orchards and vineyards. I didn't bother looking for addresses; I just found the house with all the activity.

We turned into a driveway next to a tidy but not beautiful pen that enclosed maybe a quarter of an acre. The side of the fence nearest to the driveway had been cut open.

There were four sheriff's vehicles parked next to a miniature-goat-sized barn that was painted blue with white trim. Five deputies stood near their cars and watched me drive in. About twenty yards from the deputies was a small and well-kept house with a big, friendly wraparound porch. There were four people on the porch: a woman, a child, a man, and a giant-sized man who looked as though he ate locomotives for lunch.

I parked in between the house and the sheriff's cars.

"Face-off," said Mary Jo before she opened her door and got out.

She was right. It was impossible to miss the implied hostility in the empty space between the deputies and the people on the porch. For that matter, there was some hostility between the deputies, too.

"First the sheriff's office, then the civilians," I murmured to Mary Jo.

I hung back and let her take the lead with the law enforcement. One of the deputies had misstepped with the civilians, I thought, watching the aggressive stances. He'd gotten some blowback and they were split three to two. I was betting, from his clenched shoulders, that the man with the runner's build was the culprit. But it might be his stocky buddy. He'd been reprimanded and it had stuck because he was hanging back and letting the others talk.

Body language shouts louder than words in most cases.

I half listened to what they had to say, because most of it was just a repeat of the information I'd gotten on the initial phone call. Once I had the deputies analyzed, I studied the people waiting on the porch without looking directly at them.

Family and family friend, I thought—the giant was noticeably not Hispanic.

The farm belonged to Arnoldo Salas; the goats had belonged to his ten-year-old son. Arnoldo wasn't hard to pick out.

An extremely fit man in his midforties, he stood in the center of the porch, one hand on the shoulder of a teary-eyed boy while his other arm was wrapped around a woman who looked to be his wife, who wasn't in much better condition than the child. He watched me with hostility.

Maybe he didn't like werewolves.

Mary Jo's voice broke into my concentration. "Why in the world would someone make zombie goats?"

"I don't know," I told her. "Let's see what we can find out."

We headed toward the house, the deputies trailing after us.

According to what I'd been told, the Salas parents spoke only a little English. The giant—who looked even more hard-bitten up close, an impression not detracted from by the Marine tattoos he wore—stepped forward.

"Mr. Salas did not call the werewolves in," he said.

I weighed a dozen responses, glad I had Mary Jo with me and not Ben. I could count on Mary Jo to let me take point.

"There are zombie goats running around," I said. "We

can deal with them without getting hurt. It would help to know as much as possible."

"They were my goats," said the boy in a soggy voice. "I milk them and breed them for money to pay for college."

The Marine reached back and rubbed the boy's head.

"Mercy is one of the good guys," the boy said. "She killed the troll on the Cable Bridge. I saw it on TV."

Not me, but the pack.

The man looked at Salas. The boy said something in Spanish.

Salas met my gaze and held it. Then his wife patted his arm and said something to the Marine.

He nodded respectfully to her, and when he turned back to me he dropped most of the hostility. "They were his idea. His pets. Some"—he changed the word he was going to use at the last moment—"jerk killed them all. He found them at feeding time, about seven at night last night."

"It took the sheriff's office this long to get here?" I asked.

He glanced around at the uniformed people behind me and hesitated. Finally, he said, "Arnoldo thought they would wait until morning, ma'am. They thought they would ask their neighbors if anyone saw anything."

"The police have important things to do," said the boy. "Maybe dead goats, even twenty of them, would not be important."

The hostile deputy snorted, the one with the runner's build. "If your parents are both legal, why wouldn't they call the police?"

And the figurative temperature shot to the ceiling.

"With an attitude like that, I wonder why they didn't call you in," the big Marine standing next to Salas said.

Time to take control of this situation so that Mary Jo and I could go looking for zombies and no one would get arrested or shot.

"I know of a few incidents around here that might make some people a little worried about calling the law in," I said softly. I met the hostile deputy's eyes. His name tag read

Fedders. He saw the color of my skin, I could see it in his eyes.

"You probably know about those incidents, too," I said.

He started to say something, but I interrupted him.

"Be very careful," I said softly. "I'm not afraid of you. Before you say anything more, you should take a deep breath and remember that I'm also second in the Columbia Basin werewolf pack." His face tightened and I continued. "And we have a very good lawyer."

"And she kills trolls," said the boy.

I nodded. "And I kill trolls."

The deputy's friend nudged him. "My brother, the one in the Pasco PD, was on that bridge," he said. "Time to stand down."

Fedders's face flushed, but he took a deep breath. I don't know whether it was his friend's urging, the thought of the lawyer, or the troll killing, but he backed down. He didn't say anything, but it was in his body language. He lost three inches of height and he took a step back. Good enough for me.

"The Salases are legal," the Marine told me firmly.

"I don't care," I told him. "As these gentlemen aren't with immigration, they shouldn't, either." I didn't actually know if that was true or not, but it should have been.

A young, very blond deputy, who had remained quiet, said a few words in liquid Spanish.

I caught "how" and "killed."

Salas looked at the Spanish-speaking deputy and frowned.

The deputy said something else and Mrs. Salas laughed, then covered her mouth and carefully looked away from Fedders.

Salas looked at his wife, at his friend, then began speaking, and the young deputy took notes.

"He says," the deputy told me when Salas had finished, "that they all had their throats cut. There was no sign of a struggle. Someone collected their blood." He glanced around at the other deputies. "I think, given the circumstances, that we should believe him?" At the last he looked at me.

I shrugged. "I'm not an expert in zombies," I told them. "I've never had much to do with them." But I knew that they were witchcraft, and witchcraft was powered by body parts with a leaning toward blood and bone. "But if something weird happened, any weirdness that preceded that is probably connected. We"—I indicated Mary Jo—"can find the goats. I don't know exactly what to do with them, but I have resources. Let me make another call."

Elizaveta Arkadyevna was our witch on retainer. It sometimes amazes me how much of the supernatural world has adopted lawyerlike techniques. I don't know whether that says something about lawyers—or something about the supernatural.

Elizaveta was in Europe. She'd gone to help me, and stayed when Bonarata had made her an interesting temporary job offer. But her family was still here and obliged to our pack.

I called Elizaveta's number and a woman's voice answered it, soft and Southern. "This is the home of Elizaveta Arkadyevna," she said. "I'm afraid that she's not here and her family is all tied up right now. What can I do to help you?"

No one in Elizaveta's family had an accent like that. Elizaveta clung to her Russian accent, but everyone else sounded newscaster American, the born-in-the-Pacific-Northwest kind of voice.

I had a very bad feeling. Especially since I was pretty sure that her "all tied up" wasn't a figure of speech. It wasn't that I could tell if she was lying or not—over the phone, sometimes I can tell and sometimes I can't. It was that I heard the sound of people in pain.

I cut the line. There was nothing I could say that would be useful under the circumstances. Zombies and something off at our local witch's home. Coincidences are always possible, even if unlikely.

I thought a moment and called Adam. His voice mail picked up again and I said, "We have miniature zombie goats in Benton City and when I called Elizaveta's house, a strange woman with a thick Southern accent picked up the phone. Background noises suggest that Elizaveta's family is in trouble." Then I called Darryl.

Darryl Zao was our pack's second. Unless you included me, who, as Adam's mate, was technically above Darryl. Our pack's ranks were currently a little convoluted as tradition belatedly met women's liberation and sputtered. The road to enlightenment was a little bumpy, but we were on the right path.

Anyway, I called Darryl. He'd be up. He ran every morning at six A.M.

He answered, his voice distorted by his car's phone system. "Yes."

I explained the situation to him. "I have the goats covered, more or less. We'll figure out what to do with them until better-educated minds can be put to the problem."

"I'll grab a few wolves and head over to Elizaveta's," he said.

"Just recon," I told him. "Unless Adam picks up his phone or listens to the message I just gave him. See what is going on over there. Then we contact the wicked witch herself and let her make the calls. There are witches who can control wolves," I reminded him.

He paused. "Should I bring Post, or leave him out of it?"

I frowned. "He doesn't remember anything. Why bring him in?"

Sherwood Post (not his real name—but it would do until he figured out what that was) had been discovered when the Seattle pack cleaned out a nasty coven of witches. It had taken a while for him to regain human form—and he was never able to regenerate one of his legs, which was weird. Werewolves either regenerate or they die. He didn't remember anything and no one knew who he was except (we all thought) Bran, the Marrok. Bran had gifted Sherwood with his unusual name and sent him off to our pack.

"Because," said Darryl, "he's sitting right next to me."

"Well, then," I told him, exasperated. "Ask him if he

wants to go or not. Take him if he wants to go, drop him off somewhere if he doesn't. This isn't a war mission, it's a recon. We've got enough on our plate. We'll leave any warfare to Elizaveta unless she asks otherwise."

"Problems?" asked the Spanish-speaking deputy.

"I hope not," I said. "But I think we're on our own."

3

~~~~~~~~

MARY JO AND I SPENT THE NEXT COUPLE OF hours catching adorable zombie goats. She could just pick them up in her massive jaws and deliver them. I had to let my coyote find them, then shift back to my human self to catch and carry them back. They might be small for goats, but the adults weighed nearly what my coyote did.

Luckily I usually carried a backpack in my car that I could shove my clothes into. Otherwise, I'd have spent the morning walking around naked, carrying dead goats with red eyes and a taste for blood.

Not that the zombies could actually eat anything. In the first place, their throats were cut. One of the adults I'd caught was so deeply wounded that its head just lolled around; there was no muscle to move its neck. In the second place, they were dead. No systems go. But it didn't stop them from causing lots of mayhem. Small animals—squirrels, quail, chickens, and the like—didn't fare well. I would have thought that zombies would be slow, like in the movies. But these, at least, were not.

Because we were using our animal forms, we had to

leave our phones in the car. I had to trust that Adam got my messages and that Darryl was staying safe.

I finally figured out that Darryl would rather have left Sherwood behind, and he'd been hoping that I would give the order. It was interesting that Adam's second didn't feel comfortable giving orders to Sherwood, who was, supposedly, below him in the pack structure. I tried to figure out whether that was a new thing or not, but then I detected another zombie miniature goat.

Detected, not scented. I put that aside, too.

Darryl and Sherwood had their jobs; Mary Jo and I had ours. Mine was to find as many of the miniature zombie goats as I could, not to explore too hard how I was finding them. Concentrate on the job at hand and sort everything else out later.

I found my last escapee about two miles from the Salases' house. It was a baby goat, black with a big white spot in the middle of its chest, nearly as short as the dachshund it was attacking. And I didn't find this one because of my coyote nose, either.

The goat must have backtracked, because the scent I was following continued down the road. But I *felt* the zombie and it was directly on my left. I stopped running but stayed where I was.

I had an odd grab bag of talents. I could sense magic better than the werewolves. Magic didn't always work on me, and when it did, sometimes it didn't work as intended. I could turn into a coyote. And I saw ghosts, which I'd always dismissed as mostly useless.

But over the last few years, I've been learning that I could do a little more.

Just then, standing on the verge of a dirt road in the maze of rural roads above the Yakima River, I could feel something both animate and dead, and it was on the other side of a hedge where a small dog was yapping its head off.

I burrowed under the hedge and found the goat-dachshund standoff. I changed to human, pulled on my jeans and T-shirt, and hoped that my faith in the little dog wasn't misplaced. I'd hate to live with the guilt of the death of some-one's pet just because I didn't want to run around in late-morning traffic naked as a jaybird.

I did not think, as hard as I could manage to not-think, about the fact that I had felt where it was. Ghosts were one thing. I'd been seeing them as long as I could remember. I was kind of used to my interaction with them. I didn't want to have the same connection to zombies.

Dachshunds are tough; she held her own just fine until I zipped my jeans. Hard to tell who would have won, zombie or dog. When I snagged the zombie kid and hauled it away, kicking and snapping, the dog pranced off with her tail in the air. Whatever my doubts, that dog was sure she had beaten the nasty intruder.

I jogged back at a pretty good clip despite my bare feet—my carry bag wasn't big enough for shoes. I met Mary Jo, who was following the same trail I'd picked up—she must have found her last goat faster than I did and come back to help me. The sight of her had a few cars pulling over so that people could take pictures with their cell phones.

Yes, it was a good thing I'd taken time to put my clothes on.

One of the deputies raised the lid on the zombie goat corral, an empty dumpster that had been hauled over next to the damaged goat pen—Salas's Marine friend's idea. So far, the big, green, smelly metal box had proven to be escape-proof.

I could feel them in the dumpster without looking. As if I'd become sensitized to the way the zombies felt. I could tell how many of the little zombies were bumping around just as I could tell when there was a ghost around, even if I might not be able to see it.

It wasn't so bad if I could tell there were zombies around, I thought. I'd made it thirty-odd years before running into my first zombies; it might be another thirty years before I met another.

By now, all of the sheriff's cars except for two were gone. Three of the original deputies remained, but we'd been getting drop-ins from law enforcement from as far away as Prosser and Pasco, including the highway patrol. Everyone wanted to see the miniature zombie goats.

"It could have been worse," I told the deputy who opened one side of the dumpster lid for me so I could drop my little zombie in with the rest of the adorable, blood-hungry fiends.

She said, "Right? They could have been full-sized goats and we wouldn't have any idea what to do with them. Hard enough to keep goats in without them being impervious to pain. This dumpster is picking up a lot of dents that it didn't have when we started. What do you plan on doing with these things?" She glanced at the dumpster. "You *are* planning on doing something with them?" *And not leave them to us, please*; half of that thought was unsaid but not unheard.

"I don't know," I told her, not quite honestly.

I wasn't sure exactly how to kill . . . how to eliminate zombies. But I was pretty sure we could burn them. I didn't know if real fire would do the trick, but we had Joel, inhabited by the spirit of a volcano dog.

If he couldn't manage it by himself, we could bring in the big guns—Aiden, my fire-wielding ward. He wasn't officially our ward yet, actually. We were finding it very difficult to become the legal guardians of a boy who had no paperwork trail. I was sure either Joel or Aiden could reduce the goats to ash—even zombie goats couldn't come back from ash.

I just didn't know if I wanted to advertise that we could call upon that kind of power. And I wasn't sure either Joel or Aiden had enough control to just burn the goats and stop.

"Are any of the Salases still around? I'd like to ask a few questions."

She nodded. "Jimmy, Mr. Salas, and Mr. Salas's very large friend are all sitting on the porch talking about their days in the Marines. The mom is fending off the hoi polloi from the front yard."

"Mr. Salas was a Marine, too?" I asked.

She nodded. "And English is his native tongue; he was born and raised on a quarter-horse ranch outside San Diego.

I don't think Mrs. Salas speaks English, but he is certainly bilingual. Not the first time I've seen the 'speak no English' used when people are facing hostile law enforcement."

She glanced over at the Salas house and then back at me.

"Fedders is a problem," she admitted with a sigh. "Apparently he's better known in the Spanish-speaking community around here than we thought. He was first on scene."

She gave me a quick smile. "He's like a black sheep—part of the family but also awkward and occasionally dangerous. You wouldn't think it from today's performance, but he's really good with trauma victims—even those from our Spanish-speaking communities. When he's helping someone who is hurt, he drops all that crap. I'm sure Captain Gonzales will explain, again, why antagonizing people isn't useful. Someday it will stick, or he'll cause such a big problem they'll promote him right off the streets."

She glanced at Mary Jo, who was keeping back far enough to give the officer a false sense of safety. "Maybe some big werewolf will get tired of him, chew him up, and spit him out with an attitude adjustment."

Mary Jo grinned at her.

"My, what big teeth," said the deputy with a smile, though her hand slipped toward her gun. Funny how Little Red Riding Hood came up whenever the werewolves were about.

Mary Jo closed her mouth and wagged her tail.

A nice path opened up for us through the gathering crowd—werewolves are useful like that—and we slipped past the hordes unmolested. It wasn't really a big group of people, maybe fifteen or twenty.

"Mr. Salas," I said. "Mary Jo and I were able to round up all the goats. I'll make sure they are taken care of. If anyone gives you trouble or asks you to pay for damages, you call us." I gave him a card. "This is not your fault in any way. You are not responsible for any damages, and if someone needs to be reminded of that, my husband will take care of it."

He took the card and looked thoughtful.

Mary Jo nudged me to get my attention, then she trotted off. I assumed that she was going to regain her human shape. I didn't let my gaze linger on her; instead, I considered the Salases' situation.

"Did you, your wife, or your children have any trouble with anyone lately?" I asked. "With a stranger, probably." Certainly.

There were, I understood, several kinds of practitioners who could create zombies. But this was witchcraft. As soon as I touched the first goat, I could feel the black magic humming in my bones and turning my stomach.

Leaving aside the black magic—because there were no black-magic witches in the Tri-Cities—no local witches would have done anything like it. They were too afraid of Elizaveta and her family. And we didn't, to my knowledge, have anyone with this kind of power except for Elizaveta herself. Zombies took serious mojo—I knew that much.

But I couldn't explain our local witch population to Salas or the police; I didn't want to cause anyone to go out hunting witches. That was Elizaveta's job.

Salas shook his head. He called a question to his wife, who shook her head. "A moment," he said. "I will ask my son."

"He served this country for eight years," the blond deputy (presumably Jimmy) told us, a snap in his voice. "And he has to hide when the police come to call?"

"No," I said. "Because there are deputies like you here."

Salas returned to the porch, shaking his head. "No. No unusual arguments. But Santiago, my son, he says there was a lady who stopped yesterday morning while he was feeding his goats. She wanted to buy them all, all twenty, but he didn't like her so he told her they were not for sale. He stayed inside the pen while she talked—the way he said it makes me think that maybe she wanted him to come out to her car. He told me that she sounded like one of my friends from the Corps—Porter. Porter is from Georgia."

Southern was how the witch at Elizaveta's sounded. I wondered if they were the same witch.

Twenty goats she couldn't buy, twenty goats that were

killed and turned into zombies. Then I had a terrible thought. If she could take the goats, why couldn't she take the boy? And what did she need with twenty zombie goats? She didn't even take them with her. That sounded like spite to me.

I looked at the pen that was next to the house. It was the side farthest from the house where the fence was torn open. That section of fence wasn't visible from the road. "Did the goats damage the pen, or did that happen earlier?"

"Whoever killed the goats cut open the pen," Salas said. "The goats were dead, so we didn't bother to repair it."

I wondered if the witch who had killed them had returned later that night and reanimated them, or if there was a time component. That the goats had been spelled as they died, but it had taken a few hours for them to turn to zombies.

Today that didn't matter, but I would find out. I didn't know as much about witches or zombies as I obviously should.

Had she taken the goats because she hadn't been able to persuade Santiago to come to her? Consent had magical implications for most of the magic-using folk; I didn't know how it played for witches.

"I think," I said slowly, "that your son was smart to stay in the pen when the lady came by."

If the witch had taken the goats, surely she would have been able to walk in and take the boy if she had wanted to. But maybe, I thought, not in the middle of the day. If Salas's son had come out of the pen and up to her car, she could have taken him then and there with no one thinking anything of it.

Maybe the goats had been second choice.

"Tell him—Santiago? Tell Santiago that if he sees her again, he should go inside the house, lock the doors, and call the number on that card."

His eyes narrowed and his bearing changed. It was like he had put on the same invisible cloak of readiness that Adam carried around all of the time. Deputy Jimmy had that, too. It was a matter of posture, mostly—head up, shoulders back—but also of intensity. Had Salas looked like that when I'd driven up, I'd have picked him for ex-military of some sort right off the bat.

"You think she is the one who did this? A *bruja*?"

I shrugged. "A witch did this, I can smell it. I don't know who that witch was."

Though for some reason her scent twigged my memory. As if I might not have scented her before, but maybe something about her. Irritating, but until my subconscious worked it through, there was no use trying to figure out what the connection was. When I met her, maybe I would figure it out. I had a feeling I was going to get a chance to do that—predators don't usually just wander off after they make a bold move on another predator's territory.

"Maybe," I said carefully, "the lady who talked to your son was just someone fascinated with your dwarf goats. But she made him uneasy. I'd pay attention to that."

"I have noticed that people who listen to their instincts live longer," Salas agreed.

THERE WERE THREE MESSAGES ON MY PHONE when I got into the car. The first was from someone who wanted to talk to me about my credit card. It was a scam and I erased it.

The second was from Adam.

"Got your messages, sweetheart," he said. "I called Darryl, who is on his way to Elizaveta's. I can meet him there if I hurry. Good luck with the zombie miniature goats."

The third one was from my mother.

"I haven't heard from you in a month," she said. "Are you alive?" And she hung up.

Mary Jo, who'd been checking her own phone, snorted.

My phone rang while I was texting *yes* to Mom. I checked the number and smiled.

"Hey, Adam. You missed out on the miniature zombie goat hunt."

"About those zombies," he said, his voice solemn. "You

have a better nose for magic than any of us. Do you think you could pick between one practitioner's magic and another's?"

"Like could I compare the zombie goat magic to whatever you've found at Elizaveta's?" I asked. "There are a lot of witches practicing in Elizaveta's house. That will make it hard. But I would recognize the scent of the witch who made the zombies. I don't know that I would recognize the feel of her magic. Maybe?"

"When a witch is dead, their magic dies, too, right?" he asked.

"I don't know," I told him. "Can't you ask any of Elizaveta's people?"

"No," he said with finality.

I inhaled. "Adam?"

"Everyone at Elizaveta's home is dead," he said.

"How many?" I asked.

"As far as we can tell, everyone in Elizaveta's family," he said. "We found fourteen bodies. I'm waiting for Elizaveta to confirm that."

I didn't know any of them, could have picked maybe two out of a police lineup—but fourteen? I didn't like Elizaveta; she scared me. I had a hard time liking people who scared me. But I had known her for a long time, and she was ours.

And anyone who could wipe out Elizaveta's family would have a shot at doing the same to a bunch of werewolves. Elizaveta might be the real powerhouse, but her whole family was formidable—or so it had been explained to me.

"Okay, then," I said, thinking hard. "I'm not a witch. The only witch I've dealt with is Elizaveta. If this is important, maybe we should get a witch to look into it instead of me. There is that witch in Seattle that Anna knows. Should I call Anna and get her name?"

He considered it. Exhaled noisily through his nose and then said, "I think we have enough unknown players in the Tri-Cities right now. Maybe if we need an expert. I will check with Elizaveta when she gets back to me. As for the rest, I think you should come to Elizaveta's house and see what we found. You have a better feel for magic, and that might be important. Even if Elizaveta comes as fast as she can, it will be days, not hours. Whatever traces of magic are there might dissipate before then."

There was another little pause and he said, "And I need to get *your* take on what we found, not the opinion of a witch we don't know and can't trust. I need to make some decisions, and I'd like to see if your conclusions match mine."

I disconnected and looked at Mary Jo, who was looking as shell-shocked as I was. "Do you think you could get Joel or Aiden . . . um—maybe Joel *and* Aiden might be better—to come and incinerate our poor victims? Preferably with some discretion? I don't want Aiden's picture all over the Internet."

Joel wouldn't have that problem. No one would associate the volcanic tibicena with Joel's human form.

"Yes." Mary Jo opened the car door and got out again. The seat tried to follow her and she set it back into the car. "Stay there," she told it. To me she said, "No worries, Mercy. I'll figure out how to do it out of sight. I have all the tools I need." She held up her cell phone. "Go do what you need to do, Mercy. I've got your back."

ELIZAVETA ARKADYEVNA VYSHNEVETSKAYA HAD a sprawling house just a few miles from my home.

She used to live in town. But after the neighbors complained about the sound of her granddaughter's nightly oboe practicing, she moved out to a house on five acres. She leased the land to a hay company—they didn't come out at night, so no one was around to be kept up by Elizaveta's granddaughter practicing her oboe.

I was sure her granddaughter had an oboe and that it was just coincidence that bad oboe playing can sound remarkably like screaming.

I hadn't lied to Adam; I didn't know much about witches, and the more I learned, the less certain I was about what I did know. As I understood it, witches had power over living things. Magic practitioners who could work with inanimate objects were wizards.

Witches got power from things of spiritual consequence. These included life-changing events: birth, death, dying, but also lesser things like emotions. Sacrifice, willing or unwilling, was supposed to have an especially great effect. They also did a lot of their work using body parts, bodily fluids—blood, hair, spit. I was a little vague on how that worked exactly.

Though there were three different types of witches, they all started the same way—they were born with certain abilities. At some point after that, they chose what they were willing to trade for power, staying white or becoming gray or black.

White witches generated power from themselves and the environment around them. They were less powerful than the other two kinds. The black witches tended to view them as fast food (and I wasn't sure about the gray witches, either). Most white witches were paranoid and secretive. I had only met a few of them.

Black witches were power hungry. They went for the big power boosts—death, yes. But torture-then-death generated more power from the same victim. They fed more easily off their own kind, but they could use any living being. They actively pursued victims with magical connections. That probably accounted for the fact that few supernatural communities tolerated witches who practiced black magic. That and the fact that anything that scared the humans— and black magic was difficult to keep hidden—was bad for everyone else.

Black witches were the most powerful of all witches.

Most of the witches I knew were gray witches. I wasn't sure of the exact line between gray and black, not from the witches' side, anyway. I could tell the difference from a good distance—black magic reeks.

I thought that the difference between black and gray had something to do with consent. A gray witch could cut off a person's finger and feed on the generated power of the sacrifice and pain, as long as their victim agreed to it. I was pretty sure that a gray witch could make zombies, but these had smelled of black magic.

As soon as I drove past the wall of poplar trees that marked the border of Elizaveta's property, I could see that there were a lot of pack vehicles at the house. As I approached, Warren's old truck pulled out of the drive. He slowed as he saw me, stopping in the middle of the road.

Since there wasn't anyone coming, I did the same. He rolled down his window. The Jetta's driver's-side window didn't work yet. I got out of the car and walked to Warren's truck.

Aiden was in the front seat, looking like he should have had a booster chair. Joel, in his presa Canario dog form, took up the space between Warren and Aiden on the bench seat with some of him left over to spill onto the floor. It didn't look comfortable, but Joel smiled at me anyway. Compared to his tibicena form, the presa Canario looked positively friendly.

"Heading to Benton City to burn some miniature goat zombies?" I asked.

Warren shook his head. "No, ma'am. Mary Jo had a disposal company come haul the dumpster out to the Richland landfill. We'll turn the goats to ash out of sight and away from anything else that might catch fire."

Yep. Mary Jo was competent. Too bad for her, because this was not how to get off my emergency call list.

"Then we come back here," Warren said. He grimaced. "There are some things we need to burn here, too. But not until you check things out and the boss gets the okay from Elizaveta."

"Bad?" I asked. "I mean, I know that Elizaveta's family is all dead."

He glanced at Aiden and sighed. "I think this gives 'bad' a new low."

Aiden frowned at him. "I lived in *Underhill*, Warren. I don't know what you all think you are protecting me from."

"Just because you've seen bad things doesn't mean you have to see any more," said Warren with dignity.

I waved Warren off and got back in the Jetta. I hadn't really needed to ask him if it was bad at Elizaveta's house. My answer was in the massing of the pack. It was a Wednesday, and most of the people here should have been at work. Adam wouldn't have called them all just to deal with bodies. He must have been worried that the people who had killed Elizaveta's family might be coming back.

I parked the Jetta next to Adam's SUV. Before I got out, Adam was beside my car.

He wrapped his arms around me and lifted me off my feet, his face buried in the crook of my neck as if he hadn't seen me for a decade instead of . . . at lunchtime yesterday. I could feel his chest lift as he breathed in my scent and it made me do the same to him. Musk and mint and Adam. Yum.

He put me on the ground, started to release me, then thought better of it (that might have had something to do with the grip I had around his waist). He bent down and kissed me.

His kiss told me a lot of things. It told me he loved me. The careful tightness of his grip told me that he was too tired to trust his control. The desperation . . . our sex life is very good and enthusiasm is a normal part of it, but that kiss was more like the ones I got when we were both naked and ready rather than a "hello, am I glad to see you" kind of kiss. So the desperation told me that whatever they'd found in Elizaveta's house had disturbed him a great deal.

I kissed him back, trying to give him whatever he needed from me. At least that was my motivation at first. After about five seconds it wasn't about anything other than his hands on my skin, my hands on his, the taste of his mouth, and the scent of his rapidly aroused body.

I felt the buzz of electric connections sitting up and taking notice of his strong hand on the back of my neck and the shape of his body against my hips. He was hot against my bare skin where my shirt was rising up and exposing my midriff. Even through the thickness of my jeans, I could feel his warmth.

I loved it.

Adam laughed softly against me, running his lips over my neck, biting down lightly on the tendon, and sending shivers right down to my toes. Then he took my lips again.

"Don't give in to the nudge!" called Paul urgently. "You know you'll regret it!"

"Quick," said Zack, "does anyone have any of that essential oil stuff that Jesse's friend's mom sold Mercy?"

Adam stifled another laugh, this one a laugh of self-amusement mixed with frustration as he pulled back. He steadied me and waited for his own breath to calm down.

"The nudge always wins," he murmured to me. "Thank God."

"Just not right here and now," I murmured back.

I should have been appalled, I suppose. Here we were in public, in full view of a good percentage of the pack, in front of what I was pretty sure was a murder scene.

But I've learned that there are always terrible things, and sometimes it is very important to grasp what joy and beauty you can, whenever you can. And Adam is beautiful, inside and out. Better than that—he is mine.

Adam is average height, and that's the only average thing about him. Even back when I disliked him heartily, I never denied that he was about the most gorgeous man I'd ever seen. Even married and mated, at odd moments I was surprised by the sheer power of his looks.

I think it was because normally, his looks are not the things that make me love him. I love his intelligence, his care for his pack—and even for me. Though I have to admit that I chafe under his protectiveness sometimes. I spent a lifetime taking care of myself; I did not need protection. Still, when I was facing vampires, trolls, or the IRS (my business had just gotten that dreaded audit letter), Adam was the person I most wanted at my side.

I love his honesty, his temper, his dedication to his word

and his duty. I love his humor, the way it creases the edges of his eyes and softens the usual hard line of his mouth.

Yep, I have it bad.

We leaned against each other for a few seconds more, and then he stepped back reluctantly.

"Okay," he said to me, his hands lingering on my shoulders (I found that my hands were reluctant to let go of him, too). "Back to business."

"Yep," I said. "Okay. Back to business." I pulled my shirt down to cover my belly and then stood at mock attention. "I'm ready."

He nodded. "I need you to go into Elizaveta's house and see if you can find out if the person who created your miniature zombie goats in Benton City is the person who killed all of Elizaveta's family. And if it isn't, see if you can pick up anyone else's scent." He frowned. "Look for the magic that is left, Mercy, and see what it tells you. Look for strangers."

"I can do that," I told him slowly. "Just because I can't pick out our zombie-making witch's magic doesn't mean it isn't there, though. Differentiation between magic users isn't something I've done. I don't know that I've felt the magic of all of Elizaveta's people."

He nodded. "I need you to keep your eyes open while you go through the house. Tell me what you think."

I frowned at him. I could tell something had really bothered him about what he'd found in there. Something more than all of the dead bodies. "Elizaveta isn't a black witch—there is a stench to that." She skirted the line pretty hard, but we'd know if she had started practicing black magic.

"Yes," Adam said, and I relaxed a little.

Elizaveta and I were on shaky terms, but there was real affection between her and Adam. She liked him because he spoke Russian with a Moscow accent, and because, when she flirted with him, he flirted back. He liked her because she reminded him of some relative of his mother's, an aunt I think, who came to visit them when he was nine or ten. I didn't want Adam hurt.

"It'll work best in my coyote form," I told him and then added, because I didn't want him to worry, "I've been bouncing back and forth capturing goats this morning. I can change again"—I could feel that—"but I'm not sure I can change back right away."

He nodded. "Okay. I don't think that time is so much of a factor that what you have to say can't wait a couple of hours."

What was it that he expected me to find?

"You coming with?" I asked.

He shook his head with a faint smile. He stepped back from me, finally, and I felt the loss of his touch. I'd been neck-deep in the craziness of reopening my garage. He'd been busy attending all his secret, hush-hush, middle-of-the-night meetings. We hadn't had as much time together over the past few weeks as I was used to.

"If I come in, I might prejudice what you see," he said. "Sherwood will go with you." He glanced around and nodded to the peg-legged man who was in the middle of a quiet discussion with some other pack members.

Sherwood started over to us, his gait smooth in spite of the peg leg. He had a better prosthetic, and with that one on no one would ever have thought he was missing a leg. But most of the time when he thought there might be some action, he wore the peg leg, because the artificial limb was a lot more delicate and correspondingly more expensive.

"Sherwood?" I asked. Asking him to go into a witch's house was unkind, I thought. It hadn't been that long ago that he'd been discovered three-legged and half-crazed in a cage in a black witch's den.

Adam said, "Sherwood knows the dangers better than anyone else here. I trust him to keep you safe."

I looked up into Sherwood's face with its wolf-wild eyes and said, "I thought you didn't remember anything of your captivity?"

"Apparently some things are imprinted in my skin," he said, his voice a few notes darker than usual. "Like the—" He broke off, shivered, and shook his head. "Never mind."

"As soon as you're done, we'll gather the dead," Adam told me. "Warren will bring our firestarters back with him as soon as he can. I've spoken to Elizaveta and told her we need to burn the bodies. She wasn't convinced until I told her about the goats. She said that if there is a necromancer with that much power to burn running around, she'd rather her family be turned to ash than become another witch's puppet."

There was something in his voice that concerned me. But I let it lie. I'd find out soon enough what had turned this from a tragedy for our pack's witch into something more.

———

GOING INTO A HOUSE FULL OF DEAD BODIES wasn't on the top ten of my bucket list. Going into a *witch's* house with dead bodies was even lower on my scale of happy.

But Adam had asked it of me, so I went. Sherwood stayed in human form, but he didn't look any happier about going in than I felt.

He opened the front door and turned on the lights.

"This house is dark," he told me. "A little light doesn't hurt anything."

The front door opened directly into a living room that looked warm and friendly. Light-colored walls set off wooden floors that were covered in expensive-looking carpets that were, in turn, covered with comfortable-looking furniture. Big windows let in a lot of natural light, and two skylights let in more.

There was plenty of natural light. I gave Sherwood a puzzled glance, and then I walked through the door.

It didn't *feel* light and friendly. It smelled like death, witchcraft, and black magic. The combination was stomach-turning. Suddenly the extra little bit of brightness from the lights didn't seem like overkill at all. Anything that might brighten up the spiritual atmosphere, however insignificantly, was welcome.

"I know," said Sherwood grimly when I sneezed in protest of the smell. "But you get used to it."

There were no bodies in this room, but I looked around thoroughly anyway. Adam had noticed something that bothered him in this house, bothered him more than Elizaveta's dead family, and I needed to figure out what it was.

The bodies began in the kitchen, three of them. I am not a medical professional. I'm a predator, yes, and I kill things. But my victims (mice and other small rodents, usually) die quickly from broken necks. I'm not a cat; I don't play with my food.

Elizaveta's family members—I recognized each of these, though I didn't know their names—were missing pieces. Mostly fingers, ears, toes—survivable amputations. The woman was missing her nose.

They all wore pants and the woman had on a loose unbuttoned dress shirt—no shoes, no socks. The clothes were filthy and smelled of blood and other things. Some of that was because of the usual effects of death, but some was older. Elizaveta would never have tolerated slovenliness in her family, so whoever had held them had not allowed them to bathe or change their clothes.

The woman's body was folded over a bowl that contained beaten egg that had been fresh a couple of hours ago. When I came to that, I took a good look at the room and where the bodies were. There was toast in the toaster and several slices on a large plate next to it. The stove was off, but there was a frying pan on it. On the counter next to the stove was a package of bacon—unopened, which was why I hadn't smelled it earlier.

These people had been tortured—and some of the wounds were very fresh. All three of them had been in the middle of making breakfast, judging by the condition of the kitchen. Who gets tortured and then decides to make a meal? Witches, evidently. Strange. Even more strange was that they had died very quickly and all at the same time.

I examined each of them, sniffing their bodies. Then I went through the kitchen itself, pantry and all. The next room, a workroom of some sort, had four more bodies.

There was nothing wrong with any of these people, no

wounds new or old. It looked as though they had dropped where they stood. I recognized only the teenaged girl. Her name had been Militza. She went to school with my step-daughter, Jesse, though Militza was a couple of years younger. Jesse sometimes gave her rides home from school, though not recently.

Jesse had privately told me that Militza gave her the creeps. I'd told Jesse to tell Militza to find another ride. I think Jesse had been more polite than that.

"There are fourteen bodies," Sherwood said dispassionately, as I explored the room. "Adam described them to Elizaveta, and she identified them. No survivors. Stop right there, don't open that cabinet. There's a sigil on the door. I don't know what it will do, but I doubt it is anything nice."

I stopped. I couldn't sense anything over and above the magical-crafting residue that impregnated everything in the room. It was strong inside the cabinet I stood in front of, but no stronger than it had been other places. Apparently, Sherwood had a more subtle understanding of magic than I did. I found that very interesting.

Sherwood didn't speak again until I'd moved on.

He picked up the one-sided conversation as easily as if he'd never stopped. "Whoever did this wiped Elizaveta's people out. Elizaveta thinks it was probably another coven, trying to take over her territory while she is in Europe. She will be here as soon as she can."

There were no more bodies on the first floor, though I noted that two chairs were missing from the dining room set. I went upstairs then, to search six bedrooms and three bathrooms. I found a lot of interesting things, but there weren't any more bodies.

So I was prepared to find the other seven in the basement. Or at least I knew that there would be seven dead people in the basement, most of whom I'd probably met at one time or another. "Prepared" was probably too strong a word. I don't know how I'd have been prepared for what I saw.

I have seen horrible things, things that haunt me in my dreams. But Elizaveta's basement was one of the worst.

The basement was one big room, forty feet by twenty-five feet at a rough estimate, with a nine-foot ceiling and two doors that I assumed were bathrooms in opposite corners. Like the floor above it, the basement was well lit—though with daylight bulbs in LED fixtures, rather than windows.

A big utility sink was set up on one end of the room, and next to it was a pressure washer, the kind I use for cleaning cars. All of the rest of the walls were covered with metal racks containing various sizes of cages.

The center of the room looked almost like a doctor's office, with twin metal examination tables. Near each bathroom was a chair that looked more like a dentist's chair. All of them had manacles. All of them were occupied by bodies. Two additional bodies were tied to sturdy chairs that matched the ones I'd seen upstairs around the dining table. That meant there was another body down here somewhere.

Reluctantly, I approached the bodies. It had taken a very long time for them to die. Days, I thought, though never having tortured someone to death, I couldn't be sure. Weeks maybe. The kitchen people had been in better shape than the ones down here. I searched each body carefully with both my nose and eyes.

The floor was cement with a drain. The killers hadn't bothered to use the pressure washer to clean up after themselves, so I could see that the floor had been poured so that liquids would tend to flow to the drain without urging. Effluent from the bodies had made streams from their source to the drain.

But Elizaveta's family weren't the only dead bodies in the basement; the rest just didn't happen to be human. The cages along the two long walls held dead birds—pigeons, doves, and chickens mostly, but there was an African gray parrot, a golden eagle, and a handful of parakeets. Next to the utility sink were cages of dead reptiles and amphibians.

On the wall opposite the utility sink were cages of dead small mammals. The top shelves were mice and rats. The rest were kittens and puppies.

Kittens and puppies tortured to death. If I'd been in my human body, I would have cried. I was not apologetic that their deaths bothered me more than the deaths of Elizaveta's family. Those animals had been innocent, and I was not willing to say that of anyone else who had died here.

There were no flies, though the smell of rot was incredible. I had to assume that something kept the insects away, and it was probably not the stench—physical and spiritual— that permeated the room. Some of the smell was putrefaction, but most of it was the reek of black magic. Maybe flies were repelled by the scent of black magic. Or maybe the magic that had killed Elizaveta's family had also killed all of the insects.

I started to go do my job, to leave the small dead creatures and search the corners for the missing dead body, when a movement caught my eye. I yipped for Sherwood, who was pacing with intent by the sink. I couldn't smell him over the rest of it, but his skin was covered with sweat. He stopped and came over.

Without a word, he opened the cage I indicated and pulled out the body of one half-grown orange tabby kitten with gentle hands and set it aside.

"We missed this," he said as he eased a black-and-white body out of the cage. Like the tabby, it was somewhere between kitten and cat.

The kitten twitched and tried to move away from him. "Poor thing," he murmured. "Shh now, you're safe."

He pulled off his shirt and swaddled the cat in it, gently immobilizing it. He set the cat on the floor next to its cage-mate.

He did a quick and complete check of the rest of the cages, but the black-and-white kitten was the only survivor. He picked up his shirt with the kitten and examined the animal more thoroughly while it struggled weakly.

Sherwood's eyes were wholly human and raw with emotion when he met mine. "Missing an eye" was all he said.

You were missing a leg, I thought. Maybe it was a good thing I couldn't talk in my coyote form.

I licked the face of the kitten gently. It tasted as foul as the whole basement smelled. But the touch of my tongue seemed to reassure it more than the werewolf's voice.

Cats don't like werewolves. The only exception I've ever seen to that is my own cat, Medea. I guessed that we were about to see if we could get this one to warm up to us.

"Have you seen enough?" he asked.

I started toward what I thought was the nearest bathroom, and he stepped between me and it. "No. You don't want to go into the freezer. There are some things you don't need to see. We should go."

I looked pointedly at the dead bodies, scratching the floor once per body I could see. One on each of the two tables, two in the dentist chairs, two tied up on dining room chairs. I sneezed and looked around.

"I forgot," he said.

He gave the kitten he held a worried look, but told it, "This should only take a minute."

He strode briskly to a large storage bin near one of the corner rooms and pulled off the lid. It was a big, sturdy bin, but it shouldn't have been big enough to store a body.

I peered inside and wished I hadn't. The body inside was missing legs and arms—which explained the size of the bin. My brain wanted to turn the corpse into a stage prop. His face was almost featureless because his eyes, lips, nose, and ears had been removed long enough ago that the wounds had healed over with scar tissue.

He looked mummified, but my nose told me that he, like everyone else in the room, had been alive only a few hours earlier. I didn't recognize him, but I knew the ghost who lingered, petting the corpse.

Sherwood's voice was grim. "Adam said this was Elizaveta's grandson and that likely Elizaveta had done most of the damage to him herself."

His name had been Robert. The ghost looked at me, then spat over his shoulder and scowled. I ignored him as I sniffed dutifully at the pitiful body.

I made Sherwood wait until I'd sniffed around all of the

bodies again, paying special attention to fingers and faces. Then we both escaped the basement of Elizaveta's house. I don't know who was more relieved: me, Sherwood, or that poor kitten.

I COULDN'T CHANGE BACK. ADAM ASSIGNED SOMEone to take my car back to our house. Then he packed me, Sherwood, and the kitten into his SUV to head for the veterinary clinic while the pack pulled the bodies, human and otherwise, from the house. Pack magic would keep neighbors or low-flying aircraft from noticing what the pack was doing.

Everyone would wait for Warren to return with the firestarters. The plan was for Joel and Aiden to turn Elizaveta's family—and all the dead animals—to ash.

Sherwood suggested that the house be burned down, too—which I was highly in favor of. Given the state of things that I'd seen, I doubted that anyone would ever be able to get a peaceful night's sleep in that building without someone doing a major exorcism or something of the sort to lay the ghosts to rest. I'd never seen an exorcism performed in person, so I didn't know if one would work.

Adam decided against burning Elizaveta's house because he didn't want to draw the attention of the authorities. And because it was a decision that should not be made without Elizaveta's say-so.

I was glad to be in the SUV headed away from that charnel house. Adam didn't say anything—and Sherwood was never exactly a font of words. The only sound for most of the trip was the kitten's squeaky moans. I'd never heard a cat make that sound before—and I hoped I never did again.

"He's dying," said Sherwood, breaking the silence. His attention was on the animal he held on his lap. He sounded casual, but my nose told me better. It didn't take a psychologist to understand why he'd be concerned with an animal rescued from a witch's lair.

"He made it this far," Adam said bracingly, proving that

he'd understood Sherwood, too. "It's just a mile more to the clinic."

Sherwood pulled the kitten up to his face with big hands that supported its whole body evenly and breathed its scent. "Did you know?" he asked. "About the black magic in that house?" His head tilted away from Adam told both of us how important it was to him.

Adam shook his head. "No. I'd have put a stop to it. I had no idea."

Sherwood nodded. "And what are we going to do about it?"

"*We* will do nothing," Adam said. "This is something for me to do."

Sherwood studied Adam for a long moment.

"There will be no black magic in my territory," Adam said softly. He gets quiet when he is very angry.

Sherwood relaxed in his seat.

The kitten survived until we reached the clinic.

I waited behind the very black windows in the SUV while Adam and Sherwood took the kitten in to the emergency vet. I wasn't advertising what I was—there had been a couple of times that the only reason I survived the bad guys was that they didn't know I could change into a coyote. The fight with the goblin this morning was a good example.

They came out about a half hour later, looking grim.

Adam told me as he got in the car, "Touch and go. Lots of broken bones, some of them half-healed. Lots of superficial and not so superficial damage. Minor skull fracture. Dehydrated and starving. They have him on IVs and have treated everything they can treat. It's up to him now."

"They thought it was us who had tortured the kitten," said Sherwood.

Adam nodded. "Until a lady in the waiting room recognized me and got so excited. Sometimes the publicity can be useful."

"There will be headlines," said Sherwood, sounding more settled now that the cat was out of the car and out of his care. "Werewolves rescue tortured kitten."

Adam grinned suddenly and said, "Spotlight will be on

you this time. That useful lady took a picture when you kissed the kitten's nose."

Sherwood snorted. "I posed for her."

"Sure you did, softy," Adam said as we pulled out of the parking lot and headed for home. "That photo will be all over the social media sites by morning."

"Werewolf contemplates dinner," said Sherwood. "Dinner contemplates werewolf back." Then the humor left his voice. "I hope he makes it."

Adam reached out and put his hand on Sherwood's shoulder. "Whatever happens, we've done all that we can."

4

~~~~~

UNUSUALLY, THERE WAS NO ONE HOME WHEN WE arrived. Our house serves the pack as hotel/hospital/meeting place as well as host to the weekly pirate video game tournament that was the pack's obsession. Not even Joel's rescue dog, Cookie, greeted us. Medea was, presumably, around somewhere, but like most cats, she usually didn't bother to greet her people when they first came in the door. I desperately wanted a shower, but for that I wanted to be in my human shape. I don't mind wet fur, but the whole process is simpler without it.

Adam went directly to the kitchen and we followed him.

He looked in the fridge, made a growly noise, and said, "I don't know why I thought there might be leftovers in this house."

We had werewolves living here. Food did not go to waste.

Adam sighed, opened a cupboard, and said, "Toasted tuna sandwiches it is."

He sent Sherwood out to the freezer in the garage to grab a couple of loaves of bread, then set him to thawing the bread in the microwave.

Adam made the tuna mixture with the swift economy of someone who knows what it is like to cook for a lot of people. Darryl was our usual cook, but Adam sometimes fed everyone, too. He'd told me once that it satisfied his wolf's need to care for the pack.

"Two or three?" he asked me as he diced dill pickles.

I yipped twice.

"Three," he said, grinning when I flattened my ears at him. "When you can talk, you can crab at me. Sherwood?"

"Four," said Sherwood, pulling one loaf out of the microwave and putting the other one in.

Despite my best intentions of sticking to my guns (if Adam hadn't planned on listening to me, why did he bother asking?), I ate all three sandwiches—and half of a fourth. Then I tried changing. Adam made more sandwiches.

Sherwood finished his four, then looked at me. He said abruptly, "I need to shower."

Adam looked up. "Are you okay?"

Sherwood started to nod, but stopped. "I stink like that house—and I have no wish to listen to Mercy revisit what we found there."

"Go shower," Adam said. "I have some business to discuss with you and Mercy, but it can wait. I'll get Mercy's impressions. When we're done, I'll let you know."

Sherwood nodded, got up from the table, and left. Though there was a shower he could have used upstairs, I heard him take the stairs to the basement.

The downstairs shower was the one the pack usually used if they needed to. We kept a variety of clean clothes in a closet next to the basement bathroom, sweats mostly, but some of the pack kept full changes—so his decision to go downstairs instead of upstairs made all sorts of sense. However, I was pretty sure it would be a day or two before *I* could go down to any basement, even our own, without trepidation. Sherwood, evidently, was made of sterner stuff.

I ate the other half of the fourth sandwich, two more sandwiches, and two chocolate chip cookies that Adam had apparently secreted in the garage freezer along with the bread. And then I tried changing again.

Usually my change is instantaneous and painless, but sometimes, when I've pushed it too far, it sucks. It doesn't happen often, because there just aren't that many situations, miniature zombie goats aside, that require me to bounce back and forth between shapes.

It took a subjective hour, probably no more than five or six minutes, but I managed the shift. I lay on the floor panting, too tired to move, and waited for my eyes to focus. How, I wondered, did the werewolves put up with this or worse every change? There were a lot of things that made me happy to be what I was instead of a werewolf.

"Okay, then," Adam said. "Let's get you something to wear." I heard him run up the stairs.

By the time he dumped clean clothes on my stomach, I was sitting up. I was going to need a nap soon, but I wasn't going to go to our bed smelling like Elizaveta's house— even a pigsty smells better than black magic. Shower first, nap second. But all that had to wait for the interrogation.

I sorted out the clothes and started to put them on.

"Wait," Adam said, crouching beside me. He ran a light hand over a tender spot on my shoulder—and I winced.

"Oh," I said. "That must have been the goblin." I didn't remember getting the bruise or scrape Adam had found, but it hadn't been the goats.

One of the goats had kicked me in the shin, and another had bitten me in the arm. The arm was bruised, but I'd knocked the little goat loose before he'd broken the skin. Getting bitten by a zombie wouldn't make someone turn into one, I was pretty sure, though getting bitten by something that was dead might result in the mother of all infections. But I knew they hadn't gotten the shoulder, so that must have happened when I was fighting the goblin.

Adam leaned his forehead against my uninjured shoulder and wrapped his hands around both of my arms. The weight of him was bracing against my back.

"I wish," he said, his voice muffled a little against my

skin, "that you healed as quickly as one of the pack. I wish I didn't need you to go fight goblins and zombie goats because I am stuck in stupid meetings with idiots."

"Miniature zombie goats," I corrected. "Or miniature goat zombies. The 'miniature' is important. 'Zombie goats' just sound satanic."

His hands tightened on my upper arms. "I am so grateful that you are quick and smart. That you work at staying alive, Mercy. But I worry that someday that won't be enough."

"I worry about you, too," I told him. "But I would rather worry than try to make you into a . . . an accountant or something."

My stepfather was a dentist. I had, for years, wondered if part of his appeal to my mother was that he was as unlike the danger-seeking bull rider who had been my father (he had also been Coyote, but she didn't know that part) as she could find.

Adam laughed, but there wasn't a lot of humor in it. "For nearly ten years, you led a quiet, blameless life. Danger didn't visit on a daily basis. I keep looking for the cause. For the reason all hell broke loose in your life. I can't escape that the impetus might have been me."

I shook my head firmly. "No. You didn't start the weird stuff. You were just there to help when bad things began happening. The boy, Mac, who came to my door, that had nothing to do with you."

Alan MacKenzie Frazier's appearance had broken a nearly decade-long peace, when I had repaired cars and mostly ignored and been ignored by most of the rest of the supernatural world. Mac had been a ragged harbinger of trouble to come. Poor boy, he'd been dead more than three years.

"If there is a need for someone to blame," I said, "I choose to blame Coyote. That's what Gary"—my half brother—"does. He says that nine times in ten he is right. And the one time left over might be Coyote's fault, too, it's just that he didn't leave enough evidence to pin it on him."

Adam hugged me. "Okay, okay." He sighed, and there

was enough guilt in his sigh that I was pretty sure he didn't
ascribe to my perspective.

He rubbed my arms lightly. "You're getting goose bumps."
He released me and stood up. "You need to get dressed, tell
me all about what you noticed at Elizaveta's house—"

"Dead people," I told him.

"—besides dead people," he continued smoothly. "And
then you need to go shower and rest."

I sighed. "Nope." Because as the ache of the return to
my human self subsided, I realized that a nap was not in my
near future. "After my debriefing, I need to shower and
head to work. No rest for the wicked."

He started to say something, then put his hands up in the
air. "Okay. But I'll bring pizza home for dinner."

Today was my turn to cook.

"Deal," I said.

He helped me to my feet and I let him. My hands felt
clumsy and I was off-balance and had to lean on him to drag
on my jeans. My hair smelled horrid—or at least smelled
more horrid than the rest of me did. And I kept getting a
whiff of Robert. I didn't want to think about, let alone smell
like, Elizaveta's grandson. I pulled my hair back from my
face and rebraided it. It didn't help much, but at least it
wasn't brushing against my skin every time I moved.

He watched me get dressed with what some people
might think was solely an appreciative eye. They just didn't
share a mate bond with Adam. My husband gave the lie to
that old adage that men have only one idea in their heads at
a time and usually that one thing was sex.

Part of him was cataloging my bruises. Part of him was
noticing how wobbly I was. Part of him was worrying about
things he couldn't change. And part of him was thinking
about sex.

I gave that part of him a wiggle of my hips, and he
laughed.

"Hey," he said. "No fair teasing when you know if you
made it to horizontal, you'd be asleep before I got to first
base."

I stuck my tongue out at him.

"Careful," he warned. "Or someone will take you up on your offer." Then, with a quick, rueful smile, he switched gears. "So what did you find at Elizaveta's?"

"What were you looking for?" I asked as I buttoned my jeans.

I pulled my shirt over my head instead of unbuttoning it, then paid for that bit of laziness with having to struggle when one of the shirtsleeves wouldn't turn out properly.

Adam helped me get untangled. "Just tell me whatever you noticed."

"Well, you know about the black magic, obviously," I said. "It was all of them. All of the dead people were black practitioners—even Militza."

No wonder Jesse had gotten a funny feeling about her. Maybe if she'd kept giving Militza rides, though, we'd have discovered what had been going on in our own backyard.

"What do you think about Elizaveta?" he asked. "Could she have lived in that house, with all of her family practicing black magic, and still be a gray witch?"

I shrugged. "Maybe? I don't know about how witches operate on quite that intimate a detail. But she didn't. Didn't avoid it. Is that what you wanted me to find out?" That's why he'd asked me if I could distinguish one witch's magic from another's. I hadn't actually had to do that—Elizaveta's confession had been in her bedroom.

He nodded, his face tight. He'd expected that answer, but he'd hoped for a different one.

"I don't know how she hid it from us," I told him, or maybe told myself. "I swear she doesn't smell or feel like a black witch, Adam. But when I went snooping in her bedroom, there was a secret compartment in her closet."

It had been the most interesting thing I'd found upstairs. The cubby had been well hidden, too. But it's difficult to keep a compartment secret when it is often used and the person who is searching has the nose of a coyote.

"Did Sherwood vet that compartment before you opened it?" Adam asked sharply.

I waved a hand in reassurance. "Yes, of course he did. My guess is that she didn't booby-trap it because she uses it too often. She keeps her working clothes there." She'd washed the blood out but I could still smell it—blood and other things. I hoped that my hair would wash cleaner than Elizaveta's shirt. "They smelled like death, those clothes. Like pain and rot."

"Black magic," Adam acknowledged with something like defeat. "F . . . Freaking son of a gun. Could they have belonged to someone else?"

"In her room?" I asked, but shook my head. "No. They *also* smelled like her."

"How did she hide it from me?" Adam asked.

I didn't think he was asking me, but I answered anyway. "She is a witch, Adam. I expect she used magic." I swayed a little on my feet. The food had helped, but it needed a little more time to have the full effect. I'd be okay in a bit.

"I'm not an expert," I told him. "I didn't know they could do that—hide black magic from our senses. But she did it somehow, and she's a witch. Makes sense it would be witch-craft. But it's a guess."

Adam steadied me with a hand on my back, avoiding the sore places. "Sorry, Mercy. I know you're exhausted, but there is more that we need to go over."

"I'm fine," I told him. "Or I'll be fine in a half hour or so. But if we're going to have a drawn-out conversation, right this minute, then I need to sit down."

Adam pulled a chair out from the table and plunked me down on it.

"The black magic is new, right?" I asked him. "Before we got together, when her house was in town, she'd have you and Jesse over for dinner sometimes. I don't care how good she is, she couldn't have hidden that—" Greasy cloud of magic—but the werewolves wouldn't have felt that. "—odor that permeated the house from you."

Adam sat next to me, absently taking my hand in his and playing with my fingers. I liked it when he touched me like that, without thought, as though there were some magnetic force between us. The only thing better was that I could touch him, whenever I wished.

Thoughtfully he said, "Right. I never even noticed when that feeling that she was a part of our pack stopped. Before we got together, for sure."

He thought about it some more, then grunted. "Whatever she's doing to cover up her foray into black magic, it's powerful stuff because . . . well, just think of all the people who were on that airplane on the way to Europe. She hid it from all of us."

"Passive magic," I agreed. "Because I'd have noticed anything active. Some kind of charm? If you want to know how, I think you're going to have to find an expert."

But how Elizaveta had hidden what she'd become wasn't at the top of his to-do list. Adam looked out the window and gripped my hand.

When he spoke it was soft with hurt. "I wonder when she . . . changed. And why."

He liked Elizaveta. She charmed and teased him. She spoke Russian to him, like his mother had. Despite being clear-eyed about what even gray witches did to keep their power, he'd thought of Elizaveta as family, or something near to it. Adam didn't give up on the people he cared about easily or without pain.

"Maybe it was when that sorcerer vampire scared her," I suggested softly after a minute, when he didn't say anything more. I hoped that if we could figure out a reason, then Adam would hurt less. "Remember? He scared her enough that she left town until he was gone."

Sorcerers are possessed by demons, and those demons can control people who have given up following a path of goodness. That included gray witches, and certainly included black witches.

He shook his head. "No, back then I was in and out of her house a lot. So were the rest of the pack. It was almost a second HQ, because it was in town and more central than our house is. Her switch to black magic couldn't have gone back more than a year or so."

I'd never been inside Elizaveta's house, either house, before. She didn't like me much, and I was afraid of her. The combination, as I've observed before, did not make us friends.

"I've never been in her new place before today," he said. "I'll ask the pack and see if anyone has been in her new house, but I don't think so. We gave her some space right after she moved, and never quite regained our old relationship."

"She moved last year, right? Just before Christmas."

The timing was interesting. It would have been difficult to work black magic with neighbors too close. Mundane humans wouldn't necessarily feel the magic—though that isn't always true—but black magic produces bodies and also smells and sounds. Things that are easier to hide when the neighbors are more distant.

"That's right," he agreed. "I'm following you. Maybe she had to move when she slid from gray to black magic. She picked up her whole family—because the adults mostly had their own places before then—and took them out to the country where people might not notice they were burying a lot of dead animals."

I tried to remember what had been going on around Christmastime. Not because I cared about finding Elizaveta an excuse. Black practitioners tortured and killed unwilling prey. As far as I was concerned, Elizaveta was anathema from this point forward and I didn't need anything more than that. I'd seen those dead animals in cages. I'd probably see them again in my nightmares.

But *Adam* might feel better with a reason.

"Right after Thanksgiving, that necromancer vampire challenged Marsilia—Frost," I said before I thought. If I'd been thinking, I wouldn't have mentioned Frost.

His mouth tightened. Frost was a sore point. I'd been maneuvered into fighting beside Marsilia against Frost in a sort of vampire shoot-out. Frost could command the dead—and so could I, sort of. Marsilia had thought that pulling me onto her team would give her a better chance. Adam needed to get over it because I would have killed Frost if Adam hadn't done it first. Probably. Maybe.

"Do you think Frost might have scared Elizaveta?" I asked.

"Scared me," he said. "I don't ever want to see you fighting a vampire again, Mercy, any vampire. That was too damned close."

Okay, I needed to redirect this conversation because my rules were that he only got to chew on me one time per incident. And he'd already had his say about Frost.

"We were talking about *Elizaveta*," I told him. "Would he have scared Elizaveta?"

He snorted at me, but answered the question. "She doesn't have much to do with vampires." Then his face grew serious. "You told me that necromancy is a rare talent for a vampire."

"One of the vampires told me that," I agreed. I'd relayed that information to Adam so he wouldn't think that Marsilia would be likely to volunteer me to fight more of her rivals anytime soon. "It's why Frost was so powerful."

"Necromancy is more properly a witch thing, right?" Adam said. Then he shook his head and said again, "Elizaveta doesn't have much to do with the vampires. I don't think she ever met Frost." He frowned. "But if he was witchborn, maybe she sensed something . . . It wouldn't be an excuse for what we found at her house, but it would be an explanation."

"When you talked to her," I said, "what did she say when you asked her about the black magic?"

Adam sighed. "I didn't. She would know that I understood what she'd been doing. But I think we both decided that was a conversation best not held over a transatlantic phone call." He was the one who decided to change the conversation this time. "When was the first time you saw Frost?"

"When he tried that coup on Marsilia," I said. "Um. Two years ago? Okay, right. That means it can't have been Frost. Elizaveta didn't meet him when he was here in November.

And if she knew about him by some other means, that would have happened a long time ago."

"If his power was witchborn," Adam said, "Elizaveta would have known when he entered the Tri-Cities the first time. She has ways. So the timing isn't right. At least if all she is responding to is his mere presence. Frost didn't cause her to turn."

He shrugged off the search for the answer to "why" and focused back on more immediate events.

"Who did you scent in the house?"

"All of the dead, Elizaveta, two strange witches—and I think, faintly in an upstairs bedroom, that missing man that we were helping the police look for two months ago—the guy with Alzheimer's."

Adam nodded. "Zack and Darryl caught that, too." He looked away for a moment. "She helped us search for him, too, remember? I should have seen what was going on before this."

"How?" I asked him. "She was hiding from you, Adam. That's something she's very good at."

After a moment, he said, "So you only picked up two strange witches, also. Black witches." I nodded. "And Elizaveta and her whole clan are . . . were black-magic practitioners. Did you find anything else?"

"A few things," I told him. "And I don't know what to make of them. Everyone in the house died at exactly the same time."

"How do you know that?" But before I could answer, he snapped the fingers of his free hand, the one not touching me. "Ghosts."

I shook my head. "They are all over in that house, but I didn't get anything coherent out of them. Trauma might make for strong ghosts, but it doesn't always make them good communicators."

"So how did you know they all died at the same time?" Adam asked.

I frowned, because I wasn't happy about this. "I just knew, Adam. I could feel it in that house—that life just stopped being possible in a single moment, and everything died."

He grunted unhappily, which is how I felt. I did not like knowing that there was a witch out there who could do something like that. Fourteen people and dozens of animals died under her magic. If she could do that to a house full of witches, could she do it to a house full of werewolves?

I also did not like knowing how strongly I'd felt the moment of their death. I was beginning to understand how closely Coyote was connected to the transition between life and death—Coyote was the spirit of change, after all. The implications for me were unsettling.

Moving right along, then. "There were a lot of ghosts in that house," I told him. "If you dig on her land, I bet you'll turn up human remains along with the animals. More than just the gentleman with Alzheimer's."

He grimaced. "That's something we'll figure out when Elizaveta gets back."

"Did she have any theory about who might have done this?" I asked.

He shook his head, then shrugged. "Someone trying to take over her territory while she was away."

Frost was sort of in my head because of our earlier discussion. And he'd come to the Tri-Cities to take over Marsilia's territory. And then my subconscious, which had evidently been plodding along most of the morning, finally connected a few dots.

Adam frowned at me. "Mercy?"

"Huh," I said. "Frost."

"What?" Adam asked.

"I just figured out who the witch that made those zombies smelled like," I told him. "You know how scents are, after a while it takes a bit of jogging to remember when you smelled someone before."

"Yes," Adam said.

I nodded. "I knew that she smelled like someone I'd scented before. But I kept running through the witches I've met—there haven't actually been all that many—and came up blank. But the parts of her that didn't smell like black magic and witch smelled like Frost. Enough like him to be a close relative, sibling, child—even parent. But no further removed than that."

"Huh." Adam made the same noise I had, sounding unusually nonplussed. Then he seemed to gather himself together.

"Frost," he said. "Do you think that this attack had something to do with vampires?"

"Or," I said slowly, "maybe the whole Frost thing had something to do with witches."

He pulled his hand free and used both hands to rub his face tiredly. He hadn't had a full night's sleep in nearly a week. Me, either, actually.

"Terrific," he said. "Just what we need right now, a witch-maybe-vampire territorial dispute."

"I've given you my current conspiracy theory," I told him. "Maybe it is a coincidence?"

"But it makes me go hmm," he said.

I leaned my head on his shoulder. "Sorry."

"Not your fault," he said. After a moment he said, "Did you hear Sherwood turn on the water?"

"No," I said, sitting up. If Sherwood had taken a shower, we should have heard it. "Sherwood?" I called his name. He was a werewolf; he should hear me easily.

There was no reply.

"I can't reach him through the pack bonds," Adam said, getting out of his chair and heading toward the basement. "He's there, but I can't contact him."

Adam didn't run, but he didn't waste any time, either. At the top of the stairs, he stopped and held up a hand for me to pause, too.

The basement was quiet, too quiet, and dark. Now that I was looking for it, I could feel magic at work. I would have sworn there had been nothing there when Sherwood had headed down. Come to think of it, Sherwood, unlike most werewolves, was sensitive to witchcraft—and this was witchcraft. If it had been there, he'd never have gone down.

Adam started down the stairs, but I grabbed the back of his jeans. He could see the darkness and hear the silence, but he couldn't feel what I could.

"Wait up," I whispered. "There's a lot of magic right here on the stairs."

Adam turned and gave me a quick kiss. "Mercy," he said in a normal voice. "Neither you nor I can do anything about the magic, and one of my wolves is on the other side."

I released him. "When you put it like that . . ."

He continued down, and I followed. As his foot hit the fourth step down, inky shadow boiled up, like a weird, black, dry-ice fog. Adam didn't even hesitate. I put a hand on his back as he waded into the darkness ahead of me.

Maybe I should have stayed upstairs where I could have called for help if no one came back up. But he hadn't asked me to do that, and I wasn't going to suggest it. One of our wolves was trapped down there.

I knew when we came to the bottom of the stairs because I was counting, and because Adam stopped abruptly. He snarled and the muscles under my hand tightened to rock-hard as he put pressure on whatever lay in front of him.

"Blocked," he grunted.

"Let me try," I said, slipping by him.

The barrier that had stopped him felt like a giant warm cushion blocking the way. It tried to keep me out, as it had Adam, but everywhere it pressed against me, it softened and yielded. Going forward felt like I was voluntarily suffocating myself in warm wax that slid into my ears and nose and required almost more bravery than I possessed. But Adam had my back, and that knowledge combined with Sherwood's need kept me moving forward.

I shut my mouth before any of the nasty, witchcrafted jelly goop could invade my mouth as well. I grabbed Adam's hand as I struggled forward, hoping I could pull him in my wake.

It wasn't easy or quick, but I made progress. Cool air touched the top of my head, and then I could hear the furious roar of Sherwood's wolf as the warm, insidious magic slid reluctantly away.

As soon as my nostrils were free, I could scent black magic and . . . a strange werewolf whose scent was overlaid with something I'd smelled a lot today. I didn't dare open my eyes until my lids were clear of the barrier, but my nose told me enough.

We had a zombie werewolf in the basement.

I'd leaned forward, so my upper body cleared the barrier first, which meant I was trapped from the waist down and blind when there was a zombie werewolf less than thirty feet away.

I wiped at my face with my free hand, pushing aside the magic until it felt safe to open my eyes. My legs were still stuck in slow motion, but at least I could see.

This zombie was different from the goats, better made. His black coat didn't exactly glisten with health, but it wasn't ragged, either. Hard to tell for sure, with both combatants moving so fast, but I thought the zombie wolf was a little bigger than Sherwood, which would put it in the same size category as Samuel or Charles. If it hadn't been for the smell, I might have believed that it was a living werewolf.

The goats I'd dealt with this morning had been driven by one purpose: to feed. That had made them easy to hunt because they had been blind and deaf to anything else. But this dead wolf fought with intelligence and training.

Sherwood was missing one back leg—which was annoying, I'm sure, even in his human shape. But it was a huge liability in a fight where he was a wolf, as he was now. He compensated for the lack with tactics, forcing his opponent to move into his space, where his hampered maneuverability wasn't such a problem.

Outside of Adam, I don't think there would have been a wolf in the pack who could have taken Sherwood if he'd had four legs. But he was losing his battle against the zombie.

"Mechanical damage," I yelled to Sherwood, as if he

needed my help. With my newly acquired experience with zombies, I continued more quietly, "They don't feel pain. So you have to do mechanical damage. Getting you some help in a minute."

I redoubled my struggle to get my legs free without losing my balance. I pulled my left foot out, turned, and reached back into the barrier and locked my free hand on Adam's, so I could haul with both of my hands. I wasn't going to be a lot of help with a zombie werewolf—we needed Adam.

Pulling him through was like a game of tug-of-war. I made progress, but it was unholy slow. At some point in the process, my left foot came free. In helping Adam, I'd reburied my face in the muck. I couldn't see Adam, just felt the grip of his hands in mine as we both strained to pull him through.

There was a terrible moment when I thought it wasn't going to work—that both of us were just going to suffocate in the blasted barrier. Then finally, with a vast, horrid sucking sound and a zing that went through me like that time I touched an electric fence in the rain, the spell was gone.

Adam stumbled forward, pulled off-balance by the sudden lack of resistance. But he regained his footing almost immediately, his attention on the fight. I dropped his hand and stepped back, gasping for air, as he stripped off his clothes and called on the pack bonds to quicken his change. But he didn't wait for it to take him before he waded into the fray.

Even with the help of the bonds, it would take him five or ten minutes to change. He might have been better off staying human—but he didn't have any weapons and we didn't keep any down here.

"Zombies," I muttered, staring at the dead wolf who fought like a demon. "What do I know about zombies?"

Since the magic was gone from the stairs, I bolted up them to the main floor, then paused.

"Burn zombies," I muttered. "Behead them." I had visions of a dozen horror movies with moving body parts, but I couldn't remember what part of that lore was fiction. I wished we'd experimented a bit with the miniature goat zombies. It would be helpful right now to know if beheading would work. Burning a zombie while we were all in the basement seemed like a doubtfully useful thing. If I succeed in dousing it with enough lighter fluid to actually catch the flesh on fire, there was a good chance that I'd catch everyone and everything else on fire. And no matter what caught on fire, thanks to Aiden and Joel we had a dandy fire suppression system in the house. Beheading seemed the better option with my limited knowledge.

I ran up the second flight of steps toward our bedroom instead of running to the barbecue supplies in the garage. The kitchen knives had been closer, but only a few seconds closer and they weren't big enough.

Adam had a gun safe in the walk-in closet and a locked wardrobe filled with other kinds of weapons. I regretted my cutlass—left in the trunk of my car, which was at Elizaveta's house awaiting one of the pack to drive it home. But there were a lot of sharp and pointy things in the wardrobe.

The first thing I saw in the weapons store was the .444 Marlin. I'd almost forgotten; we'd run out of room in the gun safe and put the Marlin in the weapons store instead.

In the basement, I didn't have to worry about killing innocent bystanders with the gun designed to shoot Kodiak bears. The lipstick-sized bullets might even give a zombie trouble.

No time to dither. I grabbed the rifle, which we kept loaded, with my left hand and grabbed a random sword in my right. I was back in the hallway when I realized what weapon I'd grabbed. Peter's saber.

Peter had been one of our wolves. His German cavalry saber had been at our house when he died—he had brought it over to demonstrate something to one of the other wolves. Or maybe that had been when he was teaching Jesse how to fight with a sword. Honey, his mate, had not taken it back—though she knew where it was.

German steel was more forgiving than the steel of the five katanas that also hung in that closet—it would flex where a katana might shatter. That was the only thing it had going for it as far as I was concerned. It was a heavy cavalry saber.

I'd handled katanas for years and switched to the even shorter, lighter cutlass. But a cavalry sword was designed to be wielded from horseback, as much hatchet as blade, and this one was built for a man who had been taller and stronger than I was. It was better than a kitchen knife.

At least I had the .444.

My foot hit the top step of the stairs to the main floor less than a full minute after I'd run up from the basement. I'd kept a count in my head. Fifty-three seconds is a long time in a real battle. People die in seconds. Heartbeats. I took comfort from the bestial sounds coming from the basement and the burning of the pack bonds. If Adam was drawing upon them still to hasten his change, he was alive.

Then silence fell.

I paused halfway down the upper stairway.

The zombie werewolf cleared the top of the basement stairway and stopped. It looked around as if searching for something. I dropped the sword so I could use the rifle.

The sound drew its attention, and it jumped across the space between the basement stairs and the ones I stood on top of and headed up.

I shot it, twice, as fast as I could work the action on the rifle. The Marlin kicked like a mule, and even the ported barrel didn't make up for the fact that the gun was relatively light and the bullet was huge. I should have waited on the second shot and I knew it even as my finger pulled the trigger. It only carried five bullets and I'd just wasted one.

But my first shot had taken it in the chest. I had been aiming for the forehead, but the zombie was moving fast. The bullet knocked it back, rolling it down about five steps and onto the space between the staircases before it caught its balance again.

Ears ringing with the cannonlike bellow of the rifle, I drew a deep breath, reminded myself I needed to cause mechanical damage, and hit the wolf's front left leg with the third bullet, as it attempted my stairs again. Because of the porting of the barrel, the muzzle flash from the Marlin was over two feet long and, for some weird reason, explainable only by battlefield conditions because a muzzle flash doesn't *do* anything, that reassured me.

The next shot took the bottom of its jaw off, but the next and last bullet went into the wall when the wolf moved faster than I'd seen it move before and swiped the end of the rifle barrel.

I let it go—I was out of bullets anyway—and the rifle hit the wall with a noise that left me pretty sure that weapon wasn't going to be useful ever again. But I was too busy dodging a swipe of the wicked-sharp claws to mourn my long-dead foster father's rifle. That swipe had more in common with a bear's attack than a timber wolf's. If it hit me, it could kill me with a single blow.

I leaped for the sword and stabbed the wolf with the reflexes I'd been working on since well before I'd been gifted with my cutlass. I'd executed the move smoothly, and if I'd been using my cutlass or a katana, it would have slid into its heart.

But Peter's sword was a freaking cavalry saber and the tip was heavier than I was used to—and the tip and the handle were not in line. The only thing my sword thrust did was release a vile-smelling stream of effluvia all over the white carpet. And then it got stuck in the zombie.

I didn't bother trying to hold on to the sword. Instead I leaped over it, over the railing of the stairwell, landing right on the edge of the first step of the basement stairway.

The zombie had a little trouble turning . . . but I saw to my horror that it was healing the damage I'd done. Its destroyed leg wasn't bearing weight yet, but it no longer hung from the shoulder. And when it bared its fangs at me, the lower jaw I'd all but shot off was fully functional.

It was healing itself faster than a werewolf could. That wasn't something the miniature goat zombies had done.

The zombie followed my jump, but betrayed by the bad leg, it fell badly when it landed and struggled to get to its feet. It acted as though it hadn't yet realized that one of its front legs wasn't working.

I scrambled into the kitchen and grabbed a knife out of the block and turned to face the zombie, but it hadn't followed me. I heard a battle by the stairs and ran back until I could see what was going on.

Adam had stopped the zombie werewolf from following me. There was fresh blood all over my mate, but like the zombie, he had already healed most of the damage. He was still changing, and if he'd healed as much damage as it looked like, he'd been drawing heavily from the pack to do so. That was probably why the pack bond felt like it was on fire.

I wondered where the zombie was getting its power from.

It saw me and lunged. Adam grabbed the dead wolf by its shoulder and ripped it (literally, because its claws were dug into the carpet) away from me. The creature fell all the way to the foot of the stairs and . . .

Magic hit me, as it had earlier this morning when the goblin had flung his magic around. This power surged from the bottom of my feet and traveled up my body in a shock so hard that for an instant, every muscle in my body locked up with painful intensity in a giant, hellish charley horse–like cramp and I couldn't breathe, couldn't stand, couldn't think. When that subsided and I drew in a first, panicked breath, I smelled ozone, as if I'd been too close to a lightning strike.

I collapsed in a heap on the ground and my body vibrated to even more magic, gentler magic this time that my senses wanted to interpret as music, a wild wailing sound of grief and rage echoing through my flesh and not my ears.

And then it was over. I scrambled instinctively to my feet—the floor is a terrible place to be in a fight. Adam stuck his side against me so that I didn't go right back down to the floor.

The last I'd seen Adam, his body had been poised to follow the zombie down the stairs. Evidently my weird reaction had kept him upstairs.

"I don't know," I told his worried eyes breathlessly. "Some big magic." I rubbed my arms.

There was a scraping noise from the basement.

We both looked down the stairs, but the zombie was nowhere to be seen—though I could certainly still smell him. There was a puddle of the same foul, squishy liquid muck that Peter's sword had extracted in the carpet at the foot of the stairs. Something big had been dragged through it.

"Sherwood?" I called.

The sound of his growl should have reassured me.

Adam's ears flattened. He glanced at me.

"Okay," I said reluctantly.

So I waited while my mate went down the stairs to see what had happened.

5

SHERWOOD GROWLED AGAIN. THIS TIME IT WAS A pained sound that had elements of human vocal cords in it. He had been all the way wolf when I'd seen him, not five minutes ago.

Adam, out of view, didn't make any noise at all. And a wave of magic rolled over me again. I always had trouble with heavy magic use, but it seemed to me that my reaction to it was getting worse over time. That, or I was just being exposed to more powerful magic users.

As soon as I could stand up, I took a deep breath and decided I was done waiting. I traveled cautiously down the stairs. The bottom two were wet with repulsive goo from the original barrier that we, Adam and I between us, had brought down. But beyond a certain squick factor because I was barefoot, I didn't pay much attention to that. What I saw in the room stopped me cold, right in the middle of the gooey spot.

Adam had paused about halfway across the room, presumably for the same reason I had.

At the far end of the room, where the shadows were

deepest even in the middle of the day, was a giant beanbag chair. Beanbag chairs were one of the few pieces of furniture that were equally comfortable for wolf and human, so we had a few scattered around the room.

The remains of the zombie wolf were laid on the chair as if his comfort mattered. The dead werewolf looked lifeless, really dead and going to stay that way. Sherwood knelt on the floor next to the beanbag. He was a mess. I'd heard his human voice amid the wolf, and his body was like that, caught halfway back to human in a way I'd never seen before. He was stuck in a bizarre mismatch of human and wolf limbs and features that looked incredibly painful and completely unsustainable. If his outside was so wrong, I couldn't imagine what his internal organs looked like.

But he had two human-shaped hands resting on top of the pile of hide-covered bones. Sherwood's eyes—golden, feral eyes—tracked from Adam to me and back.

Adam sat on the ground where he was, all the way down, belly to the floor. I'd have sat down, too, but there was a deep puddle of goo under my bare feet. I hoped that the combination of how much less of a threat I was than Adam and the fact that I was farther away would be enough to make my presence not an issue for Sherwood.

Sherwood apparently agreed with me. He watched Adam for a moment more, then, satisfied that we would leave him to his work, he turned his attention to the dead-again werewolf.

And he sang.

The words were mangled by the caught-between-change shape of his mouth, but he was pitch-perfect and the song ruffled the hair on the back of my neck and broke my heart with its magic-carried grief.

We waited where we were, Adam and I, while the scent of black magic dissipated. The scent, the feeling of black magic, lingers for a long time, years or even decades. But the dead wolf and the basement—and me and even my unholy rank-smelling hair—were all being cleansed as Sherwood sang.

I don't know what Adam could feel, but it seemed to me as if magic swept out from Sherwood and washed over us all. I couldn't tell what kind of magic it was—a rarity for me. It just felt like Sherwood, masculine and reserved, werewolf and gruffly kind. Not werewolf magic—that's another thing altogether. This was something . . . more primal. More wild. And I didn't think there was a thing more wild than pack magic.

As I observed Sherwood grieving over this werewolf who had been a zombie, I thought about the power of what he was doing. Of what I'd felt course through me.

I thought about how Sherwood had ended up in our pack, sent by the Marrok who had ruled us all and now ruled all of the werewolves except for our pack. And how short a period of time lay between when Sherwood got here and when those ties had been cut.

I thought of what I knew of Sherwood, whose voice was so beautiful that tears coursed down my cheeks from his sorrow when I could not even understand the words of the song he sang. But I knew the music's content because its intent was made magically clear.

Bran, the Marrok, had rescued Sherwood from a witch's coven that the Seattle wolves had uncovered. Sherwood had been missing a leg that nothing could help him regenerate and no trace of memory that predated his stay with the witches. He hadn't really answered me about how much of his captivity he remembered when I asked him how we'd headed into the witch's house earlier today.

Eventually Bran had given him a name—in a fit of exasperation, from how Sherwood himself had recounted it to me: Sherwood Post. It wasn't a . . . usual name, gleaned as it was from the authors of two books on Bran's desk, a collection of short stories by Sherwood Anderson and Emily Post's treatise on etiquette. Bran read all the time, but I had never known Bran to read either of those authors.

I'd had a class in American lit in college and the professor had made us memorize quotes, I'm not sure why. I'd thought Anderson a little too self-aware in his writing, and had much

preferred F. Scott Fitzgerald, who was more readable, and
Faulkner, who was a better wordsmith. But as Sherwood sang
his mourning song, I remembered that Anderson had said
something about people who were deliberately stupid, burying deeper thoughts beneath a steel barricade so they wouldn't
have to look at them. It made me wonder if Bran's choice of
name had been less impulse of the moment and more a rea-
soned epithet.

I *had* been mostly convinced that Bran knew who Sherwood had been before the witches had taken him. Standing
at the foot of the stairs in a puddle of rotting slime with
Sherwood's magic washing over me, I was certain of it.
There just weren't that many werewolves who could gener-
ate this kind of magic; I could not fathom a world in which
Bran would not know of him. Bran kept track of werewolf-
kind as closely as any dragon kept watch on its treasure.

I was getting an odd feeling, and I don't know where it
came from exactly, though it solidified as I watched Sherwood sing to the dead wolf as he drove the filthy magic out
of it and away. I thought that maybe Bran had also known,
somehow, that Adam and our pack would end up alone
against the world, and he'd sent this broken wolf to help us
survive. This wolf he would not be careless with. If Sherwood was here, it was because Bran wanted him here.

As he sang, Sherwood became human. Not as quickly as
I could shift—but more quickly than I'd seen anyone else
change except Bran's son Charles or an Alpha wolf pulling
power from the pack. The last few minutes, as he sang,
fully human, I could pick out words, though not meaning,
because he wasn't singing in Welsh or any other language
I recognized.

After the last note fell and silence reigned, Sherwood
kissed the dead wolf on the muzzle, ichor- and blood-
drenched though it was. Our broken wolf closed his eyes,
rested his forehead on the hide-covered bones, and blasted
the body to ashes in a burst of magic that sent me down on
my butt in the cooling, fetid goo I'd been trying to avoid
sitting in.

By the time I could see again, Sherwood was in a heap on the floor, unconscious, and Adam was licking my face.

"I'm fine," I told him. "It's just the magic." Even the thought of how much power Sherwood had used made me shiver in reflex. "Go check on Sherwood."

I lurched to my feet to do the same.

———————

"HUH," SAID SHERWOOD, DRINKING HIS THIRD CUP of cocoa and staring at the crumbs on his plate. He was bathed and wearing a set of black sweats a little too small for him, sitting at the kitchen table with his back to the wall.

The house reeked, and would until Adam's contractor got his guys to come rip out the carpet where the zombie werewolf had left generous amounts of putrid fluids behind. I would finally get to replace all the white, and tomorrow I'd be happy about that. But the smell was only the organic part of the foulness that had invaded our house, and that wasn't nearly as troubling as it might have been had Sherwood not banished the stink of black magic with his song.

My hair was wet and I had shoes on to protect me from standing in any more horrid stuff. I was on my third set of clothes today and it wasn't even noon. I'd like to say it was a record, but it wasn't even close. The washing machine, fortified with a cup of the orange cleaner I used to get grease off my hands, was attempting to remove the goo from the seat of my jeans. If that didn't work, I'd throw those jeans away.

Adam, fully human again, had been in the middle of recounting the events following Sherwood's expedition to the basement shower when I'd arrived freshly showered and clean. While he finished the tale, I made more sandwiches for all of us—and lots of hot, spicy cocoa.

As Adam finished describing what Sherwood had done to the zombie's body, Sherwood shook his head.

"I don't remember that," he mumbled into his cup. He set the cup down, stared at it, then said, "I remember nothing after I headed down and set off the witch's trap—not until I came to myself in the shower upstairs. I don't remember a zombie werewolf. I don't remember singing. I don't sing. I don't do magic." He glanced up at Adam with shadowed eyes. "I don't *think* I remember." He clenched his hands.

The sorrow I sensed from him, through the pack bonds and through his scent, did not waver. But I was almost certain he was lying about not remembering, I just didn't think that Adam and I were the people the lie was aimed at. Only his last sentence rang true, and I could see from his face that he realized that.

"Why did he change like that?" I asked Adam, because it had been bothering me—and Sherwood didn't even remember doing it.

Adam had stopped his change midway once—and the result had been monstrous. I still wasn't sure whether it had been on purpose. But what Sherwood had done had been different.

"Like what?" asked Sherwood.

"He couldn't change his whole body quickly enough for his purposes," said Adam. He spoke to me, but he was looking at Sherwood. "He just changed what he needed. I can't do it—but the Moor and a few of the other older werewolves can."

We all absorbed that for a few minutes.

"So," I said briskly, "we need to figure out how the zombie got in."

Adam frowned. "We can try, but without a witch, I'm not sure we'll get anywhere."

"I can ask Zee to help," I suggested. "He's not a witch, but he's been around a long time." I hesitated. "I could call Bran or Charles."

Adam shook his head. "Zee, but not Bran or Charles. There are too many eyes on us right now. I think it's more important than ever that the supernatural community knows that we are not part of Bran's people right now."

Sherwood frowned at Adam. "What's so important about right now?"

Adam looked at him for a long moment. "So," he said, "let us leave aside why you wept over a long-dead wolf, shall we? Or how you cleansed the stink of the dark magic from our home."

Sherwood looked away. *"Please?"*

"We have to figure out how they got in and planted that trap," I said. "If Sherwood hadn't been here, Adam—what if Jesse had found that thing? What if they plant another zombie werewolf?"

"They have no more," Sherwood said, his eyes wolf-bright and his voice nearly guttural. The change was so sudden, his voice so powerful, that I found myself scooting back in my chair.

"The one who made that poor shadow is long dead." The wolf in human-seeming almost glowed with power. "They have neither the learning nor the power to make him again. They would not have risked him if they had known who was here. I have made him free, my poor brother that was."

He looked at Adam, but his eyes did not meet those of my mate. "As for other mischief—my song has claimed this place for now. No evil may enter without invitation. They *cannot* come in." He glanced beyond us, behind Adam and me, toward the basement. "Not for a while."

"Sherwood?" Adam asked.

"No," growled Sherwood's wolf, a hint of contempt in his voice. Then his voice gentled a bit. "Not yet. He still hides."

"Wolf," I asked, "who are you?"

"Witchbane," he said. *"Witch's Spawn."* He grimaced, or maybe he smiled. "Something like that, maybe. I forget. Who are you?"

"Nothing that grand," I said.

He bared his teeth. "Coyote's Daughter," he said. "We shall sing them to the great death."

Then he shuddered, closed his eyes, and passed out cold. If Adam hadn't been as quick as he was, he would have fallen all the way to the floor.

"Well," Adam said, hefting Sherwood's limp form and striding out to the living room, where he could put him down on the couch. "That was unexpected."

"Not as unexpected as having him turn into a full-formed whatsit who obliterated a zombie werewolf," I said.

Adam grinned at me. "That which doesn't destroy us . . ."

"Leaves us scratching our heads and saying, 'What's next?'" I said. "Is he okay?"

Sherwood had already begun to stir.

"Pack bond says he's fine," Adam said. "Just worn-out. Maybe another couple of sandwiches?"

I made food—at this rate I was going to have to go shopping again. When I brought the food into the living room and set it on an end table, Sherwood was sitting up again.

He squinted at the food and began to eat like a . . . well, like a ravening wolf.

"I remember that," he growled. "Whatever that was." Then he looked a little sick and he quit eating. When he spoke again his voice was soft and uncertain. "Unsettling to have that inside me all this time. To know that it is there, all of it, waiting for me."

I didn't think he was talking about his wolf.

"What will come, will come," Adam said. "That's enough for now."

Sherwood gave a derisive half laugh. "Right."

"You saved the day," Adam told him firmly. "Let it go."

"Apparently that is something I'm good at." Despite the self-directed bitterness of his words, when Sherwood gave another half laugh, this time it was genuine.

"Okay?" Adam asked.

"All right," Sherwood said. To prove it, he started eating again.

Adam gave me a rueful look. "I planned on matters going a little differently, but I still have to discuss some things with you." He turned to Sherwood. "And you, too. It feels a little anticlimactic after all of this—" He tipped his head toward the mess that started at the top of the stairway to the upstairs and continued in a trail of interesting stains and broken things down toward the basement. "But it is still important—in the long run, it might be more important."

I swallowed, because Sherwood wasn't the only one

chowing down. Adam had not eaten—and he should because he'd changed back and forth, fought a zombie werewolf thingie, and healed himself really quickly. "You need to eat," I told him.

"I ate while you were in the shower," he said. "I promise."

I glanced at Sherwood, who raised both eyebrows to Adam but then nodded.

"I'm not doubting his word," I said with dignity. "But it's my privilege to make sure while he's looking out for everyone else that he looks out for himself, too."

Adam moved the few inches between where he stood and where I sat on a little round ottoman. He leaned down and kissed me.

When he straightened up, he didn't move away. "So," he said, "the late-night meetings I've been having are the forerunner of meetings between the government and the Gray Lords. No one really expects firm results, but it is the first nonhostile negotiation."

Sherwood pursed his lips. "So why are you telling just Mercy and me? Why not the whole pack?"

"Neither of you appears on the list of active members of the Columbia Basin Pack that someone presented to my old friend General Gerald Piotrowski," Adam said dryly. His voice was especially dry when he said "my old friend."

"The vice chairman of the Joint Chiefs of Staff?" asked Sherwood.

I was impressed that he knew who Piotrowski was. Not many people could tell you who the chairman of the Joint Chiefs of Staff was, let alone the vice chairman. And Sherwood was an amnesiac who didn't remember his own name—unless he was attacked by zombie werewolves, apparently—so in-depth knowledge about the government wasn't something I'd have expected of him. Heck, I had a degree in history so I was supposed to be interested in things like that, and *I* didn't know who the participants on the Joint Chiefs were.

"That's the one," agreed Adam. "And factually, it was you, Mercy, and Zack."

"Someone has an old list of who is in the pack," I said. "And maybe they missed me because I'm not a werewolf; I shouldn't be pack, except in an auxiliary sense." Something chilled in my veins, foreboding maybe. "The group of rogue Cantrip agents that kidnapped the pack in order to make you go assassinate their target had a list, didn't they?" Last November, at the same time that Frost had been trying to take over Marsilia's territory.

Adam put a hand on my shoulder and let it rest there. "I think that it's the same list. I don't know if they got it from the rogue group, the rogue group got it from them, or someone gave it to both parties."

"I was," I said slowly, "under the impression that it was Frost who gave the rogue agents that list."

Adam gave me a quick nod. "That's what I thought, too."

"Is it important where their information came from?" asked Sherwood.

"Not to the immediate discussion," Adam agreed. "But maybe for later investigation. I'll see to it that Charles gets word—maybe he can figure it out."

"Okay," said Sherwood. "So why is it important that Mercy and I aren't on this list?"

Adam gave me a very apologetic look. "Because the rest of the pack is going to be playing bodyguards for the governmental delegation."

I twisted so I could look up into Adam's face. "Can we do that? In a meeting between the government and the fae. Aren't we supposed to be . . . I don't know . . . neutral?"

"Yes," said Adam. "At least if we are to keep to the spirit of the bargain. But the pack isn't attacking the fae, just trying to keep the humans safe—from all threats." He didn't sound happy. "If the fae don't attack us, we won't attack them—and that is the essence of our agreement."

"How did you get maneuvered into splitting hairs that fine?" Sherwood asked.

"How did the pack get wrangled into Hauptman Security business?" I asked. Because it had been HS business that had kept him in late-night meetings recently, not pack business. There were pack members who worked for Adam's company and more who could be called in to substitute if needed. But most of the pack had their own careers elsewhere, and that was how Adam liked it.

"Remind me to fire the head of my contracts department in New Mexico," Adam told me. There was heat in his voice that made firing the better of two options for the person in question.

"Okay," I said.

Adam shook off his anger and continued briskly. "A contract with a small government project gave the US government access, not to Hauptman Security, but to 'Hauptman Security and all of its adjunct personnel'—which is a phrase that snuck into our government contracts about two years ago so it didn't raise any flags."

"The pack isn't adjunct to Hauptman Security," I said.

"You'd think that, wouldn't you?" Adam agreed. "But on this ten-thousand-dollar contract, on page forty-eight, 'adjunct personnel' was defined as anyone under my aegis."

Sherwood rocked back in his chair. "The pack."

"So the rest of the pack is on guard duty?" I said.

"Protection," Adam agreed. "This will be pretty high-level. The secretary of state, the vice president, the Senate majority leader, and a few other key people are all coming here with their staff to meet with a triumvirate of Gray Lords. They are trying to put together an agreement that will define the relationship of the fae to the human government of the United States that won't lead to genocide."

"Genocide of fae or humans?" asked Sherwood.

"Both," I told him, because I could do that math. "Or either."

"And they had to *blackmail* you into playing bodyguard?" Sherwood asked.

Adam gave him a wolf smile. "Funny that you noticed right off that it is a bad idea. It took me two days and a call to a friend who was fishing in Alaska at the time to convince the general of that."

The friend was probably the retired military man—

someone who'd known what Adam was—who had been in charge of hiring Adam (not Adam's company, which was strictly security) over the years. I knew that Adam had done a lot of contract work for the government during the Cold War era. I was pretty sure that had included some assassinations, but Adam never talked about what he'd done. All of that had stopped by the time Adam and I had become more than acquaintances, so I didn't know who his "friend" was.

Sherwood grunted. "That little contractual nudge took a lot of planning." He said it with regrettable admiration.

"Why didn't they just hire Hauptman Security?" I asked. "And ask if you could pull the pack into it?"

Adam grunted. "Some of the people in the government want a better guarantee than my word and a paycheck. Because I'm a monster."

"Wow," said Sherwood. "A blackmailed monster is just what I'd want guarding my back."

"Insulting," I said.

Adam gave me a wry grin. "Exactly. At any rate, we have ironed out a deal. Mercy, you will be in charge of orchestrating the meeting—where and when." I gave him a horrified look, which he ignored. "I give you Sherwood and Zack as your muscle. The pack will do guard duty for the government and get paid royally for it. When this is done, I'll get a better contracts lawyer." He sighed. "Or go back to reading every damned contract myself, which is how I used to do it."

"What are you thinking?" I asked. "What idiot would put me in charge of a government meeting? I can't organize a pack barbecue without Kyle. Why isn't someone else doing it? Marsilia? Or one of the fae? Or one of the government people? I bet they do this all the time."

"Kyle is a good idea," said Adam, ignoring my objections. "I'll see if he will consent to help us out. I can bill the government for him." It sounded as though that last would make Adam very happy.

"Adam," I said. "Why am I elected?"

"Because," said Adam patiently, "you put us in charge of the Tri-Cities, Mercy. Our pack. That means the fae will only meet with the government if our pack hosts the meeting. We need a representative of our pack to be an intermediary between the government and the fae. It's lucky that the fae are willing to accept you."

Sherwood, watching me, laughed. "Don't worry, Mercy. We won't actually have to *do* anything difficult. We're just glorified messengers. All the decisions will be made by the government and the fae."

I swallowed. It didn't sound like an easy job. Adam's hand cupped the back of my head.

"I believe in you, little coyote," he whispered into my ear.

I gave him an annoyed huff. "I'm not going to start reciting 'I think I can, I think I can' anytime real soon now."

Adam laughed and straightened back up. This time, his hand came off my shoulder. I missed it.

"I have every confidence that you could do just fine if we put you in charge of everything," he told me. "But Sherwood is right. It is mostly a ceremonial position with a lot of running around. The government will make their own arrangements for lodging and"—he grimaced—"security. As will the fae. Mostly you will be in charge of finding a venue that's acceptable to everyone. And, once we have the dates, you'll reserve the meeting place, show up on time, and give a very short speech that probably both the fae and the government will insist on editing."

"How *will* this play with the fae?" I asked. "Not my bit in this. I mean, really, how will they think about the pack playing security for the government? Not just how we're going to spin it. We are supposed to be a neutral party, right?"

"I checked with Beauclaire," Adam said. "Not all of my meetings have been with the government. He thinks we can squeak by."

Beauclaire was a Gray Lord, one we had a working relationship with. As close to a working relationship as you could have with someone who, I had reason to believe, could raise the sea and bring down mountains.

"Whatever the public thinks," I said, "the fae know that the only reason our compact works is because the fae want it to work. We don't have the horsepower to make a real stand against the whole might of the fae. Or, probably, even one of the Gray Lords. Not without the support of the Marrok."

"Which they don't know that we have," said Sherwood.

"Which we don't have," I said gently.

"He loves you," Sherwood said, his voice certain.

I nodded. "He does." Bran had more than demonstrated that he thought of me as a daughter. "But he loves the werewolves more. He has fought for centuries for them." I sought for words and found them in an unexpected place. "To give them 'life, liberty, and the pursuit of happiness.' He can't help us without risking that."

"He would risk the werewolves for you," Adam said.

He had risked everything for me. That knowledge had healed a wound going back to when he had driven me from his pack, from the only home I'd ever known, when I was sixteen. Bran had not abandoned me.

But that was a dangerous secret. Only a few people knew what Bran had done, and we needed to keep it that way. The fae especially couldn't know that Bran still felt responsible for me. They were a feudal society, for the most part. If they thought that our ties with Bran were still in place, then they would look upon our treaty with them as a treaty with all of the werewolves.

Our treaty with the fae had to stay small, only our territory, only our pack. That meant that Sherwood and the rest of the pack needed to believe we were on our own, too.

"Bran won't help us," I said firmly, believing it. Bran wouldn't help us because he wouldn't need to. "And that keeps him, and us, out of a power struggle between werewolf and fae that could escalate into a war that everyone loses. If we screw up here, the fae won't go after the rest of the werewolves on the planet for it. Our separation from the other packs in North America makes everyone safer."

Sherwood made a noise, but then said, "Therefore we

don't have the support of the Marrok. We only have ourselves to count on."

It didn't smell like he thought he was lying, precisely. That "therefore" was a wiggle word. He believed that the Marrok would help us if needed, but he understood that it would be a bad thing if other people thought so, too.

"And a treaty with the fae, in which they agree to abide by our rules within the bounds of our territory," said Adam. "Beauclaire understood that guarding the humans is the business of my security firm, which has retained most of the members of my pack. He agrees that Mercy is acceptable to act as our liaison and our ringmaster. Since any fae who harms a human here is breaking the agreement the fae have signed, we, the pack, are not being put into a position where our honor would be compromised. Instead, Beauclaire assures me, I am a good businessman and dealmaker for getting the government to pay me to do something that we are already bound, by our word to the fae, to do anyway."

Adam sounded a little bemused. I didn't blame him. Being coerced didn't sound like a smart business decision to me. But the fae had a twisted view of a lot of things.

"Are you charging them more, since they are taking not just your regular security detail but also most of the pack?" I asked.

"Of course," he said. "I also added a premium for being a bunch of jack . . . rabbits."

"You can say 'jackass' in front of me," said Sherwood, batting his eyelashes.

"You swear in front of my wife again," purred Adam, "and we'll discuss what I will say in front of you."

Sometimes I forgot how old my mate was. In most ways he was thoroughly modern. But he always opened the door for me, pulled out my chair at restaurants—and avoided swearing in front of me. None of which I minded.

Sherwood slid to the front of the couch—so he could get out of it in a hurry—and it wasn't to run away. The events of this morning had left both werewolves on edge. It wasn't beyond the pair of them to engage in what Adam liked to call "a good tussle" to blow off steam.

"Wait a minute," I said. "Does that mean that the government can force the pack to work for them whenever they want to?"

Adam said, "Point to you. That's what the contract says, and it says it with no out date. However, I told them I would give in this one time—because of the importance of these negotiations. But I also told them that I'd take them to court to fight that contract if they didn't add an addendum limiting them to this one time."

"Slippery slope giving in to them at all," said Sherwood.

"You make sure to fire that contract lawyer," I told Adam. "Because the real problem if this came to a court battle isn't privacy for the government; it's making the fae think that we won't keep our word."

Adam nodded tiredly. "And if the government ever figures that out, it might give them the idea that if they want to get the best of us, they just need to go to Los Alamos, talk to one of my business directors, and get them to sign off on a contract with an obscure and useful clause."

He took a breath and let it out. "The government, in the embodiment of Piotrowski, is anxious to move while the fae are willing to meet. It wasn't in their interest to fight me. So I got more money and an addendum to that contract that ends any obligation my pack has to the government directly after the meeting is held. It isn't always a bad thing that the government doesn't know the fae as well as they might. As well as we do."

We all fell silent, contemplating the complexities of a close personal relationship with the fae.

Finally, Adam slapped his hands together and dusted them. "But that's a problem for another day. I think we have sufficient problems at hand."

"Right?" I said. "How many of you think that the attack on Elizaveta has something to do with this meeting?"

We all raised our hands, including Adam.

"That goblin this morning could have been involved, too," I said. "He told us that 'she' told him that he could come here, that we would keep him safe from the authorities—or words to that effect."

"Checking our response time?" asked Sherwood.

I yawned. "Or exhausting our resources."

"Or we are jumping to unwarranted conclusions," cautioned Adam. "Getting from 'she' to 'a witch' to 'the witches who attacked Elizaveta's family' is a leap of Olympian scale. And adding that this meeting has nothing to do with witches at all . . . and yet."

"Right?" I said.

"Coincidences sometimes happen," Sherwood said heavily. "But when they happen around witches, they aren't usually coincidences."

———

WHEN I GOT TO WORK, FINALLY, THE IMAGINARY parking lot full of cars with scheduled appointments that I hadn't been there to repair wasn't there. The customer parking lot was empty, as were the three repair bays.

Maybe Tad had called everyone and told them not to come in—but that didn't sound like Tad. Answers came when I opened the office door and saw Zee at the computer inputting invoices.

Siebold Adelbertsmiter looked like a wiry old man, balding and nimble for his age. Looks, in his case, were very deceiving. Zee was an ancient fae smith, a gremlin, if you read his official government ID. Since gremlins were an invention of the twentieth century and Zee had been ancient when Columbus was commissioned to find a new route to Asia, I had my doubts. But I seldom contradicted Zee on matters that didn't involve me.

He glanced up at me but didn't stop the rapid keystrokes. "Your inventory is too low," he said. "You will be out of parts this time next week."

"I have a large order coming in day after tomorrow," I said.

He grunted. "You are charging too much for labor. It is more than the dealership."

"They charge what their faraway masters tell them a job should take. We charge actual time. Since I was trained by the best mechanic in the world, I am a lot faster. My right hand is arguably better and faster than I am, since his father is that same mechanic. Our clients usually get out cheaper— and they know that our repairs are solid."

Zee grunted again.

Since he'd given me that same speech in the past—not quite verbatim, but close enough—I assumed that grunt was a grunt of approval.

"It is good," he said after a moment, "when children prove they actually listen to their elders."

"It is good," I said carefully, because the old fae was as prickly as an Alpha werewolf about people noticing weaknesses, "to see someone who can really type. It takes me twice the time to do those entries as it does you."

He huffed, but we both knew that not very long ago, his hands had been in no shape for quick typing. He'd been held and tortured by the fae who had been trying to find out just how powerful Zee's half-human son was. That was why I hadn't called him in to help Tad this morning. My comment amounted to "I'm glad to see you're feeling better" in such a way that he wouldn't take offense.

"This shop," he said, changing the subject away from his hands. "Everything works correctly. It has no character."

"Give it a few months," I said. "Things will start breaking down just when we need them. It will be back to usual before you know it."

He looked at me over the rims of the wire-framed glasses that he wore when doing close work. I was pretty sure they were an affectation. "Are you patronizing me?"

I hitched a hip on the padded stool that was on the customer side of the counter. "Nope." I looked around at the clean walls and neatly organized matching shelving units. Even the bays smelled clean and new. "This shop makes me feel itchy, too."

He hit the enter key and set his work aside. He took off his glasses and set them on the counter.

"You do not smell like a goblin," he said.

Zee could smell goblins? I mean, I could smell goblins, and the werewolves could smell goblins, but I didn't know that Zee could smell goblins.

"That was this morning," I told him. "Very early this morning. I've showered since then. The more recent thing was a zombie werewolf set loose in the basement of my house."

I gave him a general rundown of everything that had happened. Except for the secret part—that Elizaveta and her family had all been practicing black magic. I didn't leave out the fae-government meeting. Zee was in a precarious place with the Gray Lords. They had wronged him and he'd avenged himself on the responsible parties. I wasn't sure how safe he was, and I wouldn't leave out any information about the Gray Lords for fear that it could affect his safety.

"Witches," Zee said when I was done, ignoring the information about the meeting, which told me that he'd probably already known. "I have not had much to do with witches. In the old days, if one became troublesome, I killed them. Mostly they died off on their own before I felt the need to bestir myself."

Witches were mortal, I was pretty sure. I had the feeling that they probably avoided the fae. It was a question that I might have thrown to Elizaveta—but not anymore.

"Do you think that we should warn the fae that there is a new group of witches in town?" I asked.

Zee grunted. "If they do not know, then they deserve to be blindsided. But I expect they know; they are planning their meeting with the government and so are more concerned with the doings of the mortals here than usual."

I guess the meeting wasn't as secret as all that, at least not among the fae.

Zee grunted again, then picked out a single inconsequential detail from my whole recitation of witches and zombies and said, "That rifle that was damaged—it was the one your father bequeathed you?"

I blinked at him a moment, then said, "Yes. The Marlin."

He nodded. "Bring to me your father's rifle, and I will fix it."

Adam had looked at it and determined that the zombie had bent more than just the barrel. He didn't think it could be fixed.

Neither of us had thought about bringing it to Zee. If Peter's sword had been broken, Zee would have been the first person I'd have taken it to. But I just didn't think of Zee and rifles at the same time.

"I will," I said in a voice that was a little rougher than I meant it to be.

He frowned at me. "What are you leaking about, child? Go work on that carburetor. You have the mixture too rich, I can smell it from here."

I huffed and went back to the car I'd been working on yesterday. I hadn't been crying, no matter what Zee had said. Though it had been a close call. Bryan had really loved that rifle.

Tad returned with lunch. It was Chinese, so splitting it between the three of us instead of two was pretty easy. I shared the same information with Tad that I had with Zee. He was still mulling it over when an old customer stopped in with a stalling Passat and no appointment.

"I heard you were back in business," Betty said, handing me the keys. "Thank goodness. I've had it to the dealership twice and they can't figure out what it is."

The dealership had a couple of decent mechanics in their mix. If someone brought a problem back to them, the car went to one of their good people. If they hadn't been able to fix her Passat, then I was glad Zee had decided to spend the day here.

"We'll take a look at it and call you when we know more," I told her. "Do you want Tad to give you a ride home?"

Betty was in her eighties, though she didn't look a day over sixty-five. Even if the waiting area was cleaner than it used to be, I wasn't going to make her sit around until we knew what was up.

"Bless you, Mercy," she said. "That would be wonderful."

As Tad drove off with her, our two o'clock appointment drove in. I took that one and left the Passat with its mystery problem to Zee.

The rest of the day was pretty normal. We fixed a few cars, including the Passat. I never did figure out what was wrong with it—Zee told me he had to let the bad mojo out. I thought he was kidding, but that was what I put on the bill.

Betty had been Zee's customer before I started working at the shop. She just laughed as she paid for the work when Tad and I dropped the car off.

"That Zee," she said. "He likes his little jokes. One time he said that he told my car to behave itself. He didn't charge me for that one—but the car ran fine for another six months. If Zee says he fixed the car, it will be fixed."

We sent one old BMW to the eternal resting place (a scrap yard) and mourned with her owner. When there weren't customers around, we chatted about odd topics. Zee, Tad, and I had spent a lot of days like this. It felt like coming home in a way the previous weeks had not, as if with Zee's presence, the shop had regained its heart.

Working on a car cleared my head. When there was a gnarly mechanical problem to fix, I would concentrate on that—and all the other things going on in my life got sorted out by my subconscious. But most of the work I did in the shop was more like building with Legos. Once I had the plan of attack laid out, and understood the steps to take—then there was this Zen time where my head cleared and I could examine things without the hefty weight of emotion.

The first thing I decided was that now that there were witches added into the mix, Adam could not have left the humans in the government to guard themselves. There was only so much that mundane security could do against supernatural forces. Because of the badly written contract, he had an excuse to give to the fae—so that contract had actually turned out to be useful. And it was nice that he was charging them more money.

"Why are you humming, Mercy?" asked Tad, shutting the hood of a car with his elbow because his hands were covered with grease. Neither Tad nor Zee had adopted my new habit of using nitrile gloves to keep their hands cleaner.

"Humming is fine," proclaimed Zee more directly from under the new bug (as opposed to the old ones) he was working on. He didn't like the new version as well—he had a whole spiel in German that he would occasionally lapse into about the beauty of a simple car.

"But do not, please," he continued, "hum 'Yellow Submarine' anymore today. I may be working on a Beetle, but it is not necessary to also sing songs of the Beatles."

I switched to "Billie Jean" and Tad sighed. Zee snorted but didn't object.

The second thing I thought about were the witches who had killed Elizaveta's family. There weren't a lot of clues about who they were. The only clue I could think of was that one of the witches shared a close bloodline with Frost.

I didn't know much about Frost's background, but I knew where to go looking.

I should talk to Stefan.

And all of my Zen disappeared in one thought. Stefan was my friend. He had risked his life for mine on a number of occasions, the most recent being my involuntary trip to Europe.

He had never done anything to me that was not my choice. But that didn't matter. I didn't want to talk to him at all.

Maybe Adam could.

6

~~~

ADAM CALLED ABOUT FIVE MINUTES BEFORE closing time to say that he had another meeting and Jesse was staying over with a friend. He sounded tired. I told him it was no trouble; I'd just stop and grab something on the way home.

Zee had gone for the day, but Tad was helping me tidy the office.

"You know," he said, swinging his mop with practiced ease. "You and my dad have been whining all day about how sterile the garage is. But now you're insisting on cleaning all the nooks and crannies that might have gotten even a smudge of dirt."

"I don't know why I surround myself with insubordinate smart alecks," I said, getting a smudge off the big window with a little elbow grease. "Maybe I should fire a few."

He gave me a companionable grin. "If you're going to start firing smart alecks, you'd have to start with the biggest one of all. I dare you to fire my dad, I just dare you."

I looked around. "You know that he's going to give us

both the edge of his tongue if we don't have this immaculate when he gets in tomorrow."

"Yep. Hypocrites, the both of you," he said affectionately.

We were getting ready to lock up when a battered bug sporting a rattle-can, glitter-gold paint job drove into the lot. The VW known as Stella chugged roughly, coughed, and died as soon as she stopped moving.

"Sorry," Nick, Stella's owner and devoted fan, said. "I know it's closing time, but Stella isn't doing well—I can't figure it out. And I need her to run for another three weeks before I can afford to fix her again."

It took Tad and me and the young man about three hours to fix Stella to our satisfaction. Nick wasn't an absolute newbie; buying Stella two years ago had turned him from someone who had never put a wrench on a bolt to someone who could change his own oil and spark plugs. But Stella was a diva who would be a challenge for the most experienced mechanic to keep running.

Darkness had fallen by the time Nick drove off, but Stella was purring like a kitten.

"Softy," said Tad as we cleaned up.

"You donated your time, too," I reminded him. I'd told Nick that we'd throw in labor because he'd been sending people to the reopened shop. He could pay for the parts when he caught his breath. If money was too tight, he could come put in a few hours—he knew enough to run tools.

I expected Tad to continue teasing, but he turned grim instead. "Last time I left you alone here," he said shortly and half-embarrassed, "you almost died. Not going to do that again anytime soon. Nick wouldn't have even slowed your kind of bad guys down."

And that explained why he'd been coming to the shop before I got here and insisted on locking up afterward. We all had our scars.

"Thank you," I said. "I appreciate it." Contrary to popular belief, I did know my limits. Having Tad guard my back was comforting.

He nodded without meeting my eyes. And he waited until I was safely in my car before he got into his own.

I decided to celebrate surviving the day by driving the extra few miles to a local fast-food place that served an Asian-Mexican fusion that could take the roof of your mouth off with heat and still taste amazing. I grabbed enough food to feed half the pack, just in case, and headed home. Traffic made me turn right instead of left and I found myself taking the long way back.

The long way took me past the turn to Stefan's house. I had decided that Adam could talk to Stefan. I slowed the car, giving it a bit more gas when it stuttered. I needed to do some fine adjustments still.

Without letting myself think too much, I turned the car and drove to Stefan's house. I pulled into the driveway and parked next to the dust-covered VW bus that had been painted to match the Scooby-Doo Mystery Machine.

I got out of the Jetta but couldn't make myself go to the house. Instead I wandered around the bus. Life-sized and stuffed, Scooby watched me sadly from the front passenger seat. His coat was getting sun faded.

Stefan opened his front door and walked out, stopping well clear of me, but close enough to engage. He didn't say anything.

"Shame to let it sit there," I said finally, not looking at him. "I've spent a lot of hours keeping her running. If you leave her there, she's going to need rebuilding again."

"I need to drain the gas tank and refill it before I drive it again," he said. "I confess, the prospect is a little daunting."

"Call Dale and have him tow it to the garage," I suggested. Dale was one of the towing guys we both knew. One of the perks of driving old cars is getting to know towing guys. "You might air up the tires first, though; the right front tire is a little low."

"And having you fix her is messy, too," Stefan said. "If I pay you, Marsilia might take it into her head that you should be punished for charging me money. If I don't pay you, I'm telling her that I consider myself a part of her seethe again—which I do not. I'm an ally, certainly. But never again will I owe her fealty."

Marsilia ruled the vampires in the Tri-Cities. We had a long-standing agreement that I would provide whatever maintenance her cars needed and she would keep her vampires from attacking me. She had destroyed Stefan, who had been her loyal wingman, for her own needs. If that had been the extent of it, I thought Stefan would have forgiven her for that. But to do it, she'd gone after the people Stefan kept in his household to feed upon, his sheep. Most vampires would not have cared, but Stefan believed in taking care and responsibility for his people.

I pursed my lips, took a deep breath, and turned to face him. "How about an exchange of favors?" I proposed. "I came here for information—and I am happy to fix the Mystery Machine to get it."

"What do you need?" he asked.

The yard light did a decent job of illuminating Stefan. He looked good. Back to his usual self, even. He was tall and lean, but not skinny now. And he looked entirely human again, something in the way he balanced on his feet and the energy with which he moved. For a while he'd moved more like a vampire—some of the very young or the very old have this odd jerkiness to their movements, like somewhere there might be a puppeteer making them move.

Stefan also looked like a cat contemplating a strange dog.

I laughed. "Nothing to put that look on your face. I just stopped in to ask a question. If we can turn that into an exchange that gets you out of a dilemma, that's all the better."

He relaxed fractionally. "What did you need to know? Or do we need privacy for it?"

"I just need to know whatever you can tell me about Frost. I don't think that we need privacy."

"Frost?" said Stefan. "He is dead, Mercy." Then, very un-Stefan-like, he stumbled a little. "All the way dead, I mean."

"I know that—I accomplished his demise," I said, putting him out of his apparent misery. I'd have thought a vampire

as old as he was would have gotten around the awkwardness of how to announce the extinction of a vampire.
Maybe that awkwardness was more about what was between us, though. "Or at least I was there when Adam finished him off—but Adam wouldn't have been there without
me. However you'd prefer."

Frost had been finished, I was pretty sure, before Adam
got there to complete the business. But there was no arguing that Adam had ended Frost with absolute finality.

"But here's the thing," I said. "I stumbled into someone
who smells a lot like Frost recently. Since it is the only
identifier anyone has picked up in the whole mess, I decided it might help to get more information."

"Today's mystery?" asked Stefan.

And because he was a friend, and because Marsilia
needed to know about the attack on Elizaveta's family and
I wasn't about to call her, I told Stefan about my morning,
stopping just after the werewolf zombie in the basement—
and I tidied up the zombie wolf's attack and end without
much detail, leaving out Sherwood's spectacular performance
entirely. His secrets didn't belong to me.

Unlike with Zee, I left out the upcoming meeting between the fae and the government. I would have been surprised if the vampires didn't know about the meeting—the
vampires had ties pretty high up in politics. But if they
didn't know, they weren't going to learn about it from me.

I also didn't tell him about the evidence that Elizaveta
and her brood were working black magic—just as I had not
told Zee. That was pack business. We paid her a retainer for
her services. We had been supporting her while she tortured unwilling subjects for the power she used to aid us.

"Elizaveta's family is gone?" he murmured.

I couldn't tell what he felt about that.

"Yes."

"And you and Adam were attacked by a zombie werewolf at your home and"—he did air quotes—"'the werewolves took care of him.'"

"Not a lie," I told him. I don't lie very often, so I'd been very brief instead. "I can't tell you things that aren't mine to tell."

He watched me for a moment, and then his face relaxed and he nodded. "Okay." Looking away, he continued, "You could have called on me for help with the goblin."

I knew what he meant. Just as I bore bonds to my mate and to our pack, I also had a bond to Stefan. Through it, he could control me, not just my actions, but my thoughts. He could take away my ability to make decisions for myself. All I could do was trust that he would not do that, that he would continue as he had since I'd asked for his help against another vampire.

That was why I'd been avoiding him.

He didn't deserve my first response, so I kept my mouth shut until I could give him the real truth.

Finally I said, "I didn't think about it. It was pack business, so I took a pair of werewolves. He was a goblin, so I called Larry."

"Fair enough," he acknowledged. "But it could have killed you when it came out of the barn. You are no match for a goblin. You could have called me." And he could have come. Like his former Mistress, Marsilia, Stefan could teleport. I'd never heard of any other vampires who could do that.

He paced away from me and stood, arms crossed, with his back to me. "Once you married Adam, you pulled yourself out of your weight class. Someday I will be looking at your dead body, because you were too stubborn to call me."

There was real anger in his voice. I thought about telling him that it wasn't his job to protect me—but I actually didn't know the vampire protocol about situations like ours. I thought about telling him I could protect myself—but he was right.

"If I had thought about it," I told him, "I might have called you. But that would have been a mistake. Marsilia leaves you alone now."

He laughed and it sounded harsh, like broken dreams.

"She allows you to stay here, Stefan. In relative safety. Instead of forcing you to move into another vampire's territory. She allows you to be independent when you might not have that luxury elsewhere."

He nodded. "She is generous," he told me, meaning the opposite.

"If she thinks that your first loyalty is to our pack—or me . . . especially me—she will not abide it." I held up a finger to make him pause. "And if the pack thinks that I have a tame vampire that I call upon whenever things might get hairy, it will be equally bad for me."

I put a hand on his arm and he stiffened. "But I am very happy to come over to your house and ask you to help me solve mysteries."

He drew in a deep breath he didn't need. Then he turned around and let his arms drop to his side. My hand fell away when he moved.

"All right," he said. "All right, Mercy. We are friends as well as allies? But I am not pack—nor should I be."

And I realized that Stefan was lonely. Werewolves are like that. They need a pack to belong to, to be safe with. Some of them don't like it much, but that doesn't change the nature of the beast. I knew vampires lived in seethes, but it had never occurred to me that one of the reasons they did so was that they, like the wolves, needed to belong.

There was not much I could do about that. Stefan did not want to be a member of the pack—and the pack would not, could not, make him a member.

Stefan was apparently finished with that conversation, because when he spoke again it was on a different topic. "I don't know a lot more about Frost than you do. He showed up as a Power maybe twenty or thirty years ago—I don't keep track of time on that level, so I'm not sure. He seemed to be acting as a minion of Bonarata for most of that, so I watched Bonarata, and not him." Bonarata was the Lord of Night, ruler of the European vampires, who had, I was assured, long tentacles of power that dug deeply on this continent, too.

Stefan frowned deeply. "I don't know who made him or why. I don't know who his affiliates are. But I should be able to find out."

"What nationality is he?" I asked.

"I don't know. I had assumed that he was European, given that he initially came as an agent of Bonarata. I can find that out, too." Stefan rubbed his hands briskly together. "Give me some time to run some things down. I do think it is interesting that a vampire who has power over the dead and a witch who creates zombie goats share a close familial scent. If he was born a witch and someone turned him—that someone needs to be stopped."

"Creates miniature zombie goats," I corrected him.

He nodded at me. "'Zombie goat' sounds satanic."

There are reasons that Stefan and I became friends.

MY PHONE RANG WHEN I WAS ABOUT HALFWAY home from Stefan's house.

I glanced down at my cell phone, which was faceup on the passenger seat. Whoever was calling wasn't a number my phone knew, but it was a Benton City number. Benton City is not a hotbed of robocallers trying to sell auto warranties or time-shares. I let the phone ring three times before I gave in to curiosity and pulled over to the side of the road.

"Ms. Hauptman? This is Arnoldo Salas. You were at my house this morning with the zombie goats."

"Mr. Salas," I said. "What can I do for you?"

"There is a car that has been driving back and forth in front of my house. It matches the car my boy saw yesterday. I do not know if it means anything. Maybe whoever is driving the car is lost—we get that here a lot."

"And maybe we should get you some help right now," I said. "Okay. Don't go outside your house. Don't answer your door if anyone knocks. I will call you from this phone when I get there."

I called Adam and got his voice mail. I called Warren and got his voice mail.

I called Stefan.

———————

"WHAT DO YOU THINK THAT YOU AND I CAN DO against a witch?" asked Stefan, sounding not overly concerned.

I glanced over at him. He was driving his two-year-old baby blue BMW because my Jetta now only had one usable seat.

"Do you think I should call for some more backup?" I asked. I'd left a message for Adam. I could have called more werewolves, but I wasn't sure how much help they would be. I, at least, had my undependable resistance to magic. Stefan was Stefan.

I didn't want to call Sherwood. Not because he wouldn't be useful, but because he'd been pushed enough today.

"I could call Wulfe," he said.

I straightened in my seat. "No."

"He can deal with witches," he continued. "They are very nearly his favorite playthings."

"No," I said again. More firmly.

Stefan grinned at me. "Yes, the 'very nearly' thing is a problem. He might just throw in with the enemy because you are 'more fun as an opponent than any witch.' I'm afraid that last bit is a quote. A recent quote. I didn't know, yesterday, why he'd suddenly started blathering on about witches. He must have known about Elizaveta's visitors."

A chill ran down my spine. I did not want to be within a mile of Wulfe if I could help it. The crazy-like-a-tornado-in-the-land-of-Oz vampire wasn't anyone I wanted thinking about me at all. Let alone looking forward to having me as an opponent.

"Hmm," I said.

"So now you are warned," Stefan said, his voice remote. The reason for that became apparent in his next sentence.

"I need your promise that you will summon me should Wulfe become a problem. Wulfe is not werewolf business."

I stiffened. But I didn't think that he was influencing me. I *thought* that it sounded like a good idea. That right there is the reason vampires are so scary.

"I understand your reasoning," I said slowly.

"But?" Stefan supplied.

"But," I agreed. "How about if I make you a promise when I am not sitting in the car next to you?"

A distinct chill settled in the air. "You do know that if I were going to influence you like that, I could do it if I were here and you in Seattle."

"Thanks for that," I told him sourly. "How about I promise to consider what you've said should the occasion arise?"

"Fine," he said.

I knew I'd hurt his feelings. But there was a tie between us through which he could make me think and do whatever he wanted—and unlike hypnotism, I was pretty sure that "whatever he wanted" was limitless. I saw a man participate happily in his own death. The vampire involved wasn't Stefan—it was Wulfe. That knowledge made me understand why trapped animals have been known to gnaw their own legs off. It was a peculiar kind of claustrophobia and there was nothing I could do about it.

Nothing Stefan could do about it, either.

"I am being unfair," I said grudgingly. "I know it. But . . ." I made a frustrated sound.

"But," agreed Stefan heavily.

And we drove the rest of the way to Benton City in silence.

———————

STEFAN'S WAS THE ONLY CAR ON THE ROAD IN front of the Salas house. As we turned down the long drive, the porch light came on and Arnoldo Salas came out.

"She quit driving by as soon as I called you," he said grimly. He had a gun in a holster on his hip and he was wearing his military posture. His breathing was slow and even—deliberately so, I thought. I didn't know him, but I thought he was pretty spooked.

I shrugged. "I'm not a witch," I told him. "I don't know how they think—and only some of what they can do."

"I don't want her near my family," he said.

"I don't blame you," I agreed. "Let me introduce my associate. Arnoldo Salas, this is my friend Stefan Uccello. We'll wait here for a bit—*don't* invite us inside your house— to see if she returns. If she does, we'll find out if she wants to talk."

I could hear the sound of a car's engine in the distance. It might just have been one of his neighbors.

"Do you know why she is stalking my family?" he asked.

I shook my head. "I don't know the why of any of this. Witches are hungry for power—and killing the goats would give her power. But it would take more power than the goats' deaths to allow her to do something as spectacular as turning them all into zombies. And that accomplished nothing except to make your family sad and scared. Do you know any reason anyone would have had for that?"

"Scaring people is fun," said the witch, stepping out of the shadows about ten feet from the porch.

I had not sensed her in any way—and, I could tell by Stefan's complete stillness, neither had the vampire. Usually supernatural creatures who can hide from sight forget about other things—scent or sound.

I, of course, jumped—as she evidently intended.

Arnoldo Salas pulled his gun.

She smiled at him. I noted that she was tall for a woman and built on a graceful frame. Her hair was dark and her eyes were some light color but I couldn't tell for certain if they were green, gray, or blue in the dimness of the night. I see very well in the darkness, but colors tend to fade to shades of gray.

Her face had been relatively plain until she smiled and the expression gave definition to her features. She reminded me of someone, but I couldn't place who. It wasn't Frost, though she did indeed share a close family resemblance to his scent under the foulness of her magic. Smelling her again, I was absolutely certain of the connection between her and Frost.

I hadn't been able to scent her until she'd come out of the shadows, though. I didn't like that at all.

"Aren't you a darling?" she told Salas in a husky voice with an accent that originated in the Deep South. "But you won't have any luck with that old thing, so you might as well put it away." There was magic in her voice that made the hair on the back of my neck stand up.

He held his stance, cradling the gun in a classic grip. A light sweat broke out on his face—but the gun held steady.

She turned her smile to me. "And that is the reason I picked this family, Mercedes Thompson Hauptman. I find it so interesting when people don't do as I tell them. It doesn't happen too often."

I wondered if the three tortured members of Elizaveta's family had been told to go make breakfast. Time to think about that later. Right this moment, I needed to distract her from Salas. I didn't like the attention she was paying to him, even with her face turned toward me.

Last moon hunt, which we held out on the Hanford Reservation, the pack had been on the trail of an elk when a rabbit broke cover just in front of us. Just for an instant, the pack weighed switching their prey before continuing after the elk.

Salas was the witch's version of that rabbit and I wanted her focus on me instead.

"Picked them for what?" I asked.

"To get your attention," she said. "We need to talk." She glanced at Arnoldo and said softly, "Why are you still pointing that gun at me? Stefan Uccello is a vampire. Shoot him."

This time Arnoldo didn't react at all.

The witch frowned at him. "That's not nice," she said. "I asked you politely."

"Mr. Salas," said Stefan softly. "I think that if you put

the gun away, you won't be so interesting to her. That might be a good thing."

"Ms. Hauptman," said Salas. "If I shoot her, will she die?"

"Probably," I said. "But then you'll have a dead woman on your front lawn. I'll stand witness for you that she was a witch, but she is not trying to harm you just now. I think that she is responsible for the killing of your son's goats, but that won't get you out of a murder charge. Worse, I am fairly certain that she is part of a group of witches. If you kill her, they will come for you. I promise that our pack will try to keep them away, but our resources are limited."

"Werewolves protecting humans," drawled the witch. "I never thought I'd see the day. It's kind of cute."

Salas nodded at me and put his gun away. He glanced at Stefan and then away. He'd heard her call Stefan a vampire, but he was willing to give us the benefit of the doubt. Which was pretty amazing in a man I'd only met this morning.

"You wanted our attention," I said. "You have it. What do you want?"

"We have pushed out the local coven," she said. "My lady, our Ishtar, has told me that you have found the results."

"Yes," I said. Who was Ishtar? It sounded, from the way she said it, more like a title than a name, but I couldn't be certain.

"Good. Then you will have no trouble with us assuming their place. We find that this town, which previously we knew nothing about, has become very interesting—a place where the werewolves make certain everyone feels safe. You will stay out of our way—and we will allow you to remain here."

"No," I said. I'd heard the "feels" safe. "Feels safe" is a lot different from "is safe."

She smiled. "Ms. Hauptman, you are young." Which was a weird thing for her to say. I'd have put her in her midtwenties, maybe, given the kindness of night shadows, even midthirties. "I doubt you know your history. Until the arrival

of the Marrok, werewolves were the vermin of the supernatural world. Dangerous individually, of course, if one were
such a fool as to put yourself in a bad position, but ultimately
not much of a threat. Nuisances. Your pack does not belong
to the witchborn Marrok, he who has abandoned his birth-
right. Alone, you and your pack are no match for us."

She was guessing about Bran being witchborn, I was
pretty sure. Bran made a point of not confirming that ru-
mor.

The witch looked at Stefan. "I understand that you do
not represent the Mistress of the Seethe, but that she listens
to you. Please inform her that we will send a delegate to
speak with her sometime in the next few days."

"No," I said. "You are not staying here."

She turned her pleasant face to me.

"We will not allow black witches in our territory," I said.

"Darling," she said. "You already did." She turned to
walk away. "Oh, and about that meeting your mate is planning. When we act, don't interfere."

Shadows cloaked her. The three of us waited on Arnoldo
Salas's porch until she was gone.

"Do you know why the witch could not make you do as
she asked?" Stefan asked Salas.

Salas let air out through his nose like a spooked horse.
"My mother had the pope bless me when I was a child. She
asked him to bless me that witchcraft would not touch me
or my children. It is a story my father liked to tell. My
mother was afraid of witches."

"Me, too," I said, still looking around.

"She is gone," Stefan said.

"You're sure?" I asked.

He nodded. "I am certain."

"Mr. Salas," I said earnestly. "Do you have the ability to
leave town for a week or two? You've caught the attention
of the witches and I don't think it's a good idea."

He nodded. "I have some vacation coming. My wife's
mother lives in California, and she has been asking us to
come visit."

"I would go."

His mouth tightened. "It does not make me happy to leave the field because of a witch."

"You have a family to protect," I said.

"I can leave for two weeks. I have neighbors who can mind our place, but we still have to come home."

"That will give her time to forget about you," said Stefan. "Why don't you call Mercy when you are ready to head back?"

"And if no one answers," I told him grimly, "maybe you should consider staying away. I have a feeling that she's not going to forget about you very easily."

ALL OF THE LIGHTS WERE BLAZING AT THE SALAS household when we left. I didn't blame him in the least.

I called Adam's cell phone and left the message that I was headed home. I called Warren's phone and left the same message. Feeling Stefan's attention on the matter, I said, "My recent kidnapping has left everyone a little on edge. So I check in."

He nodded.

Eventually he asked, "What do you intend to do about the witches?"

"Not my call," I told him. "I'll let Adam know and he'll take it from there."

Not that I wouldn't give him suggestions. I hesitated, but I needed to talk this out. And Stefan had a tactical mind— he could pick out things that I missed sometimes.

"Why didn't the witch just pick up the phone and call us? Our pack isn't exactly hiding out. She killed the goats, turned them into zombies, to get our attention? That is a serious waste of power right before what might be a real fight. Killing Elizaveta's people would get our attention all on its own. She doesn't make sense. But, Stefan, she wasn't lying."

"Just because something is stupid doesn't mean it is not true," said Stefan.

I tapped my fingers on the dashboard. "No, but it's still stupid." I thought a little more. "I can understand tonight—just now at Salas's house. There was no power wasted. She was testing us, to see if we would protect someone who we met just this morning."

"Probing for weakness, yes," said Stefan. "I agree. I have another thought you are not going to like. She meant to take the boy—you could see it in her. She took the goats as revenge because that boy stood up to her. She tested the father, but it didn't anger her. She expected it. Witches have different affinities, but most of them are good with things like bloodline powers."

"The boy resisted her—and she divined that it was something that might run in his family?" I asked. "Because she could normally control someone? If she asked someone to come to her, they would have to do it?" I swallowed. "I thought they needed artifacts—like the collar Bonarata had on that poor werewolf in Italy."

"For werewolves," he said. "But people with no magic?" He shrugged. At least he didn't sound happy about it. "If it helps," he added, "it is a rare thing. Back in the days when covens dotted the landscape of Europe, they were highly prized. They called them Love Talkers."

"Love Talkers are fae," I told him. "And they are male."

"In fairy tales," he said. "But most of those stories are about witches, not the fae. And I think it is one of the few witch traits that is equally strong in men and women."

I supposed if Baba Yaga was fae, it was only fair that some of the stories about the fae were really about witches.

He continued, "We are safe enough, but I am not sure a blessing, even one given by the pope, could make a human resistant to witchcraft." He pursed his lips thoughtfully. "But witchborn families can be resistant to magic."

I didn't think, upon reflection, that the Salases were even a little bit safe while that witch knew where they were. If they were witchborn and didn't know it, that would explain why the witch singled them out. It also meant that, like any other white witches, they were prey.

I picked up my phone and called Mary Jo.

She listened while I explained everything.

"You want me to protect them?" she asked.

"I want you to find another two wolves and go keep watch. Call us—me, I suppose, because Adam is in another freaking long meeting—if you notice anything awry. Do not engage unless it can't be helped. But this man's whole family has a target painted on their backs."

"You have any objection to me grabbing Sherwood and Joel?" she asked.

I hesitated. "Only if you don't force Sherwood," I said finally. "Accept no for an answer."

"Done," she said and disconnected.

———

THE BILLBOARD ON CHEMICAL DRIVE WAS NEW. *Don't let the monsters win in our city* was sprawled menacingly over a picture of a cute little girl with a terrified expression on her face, down which slid a single tear. A shadow of a wolflike creature fell over her white dress. In case I was in any doubt of who funded the billboard, eight-foot-tall letters on the right-hand corner proclaimed the website address for the John Lauren Society.

The Citizens for a Bright Future were more active in the Tri-Cities, so I was more familiar with their tactics. Bright Future's focus was more protest marches, graffiti, and vandalism. My builder had spent a lot of time and money (for which I was billed) keeping them away from the garage. Now that the garage was rebuilt, Hauptman Security had run people off twice in the last two weeks. I had killed one of Bright Future's members a while back. It had been self-defense, but they didn't intend to let it go. Not as long as his cousin ran the local chapter, anyway.

The John Lauren Society was a different enemy altogether. They had money and their attacks were better planned. The billboards that had begun springing up all over town after the incident with the troll and the bridge were the first hint we'd had that they were interested in the Tri-Cities.

Two of the signs on the farmer's field this morning had been smaller versions of JLS billboards.

It was good, I thought as I drove past the billboard, to remember that not everyone was enamored of living in a city under the protection of a werewolf pack.

I wondered what the JLS would think about witches.

———

HORDES OF HUNGRY WEREWOLVES WERE AWAIT-ing the food I brought. Okay, it was only Lucia, Aiden, George, and Honey—and only some of them were were-wolves. But they *were* hungry.

I threaded my way past the destruction between the front door and the kitchen, then passed out the cold food and ate myself, one hip on a counter, and caught up with everyone's day.

"Cookie is gone," Aiden told me sadly.

I looked up at Lucia, who nodded. "The brother of a friend of mine took her. She has a nice family now, and another shepherd to play with."

Aiden sighed. "And there are too many people coming in and out of here for her. I know."

Lucia tilted her head. "We can find another dog who needs our help. Maybe one who would enjoy all the com-motion?"

"That's where you were when the zombie wolf tried to destroy the house?" I asked.

She nodded. "Cookie saved my life." She didn't sound worried. Lucia was one of the most confident people I'd ever met. If she were a werewolf, she might give Bran a run for his money.

"And you saved hers," said Aiden, sounding happier. "Balance."

Aiden had spent a long time in Underhill. We were working on things like generosity and charity. He was more comfortable with bargains.

It was early when I headed to bed, but it had been a long

day and I was tired. I took a long, hot shower that loosened my sore muscles, then took my battered body and tucked it into our big bed.

In my dreams I was wandering down a dark road with Coyote. We were talking about . . . water, I think. Then suddenly Coyote stopped, turned to me, grabbed me by my hands, looked into my eyes, and said, *"Her name is Death."*

I woke up gasping in panic, and Adam's voice from the bathroom said, "It's all right, sweetheart, it's just me."

"It's just I," I told him, more pedantic than usual because I was scared.

"Good to know," he said, unperturbed. "I'd hate to think that someone else was in my bed."

"How did your meeting go?" I asked, shaking off the ugly feeling that had accompanied my nightmare.

He grunted without pleasure. "It would be so much easier if I could kill a few of them. Then I wouldn't have to argue for an hour to get them to see common sense. I have one more meeting tomorrow afternoon before the show is ready to start. Can you break free? They want to meet you and tell you that you don't have any real power, they just need you to be the figurehead and play messenger."

"When?" I asked.

"Two in the afternoon," he said.

If Zee didn't mind working in the shop again, it would be no trouble. "I can do that, I think. Where?"

He turned out the light in the bathroom and pulled back the covers. He looked at me. "I'll pick you up," he said absently.

And then ripped the covers all the way off.

I squeaked and ran. He caught me without much effort because he was my Adam, and I didn't really want to run away from him. I was laughing when he dragged me (not ungently) by one leg to the bed.

He picked me up and set me on the mattress.

"You are so beautiful," he told me.

He was wrong, but he wasn't lying. I can hit pretty, but

beautiful was a long way off. Christy, his ex-wife, was beautiful. Honey was beautiful. But if Adam thought I was beautiful, I wasn't going to argue with him.

"Back atcha," I said—and he snorted.

But he was intent on other things than words. And it didn't take long before I was, too. I bathed myself in him, the silken skin of his shoulders and the rougher skin of his hands, his distinctive smell, the weight of his body.

After the first time, I was in the mood to play. I tortured the both of us (in the best sense of the word) until sweat gathered on his forehead and his wolf looked out from his eyes. His hands dug into my hips harder than he'd be happy with, but he didn't force me to stop teasing. Adam would never use his strength against me.

I ratcheted us both up until we hung on that edge, like being on the top of the first hill on a wooden roller coaster. I held us both suspended, hearts pounding but bodies still. The muscles stood out on his flat belly and I put one hand there. He shuddered and our eyes met. I felt butterflies take flight in my veins as he smiled, a wolf's smile, joyous and hungry.

We fell together. And it was glorious.

Adam fell asleep afterward. But energized by good sex, I thought about motivation. After a few minutes, I poked him.

"I have a theory," I said when he grunted.

"This is going to be one of those nights when all I want to do is sleep, and you're wound up like a spinning top, isn't it?" he said.

I ignored him. "There are two possibilities to explain the witches' arrival. The first is that they found out that Sherwood is here—we've been getting a lot of press and Sherwood was in at least one of the pictures that hit the AP."

"Sleep, that blessed state . . ." intoned Adam, but he was listening to me.

"Sherwood is witchborn, I think, though his magic feels a little more wild than theirs. Still, they used him as a power source for who knows how long." No one had actually told me that, but what else would they have been doing with him? "Maybe they want him back. That would explain most of the rest."

"I listened to your messages," Adam said. "Thank you for doing that, by the way. I find it reassuring that after you escape near death, I can always expect a phone message from you. That way I only panic if I don't hear from you."

I couldn't tell if he was being sarcastic or not. Probably because he wasn't sure, either.

"You're welcome," I said with dignity. "The witch last night very kindly informed us that the witches are staging a takeover. And we—Marsilia included—are expected to sit quietly and take it. But she also mentioned that she expects us to remove ourselves from helping with the meeting between the fae and the humans."

"Yes," said Adam.

"So maybe today"—I glanced at the clock, which read two A.M.—"yesterday, I mean, had more to do with that."

"Okay," Adam said. "Can I go to sleep now?"

I thought about it a minute. "Nudge," I said.

He growled and lunged.

MEETINGS ARE BORING.

Meetings in which my whole job was to show up and let everyone get a good look at me, then sit down and shut up while they talked, were more than boring. Okay, first they told me it would be my job to find a venue for the big meeting. But they didn't actually ask me anything or give me a chance to talk.

We met in a hotel boardroom that looked a lot like a lot of other hotel boardrooms I'd been in. Maybe I'd have been more impressed by the people—all men—who represented so much governmental power if the last boardroom I'd been in hadn't held five Gray Lords of the fae.

The only person who made an impression on me was Tory Abbot, the assistant of the Senate majority whip, Jake Campbell, a Republican from Minnesota. Tory was a sharp-faced man about ten years older than I was and had a decisive manner that demanded people listen when he spoke. Which he did—quite a lot. And he said not very much, which has always seemed to me to be a quality much prized in a politician.

Most of the reason he was interesting had nothing to do with the man himself. I'd been informed (by him) that he would be my liaison with the government. And the man he worked for, Senator Campbell, was the senator that the rogue Cantrip agents had tried to force Adam to assassinate.

About forty minutes into the meeting, which was mostly an endless debate about where to hold the meeting, I started playing solitaire on my phone. The other pack members—Adam, Paul, Kelly, and Luke (the latter three all clad in Hauptman Security shirts)—were more disciplined. They simply waited, seated around the conference table, while no one talked to them.

Finally, Tory Abbot looked at me. "Do you have any suggestions about where to hold this meeting?"

I looked over my shoulder as if there might be someone there whom he was talking to.

"Smart aleck," murmured Kelly in a voice too soft for the humans to hear. Kelly's day job was working at a plant nursery, but like a lot of the wolves, he moonlighted for Adam when needed. His bright blue eyes were looking away from me, so no one would see that he was talking to me. He was a sneaky hunter.

"Ms. Hauptman," Abbot said, a little impatiently, though he was careful to stay on the far side of the room from me.

"None of the places you talked about will do," I said. "The fae won't come to the city and sit in iron and cement walls to discuss peace with the enemy."

"We're sure as fuck not going to go out to the reservation and talk with them," said Abbot.

"That's my wife you're swearing at," growled Adam, and the whole room came to a silent stillness. "Don't do that again." There was a lot more threat in his voice than there had been when he'd said the same thing to Sherwood yesterday.

"I wouldn't suggest going to the reservation," I said, as smoothly as if Adam hadn't spoken. "I doubt they'd let you in anyway. Or out, if they did let you in. What you need is a place big enough to hold everyone and their entourages as well as the fae delegation, one that also has a small room nearby where the principals can talk. Somewhere in our territory, but not actually in town, where the fae feel at a disadvantage."

I had been listening and thinking. I can do all that and play solitaire at the same time—it's a gift.

"Okay," said Abbot warily. "Where do you suggest?"

"How about one of the Red Mountain wineries? They are still in our territory." With a sweeping hand I included Adam and the other wolves. "They are built to hold company meetings and retreats—and they are situated among growing things."

I stopped speaking before I could tell them about the connections between the fae and alcoholic beverages—beer and mead more than wine, to be sure. But the wine would be something that would make the fae feel more at home.

"Security-wise that might be a good choice," said a man. I was pretty sure he was Secret Service or something like that because they hadn't told me what he did—and he'd been sitting on the sidelines like the rest of us while the others talked. "The wineries are pretty isolated, so we can keep nonparticipants away. I can go scout some out tonight and bring back suggestions."

And the talks resumed.

I looked at the time on my phone for the third time in five minutes and Adam said, breaking easily into a heated argument about the appropriateness of holding a governmental meeting at a winery, "Gentlemen. We should excuse my wife, who needs to get back to her work." He took the SUV key off his key ring (it was a diesel; diesels still had keys rather than fobs) and tossed it. "Paul, take my rig. I'll catch a ride back with Luke and Kelly."

Paul grabbed the key out of the air and saluted Adam. He opened the door for me to precede him.

I would have preferred either Kelly or Luke. Paul was one of the wolves who would rather I were not his Alpha's mate. When Adam had told the pack he would no longer tolerate anyone dissing me, Paul had been very quiet around me. Paul had gotten a divorce a couple of months ago—and that hadn't sweetened his temperament even a little bit. I wasn't afraid of Paul, but he wasn't someone I wanted to hang out with, either. That was probably why Adam had sent him with me, to force us to deal with each other.

"At least you didn't suggest Uncle Mike's," Paul said acerbically when we were far enough down the hall that Adam wouldn't hear him.

Before I could respond, we turned a corner and found ourselves in the middle of a wild rumpus of the first order. A tourist bus had evidently arrived while we'd been twiddling our toes in the boardroom. The check-in desk and the surrounding room were full of dozens of well-to-do retirees, a pizza delivery guy with a big box, and four people from a local flower shop pushing in carts of bright-colored mini-bouquets in small clear vases.

I dropped back to let Paul take point. He was a big man and people moved to let him through. I trailed in his wake through the crowd and out the revolving door into the fresh air.

"Don't worry," said Paul as we cleared the hotel, "I won't attack you or anything."

I rolled my eyes. "As if you could."

He started to say something, shook his head, and muttered, "Let me try this again."

"Try what?" I asked.

Instead of answering me, he stopped dead and turned in a slow circle. "Do you smell that?"

Having sharp senses is one thing. Paying attention to them so they do some good is another. I inhaled. The hotel was in the middle of town; there were a lot of scents in the air. One of those scents just didn't belong.

"Gunpowder?" I asked. "Why are we smelling gunpowder?"

I looked around but there weren't any people outside the hotel who were near enough that the scent could be coming off them even if they'd spent the morning out shooting— even if they had *rolled* in gunpowder.

Paul focused on the cars, which made more sense because they were closer.

What we had were two minivans, a battered car with a pizza sign on the top, and, closest to us, a tour bus.

The silver bus purred at rest, her big luggage doors open to expose the belly of the beast. I took two steps toward her, but as soon as I did, the smell of her diesel engine overpowered the smell of gunpowder.

The diesel, being a volatile organic, would travel farther than the gunpowder. If I was smelling gunpowder outside the range of the diesel, it could only be because the gunpowder smell was coming from somewhere other than the bus.

Meanwhile, Paul had examined the first of the minivans. He shook his head at me and took a step toward the little battered car with a local pizza sign on the roof. Frowning, he tilted his head.

I ran up to him and got hit in the face with a wash of garlic, tomatoes, cheese, pepperoni—the usual. He looked at me and shrugged; his stomach rumbled. He grinned, a boyish expression he'd never turned on me before, then shook his head.

We both tried the second minivan, but it smelled of flowers and baby's breath. The baby's breath made Paul sneeze.

He gave half a growl, stalked back to the pizza car, and pulled open the driver's-side door. He stuck his head in.

"Pizza is strong, but it shouldn't smell like gunpowder," he said to me. But by then I could smell it, too, wafting out of the open door. I saw him in my mind's eye, the pizza delivery boy carrying one of those big vinyl pizza bags designed to carry multiple boxes of pizzas.

Paul and I both ran, leaving the door of the pizza car open.

When two people run into a crowded room, a lot of drama

happens—shouts and shuffling and people with mouths agape. One of the things that doesn't happen is a miraculous clearing of pathways. Paul did that all by himself.

I hoped that the old woman he shoved to the ground would be okay, but I didn't hesitate when I jumped over her. Time enough to apologize and feel guilty after we hunted down the threat.

We ran for the boardroom. Once out of the crowd, I was faster than Paul, so I was in front when we turned the last corner.

"Adam," I yelled. *"Gun."*

The pizza man, one hand raised to knock at the closed door, turned a startled gaze at me. I supposed he hadn't heard us until I yelled.

"Bomb," corrected Paul, who had spent ten years in the SWAT unit of a large city back east. He'd never told me which one—we just didn't talk that much.

The pizza man screamed, "Open the goddamned door, you freaks!" And, with a panicked look at my rapid approach, he did something with the pizza box.

The world stopped in a roar of sound and light.

One moment I was upright and running, the next I was facedown on the rough hotel carpet, struggling to breathe. The air was full of dust and my lungs didn't want to work because of the heavy weight on top of me. Pain and loss shivered down the pack bonds with the even heavier weight of our dead.

Our *dead*.

"Paul," I tried to say.

Though the lifeless weight of him on my back didn't move, I felt the touch of his fingers on my cheek. They were warm, which I knew was weird.

They should have been cold. The touch of the dead is usually cold.

"Heyya, lady," Paul said, his voice gentler than I'd ever heard it. "You'll tell him, right?"

"Paul," I said. "No."

He laughed. "Yes, you will. You're fair like that." There

was a little pause and he said a bit wistfully, "Tell Mary Jo that I loved her, okay?" Then he made a sharp sound. "No. No. That wouldn't be right. Just make sure they all know what I did. So they will think well of me. I'd like that."

And then Paul was gone, even though his body lay on top of me, the smell of him, of his blood, all around me.

7

IT TOOK ADAM, KELLY, AND LUKE A WHILE TO DIG me out of the debris. By that time, Paul's extremities had cooled and his blood had stopped flowing over my skin. When they pulled Paul's body off me, we were stuck together with his blood.

Maybe it was shock or the shot the EMT people gave me, but I was pretty loopy. I remember the faces of the EMT people dealing with two unhappy wolves (Kelly and Luke had both shifted to dig rubble), which varied from terror to fascination. But other than that, I don't remember getting from the hotel to the hospital.

In the emergency room, I collected information a little haphazardly, as people came in and out of my cubby, and as I was hauled out for X-rays. Some of the people were pack, some were the nonpack who worked for Adam, but a few of them were strangers who looked like alphabet agency types. The fog increased after they decided I didn't have a head injury and gave me something stronger.

I woke up to an unfamiliar voice.

"—twenty-five years old. Grad student in viticulture at WSU."

"What does making wine have to do with making bombs?" That was Kelly. So I must have dozed off long enough ago that he'd had time to shift back. He sounded indignant, as if people who grew plants (like he did) should not contemplate blowing up hotels. It struck me as funny.

The bed moved a little, so I pried open my eyes.

A grim-faced man was sitting on the end of my bed. Apparently disaster makes us all friends because it was the caustic Secret Service guy from the meeting, now a little more battered and dusty.

He said, "Nothing. But growing up in a family with a demolition business does. I don't know what the connection with Ford is, but the FBI is working on that."

"Ford?" I asked; my voice came out a little wobbly.

Adam leaned in to look at me. He was seated on a rolling, backless chair pulled up to my bed. He and his clothing were filthy with blood and dirt, but his face and hands were clean.

It made me aware that sometime between when I was last functioning and now, I'd been stripped out of my blood-soaked clothing and put in a clean hospital gown. Parts of me were clean and parts of me were horrid. I smelled like gunpowder, muck, and Paul's blood.

Adam touched my face with gentle fingers. "Back with us again, I see," he said. "How do you feel?"

"Floaty," I said, instead of telling him I wanted to crawl out of my skin to get Paul's blood off me. "Floaty" was true, too. "It's nice. What does the bomber have to do with trucks?"

He smiled—it was a real smile, though his face was tired. "Not much, sweetheart. But Ford is the name of Rankin's man. Right now it looks like he's the one who arranged for the bombing."

"Okay." I couldn't quite remember which of the men in the meeting was Rankin's man. Rankin was one of the

Democrats, included because he was on the House commit-tee on fae and supernatural affairs. That committee had undergone so many name changes over the past few years that I couldn't, right off the top of my head, come up with what it was officially called. I knew it wasn't the Tinker Bell Committee, which is what most people called it.

The filth and the blood and the dust that everyone was wearing told me that it was probably still the day of the bombing. The position of the sun told me that it wasn't more than a few hours later.

"What's the situation?" I asked Adam.

I didn't have to spell out for him what I needed.

"Paul is dead. The bomber is dead," he said.

"Did you—" I glanced hurriedly at the Secret Service guy, who glanced blandly back at me. This was why I didn't drink. Too many minefields.

"I didn't kill the bomber, no," Adam said, his voice a little harsh. "I didn't need to because he did it for us."

"How about everyone else?" I asked. "Are you okay?"

"We got tossed around a little. The windows went and we lost chunks of ceiling and wall. No one was seriously hurt—Abbot has a broken arm. The rest of us just got bumps and bruises."

"Luke broke his shoulder," Kelly added. "But it healed up. Adam sent him home with Darryl."

Translation: Luke was too worn out by the healing to change back to human and too upset by the bombing to be trusted out in public without a wolf dominant enough to make him mind.

"Okay," I said. I looked at the Secret Service guy. "If the bomber died at the scene, how did you figure out—" I was still not at the top of my game because I had to run down truck brands until I came up with the right one. Not Dodge or Chevy. "—*Ford* was responsible?"

"I missed all but the end of it," said the Secret Service guy regretfully. "I was too busy not dying and then scram-bling out from under Kelly—thank you. But as soon as he realized he was alive, Ford started screaming that it was fifteen minutes early."

"Abbot got the whole thing on his cell phone," said Adam.

"We contacted Representative Rankin," said the Secret Service guy. "You'll be surprised to know that he was shocked and appalled."

The Secret Service guy sounded honestly regretful when he added, "Unfortunately, I think that shock was real, at least. I'd love to pin this to that slimy toad. But it's likely that the whole thing rests on Ford."

"What is your name?" I asked. "I can't just keep calling you the Secret Service guy."

"Judd Spielman," he said.

"Cool," I said, leaning forward earnestly. "Paul saved me."

"And there she goes again," murmured Kelly. "We know, Mercy. You've told us a time or two."

I turned to look at him—he was somewhere behind Adam—but I ended up burying my face against Adam's chest. It felt so good I stayed there.

When I lifted my head, the Secret Service guy whose name was Judd Spielman was gone from the end of the bed. Instead, inexplicably Tory Abbot was there in an immaculate suit that was slightly different from the one he'd worn in the meeting. The lines in his face were a little deeper, and he had a splint on his left arm.

He was saying, "—hadn't panicked we'd all have been dead and he'd have been alive."

It felt like I'd just blinked and he'd appeared out of nowhere, but his presence wasn't the only change in the room. Everything was a little grubbier than it had been—the white sheets had acquired dirty smudges.

Adam was cleaner, though. His hair was wet and he was in different clothing. Kelly was gone, and Warren sat on the windowsill, looking out at the setting sun.

"I hate drugs," I said muzzily. "My mouth is dry."

"I don't blame you," said Adam, kissing my forehead. Warren got off the window ledge and brought a glass of water with a straw. "And they won't be giving you any more. Looks like you sustained lots of cuts and bruises but nothing major."

"Probably," said Warren, going back to the window.

"Probably," agreed Adam smoothly. "Having a hotel dumped on top of someone isn't usually something people walk away from, so they're keeping you here for a couple more hours to be sure."

"You're driving them batty," said Warren. "Because a hotel fell on you and you should be dead. They can't figure out why you aren't."

"Paul saved me," I told Adam.

He kissed me again. "I know, love."

"Why does she keep saying that?" Warren asked. "Does she have a concussion?"

"He asked me to," I told Warren with drug-born earnestness. "He touched my cheek and asked me to make sure that everyone knew that when push came to shove, he was a hero."

"He died instantly," said Abbot, not ungently. "He couldn't have asked her to do anything."

"I see dead people," I told him.

"Hush," Adam said.

"That's why I don't like hospitals very much," I continued. "Paul died and the only thing he wanted me to tell people was that he saved me." I paused. "He didn't want me to tell Mary Jo he loved her."

"You see dead people?" asked Abbot, his voice arrested.

"Let's just give Abbot time to brief us, okay?" Warren said. "You're talking nonsense, Mercy."

I nodded—which hurt my neck, my shoulders, and my left toe, so I stopped.

"Your wife talks to ghosts?" Abbot asked.

"P-p-please!" I told him earnestly in the voice of Roger Rabbit—or as close to it as I could get. "Only when it's funny."

"Go to sleep," Adam told me.

I closed my eyes and listened until we were all alone.

But I must have slept a little because when I woke up, Judd Spielman the Secret Service guy was back. This time he had taken the same seat that Abbot had used.

"The FBI say that the bomb was expertly constructed. From the brass caps to the detonation wiring." Spielman was wearing clean clothes, too. Instead of another suit, though, he'd gone for jeans and a T-shirt. It made him look tougher—the shiner didn't hurt that impression, either. Some people (me) get a black eye and people ask, "Hey, who beat you up?" Other people (Spielman) get a black eye and people say, "Where did they bury the other guy?"

Adam doesn't get shiners.

"Goes with him being raised by a demolition expert," said Adam.

"Guess the kid was bright and paid attention." Spielman's tone was ironic. "But I wouldn't have sounded as admiring as my contact did. The boy killed two people, including himself. I asked them, if he was such a genius, why wasn't he working for his parents' company? They told me that he didn't like to take orders. So his father encouraged him to go into another line of work before he killed someone—hence the viticulture. His family didn't quite say it, but my guy in the FBI says that he started to get radical and his family shipped him out west to get him away from all of that."

"Well, *that* worked," said Warren.

"Like dumping a drowning boy into the ocean," agreed Spielman. "He came here and joined the local Bright Future chapter, dated a few girls from that group. Then he brought a new girl for a couple of weeks. Word from the Bright Future people is that those two said something about being tired of belonging to a useless group who didn't do anything but talk and paint graffiti—a charge BF denies, for the record. They quit coming. My guy is checking to see if they found another, more radical group, or if they headed off on their own."

"Any word on the connection to Ford?" I asked.

The whole room turned to look at me—apparently they

hadn't noticed that I'd started paying attention again. Adam's hand tightened on mine.

"Apparently Ford was a friend of the kid's family," Spielman said. "I understand that right at the moment, past tense is the correct verb form. The kid's father is ready to do murder."

"Why now?" asked Adam suddenly. "This was a meeting of—you'll forgive me—minions. Why didn't he wait until the key players were in place?"

"Because Ford had been dating Senator Campbell's youngest daughter before she broke it off," Spielman said heavily. "Apparently he was worried that if Campbell was killed, Stephanie would move back to Minnesota and he would lose his chance to get her back."

"Wow," I said, a little awed by the . . . wrongness of that thinking. "That's special."

"How do you know that?" Warren asked.

"Ford is talking like someone put a nickel in him," said Spielman. "I have no idea why. I don't see how announcing that he did it for the good of mankind because we shouldn't be bargaining with the fae, we should be nuking them out of existence, is going to help him in court. He is sounding more like someone campaigning for president than someone facing time behind bars for bombing a government meeting."

Warren growled, "For murder."

Spielman's face lost the blandly pleasant expression that seemed to be its default setting. "I know. I helped carry your man out."

Warren breathed deeply. "Sorry."

"Me, too," said Spielman.

"Paul—" I started to say, but Warren broke in.

"Saved you," the lanky cowboy said firmly. "On purpose. I never liked him, would not have thought he had it in him. I was wrong and he died a hero."

"You wouldn't have survived if he hadn't protected you," Adam said. "We won't forget what we owe him."

Eventually Spielman left with a couple of his people. The doctor came and told me I could go, but I shouldn't make any life-changing decisions for a day or two.

Warren headed to his truck as I climbed into the SUV under Adam's assessing eye.

"At least," Adam said as he started the big diesel engine, "we know that this attempt had nothing to do with witches."

"No," I told him. "Abbot smelled like the witch in Benton City. Not like Frost; I don't think they are related. But the two of them use the same laundry soap, shampoo, and toothpaste—and he carries her scent, too, a little."

"Abbot," said Adam slowly. "But not Ford."

"I couldn't tell you which one of the government minion clones in that meeting was Ford," I admitted. "And maybe the bombing was all this Ford guy in some sort of attempt to make sure that the government and the fae don't reach any sort of agreement."

"But," Adam said, "Ford is acting weirdly—and we have a witch who we think might be able to make mundane people do things."

"But," I agreed. "I don't know if it is only when the witch is present—or if it's like the vampire thing."

"I'll ask around," Adam told me.

———————

I FELT AWFUL FOR THE NEXT FOUR DAYS. NOTHING specific, just headachy and sore-muscled. When I went to the garage, Tad made me man the front desk while he worked on the cars. On the second day, Zee worked on the cars, too. On the third day, Dale brought Stefan's bus over—and I stood up to the two overprotective louts and fixed her myself.

There were things more painful than my sore muscles, like the press conference. Luckily, I didn't have to say much. The reporter was a woman, so she was much more interested in talking to Adam than to me. The debriefing by the FBI wasn't fun, either. But in my hierarchy of painful things, Paul's funeral and the tasks surrounding it topped them all.

We had him cremated—and Sherwood went to watch while it was done. We weren't going to let Paul be slipped out and donated to science while our backs were turned. Sherwood, I think, was more concerned that his body might be stolen and made into a zombie. Maybe it was just paranoia, but it gave us something to focus on.

And there were more zombies.

Our pack got called to Pasco to deal with a zombie cat— a stray this time, so at least there were no crying children. I didn't go, but apparently there was quite a chase before Ben caught it. And then there was the cow.

They didn't call us in for the cow until it had already killed two people and injured a handful more. I wish I had gone for that one, but I had to settle for a secondhand account of Warren roping it from the back of his truck at thirty miles an hour. He secured the rope and had the driver hit the brakes. The resulting snap of the rope ripped the rotting head right off.

Adam thought the witch—or witches, because we really weren't sure—was playing with us.

Adam dealt with the FBI, the Secret Service, and all of the hoopla that happens when you don't actually die when a bomb goes off. The secret meeting wasn't so secret anymore, and Bright Future, undeterred by their association with the bomber, held a sit-in at John Dam Plaza, a little park in the middle of Richland. I heard they gave out free ice cream cones.

Ford died in custody. The public was being held in suspense but our new friend in the Secret Service told Adam that no one knew why he died. It wasn't suicide, but it didn't look like murder, either.

After a couple of days, the news stories all concentrated on the upcoming meeting between the fae and the government. The bombing sort of faded to the background. After all, all of the bad guys died. They only had a driver's license photo of Paul, and a few words from Adam about how he was a good and faithful employee—not enough to make a story out of Paul.

Paul only wanted Adam and the pack to know that he was a hero. He wouldn't have cared, much, about what they said in the news.

Senator Campbell did a series of interviews with both conservative and liberal press. I caught several of those.

The senator was a handsome man—he could have starred in one of the 1950s Westerns that my foster father had been addicted to. He looked like a man you could trust.

He looked me directly in the eye. Or at least he looked in the camera and spoke as if he were talking to me.

"In the view of the fae," he said, "we broke faith with them when we denied justice to one of their own. But they are willing to step up to the table one more time. It doesn't matter what you or I feel about the fae, the fact of the matter is that we are less safe from them right this minute than we were before. An agreement will make us safer, make them safer, and make the lives of our children safer."

Still looking at me through the TV, he said, "This is not a chance that is likely to come again in our generation. And I am not going to let the actions of a homegrown terrorist get in the way of making my country a safer place to live."

He was an effective speaker. And his opinion was made more weighty by the common knowledge that he was the poster child for the anti-fae groups.

———

WHILE THE PACK WAS HERDING ZOMBIES AND Adam was dealing with investigators and reporters, Mary Jo, George, and I cleaned out Paul's apartment. It took us two evenings to pack up his things. It seemed to me that it should take more time to bundle up a person's life.

"Is his ghost here?" asked Mary Jo as we sorted books into boxes.

I looked around and shook my head. "I haven't seen anything while we've been here."

She closed up the box she was working on and taped it shut. "I called Renny. We're going on a date on Saturday."

"Good," I said.

"Is it?" she asked pensively. "Pensive" was not an emotion I'd ever seen in Mary Jo.

"He loved me, you know," she told me. "Paul, I mean. I know you didn't see the best side of him, but he could be a lot of fun." She was quiet for a moment, then she said, "I wish I had loved him back."

She cried—and didn't push me away when I gave her a hug. George came over and crouched beside her, putting a hand on her shoulder. He said what we'd all been thinking.

"He didn't have anyone but pack," he said. Then he rubbed her shoulder gently. "But he did have us, darling. We had his back when things went rough—and he had ours."

"He saved my life," I said.

I met Mary Jo's wet eyes—mostly to avoid looking at Paul's shade, who had shown up, looking lost, as soon as Mary Jo had acknowledged that he had loved her.

She nodded. "He was not an easy man, Mercy. But he was a good person to have at your back."

"I know," I told her sincerely.

"What he wasn't," George said, "was sentimental. Back to work, me hearties. Time and tide wait for no one."

"We're not sailing anywhere," said Mary Jo. "So we don't care about the tide, even if we were anywhere near the ocean. Maybe you should lay off the pirate game for a while. It's warping your brain."

"His brain is already warped," I said.

George grinned at me. "I know you are, but what am I?"

I stuck my tongue out at him and we all got back to work. Paul lingered, touching a book or two as we packed them or fingering the empty bookcase. Sometimes he would reach out and almost caress Mary Jo—but not quite.

This shade wasn't really Paul, I could tell—not like when he'd talked to me just after he'd died. But his shade made me sad. Sadder. So I didn't look at him. At it.

ELIZAVETA MADE IT BACK IN TIME TO JUST MISS the funeral. I think she planned it that way—I sure would have under the circumstances.

A taxi dropped her and her luggage at our door smelling of stale air and all the things that go with air travel. She looked . . . old.

"Adam," she said, brushing by me, and launched into a spate of Russian.

Her face crumpled with grief and loss and he held her while she cried. But his face was— It was probably a good thing she couldn't see his face. After a moment, though, he closed his eyes and grief deepened the line of his mouth.

"Elizaveta," I said. "Come sit down. We have a situation here and I think you may be the only one who can clarify what's going on."

She started to come in, but took a step back before her foot landed inside the threshold. "It is lovely outside," she said. "I have just spent most of a day inside planes and airports. Can we sit out on the porch?"

I thought of the cleansing that Sherwood had performed on the house.

"Of course," I said. "Why don't you two find a seat and I'll bring out some iced tea for everyone." Elizaveta was fond of iced tea.

Eventually we all sat in the comfortable chairs that were scattered in seating groups all over the porch. Elizaveta drank her tea. I did not doubt her grief or her fear.

It sounded like Sherwood's cat was going to make it. But Elizaveta's house had been full of the ghosts of people she and her family had tortured to death for power. I couldn't look at Elizaveta without seeing the face of that half-dead cat, as if he stood for all of her victims. She grieved, and I had not the slightest bit of sympathy.

"We buried the ashes of your family in your garden," said Adam.

And there had been a lot of bones in that garden, Warren had told us. They had reburied what they found. We were still considering what to do about that garden.

Elizaveta's face went still. "Oh?" But when he didn't say anything more, she said, "Thank you. They would have liked that."

I didn't think any of her family would like where they were now. But I didn't generally impose my beliefs on other people—especially when they wouldn't do anyone any good.

"About the black magic," she said tentatively. She was watching Adam; my reaction didn't matter to her.

Adam shook his head. "I understand. I know how witchcraft works." "Understand" did not mean "approve."

"They tried to take us once before," she said, watching him narrowly. "The Hardesty witches. Some sacrifices were necessary to ensure our survival."

"I see," Adam said. "Why didn't you come to us for help?"

"It was at the same time that you and your pack got taken by the government agents," Elizaveta said. "You were a little busy. By the time matters settled down for you"—after Frost was dead—"they had backed off." She gave Adam a grim smile. "My family was not big compared to theirs. But we had some powerful practitioners."

I was going to have to call Stefan and see what he'd found out about Frost.

"Mercy?" Adam asked.

"Sorry," I said. "I was woolgathering."

"I asked if you could describe the witch you saw," Elizaveta said.

"Tall," I said. "Dark hair. Big smile that lights up her face. She sounds like she comes from Adam's quadrant of the country, though maybe not Alabama."

"And she makes zombies," said Elizaveta, as if what I'd told her had given her the final bits she needed to make an identification. "Definitely the Hardesty family."

"Why do you think she's making so many zombies?" I asked. "We've had a werewolf, twenty miniature goats, a cat, and a cow."

"She can't help it," said Elizaveta. "It is the curse of that kind of necromancy, this uncontrollable need to create more. I am told that the euphoria that lingers after you bring the dead to life is more addictive than morphine. That's why there aren't many witches who do it. Some of the African-influenced families seem to have a better handle on that, but even they have a limit. She must be valuable if they haven't put her down yet."

"So could we track her using the zombies?" asked Adam. "How does zombie-making work?"

"It doesn't matter how it works," Elizaveta said with a dismissive wave of her hand. "By the time there are zombies running around, she could be miles away. What matters is that I can track that sort of magic in my territory." She took a deep breath. "There were two witches at my house, and one of them was this zombie-maker."

"Yes," I said. "Would being a Love Talker make her valuable enough to keep around?"

"Ha," said Elizaveta. "Is that what she is?"

"I'm not sure," I told her honestly. Then I described the incident with Salas.

Elizaveta nodded. "Your vampire is right. This man— What was his name? This man is probably witchborn—you say that he has left town?"

"Yes." I didn't give his name, and Elizaveta didn't ask for it again.

"Safer for him," she commented. "And if she is, indeed, a Love Talker, that would explain a few things I have wondered about her over the years."

"Can she influence people over distance—like when the vampires mark one of the people they feed from?" Adam asked.

Elizaveta pursed her lips. "Possibly. Some of them have been known to do that." Then her face cleared. "Oh, I see. You think that she might have been behind your explosion?"

"Ford died in custody," said Adam. "And he died very much like your family did."

"If they want to stop an alliance between the humans

and the fae—and it is my understanding that they would do that—it could be the Hardestys behind the bombing." She shrugged and waved her hands. "It might be a single incident; there are enough humans who would be appalled by this alliance. But the Hardesty family is famous for using others to do their work when they can." She compressed her lips and nodded slowly. "It *smells* like something they would come up with—and given the death of this man who was supposed to be behind it all, I think it very likely to be them behind the incident. It cost them nothing and had the potential to forward their goals."

"You think that primarily, these witches have come to take over your territory," said Adam.

She nodded decisively, but said, "It is too soon to tell. *Sometimes they come one by one, others two by two.*" She spoke that sentence in a singsong, as if it were a children's rhyme. She shivered a little, looking old.

"Ah well," she said. "I should find a hotel, do you think?" She had planned on staying here, I thought, until she found she could not cross our threshold.

"How worried should we be?" I asked her. "I mean, should we caution our werewolves?"

She frowned. "From the Love Talker, not much, I don't think. I've never heard of one who could influence a werewolf. The Hardesty lineage has had a few who had the ability to persuade vampires. From the one who killed my family? It takes a lot more power to kill werewolves than it does humans. Adam told me that it was your assessment that all of my family died at the same time, no?"

I nodded. "All of your family, all of the animals—" I wasn't going to tell her about Sherwood's cat. She might try to claim it, and that would be bad all around. "—all of the insects. Everything."

"Ah," she said. "I hadn't known it had gone that far. That's not your zombie-making Love Talker who did that, Mercy. There is only one witch I know of who can relieve others of their lives in such a manner. I suppose I should be flattered that they sent Death after my people."

My heart skipped a beat, because I heard Coyote echoing her voice in my head when she said "Death."

She smiled tightly and looked at Adam. "If they sent Death, she is after me. But you should know that allying yourself with me will put you in her crosshairs. That thing she does, eating the lives of others . . . she did it in my home. That was a mistake." Her expression grew hungry and satisfied at the same time. "She will regret attacking my family with her curse."

"I couldn't smell or feel the zombie-making witch until she wanted me to," I said. "I couldn't even sense the magic of the trap that Sherwood fell into until we were right on top of it."

"Mercy is sensitive to magic," Adam said.

"Walkers are," said Elizaveta with a nod.

"And," I said, "none of us knew that you had begun practicing black magic—you know that it has a scent that werewolves and I can pick up."

She froze with her glass halfway to her lips. She knew that we understood what she'd been doing—or she should have known. Maybe she'd been lying to herself until this moment. She glanced at Adam. I couldn't read Adam's face, so I didn't think she could, either.

"The trap in your basement," she said finally, setting her glass down gently, "that is a simple thing. If a witch knows that there is someone about who might be able to sense magic, there is an extra step that can be used to insulate the spell, separate it from the air around it. It doesn't work on active magic, but the trap you described to me is in stasis until it is triggered. It might take a few minutes or even hours for the insulating layer to dissipate after the spell is triggered. So you still wouldn't feel the magic until you walked into the spell."

"Okay," said Adam. "And the rest? How did you keep us from knowing you had changed your mind about staying to the lighter path?" "The lighter path" is what the witches themselves sometimes call gray magic. It isn't the path of light, but it isn't pure evil, either.

She sighed. "I told you that I was good at talismans, or *gris-gris*, while we were in Italy." She tugged on one of the necklaces she was wearing to display an amulet. It looked like something I'd seen displayed in craft fairs when potters tried their hands at making jewelry. It was pretty, made of green and copper glazed pottery, and vaguely resembled a flower, if that flower had been put together by Picasso.

She moved her hand until the amulet dangled away from her skin. As soon as it was no longer in contact, I felt like someone had dumped a bucket of filth over my head.

"I did not want you to know, Adam," she said. And a tear trailed down her face. She wiped it away with the edge of her free hand. "I did not want you to know what I had become. So I made this."

She tucked it back into her clothing and the awareness of black magic faded.

"It is a thing of my own devising, using secrets of my family. It is unlikely that the Hardesty witches made such a thing—their magics don't lend themselves to this kind of working. But my people knew how—and I fear that the Hardesty witches weren't without allies in my home."

"There were four who hadn't been tortured," I said.

Elizaveta nodded. "I am afraid that ambition is a problem among my kind. They were the ones who most chafed at my restrictions."

"And one of them was Robert's daughter, Militza," Adam said. "We found Robert."

"That wouldn't have bothered her," Elizaveta said. "But she minded the loss of status when her father betrayed me."

"So why did they kill the members of your family who helped them?" I asked.

"The Hardestys value family loyalty, Mercy," said Elizaveta. "Those who betrayed their blood—they would never be welcomed to the Hardestys." She looked at Adam. "I assume you have been looking for them."

Adam nodded. "We think they drove an RV here and were staying in it at an RV park for a while. They left the park two days before we discovered the bodies at your house, and they haven't been back since."

"Frustrating," I said.

Adam nodded at me. "How can we kill them if we can't find them?"

Elizaveta watched him with a little smile. "They will find us, my darling," she murmured. Then she said briskly, "Yes, well, all of this information you have now. I am an old woman and I need my rest after my long journey. I will be on my way."

"Let us know which hotel you're staying at," Adam said. "We'll keep a patrol on it."

She straightened and looked a little less old and fragile. "Thank you, darling boy. That is very kind."

Did Adam mean for the patrol to watch over her, or just watch her? Probably best not to ask that right this minute.

"I took a taxi here," she said. "Might I have someone to drive me to a hotel?"

"I'll do it," I volunteered. "I need to pick up some more eggs anyway."

Adam tensed, shook his head—not like he was indicating a negative, more like he was shedding something off. "Bad things happen when you go by yourself to get eggs, Mercy. I'll take her and pick up whatever groceries you need on the way back."

I DIDN'T TALK TO ADAM ABOUT ELIZAVETA UNTIL he closed our bedroom door behind him that night.

"The talks are still on," he told me as he unbuttoned his shirt. "The president was going to pull the plug, but apparently Campbell and a bipartisan group of senators cornered him in his office and convinced him."

"He's coming up for election next year," I said. "He's worried about how this will look."

Adam nodded and stripped out of his shirt. He made an irritated sound because he'd forgotten to unbutton the cuffs.

I started over to help him out of his shirt manacles—but he solved the problem by ripping off the sleeves. He hadn't looked particularly upset until that point—but he didn't usually destroy bespoke shirts casually, either.

"I'm sorry about Elizaveta," I said.

He ripped off the rest of his shirt and tossed it into the garbage bin, just inside our bathroom door. He then carefully unbuttoned the cuffs and threw them away, too. With his back to me, he put a hand on either side of the bathroom door and bowed his head.

"I wanted her to have a good explanation," he said.

"I know," I told him.

"I wanted her to be . . . different than she is."

"I know," I said.

He looked at me, his face stark. "She was one of mine," he said.

I slid into his arms and wrapped mine around his waist. "You can't force people to make the right choice, Adam."

He drew in a breath. "Every time I have ever asked her for help, she has come. She came to face down Bonarata because I asked her to."

I nodded and just held him. Sometimes there is no way to make things better. There is only making it through. I couldn't make Adam not hurt; I could only let him know he wasn't alone.

THE NEXT DAY, AS I PUT TOGETHER A JETTA THAT someone had tried to rewire themselves, I thought about connections. Making a car run smoothly was all about connections: fuel, air, coolant, electric.

I wondered if I was becoming a conspiracy theorist because the web I was building from bits and pieces was truly Byzantine. And if all the things that seemed to be connected were, then a family of witches I'd never heard of had been responsible for an awful lot of chaos in my life for the last four years or more.

Maybe things would become more clear when Stefan got back to me with information about Frost.

I finished the Jetta and pulled a sputtering Rabbit into the garage. It died about four feet from where I needed it to be.

"You need help with that?" asked Zee as I got out of the car.

"Nope," I said.

"*Gut*," said Zee shortly. "The boy and I are busy."

I laughed and pushed the Rabbit until it was rolling, then hopped in to hit the brakes before it traveled too far. Pushing cars wasn't a new thing for me. I propped up the hood and contemplated the engine compartment. It was surprisingly pristine given the age of the car and left me feeling a little nostalgic for *my* Rabbit.

My cell phone rang as I pulled the cover off the air filter. The filter material, which should have been whitish but more often in the Tri-Cities was brownish with dust, was an astonishingly bright orange.

Staring at the orange air filter, I answered my cell without checking ID.

"This is Tory Abbot," said Senator Campbell's assistant, who smelled like the zombie-making witch. Darn it, "zombie witch" was easier and it flowed off the tongue better—even if it left the impression that the witch was a zombie. So "zombie witch" it was.

"What can I do for you?"

"I have some documents for you to take to the fae. We need a complete list of which fae will be there—names, attributes, and all of that."

I pulled the phone away from my face and gave it an incredulous look. "Paperwork for the Gray Lords to fill out," I said slowly. "Huh. That's an interesting proposition. But they won't do it."

"They will if they want a meeting," he said. "I'll drop them by your . . . place of business this afternoon." He said the last as if he just noticed that my place of business was a garage and not, say, a lawyer's office.

"You can if you want to," I told him. "But I won't pass them on."

"I'm afraid this is nonnegotiable," he said.

"Okay," I said. "I'll tell them that the meeting is off. And I'll tell them why. You can explain to the president and the secretary of state why this meeting that they were so hot to have was canceled by your grandstanding. But maybe they will agree with you. That without some pieces of paper— that your side would have filled with lies if you were the fae—this meeting should not be held. Even though it is the first step in a process that might keep our country from being at war with the fae. You can start, maybe, by informing Senator Campbell."

A short silence fell. I think he was waiting for me to continue my rant.

"Ms. Hauptman," Abbot began, "I know that you are overset by the bombing. Maybe you should pass on your duties to someone more experienced and less obstructionist."

"Okay," I said. "Give me the name of someone the fae won't object to."

"Adam Hauptman," he said.

"Someone made sure that Adam had a job for this meeting," I said. "He won't renege on an agreement he has already made." I decided I wasn't really interested in helping him with his hunt for my replacement. "And if you think I am an obstructionist, you should try him. Good luck with your search."

I hit the red button and went back to the mystery of the Rabbit's air filter. Experimentally I brought it to my nose because it looked like someone had dusted the whole filter with cheese powder from a macaroni and cheese box. But it didn't have a smell.

I took an air hose and used it to blow off the filter, half expecting orange powder to fill the air—but nothing happened. The substance looked powdery, but it clung to the filter as if it were glue.

I poked at it with my finger. I was still wearing gloves when I worked, though Adam's ex-wife was back in Eugene and not around to make little pointed remarks about the grease I couldn't get out from under my nails. I hated the way my hands sweated in them. But that was made up for by the way my skin was less dry and cracked because I wasn't using as much caustic soap on them to get the grease off. Christy had done me a favor.

There was no orange residue on my gloves.

"Hey, Zee?" I asked, holding up the filter.

"*Was,*" he said, perched on the edge of an engine compartment with a limberness that belied his elderly appearance. "I am busy," he added.

"I have a bright orange air filter," I singsonged. "Don't you want to give it a look?"

There was the buzz of hard rubber on cement and Tad slid out from under Zee's car, a flashlight in his hand. "Orange?" he said.

"Bah," said Zee. "You've distracted the boy, Mercy."

"What is orange and keeps air from flowing—and why would someone dump that all over an air filter?" I asked.

Tad took the air filter and stared at it. He looked at the Rabbit.

"What was supposed to be wrong with the car?" he asked.

I looked at the repair sheet I'd filled out while I'd been in exile on the front desk. "Sputters and dies," I said.

"I guess I know why," Tad said. And then he dropped the filter like it was a hot potato and jumped back.

"Dad?" he said in a semipanicked voice, holding up his hands. The skin on his fingers, where he'd touched the air filter, was blistering and cracking. As I watched, the tips of his fingers blackened.

Zee grabbed Tad's hands, muttered something foul, and hauled Tad to the sink. I got there just before them and turned the water on full force. Zee held Tad's hands under the flow of water and then SPOKE.

Wasser, Freund mir sei,
komm und steh mir bei.
Fließe, wasche, binde, fasse,

Löse Fluch, trag ihn hinfort,
Lass ab von Hand und diesem Ort.

The power in his voice made my ears ring. And that made me realize that whatever was on the air filter wasn't caustic—which was what I'd thought when I'd seen Tad's skin—but magic. And as Zee's power touched it, something that cloaked that magic washed away and the whole shop smelled of witchcraft.

I thought of Elizaveta's explanation of what the witches had done to disguise the trap in my basement, and figured that they had done something like that here.

"How is he?" I asked.

"He is angry at himself for being so careless. His hands smart a bit, but they will heal up just fine now that his dad has made the bad magic go poof. And he is able to evaluate himself, thank you very much," said Tad crossly.

"He is fine," said Zee. "Grumpy as usual."

"That's a little 'pot calling kettle' of you, don't you think?" asked Tad.

Zee grunted, frowned, and tipped his head to the side. He sniffed loudly.

"I smell it, too," I said. "It's not just the air filter. If it were the air filter emitting that much magic, Tad wouldn't have any hands left."

"Hey," said Tad. "Thanks for that thought."

"Serves you right for being so careless," said Zee. "Mercy, this new shop of yours, it is equipped with fire suppression, no? Do you know if it is foam or water?"

"Water," I said. "Water was easier."

"Ja," he said. "And useless in a grease fire."

"We dealt with building codes, not practical matters," I said. "Building codes said sprinkler system. But the fire extinguishers will take on grease fires." We had lots of extinguishers.

"The sprinklers are good news for us," he said. "But maybe not for a fire. Mercy, help me get the vehicles opened up."

So we opened hoods and air filter covers and any other

kind of covers that Zee thought useful. Tad unplugged and collected various electronics and covered them with plastic—something he could do with minimal use of his poor hands.

Zee inspected the computers, cell phones, and computational equipment and gave a reluctant nod. "Those have not been affected yet. We can let them stay out of the water."

Then Zee stalked over to the test lever for the water suppression system and pulled it down. As he did, he SPOKE again.

> *Wasser, Freund mir sei,*
> *komm und steh mir bei.*
> *Fließe, löse, binde, fasse,*
> *Hexenwerk verfange dich,*
> *Schwinde Fluch, zersetz den Spruch,*
> *nimm's hinweg, erhöre mich.*

This time, since Tad wasn't writhing in pain, I paid more attention to what Zee said. My German wasn't good enough for a full poetic translation (and it sounded like poetry) but I got the rough gist of it. He called upon water—the element, I thought—and entreated it to wash away the witchcraft.

Nothing different happened after he spoke, until he pulled out his pocketknife and nicked the back of his hand, letting his blood wash into the water.

Black smoke filled the air, and the water hissed and steamed as it came down. Some of the foulness was from the water that had been sitting for months in the tanks that supplied the system, but most of it was magic-born.

"This is a cursing," Zee told me, grabbing a clean rag to stanch his hand. "The last time I saw something like this was . . ." He shook his head. "I don't remember how long ago. But it doesn't matter. If we do not take care of it now, right now—it will spread from the shop, from us, from everything here, like a virus. Gaining power from the misery it causes."

I put up the *Closed* sign and locked the door.

When the water had finished its job in the shop, Zee ran us—clothes and all—into the shower for the same treatment.

Finally, wet and shivering with nerves, I dug my phone out and called Elizaveta, just as if nothing had changed in our relationship.

I don't know that I trusted her—and I was really, really glad that Zee had been here so I didn't need to trust her with everything. But calling her for help beat calling in Wulfe, the witchblood (or something magic using, anyway) vampire.

Elizaveta, black magic and all, was preferable to Wulfe. Besides, it was daytime, so I had no choice.

Then I called Adam.

"I heard you gave up your position as organizer," he said.

"Was that what I was?" I asked. "I thought I was message girl. Yes. Abbot wanted me to get the fae to supply a list of the attending fae, by name, and what their powers were."

"Ah," he said. "And you told Abbot it wouldn't fly."

"And he said then there would be no talks," I agreed. "So it wasn't so much that I resigned as it was that if I continued in my position, there would be no talks."

"And you wouldn't have a position," Adam said dryly.

"Exactly," I agreed. "But I think he fired me anyway."

"Sounds good to me," he said. "It will be a lot less work."

"Might shorten the life span of everyone living in the US by a decade or so, but less work is good," I agreed.

He laughed. "The fae would never fill out paperwork for a meeting," he said.

"Or supply real names," I said. "Or fill out the sheets with lies. Better all the way around to establish what is possible and what is not possible before all hell breaks loose."

Back when the fae first went into the reservations, the government had required the fae to give names and tell them what kind of fae they were. I don't know about the other fae, but I know that Zee gave them the name he was going by right now—and the human-made category of gremlin. That probably fit him as well as anything else, but it trivialized the kind of power he could manifest. The one thing I did know was that *none* of the fae who filled out those forms were Gray Lords.

"So if you weren't calling about that," Adam said, "what *are* you calling about? And does it have anything to do with the reason my people tell me that the fire suppression system in your shop has been drained?"

"Yep," I said. "The shop was cursed."

"I will be right there," he said. Then he said, in a low tone, "Did you call Elizaveta?"

"It was either her or Wulfe," I said.

"And it's daytime," he agreed. "I'm leaving now."

8

~~~~~~

"IT STARTED WITH THIS?" ASKED ELIZAVETA, HOLD-ing up the air filter.

She had been stalking around the garage for five minutes, muttering about the puddles everywhere. I was actually surprised that there wasn't more water—but she hadn't been here during the deluge.

Tad was in the office calling (with his poor sore fingers) the clients whose cars we had doused with water. We were offering them the repairs free of charge, but not delivering the cars until tomorrow or the next day, depending on how long cleanup took us. A problem, I could hear Tad explaining, with the new fire suppression system.

I'd found a spot near the wall that separated garage from office, and Adam had taken up a station next to me, where he proceeded to ignore Elizaveta's doings and answer texts and e-mails on his phone. Or maybe he was planning world domination—with Adam's phone it was hard to tell.

Zee took my other side, leaving the garage at large to Elizaveta.

My cell went off again. But the caller ID was blocked

and my policy was that I didn't pick up on blocked-ID calls just after I got off the hook for a nonpaying government job I didn't want.

"Yes," I said. "The air filter was the first thing we found."

She made a noise and began examining it minutely. The bright orange substance had changed to something that looked a lot more like (and maybe was) the caked-on dirt I sometimes find in cars that belong to people who do a lot of driving on dirt roads around here. A lot of our dirt is powder-fine and coats everything in its path.

"So," I said, "do you think that the cheese-colored magic plague let loose in my shop is the Hardesty witches? I know it's an obvious question, but I figured I should ask it anyway."

"Could be," drawled Adam. "Unless you've been out annoying other witches without telling me."

"The Hardestys are like . . . the Borgia family. There is seldom only one way for them to win," counseled Elizaveta absently as she continued to examine the air filter. "Their goal always is to consolidate their power. Judging by their actions, if the meetings do not take place, they win. If they take place and they blow up—literally or figuratively—they win. If you spread a mysterious and fatal magical plague wherever you go, they triumph on all fronts."

My phone rang again and she gave me an irritated look as if it were my fault that someone was calling me. There was no caller ID so I refused that call, too.

Elizaveta turned back to Adam. "The attack on your home . . . a zombie werewolf would be a treasure for a witch family, something not easily replaced. They did not expect you to defeat it. They expected it to kill whoever triggered the trap—maybe everyone in the house when it was triggered. It would not have destroyed the pack, unless they got lucky and it killed you, Adam. But if you had lost more pack members . . . I think that the meeting between you and the government would not be so important to you."

She frowned again at the air filter. "They do seem to want badly to stop it, don't they? I wonder why they do not want the government and the fae to make peace."

"If the witches are trying to stop it, maybe we should fight a little harder to see that the meeting does take place," Adam said. "To that end, Mercy, I have a dozen or so texts that tell me that you should answer your phone."

I frowned at him, but the blocked caller started calling my phone again. Adam's eyes on me, I answered the phone.

"Ms. Hauptman," said the rough-hewn voice of the man everyone thought was about to declare his candidacy for president. "This is Jake Campbell. How are you?"

"Wet and cranky," I told him. "My fire suppression system just went off and doused both me and my place of business. What can I do for you?"

There was a brief pause. "You can step back into the shoes that my assistant tried to force you out of. I have explained matters to him, and you'll be dealing directly with my personal assistant, Ruth Gillman, after this. Ruth, you will find, is a very good listener."

"Look," I told him. "Fae are what they are. The ones you will be dealing with—assuming they send anyone who can actually make a deal or has any authority—are very old. They won't give you true names because true names have power. Even names that are old, true or not, have power. They won't tell you what they can or cannot do. First, it is rude. Second, most of them do not have the kind of power that they used to before Christianity and iron swept over their territory, and that is a very sore spot for most of them. Asking them about their power, about their names, could inspire one of them to demonstrate on the spot just how much power they still do have. I have a business to run and a very happy marriage. I am not interested in being squashed like a bug because someone else wants me to do something stupid."

"Tell him how you really feel," called Tad from the front desk; he must have been in between calls.

I guess I'd gotten a little loud. I get mad when I am afraid. And I had been afraid since I walked into the killing field of Elizaveta's house.

"Okay," Campbell said. "And that is exactly why we

need you. And I am very sorry for the loss of your pack member. I think we both agree that it would be best if we proceed without incurring any more deaths if we can. So what *is* the proper approach?"

"They know you want a meeting," I said. "Before the hotel blew up, the subject of that discussion was where."

"You suggested a winery on Red Mountain," he said. "It sounds like an excellent compromise.

"I might be part of a werewolf pack," I said dryly, "but I do not require a pat on my head."

"Noted," he said. And I could hear a scratching sound, as if he were actually writing that down on a sheet of paper.

It probably said, *M. Hauptman is touchy but possibly useful. Treat with kid gloves until she proves otherwise.* Or maybe it was just his lunch order for his personal assistant, Ruth.

Being wet and scared was making me way more grumpy than usual.

"I told you I was wet and grumpy," I said. "Also thoroughly spooked." I hadn't intended to admit that last part. "It makes me snap at people who might not deserve it."

"I haven't been near a bomb since I was in the army," Campbell said. "Roadside mine took out the truck just ahead of mine. Not something I've forgotten, and I wasn't hurt. It will be a while before you feel safe again."

He was sincere. But other than the wrenching sadness that was Paul's absence, I had hardly worried about the bomb. Witches were way scarier than bombs.

"That's not what's spooking me," I said slowly. Senator Campbell and the other government officials were all at risk here.

There was a little silence. Then he asked, "I thought the fae agreed not to harm anyone in your territory."

"They won't," I said, "as long as no one insults them by trying to insist that they fill out a questionnaire."

"Not my idea," said the senator. "But I didn't object to it. It would be good to know something—anything about the fae we'll be dealing with."

"I can see how you'd feel that way," I said. "You might start by reading the *Mabinogion*."

"On my mother's knee," said Campbell. "I was afraid of that. But if you aren't worried about the fae, just what is spooking you?"

"Witches are spooking me," I said.

Elizaveta hissed, "Mercy, that is my business."

I narrowed my eyes at her.

"It ceased being your business when Paul died," said Adam; he nodded at me.

"Witches?" The senator's voice was cautious.

"Witches," I said.

And that is how you get a personal meeting with a US senator. Tomorrow, with details to follow.

———

"OKAY, THEN," I SAID, LETTING OUT A SURPRISED and appalled breath as I hit the disconnect. "That was weird."

Elizaveta gave me a long stare. Then she looked at what she still held in her hands.

"This is not the spark," she proclaimed, placing the filter back where she had found it, on the floor by the sink. She turned around, looking at the wet shop.

"Who was it who knew to flood the shop with water?" she asked. Her gaze fell on Zee. "Adam said it was the fae. Are you the fae who works for Mercy?"

Zee smiled meekly and agreed that he was. "One picks up a thing or two in a long life," he said. "It would have been better if it had been salt water, but city water seemed to do well enough."

Keeping track of who knew what about whom was eventually going to make me crazy. Elizaveta knew nothing of who Zee was beyond that he was a simple mechanic. To be fair, I'd known him for nearly ten years before I understood much more than that.

"You may have saved the lives of everyone here," she told him graciously.

He gave a slight nod. "Did what I could."

She dismissed him from her thoughts as she looked around the shop. "Let's see what they've hidden in here."

She muttered something under her breath in Russian that made Adam smile—a thing here and then gone—behind her back. And she waved her hands out as if she were shaking dust off them in a rhythm that seemed to have a specific beat. She frowned and said, "This would be easier to do without the water masking the feel of the magic."

"I am sorry," said Zee meekly. "It seemed the right thing to do at the time."

She nodded. "I see. And yes, it was. But it still makes this more difficult." She closed her eyes and made that same flick-flick gesture with her hands, but this time she started walking forward.

Adam moved closer to her. I thought it was probably to be in a better position to keep her from, say, falling into the pit under the lift or over the knee-high toolbox, a tripping hazard that had already claimed a victim today—me. And *my* eyes had been open at the time.

But she seemed to sense those hazards before she came too close to them. She walked in a hesitant, zigzag path that reminded me of the finding game of Hot and Cold. Whatever she was using to guide herself took her to one of the shelving units that covered the back wall. She reached into a cardboard box of oil containers and pulled out a rag doll dressed all in black.

She opened her eyes then and regarded the doll. "Well, look what we have here. A poppet."

Adam hit a button on his phone. "I need a review of Mercy's shop. Someone planted a doll along the east wall in the garage bay area." He met Elizaveta's eyes. "Sometime between close of shop yesterday and opening today."

Elizaveta nodded. "I concur."

Tad came into the garage and, after Adam disconnected, he nodded at what Elizaveta was examining.

"A voodoo doll?" he asked.

She made a negative noise, but then said, "Of a sort, I

suppose. Though this is nothing so crude as that, nor does it rely on sympathetic magic. This is something of a higher art."

She looked at me. "I'm surprised you weren't killed outright."

"I was wearing nitrile gloves when I picked up the air filter," I said, approaching to examine the doll with morbid curiosity.

She snorted. "I don't know why that curse didn't touch you—but it wasn't a silly pair of plastic gloves."

"Nitrile," said Zee sourly. "They were not plastic."

She ignored him, which I think was his point. There is more than one way to be unseen. If he'd been skulking in the background saying nothing at all, she might wonder about him later. If he made annoying and not too germane comments, then she'd simply dismiss him as unimportant.

Her mistake—but not one she was alone in.

Up close, the doll was unquestionably handmade, from its fabric face to its intricate clothing. Tiny, precise seams edged the black lace dress, and a plethora of black beads littered the frilly skirts. Her silk head was crowned with black and dark brown yarn confined in two even braids. Even the shoes were detailed: tiny boots laced with silvery embroidery thread. Her face was a smooth blank canvas of silk.

Looking at the braids, I asked, "Is that supposed to be me?"

She pursed her lips. "No. It represents the witch who wanted to curse you." She picked up the doll's hand to show me that a strand of black hair had been stitched into the fabric there. "This is you—to symbolize the one the curse was aimed at. I don't understand why whatever it was on the car part—"

"Air filter," said Zee.

She ignored him and kept talking. "—didn't do anything to you." She frowned at me as if that were something she deemed worse than a strange witch putting a death curse on my place of business.

"Is that safe?" asked Adam, nodding to the doll Elizaveta held.

She looked at it as if she'd forgotten what she held. "No, actually." She glanced over her shoulder and then seemed to realize that none of her usual minions were there. She looked around and her eyes found me. "Mercy, you must have something like a torch we can use to burn this, yes?"

"I do," I agreed.

We had been doing a lot of burning lately.

———————

WE BURNED THE LITTLE DOLL IN THE DIRT SECTION of the parking lot where I kept a few cars I stripped for parts. It was daylight, so the burning shouldn't attract much attention. To make sure of that, we picked a spot where the junker cars blocked the line of sight to the road.

I half expected the wet doll to be difficult to ignite. But Tad doused it with gasoline, and it seemed to catch fire easily enough. Tad was ignoring his burnt hands, which looked terribly painful.

I thought about why the curse hadn't hit me.

I was Coyote's daughter, which made me one of the walkers, people who were descended from the avatars of the first people: Coyote, Wolf, Raven, and the like. We could all assume the aspect of our ancestor—I could turn into a coyote. My friend Hank descended from Hawk and he could take that shape and fly. Otherwise we mostly all had different talents except for the two we all shared: we could see ghosts, and magic acted oddly around us.

Vampiric magic almost never affected me. I don't know how it affected Hank because, as he liked to tell me, "I don't hang out with those folk. They come near me and I skedaddle away." The other thing he liked to tell me was "I am lucky to be Hawk's get. Luckier than you. And we are both luckier than someone who descends from Iktomi."

I had to agree with Hank. Iktomi was Spider, who tended to be a trickster like Raven and Coyote, though with a crueler edge than either of them.

The witch's magic had not wanted to work on Arnoldo Salas, and we'd been assuming it was because he was a

witch. Maybe that was so—or maybe it was because he was
like me. I didn't know if I would recognize another walker.
I hadn't met enough of them to be sure.

But I didn't see how the witches could know that about
me . . . unless one of Elizaveta's family had told them so.
While I was still shaking things up in my head, Adam
asked Elizaveta the question I'd been working on.

"Why attack Mercy?" he said.

Elizaveta said, "Not now, beloved. Let me see this thing
done and we can talk." She was walking around the burning
doll clockwise, very slowly. After she finished speaking, she
began to walk backward, counterclockwise. Widdershins.
And she sang a little song in Russian.

The doll, for all that it had caught fire, did not seem to
be burning as quickly as I'd have expected from the materi-
als it was composed from.

Elizaveta's magic didn't feel like the same magic that
Sherwood had used on the zombie werewolf. But the music,
like his, had power if not beauty. I found it jarring, like
someone was petting my fur backward.

And it reeked of black magic, foul and sticky.

I grimaced at Adam. "I'm going to go back and clean up
the shop."

"I'll go with you," said Zee.

Adam gave him a nod of thanks. So I and my bodyguard
went back to see if I could earn a living.

———

MOST OF THE PACK STAYED AT OUR HOUSE THAT
night. For one, it was our weekly ISTDPB4 night, when all
our werewolves could pretend to be pirates and kill each
other for gold, for women (or men—The Dread Pirate's
Booty didn't bother with historical accuracy; Saucy Wenches
were matched with Mouthwatering Manservants), and for
the heck of it. I don't know why ISTDPB4 ended with a 4
when CAGCTDPBT (Codpieces and Golden Corsets: The
Dread Pirate's Booty Three) ended with a T. It had started as

ISTDPBF, but at some point someone had said "four," and "four" it remained.

The other reason the house was full was that Adam had issued a quiet call to the pack, welcoming wives and dependents to stay. The conditions were crowded, but they were safe from the witches. He didn't tell anyone why we were safe—that was Sherwood's secret for now. To my . . . amazement, I guess, the pack decided that it had been something I'd managed.

When I went to bed, every bed and couch was full of people (sometimes more than one) trying to sleep while the pirates (including my mate) howled and hooted from the basement.

Cries of "Put up or shut up!" "*Die*, you freaking rapscallion!" "ARGHHHHH!" sounded sort of homey. I smiled when I closed my eyes.

THE NEXT MORNING, ADAM AND I DROVE TO A house outside Pasco, situated in lonely exile on the bluffs overlooking the Columbia about ten miles away from its nearest neighbor. There was a helicopter on a pad next to the driveway we parked in, but other than that, the house could have been plopped down in any middle-class neighborhood in town and blended in.

Senator Campbell was borrowing the house, Adam had told me.

I followed Adam to the door, regretting the stubbornness that had put me in jeans and a button-down shirt instead of something more formal. Adam, of course, was wearing his working uniform, which was a well-cut suit.

We were met at the door by a smiling, middle-aged black woman who introduced herself as Ruth Gillman, Senator Campbell's personal assistant.

"Come in," she said. "The senator is on a conference call, but it should be finished up in the next few minutes. Can I get you something to drink?"

She led us through a sparsely furnished living room with
worn patches on the carpet into a kitchen that was nearly as
large as the living room and filled with cherry cabinets,
marble countertops, and expensive everything else.

"I know," she told us, "it looks like it belongs in a different house. It's going to be Bob's retirement house, and he
and Sharon are redecorating one room at a time. This year,
he told me, it will be the master bedroom."

"Bob?" I asked.

"The senator's younger brother," she said. "He's an en-
gineer and worked for twenty years in Richland at the Pa-
cific Northwest National Laboratory. He was transferred to
Virginia, but he fell in love with this country."

"Huh," I said. The Tri-Cities were my home, but I'd grown
up in the mountains of Montana. It had taken me a long while
to appreciate the barren hills and rolling landscape.

She laughed. "His wife thinks he's crazy, too. But she
loves him. I think they still have a lot of friends here."

"Are you making fun of Bob again?" asked Senator
Campbell.

"No, sir," she said. "I wouldn't do that." She lied when
she said it, and he laughed because she intended him to.

He was a big man, maybe half a foot taller than Adam
and fifty pounds heavier—not much of that was fat. His
hair was light brown fading to gray around the edges. There
were laugh lines at the corners of his eyes.

His eyes were hard and predatory. Hawk's eyes.

He gripped Adam's hand firmly—and mine less so.

"Welcome to my brother's home," he said. "Why don't
we all go into the study—you, too, Ruth. If you and Ms.
Hauptman are going to be working together, you might as
well start now."

The study had probably been a bedroom when the house
was built, but like the kitchen, it had been changed into a
better version of itself. The floor was some exotic hard-
wood, and the whole room had a masculine feel.

There was a mahogany desk, but there were four

comfortable-looking leather chairs, too. He took one of them and left it to the three of us to take the others.

"So that our cards are on the table before we begin," he said. "You know that I want to keep the fae and the were-wolves and everything else that goes bump in the night as far away from the citizens whom I represent as I possibly can. If we could come up with something that could keep the werewolves from walking around with regular people, I would. If I could hit a button right now and kill all of your kind, all of the fae, I would."

"Fair enough," said Adam. "I know a few werewolves who feel the same about you."

Campbell leaned back in his seat, his eyes steady on Adam. "So why the hell did you warn my team last fall that there was going to be an attempt on my life—that one of my security people was an assassin? I trusted him with my wife and daughters. I'd have sworn he was loyal. I told Spielman that. But he talked me into setting up a sting any-way, and damned if you weren't right."

"I said," my husband said gently, "that I knew were-wolves who felt the world would be a better place without you. But I didn't say I was one of them. You are the honor-able enemy, I suppose. But we, my kind, need you where you are. Giving voice to the fear, but also to reason. If you weren't where you are, it would be that idiot from Alabama who wanted to make it legal to hunt werewolves."

Campbell winced. "Right, her. It's like when I played dodgeball in my high school gym class. The Republicans and the Democrats both get some good players—and to make things even, we both get some idiots. We have the Honorable Ms. Pepperidge from Alabama. The Democrats get the Honorable Mr. Rankin from California."

He paused. "You should know that the reason that I'm here—that we are coming down from Washington"—he snorted—"Washington, D.C., I mean, is because of that. That you warned me when it would probably have made your life a lot easier if he'd managed to kill me."

"To be fair," Adam said, "I also did it to spite the people who tried to make me assassinate you."

Campbell laughed. "I didn't expect to like you."

"Funny what happens when you talk to people," I said.

Campbell nodded. "Fair enough." He spread his hands out, palms up. I think they teach politicians to use their hands when they talk in politician school. "So talk, Ms. Hauptman. Tell me about the witches who spooked you."

They also teach them to lie. Campbell had expected to like Adam and he wouldn't push a button to eliminate all the werewolves and fae in the world—though he'd been honest enough about keeping the werewolves away from the general population.

"There are at least two witches who entered our territory a few weeks ago. We became aware of them last week. From their actions and what one of them told me directly, they intend to stop the talks between the fae and the government," I said.

"I've been reading the *Herald*," he said. The *Tri-City Herald* is our local newspaper. "Are the witches responsible for the zombies?"

"The zombie cow made Facebook sit up and beg," said Ruth. "That cowboy is fine."

"His boyfriend thinks so, too," I said.

"Honey, I am married," she told me. "And my wife was the one who pointed out what a hunk your zombie-roping man is. There is something about a man with a lasso."

I grinned at her. "I'll tell him you said so."

"When you are through flirting with the enemy, Ruth, we could get back on topic." There was irony in the senator's tone, but no bite.

I told him about the witches, beginning with the difference between a white witch, a gray witch, and a black witch. None of that, I saw, was news to either Ruth or the senator. I began with the zombie miniature goats all the way through the poppet at my garage yesterday. I brushed over Elizaveta's fourteen dead with "a forceful attack on our local witches." After a moment's thought, I included what my nose had told me about Abbot.

"Oh no, honey," Ruth said. "Tory Abbot is a good man. He goes to church every Sunday."

"Abbot," said Campbell slowly. "Abbot changed a few months ago."

"He got married," said Ruth. "That kind of thing changes a man a little." But there was no conviction in her voice. Something about that change had bothered her, too.

"To a nice girl from Tennessee?" I was guessing, but . . . Abbot had smelled like the zombie witch.

"How'd you know?" asked Ruth.

"The Hardesty witches come from Tennessee," Adam told them. "From what we can find out, the family is large. They own businesses all over the country. But the core of their power is in Tennessee."

"You told me there was something off about Tory's new wife," Campbell said to Ruth. "You didn't like the way she treated him."

"Ordered him around like a dog," said Ruth. "You think she is a witch?" She paused, thinking about it. "I could see that. There is a core of cold in her that chills my bones."

"So what should we do?" Campbell asked.

"Don't be alone in a room with Abbot's wife," I told him. "Don't let her into your personal spaces."

"Most witches are going to avoid you like the plague," Adam told him. "They are trying to survive by hiding in plain sight. They don't want to draw notice. I don't know what's up with this bunch, but they are not acting like normal witches.

"In the meantime," Adam said, "I can send over some of my pack to keep an eye out."

"No," said Campbell heavily. "Let me think about this. I have some experts I can consult."

"Okay." Adam stood up, so I followed suit.

Ruth took out a card and gave it to me. "The senator gave me your number. Why don't we do lunch tomorrow—

just you and I. And we can discuss how best we should deal with the Gray Lords. I would be grateful for anything you could tell me."

Campbell's hawk eyes met mine. "You aren't the only person we are talking to about this, but we'll take anything you can add."

The senator had gotten to his feet when Ruth and I had, but he let Ruth lead us from the room. I got to the door and turned back to him.

"Senator, I didn't know you were Native American?"

His eyebrows climbed to his hairline. "That's because I'm not. What gave you that impression?"

I shook my head. "Sorry. Something about your eyes."

He shook his head. "Wish I were," he said. "It would help me get the Native American vote in Minnesota. Being red in a blue state, I need every vote I can get."

———

ADAM WAITED UNTIL WE WERE IN THE SUV BEFORE asking me, "What was that about?"

"Curiouser and curiouser," I murmured. "If the senator isn't one of Hawk's children, I'll eat my hat."

"You don't have a hat," Adam said.

"I feel like all I need is the right perspective and everything will become clear," I told him. "I'm calling Stefan tonight. I meant to do it last night. But I'm a lot more interested in what he managed to dig up on Frost now than before."

"You think Frost ties into all of this?" Adam asked.

I huffed. "I don't know. What do you think?"

"I think," Adam said, "that I am heartily tired of witches."

"Hear, hear," I said. "So would you vote for him for president?"

"Yes," Adam said without hesitation.

"Huh," I said. "I'd vote for Ruth. She didn't lie."

"Politicians have to lie," Adam said. "It's written into their black souls. It's only a problem when they begin to believe their own lies."

"And these are the people we are going to introduce to the fae," I said.

Adam smiled. "I'm kind of looking forward to it."

"You probably would have liked bloody gladiator sports, too," I said, leaning my head on his shoulder.

WHEN I CALLED HIS CELL THAT NIGHT, STEFAN didn't answer his phone. When I called his home phone, I didn't recognize the boy who answered it, but he called for Rachel, whom I did know.

"Hey, Mercy," she said. "I don't know where Stefan is. He left last night to go talk to Marsilia and hasn't made it back yet."

"Is that usual?" I asked.

"It's not unusual," she told me, "but I wouldn't go so far as to say it happens all the time." She paused. "She wants him back and he lets her think that might happen. He thinks that you are safer as long as she thinks she can bring him back into the fold."

"Is that dangerous for him?" I asked slowly.

She laughed bitterly. "She's a vampire, Mercy. Of course it's dangerous." Her voice softened. "But he's not dumb— and he's not an easy mark. He's been playing games with her and worse for centuries and he's not dead yet."

I didn't correct her—Stefan had been dead for a very long time. But Rachel had not had an easy life and I liked her. I tried not to pick at her unless I had to.

ADAM WENT RIGHT TO SLEEP. I HAD MORE TROU-ble. I felt like we were all standing around waiting for the other shoe to drop.

Senator Campbell was a walker like me—or rather, like my friend Hank. Though he didn't know it. Should I have told him?

That did answer the question of whether I'd know a walker when I met them—so the Salas family's resistance to witchcraft must have been because they were witchborn. I felt a little uneasy that Elizaveta knew it now, too. When Arnoldo called, assuming he would, I would see if I could talk him into moving elsewhere.

Was it important that Campbell was a walker? Was it important to the witches? Did they know?

"Adam," I said.

"I'm asleep, Mercy. It's a guy thing. We like to sleep after sex."

"Frost wanted to take over the North American vampires, and he mostly managed it," I said.

"Yes," he agreed, rolling over so he could look at me. "For this you wake me up?"

"He intended to bring them out to the public," I said. "So they could hunt like vampires of old."

"That's what he said," Adam agreed.

"But that would be stupid," I said. "If the vampires come out—especially if they are engaging in hunting in ways that terrorize the human population—they'll be hunted into extinction."

"Yes." Adam's voice was patient. "He's not the first idiot to attain power."

"He corrupted and then funded the Cantrip agents who kidnapped the pack and tried to force you to kill Senator Campbell."

"Yes," said Adam slowly—and I knew he saw it, too.

"You thought that they didn't care if you were successful or not, thought they had a backup plan to kill him. All they wanted was to pin the attempt on werewolves."

"Yes." Adam sat up. Then he got out of bed and started to pace as he ran through the patterns that I was painting. He had a better understanding of politics than I did because he actually trod the halls of power occasionally.

He stopped to look out the window. He was naked and I got a little distracted.

"Sorry," I said, "I was distracted by the scenery. What did you say?"

He grinned at me, showing a flash of dimple. "I said, what if we assume that Frost wasn't stupid?"

"Yes," I agreed.

"Let's say that he was a witchborn vampire," he said.

"Yes," I agreed.

"It's like your miniature zombie goats," he said. "The important thing isn't the 'miniature' or the 'goat,' it's the 'zombie.' With Frost, the important thing isn't the 'vampire.' It's the 'witchborn.' If we look at it like that, then he was engineering the downfall of werewolves and vampires."

I nodded. "And then he wasn't being stupid. So what does that have to do with what the witches are trying now?"

"Damned if I know," he said, after a long moment.

I pulled the covers up under my chin. "Me, either. But it clears up a few things."

"So that was what was keeping you up?" Adam asked.

I nodded.

"You can sleep now?"

"And so can you," I promised.

Adam shook his head slowly and lowered his brows, his eyes flashing gold for a moment. "Nudge," he said.

———

I FELL RIGHT ASLEEP AFTERWARD, FEELING WARM and comfortable and safe.

That didn't last long.

I dreamed that I was walking along a road. It seemed familiar, somehow. I couldn't quite place it until I realized that there was someone walking with me.

"You could have picked anywhere," I told Coyote. "Why did you choose a dirt road in the middle of Finley?"

Coyote stopped walking and I turned to face him.

"Because," he said soberly, "it is better to come home."

I frowned at him. "What do you mean?"

"I have," he said, "some information for you."

"What is that?" I asked.

Coyote didn't answer me in words.

———————

I WAS LOCKED IN A CAGE WITH MY BROTHER, AND
I hurt. I was scared and he was scared and we huddled
together in joined misery. We lived in moment-to-moment
terror, waiting in dread for when we were taken out of the
cages again. When the new witches came, when the old
ones screamed out their lives, I was glad because I thought
they'd forget about us.

I was wrong.

It was took me a while to come to myself enough to realize
what had happened. Coyote had put me into the mind of
Sherwood's cat sometime before the Hardesty witches killed
Elizaveta's people. I was dreaming, I remembered, so all I
had to do was wake up.

But I couldn't wake up.

Time did not speed up like it did in normal dreams.
Minutes crept by like minutes. Hours were hours. It hurt to
breathe, it hurt to move—but my catself cleaned my brother's face so he'd know he wasn't alone. It comforted us. All
three of us.

The cat became aware of me at some point. He didn't
seem frightened by having a visitor inside his head, though
I couldn't communicate with him very well. I crooned to
him while the witches did their work, harvesting our misery. I don't know if he heard me or not.

"Amputation and mutilation are not effective," the witch
the others called Death said disapprovingly to the young
woman who had taken our eye. "The shock can kill the
animal, and that is a waste of potential magic to be harvested. They aren't human, and they don't realize that you
have done permanent damage, so there is no additional
boost from emotional trauma."

The cat and I disagreed with her. But we didn't tell her so.

The other witch, who was Elizaveta's kin, who had spent
the last few days learning from Death, prodded our new
wound and then coated it with a paste that made us cry
piteously.

In my human life I had found that witch dead (will have found her dead) in the workroom of Elizaveta's house. Militza. I was not sorry that she would die.

The cat's senses were different from my coyote's, from my human ones. He could see the ghosts better than I could, and he saw the witches as entirely different from the humans. The witches mostly appeared oddly twisted—not visually, but to some other sense I could find no human correlation for. I knew, because the cat knew.

Death, on the other hand, was a black hole so dense that we shivered from the icy cold of it. She was scary on a level that if we could have willed ourselves to die before she ever touched us again, we would have.

The zombie witch was there, too. She had a touch of that fathomless void that watched us as we watched it. We grew to know her, as we did Elizaveta's witches. But because I knew that they all died, the cat and I ignored Elizaveta's family and watched the Hardesty witches. We learned who they were and what they wanted, and it terrified us.

After a number of days had passed, I forgot that I was not the cat.

When Death stopped the world, I huddled with my brother and felt the life leave his body. I waited for her to take me, too. I felt her magic sweep over me, but it could not take hold. I hid against my dead brother and tried not to attract her notice.

MY FACE WAS PRESSED AGAINST GRAVEL, MY paws . . . fingers dug into the ground as I curled tighter into myself and sobbed for my dead brother, making hoarse, ugly sounds. I cried for the creatures who died to feed Death's appetite, and I cried for the darkness in the world.

A man's voice crooned to me, saying words that didn't make sense. I knew that voice, but it did not bring me any comfort.

But a warm blanket was laid over me, and the night sky gave way with bewildering swiftness to golden sun that warmed the blanket and made me feel safer. I breathed in the familiar scents of sage, sun, and fresh air.

"Come home, little coyote," said Coyote. His voice was as gentle as I'd ever heard it, and he petted the top of my head. "You are safe. For now, anyway."

After a while I quit crying, though I remained curled in a ball in the middle of the road. His touch was an anchor that kept me from drifting back into the witch's lair.

"Those times are all in the past and beyond changing," he said, and then his hand stilled. "Huh. I had wondered how that single half-grown cat escaped Death. I found it was convenient because if I'd used one of the animals who died it might have killed you, too. He didn't appear to be special—and now I find that I saved him myself and didn't know it. How clever of me."

I braced myself on my arms and sat up. My whole body ached down to the bone. His hand fell away from my head, but that was okay, I didn't need it anymore.

He smiled brightly at me, rising to a crouch but keeping his face at my level. "I guess you could claim credit, too. If you hadn't been with him when Death called—resistant as you are to the magic of the dead—he would have died, too."

I cleared my throat and tried to speak but my mouth was too dry. I swallowed a couple of times and tried again. "You suck."

He beamed and rubbed his chest with false modesty. "I do try." Then all the laughter left him.

"The Hardesty witches are abominations. They take death, a change that is sacred, and they profane it. Kill them, my child. Kill them and kill their kin."

I looked at him, inclined, after my sojourn, to agree with him. Instead I held up one finger. "You aren't the boss of me." I held up a second finger. "I am not an assassin." I held up a third finger. "Who are you to complain about making the sacred profane? Isn't that what you do?" I held up a fourth finger. "I am, in this moment, more inclined to kill you than anyone else."

He threw back his head and laughed. "Good. Good. Take that anger and remember, all I did was allow you to see what they are."

"What do you care about them for?" I said. "Did one of the witches place a curse on you?"

He hung his head and looked up at me through his lashes. His eyes were mournful and sly. "Yes," he said, then shook his head. "No."

"What do you mean?" I asked.

He sat on the ground beside me and crossed his legs. "Oh, it's story time," he said. Then he sat without talking for a long time.

"Yes?" I said.

"You aren't ready to hear this story," he said. "So I'm trying to make up another one. But it isn't working. So let me just say this." He looked at me, and his face and body were suddenly very serious. "Death is sacred. It is a change . . . and I am the spirit of change. So death is sacred, specifically to me. The Hardesty witches are blood-tied, by bone, by breeding, and by choice, to death magics." He paused to give greater weight to his words, then said, "Zombies are anathema."

"I agree," I said. "I noticed. A lot of the things those witches were doing are anathema. Especially if you consider death sacred. I ask you again, why the Hardesty witches? Why not Elizaveta?"

He snorted. "Can't get one by you, can I? Let's just say that they are particularly stupid about the way they have gone about things." His face twisted and I saw, to my surprise, honest grief. "They have taken something that was pure and holy and besmirched it with their filthy magic."

"Why don't *you* kill them?" I asked.

"I can't do that," he said regretfully. "This isn't like the river monster. These are once-mortal witches whose flesh originated in a different land. They are in your realm of influence, not mine."

"I don't understand," I told him. Unhappy about the "once-mortal." "Once-mortal" is a bad thing when dealing with a witch, for whom learning is one of the keys of power. Old things have an opportunity to learn a lot.

He patted me on the head. "That's all right. You just need to kill them. I'll do the understanding for both of us."

"Mercy," Adam's voice said urgently. *"Mercy, wake up."*

9

~~~

"YOU WERE CRYING," ADAM SAID, HIS VOICE SOFT
with sleep. He brushed a finger over my cheekbone.

We were both familiar with each other's nightmares. I
couldn't recall what I'd dreamed about, but sadness still
clogged my chest.

I rubbed my head against his hand for comfort, like
a cat. A cat.

"It was something about cats," I told him. "Sherwood's
cat, I think. But I don't remember it anymore."

"Okay." He tucked me against him. "Go back to sleep."

I glanced at the clock and saw that I'd been sleeping less
than an hour. No wonder I felt so tired.

"We need to find those witches," I said.

Adam nodded. "I hate fighting a defensive battle. All
you can do is react, react, react. And you find yourself running around like Chicken Little, never knowing where the
next rock will fall from."

"Adam," I said slowly, "if you hate being on the defensive—
why are you running a security firm? Isn't security, by definition, always on defense?"

"I hear your logic," he said. "But I'm not listening."

"Ethically," I said, "defense is easier to defend than, say, assassinations or attacking people because they irritate you."

He growled, then laughed. "Defense is easier to defend."

"Hey," I told him, "it's two in the morning. I'm not responsible for anything I say after midnight." I frowned. "I have this weird feeling that we need to hunt down those witches really soon."

He kissed me long and sweet, then pulled me against him and said, again, "Go to sleep, Mercy." He rolled until I was on top of him, then rumbled, "We need all the sleep we can get if we are going to hunt witches in the morning."

"Oh goody," I said.

WE WERE ON OUR THIRD DAY OF A FULL HOUSE. Werewolves who had human families were still on virtual house arrest for their own protection. That meant breakfast was a big deal and both the kitchen and the dining room table were full.

Adam had intended to work from home this morning. But when Jesse asked him what he wanted for breakfast when he came downstairs from his shower, he said, "No time for breakfast."

That was a little unusual. Werewolves have to eat a lot. And "hangry" just doesn't describe what happens to a werewolf when he is hungry.

He saw my look and grinned at me.

"You're in a good mood today," I told him.

"You need to eat," said Jesse. "There is always time for a good breakfast."

He breezed through the kitchen, kissing her on her cheek and me, lightly, on the mouth. Aiden got a fist bump. Aiden wasn't big on touch—so we let him decide when he needed a hug.

"I got called in," Adam told us. "No rest for the wicked. Jesse, there'll be food where I'm going."

He glanced around the room and called all the werewolves to him with nothing more than a glance. After a moment, a few other werewolves appeared from other places, so Adam must have used pack bonds.

"Dress up for an official workday," he told them. "Meet me at the office. ASAP. Food will be served."

They scattered. No mistaking the rising energy of "something to do at last" that rose from them.

"No hunting witches?" I asked.

"No witch hunts today," he told me. "I expect to be late."

"Where at?" Jesse asked.

"Sorry, I can't tell you." He paused. Kissed me again. Then said, "Don't go hunting without me."

And then he was gone.

"Huh," said Jesse. "He seems awfully excited."

We exchanged mutual raised eyebrows.

"Grrr," said Kelly's wife, Hannah. "I hate secrets." She looked at me with lowered brow. "Do you know how much longer we are all stuck here?"

"Don't look at me," I said. "I told Adam we had to go witch hunting today." I waved a hand at all the werewolves bounding out the door wearing Hauptman Security shirts. "You see the result."

"Just how dangerous are these witches, really?" she asked.

A cold chill ran down my spine—and for a moment I had a glimpse of the dream I'd had last night.

"Very," I said. "You all stay inside this house today. If we don't get the situation taken care of in the next few days, maybe we should see about a camping trip or something for everyone until this all blows over."

I grabbed a piece of toast and a slice of bacon and slunk out. They all knew that my garage had just reopened and I needed to go to work. They would be safe with Joel—and Aiden for that matter—but they weren't happy.

ZEE AND I SPENT THE MORNING DETAILING THE cars that had gotten soaked the day before yesterday, using my new steam cleaner and the old Shop-Vac I'd brought over from home. For the heck of it, I detailed Stefan's van, too. It needed it. I tried the steam cleaner on Stuffed Scooby. The best that could be said about that attempt was that he didn't look any worse. I managed to reattach the spot that had fallen off his back with a little hot glue.

Tad's hands were still in rough shape, so I'd sent him home to heal up.

"It's a good thing," said Zee, cleaning the outside of the driver's-side window of the car we were working on, "that it's high summer. These should finish drying out in the sun this afternoon."

"I'll remember to thank the witches for picking this time of year when we finally catch up to them," I said.

I was working on the interior. The car was a couple of decades old, and I might have been the first person to clean the dash. I hoped that the plastic didn't dissolve in panic at the touch of my cleaner, but I wouldn't detail a car and send it out with a gunk-covered dash.

Zee paused. "*Liebling*, this might not be a battle for a little coyote. Black witches are an ugly thing. Maybe leave it for the ugly thing that your pack's witch has become."

I shook my head. "No. Adam has promised to protect the government people—and the witches have made it pretty obvious that they intend harm. And they attacked us—here and at my home. We can't just stand back and hope that Elizaveta takes them out."

I quit scrubbing for a moment so I could look him in the face. "And what if Elizaveta joins with them like some of her family did?"

"The Gray Lords tell us that no one is to interfere with the witches," he said.

"They know about them?" I asked.

He nodded. "I told them about the attack here, Mercy, but they already knew that the black witches had attacked Elizaveta." He scrubbed with a little more emphasis, then said reluctantly, "They are right to tell us not to interfere. These talks are important and it would be too easy to make ourselves look bad if we take on the witches. I may be an outcast—"

"I'm not sure you can be an outcast by choice," I told him. "They'd take you back in a moment if you wanted to go."

He shrugged. "Sometimes the English language confuses me."

"Sure it does," I said. I took out a Q-tip and started on the vent covers. "Outcast. Cast. Out. That means someone kicked you out. If you leave—then you can be something less pathetic and more adventurous-sounding. Like a rogue."

He snorted. "I may be a *rogue*, Mercy, but I don't want the fae to fade away and die." He looked thoughtful. "I don't want *all* of them to fade away and die, anyway. And the ones I'd prefer dead, I'd rather kill myself."

"Hah," I said.

My phone chimed and I checked the text message—it was from Ruth Gillman. She was reminding me of our lunch date, and requesting that I pick the venue since she wasn't familiar with the Tri-Cities.

"I'm going to talk to Senator Campbell's assistant over lunch," I told Zee. "Do you have any idea who the fae are going to send to deal with them? I won't tell her if you don't want me to, but I'd like to have a ballpark guess about how easily offended the fae who are treating with the humans are going to be."

"*Es tut mir leid*, Mercy." Zee shook his head. "I do not know. I am a rogue, you see; they do not tell me such things. But you may tell them that the majority of the fae are tired of the fuss. They would like to go and live their lives. They are not clamoring for human blood."

I gave him a look and he flashed a quick smile.

"Ah, you are right. There are fae who would love to bathe in human blood. But the fae who are making the decisions are not driven by the need to destroy. They just want a place to live in peace."

"Do you have any sense that this meeting might be dangerous?" I said. "I mean, that the humans will have to watch what they say and how they say it? Some of the fae can be very prickly." I cleared my throat. "And Adam and most of the pack are going to be putting themselves between the fae and the humans if something goes wrong."

"I don't know who they are sending," Zee said again. "But I do know that they will not send out anyone who is not familiar with working with the human government. With humans in general." He turned on the steam cleaner—and then shut it off again. "Among the more powerful of us, we have a lot who are trained in human law. Like your government, we have an overabundance of lawyers."

I HAD BEEN GOING TO MEET MS. GILLMAN AT THE Ice Harbor Brewing Company, a local pub, but changed my mind at the last minute and texted her directions for a different place.

She beat me there and was waiting for me in a white Camry that shouted "rental car." When I pulled in next to her, she unlocked her doors and got out.

"I was just about to text you to make sure I'd gotten the right place," she said. "I hope that this is like good Chinese restaurants. You know—where the more run-down the exterior is, the better the food."

She was right that it wasn't pretty. The exterior was boxy and an unlovely blend of textures and shades of white.

The wall nearest the entrance had been newly repaired. I'd been here when a snow elf had taken the whole wall out. He'd been chasing me at the time.

Getting chased by a snow elf might not sound impressive. But when a frost giant says he's a snow elf, there aren't many, even among the fae, who would argue with him about it.

The repair work, though not beautiful, had been competently done. Like the rest of the building, it had been painted white. It might have looked better if the rest of the building, also whitish, had been painted sometime this century.

The only elegant thing in sight was a hitching post that

looked like someone had lifted it from the movie set of Elrond Half-elven's home in *The Lord of the Rings*. It was new because I'd have remembered if I'd seen something so out of place before.

I didn't know what Uncle Mike's needed with a hitching post. I breathed in and paid attention to the scents—there just might have been a hint of horse in the air.

"You found the right place," I told Ruth Gillman, assistant to the most famously fae-hostile senator in Congress. "Welcome to Uncle Mike's."

The big *Uncle Mike's* sign was down today, awaiting a newer, bigger sign. But there were cars in the lot and the *Open* sign on the door was lit.

She stiffened and gave me an unsmiling look. "Do you think that it is wise to discuss our meeting here?"

Uncle Mike's had, once upon a time, been the local fae hangout—humans not allowed. It had sat empty for a while during the worst of the tensions between the fae and humans. But Uncle Mike had gone to work on it, right after the fae had signed their agreement with our pack. It had been up and running for a few weeks now. All the work, from the bussers to the brewmaster himself, was done by the fae. But this time, Uncle Mike had opened it to all customers.

He hadn't made a big deal about its reopening, and I was sure there were still locals who didn't realize it existed. But from Ruth's face, the government knew all about Uncle Mike's.

"I think that eating lunch here will teach you more than anything you can get out of me in a two-hour meal," I told her. "Whatever else you need to know, you can ask."

I hadn't called ahead, but Uncle Mike himself met us at the door. He looked better than I'd seen him in a while and had his charming-innkeeper thing he did so well blazing away like a blast furnace.

"Mercy," he said expansively. "Sure and it's been too long since you've brightened our doorstep. Who are you bringing with you, darlin'?"

I made introductions and Ruth's eyes widened when I gave her his name. Uncle Mike was one of the more accessible fae, and I was sure the government thought they knew quite a bit about him. I was equally sure they didn't know anything he didn't want them to know.

"Senator Campbell's aide," Uncle Mike said. "And you're both here for lunch, no doubt. I have just the spot for you."

He sat us at a card-table-sized table, just in front of the stage where a middle-aged man was tuning his guitar. I didn't know him—I didn't think.

The fae have glamour. They might tend to wear the same guise from day to day, but that doesn't mean that they have to. But I was pretty sure he was new to me; he didn't smell familiar. A lot of the fae forget about scent.

The crowd was tame today, and mostly human seeming. I could smell fae, thick in the air. But this looked very much like any bar-restaurant lunch crowd.

The hobgoblin who came bustling up to the table with drinks neither of us had ordered was as fae as fae get. He set down a glass full to the brim with something that was a lovely amber for Ruth. For me he brought a bottle of water. Unopened.

"Compliments of Uncle Mike," he said, his voice a bass rumble far too big for his wiry greenish-gray body, which was barely tall enough to keep his head above the height of our table. His ears, more fragile and larger than anything Mr. Spock had ever sported, moved rapidly, as if they were wings.

I'd never seen another hobgoblin with ears like his. I was curious as a cat, but it had always felt rude to ask why his ears fluttered like that.

Like the other employees he wore black pants, but there was no sign of the kelly green shirt emblazoned with Uncle Mike's logo all the rest of the staff wore, including Uncle Mike. Instead, the hobgoblin's upper body was as bare as his long-toed feet.

Hobgoblins and goblins are related, I'd been told, but

it was a long way back and they both liked to pretend it wasn't so.

"I didn't intend for Uncle Mike to treat us, Kinsey," I said.

"Pssht," said the hobgoblin. "He said nothing owed for it, Mercy, don't fuss."

"All right," I told him. He grinned and scurried off.

Ruth sat very still in her seat, almost as if she'd forgotten to breathe.

The guitarist grinned at me, briefly, and his sharp teeth were slightly blue. He slid callused fingertips over the strings to make a shivery-raspy sound, then began picking his way through a Simon and Garfunkel piece.

The music seemed to break the spell that held her still. Ruth blinked and lifted the glass to her mouth for a careful sip. She paused and drank another swallow before she put it down.

"That is lovely," she said. "Am I going to need someone to drive me home after I drink it?"

Uncle Mike, who'd bustled past us without a glance a couple of times, paused at her question. He dragged over a chair from another table and joined us.

He had a glass that looked and smelled very much like Ruth's. He hadn't been carrying it a moment ago, and I hadn't seen him pick it up. Usually he was more circumspect about using magic, especially in front of the enemy.

"Not if you only have one, Ruth Gillman," he said. "This is mead of my own making. I won't deny there's some powerful spirit in't, but it will do you no ill." I felt the magic in his words, but I was sure she hadn't. Since I was sure that the magic was attached to his guarantee, I let it pass without challenge.

"And," he continued, "not if you eat some of my lovely stew for lunch. We have sandwiches and such, but the stew is the best thing on the menu today."

For the rest of lunch, Uncle Mike set out to charm Ruth Gillman. Only once more did I catch a whiff of magic emanating from him. This time it was to amp up the power of his smile, and I tapped my toe against his leg.

He shot me an apologetic glance. "Habit," he told me.

"What is?" Ruth asked.

"Flirting with pretty ladies," he said.

"I'm married," she told him. "And happy."

"My favorite kind," he said. "Happy is a wonderful thing. Tell me about your wife?"

She had not told him that she had a wife. That told me that the fae might not let the humans know who or what was coming to their meeting, but they knew an awful lot about who the government was sending.

My phone rang. I glanced down at it. "I have to take this call," I said, slanting a concerned look at Ruth. She didn't see it, but Uncle Mike did.

"She'll be safe as houses with me," he promised.

"Where did that come from?" asked Ruth. "'Safe as houses,' I mean. I've heard it all my life and never understood it."

With Uncle Mike's promise to play guardian, I abandoned Ruth in the land of the fae, though not without misgivings. I answered the phone while I walked.

"Sorry," I said. "It's too loud in here. Give me a second and I'll be outside."

I stepped outside to, well, not silence—that area of town has a lot of noise—but it was quieter than inside the bar.

"Zack," I said. "How can I help you?"

"I'm not sure," he said. "I'm not really sure there's anything wrong. But Warren left this morning in a big hurry. Kyle just got back."

When Warren and Adam together had tried to get Kyle to stay safe at the pack house, he'd just looked at them. When he left for home, Zack and Warren had gone with him. Kyle might be just human, but making him stay would have taken more threat from either Adam or Warren than either of them was willing to be responsible for.

"Isn't it early for him to be home from work?" I asked.

Zack said, "Kyle took the afternoon off because he and

Warren were supposed to go out shopping for a new bed. He can't reach him by phone—the phone is off. We both think that it's not like Warren, but Kyle is too angry to worry."

Zack, our submissive wolf, lived with Warren, third in the pack, and Warren's boyfriend, Kyle. Zack wasn't gay, but he'd come to us damaged and everyone felt better with him living with someone in the pack—and Kyle's house was bigger than ours.

Kyle and Warren had both taken him under their protection. It was cute that most of the pack was more afraid of Kyle. It wasn't that anyone in the pack would hurt Zack. But if someone inadvertently scared him . . . well, if Kyle was around, they would *never* do it again.

"I'll try to call Adam, but if you can't reach Warren, likely Adam will be in the same boat," I told Zack.

Maybe the president had stopped in, I thought. They take away people's cell phones when the president's around, right? Something that big might be a good reason for why Warren had turned off his phone and not told Zack what was up.

Or maybe it was just another boring meeting, but the president would be a better story. And it had a better chance of pouring water on Kyle's temper than just a meeting.

I called Adam and, not unexpectedly, got his voice message. I hung up and called Zack back.

"I can't get through, either, but the pack bonds feel fine. So I don't think anything is wrong."

"Okay," Zack said. "I'll let Kyle know."

"If he decides to be worried instead of mad, you could call Hauptman Security. They won't be able to tell him anything." I paused. "Wait. They might be able to tell me more than they could either of you. I'll do that, too."

Hauptman Security answered on the second ring.

"Hey, Mercy," said Jim.

"Hey," I said. "Is the boss around?"

"Nah," he told me. "He and most of the crew—that crew, if you know what I mean—got called out this morning. Is there anything I can do for you?"

"No," I told him. "Thanks." "That crew" had to be the werewolves.

I called and told Zack that all seemed quiet on the Hauptman Security front. I promised to let him and Kyle know if I heard anything before they did.

By the time I got back to Ruth, there was food on the table. We ate, Uncle Mike flirted—and I realized that I didn't see this side of Uncle Mike very often anymore. There was a time when I wouldn't have known there was another side to him.

Ruth polished off her mead—which she told Uncle Mike she usually didn't like. We both ate the last of the stew and homemade bread and said our good-byes.

Ruth stood by her car for a moment, looking thoughtful. Then she looked at me. "Was I bespelled?"

"Nope," I told her. "He can, but he doesn't. Won't do it at his place of business." I didn't feel obligated to tell her that he'd started to—because I believed Uncle Mike that he hadn't done it intentionally.

"He was funny and kind," she said.

"Mostly people are just people when you get to know them," I told her. "Even fae people."

"Did you plan this with him?"

I shook my head. "I did not tell him we were coming. He's an old friend of mine—but he doesn't usually give me that sort of personal attention when I come here. He definitely knew who you were, and gave you the red-carpet treatment. Someone clued him in, but it wasn't me."

I wondered if it was Zee, but that didn't feel like something he'd do.

"Why did he make such a fuss?" she demanded, and there was a hint of fear in the air. "I'm nobody."

"That's not true," I told her. "As to why . . . for the same reason that anyone treating with the US government puts its best foot forward. They don't want you scared. They don't want a war. They want an agreement that everyone can live with—on both sides."

"You like him," she said. It was almost an accusation.

I nodded. "I do, and so do most people—fae or not."

"You trust him."

That was harder. "I trust him to be himself," I told her. "I won't say he isn't dangerous. But I've seen him protect two men, humans whom he did not know, at a significant risk to himself. He knew that those men were important to me—but the chance of my finding out that he had been there and done nothing was, in my estimate and his, not very great. He did it because it was the right thing to do."

"They are not Christians," she said. "They are not moral people."

She said it as if it were a mantra, something she'd been taught. I'd heard it just the other day in a JLS sound bite on Facebook. As if only Christians were moral. As if *all* Christians were moral.

My old pastor liked to say that church is a hospital for the sick, not a mausoleum for the saints.

"They do not lie," I said, choosing my words with care. "Otherwise they are, morally, a great deal like us. Their morality spans the spectrum of good and evil. Like us, they have rulers—and those rulers, pragmatically, know that they have to enforce laws that keep the peace between fae and humans."

"Okay," she said. She stared at Uncle Mike's for a moment. "You've made me think about things that I thought my mind was made up about. I'm not saying I've changed my mind. Just that I'm reconsidering."

"That is very"—what could I say that didn't sound patronizing?—"open-minded of you."

She looked at me. "You seem so straightforward. Jake thinks that you are your husband's minion, doing the great Alpha werewolf's bidding, poor human that you are. But you are your own person, aren't you? And you aren't nearly as straightforward as you appear to be."

"Stick with me," I intoned lightly, "and I'll have you thinking that Adam and I, that the werewolves, are the good guys."

She held out her hand, so I did the same and we shook.

She started to say something, shook her head, and got in her car. She gave me a wave as she drove away.

"I hope I didn't make a mistake," I muttered.

"That's both of us," said Uncle Mike, who was somehow right behind me. "But all you can do is show them your cards and hope they show you theirs. It might have been nice if you'd warned me that you were coming."

I smiled grimly at him. "You knew."

"Kinsey saw her in the parking lot," Uncle Mike told me. "But I could have used more time."

"I may trust you, Uncle Mike," I told him, "but you have twenty or more fae in there that might owe allegiance to any one of the Gray Lords. If I'd told you we were coming, it could have compromised her safety. Isn't her safety the real reason you joined us for lunch?"

"Well, now," said Uncle Mike, "can't I flirt with a pair of pretty women when they come to dine at my place without getting accused of ulterior motivation?"

I shook my head and laughed. "No."

"That's all right, then," he said happily.

———————

TAD WAS AT THE SHOP BY HIMSELF WHEN I GOT back. His hands were newly bandaged and he was reading a book.

"Hey, Mercy," he said. He held up a hand. "Look what I did. The lady at the doc-in-a-box said they'd heal in a week or so if I gave them a chance."

"What are you doing here?" I demanded. "I sent you home."

"Dad had to step out for lunch," he said. "We didn't want to leave the garage unattended, given what happened yesterday."

"I don't know that it matters," I told him. "Adam's people watched the tapes and found when the poppet was placed in the box. Someone came through the front door without setting off the alarm. They walked into the garage, put the poppet in the box, and walked out the way they came in."

"How did they do that?" asked Tad, putting down his book. "Did they see a face?"

I nodded. "It was one of Adam's security people. But when Adam questioned him, the guy said with perfect honesty that he didn't remember doing any of it. Adam gave him a leave of absence and tickets to California for him and his girlfriend—to get them out of the range of the witches."

"If they can get one of Adam's people," Tad said slowly, "they can get more."

I nodded. "That's what we think."

"Better find them and take care of them soon, eh?" Tad said. "Dad says that the Gray Lords told everyone hands off." He gave me a firm look. "But he also pointed out that he and I are rogues. Cast-outs—did you have an argument with him over that term, Mercy? He said cast-outs don't need to follow the rules. If you need help, you let us know."

I GOT HOME AFTER DARK BECAUSE CLEANING THE waterlogged cars had put us behind, and Tad's necessary medical leave had put us even further behind.

There was a gaggle of people wandering around the house, children and wives, but the only pack there were Sherwood (back from work) and Joel.

I pulled Sherwood aside. "Has anyone heard from any of the other wolves?"

"You mean the pack?" he asked. "No. I thought Adam might have told you. Maybe the president showed up and they needed Adam to provide security unexpectedly."

Funny how both of our minds went to the same place. But how else to explain the radio silence? I couldn't help it; my mind went back to last November when the whole pack had been taken by a bunch of nutjobs taking orders, whether they knew it or not, from Frost. Who, I was pretty sure by now, was not only a vampire but a Hardesty witch.

I called Kyle.

"Hey, Mercy," he said. "Do you know when I can expect Warren to come home?"

Yep, he was still mad.

"No," I said. "Is Zack still there?"

"Yes."

"I think you and he should come to pack headquarters," I said. "Please. I don't like it that the whole pack is out of contact."

I could practically feel the worry win out over anger. But all he said was "Okay." Then he disconnected.

My phone rang. I looked down and saw that it was Stefan.

"Hey," I said. "I've been trying to get in touch. I was about ready to drive over again."

"I have the information you need on Frost," Stefan said. "But I had to go to Marsilia to get it, and it comes with a price."

"What price?" I asked.

Marsilia's voice gave me my answer. "Stefan needs to stay here until this is over. This family, the Hardesty family, they produce people who control the dead, Mercy. More people like Frost. I do not want to lose Stefan to them, or worse, have him turned against me as a weapon."

Sherwood was listening intently. He made a motion and Joel, in his dog form, got up from where he'd been playing with one of Kelly's boys and walked over to us so he could listen, too.

"Okay," I told Marsilia. "I can agree with that reasoning."

"I am so pleased," said Marsilia with a bite in her voice, "that you approve. Particularly as Stefan does not. I will tell him that his pet doesn't think that he can defend himself, either."

I thought of all the replies I could make. I was reasonably sure that Stefan could hear me—though he wasn't saying anything.

"Stefan is dear to me," I said at last. "I would not have him take unreasonable risks for doubtful outcomes. If Death or the witch she brought with her can command the dead as Frost did"—and didn't that sound stupid?—"if one of them is better at it than Frost was, I would rather that all my vampire allies stay as far away from the witches as possible. For their sakes and my own."

"Why, Mercy," she purred, "you've been spending too much time with politicians. Be careful or you'll end up just like them."

I didn't respond.

Finally she said, in a brisk and businesslike fashion, "I did not connect Frost to the witch family until Stefan asked me about him."

"They are connected, then?" I asked.

"Yes. I knew he'd come from Bonarata to monitor me, and I assumed he was one of Bonarata's. I did not examine him closely—such things can be misunderstood. I did not want to give Bonarata reason to come boiling out of Europe so he could stick his big feet in the middle of my affairs."

"Understandable," I said.

"But, since matters between me and the Master of Milan have been altered in the past few months, when Stefan asked me to check into Frost, I called Jacob." Iacopo Bonarata, she meant, the Master of Milan himself.

That was a lot more action than I'd expected. I hadn't expected Stefan to take matters to Marsilia at all.

"Jacob assured me that Frost showed up at his doorstep twenty years ago, a full-fledged vampire. He was, I am fairly sure, though it is difficult to ascertain such things over the phone, surprised to find that Frost was young enough that we had to dispose of his body. From the condition of that body, Wulfe and I estimate that Frost was no more than seventy years old—dating from his human birth, not his vampiric rebirth."

"Who made him?" I asked.

"We don't know," Marsilia said. "But I have called around to seethes where I have allies. I found that there are at least three other vampires who share his bloodline."

"I thought Frost took over all the other seethes," I said.

"Do you think Bonarata would have allowed that?" she

said. "No. But he took over most of the seethes of the western United States, all of them except for Hao's and mine, before he died. Hao's probably doesn't count, since he is the only vampire in his seethe. Seattle doesn't count because it was the werewolves who kept him away from there, not the vampires. The vampires in Seattle barely qualify as a seethe at all."

"Okay," I said. "But how did you discover that there were vampires made by Frost's maker in your allies' seethes?"

I didn't know if she'd answer that question. Vampires are a secretive bunch. I could feel her hesitation, but Stefan made a muffled noise.

They had gagged him.

"If Stefan doesn't come out of the seethe as soon as we deal with the witches," I murmured softly, "then Adam and I will have to come visit."

"Adam and I will have to come visit," repeated Lilly's little-girl voice. *"Adam and I will have to come visit.* Yummy."

Lilly was a special vampire, extraordinarily gifted with music, but incapable of taking care of herself. See also "homicidally inclined."

"Lilly, what did I tell you?" Marsilia said.

"Behave," Lilly said sullenly, "or I can't listen in."

"That's it," Marsilia said. "Now, where were we?"

"How did you discover that there were other vampires made by Frost's maker in other seethes?"

She sighed. "I did tell Stefan I would answer all of your questions, as long as they pertained to Frost or the Hardesty witches."

"Wow," I said involuntarily. Both that she'd agreed to it—and that she'd told me what she had agreed to.

"We are not enemies," Marsilia told me. "Uneasy allies, perhaps, but not enemies."

"I agree," I told her. "I just didn't know that you did, too."

"I don't like you, Mercy—though watching Bonarata run around in circles was almost enough to change my mind—but I do like Adam. More importantly, I trust him." She sighed again. "And, I suppose, you as well."

I didn't trust her at all, so I didn't say anything.

After a moment, she answered my question. "I asked my allies and my friends if they had vampires whose makers they were unsure of. In those places where that was true, I visited their seethes myself. I knew what Frost . . . smelled like, I suppose, though that isn't quite the way it works. A Master Vampire can tell if a vampire is made by someone other than themselves. Eventually, with practice, we learn to tell which other Master made a vampire. So I went to those seethes where there were unknowns—vampires made by someone their own Master could not identify for certain. In three of those cases, the maker was the same as the vampire who made Frost."

She paused, while I absorbed the fact that Marsilia could apparently teleport herself a lot farther than Stefan could. I was pretty sure she wasn't talking about seethes that were nearby—and there had not been enough time for her, who could only travel at night, to go to very many places. She'd been teleporting a lot. I wasn't sure how I felt about that.

I wasn't the only one unsettled by matters, though.

"We owe you our gratitude, Mercy," Marsilia said reluctantly. "These people were definitely sent in as spies and worse for the Hardesty witches. If you had not asked Stefan to look into it, I would not have taken up the trail. We destroyed the ones we found, and now all of the vampires in those seethes know what scent to follow. They are, in turn, consulting with their allies. We will find all of them.

"We are also presently trying to locate the vampire who made them all. He or she seemed to be active between thirty and forty years ago—approximately when all of the vampires I found were made. Since we did not find any newer ones, like as not that vampire was disposed of. But I do not want those witches to own a Master Vampire they can make do their bidding."

Only Master Vampires could make other vampires.

"You are giving me a lot of information," I said. "Let me give you some in return."

"That is not the bargain I had with Stefan," she warned me.

"We are allies," I said. "But be warned that some of this is speculation."

"So noted," she said.

"I think that Frost wanted to destroy the vampires," I told her. "And the werewolves as well. He engineered the whole rogue Cantrip debacle—with the end goal of having Adam assassinate Senator Campbell. We assume that it would have been revealed to be a werewolf kill."

"Whereas Frost would have brought the vampires out to the public," she said. "Yes, we figured that one out as soon as we realized he was Hardesty-bred. I had not made the werewolf connection, though I don't know if that will be useful to me." She made an exasperated noise that might have been more effective if I didn't know that she feared those witches enough to force Stefan—and presumably all of her vampires—into the seethe for protection. "Filthy witches."

"You are sure that you are safe in your seethe?" I asked.

"We have Wulfe, Mercy, but thank you for your concern," she said dryly.

"Do you know how many of the Hardesty witches there are here in the Tri-Cities?"

"You should ask your goblins that," she said. "But they will tell you that there are only two. They checked into a hotel for a few days before moving in with Elizaveta's brood."

"Huh," I said. "Adam's people have them in an RV in an RV park—though they've moved on."

"I will give that information to my people," she said. "We might be able to help. Do you have a description of the RV?"

"Adam will," I told her. "Shall I have him call?"

"It might be useful." She paused. "There is a saying about the Hardesty witches—they travel in pairs. I don't know much about them, Mercy, though I am fixing that. They have stayed under my radar. I have inquiries out with seethes that are closer to their home base. The vampires who live near them are unwilling or unable to talk about them. But a vampire from Kentucky told me this creepy little bit of doggerel verse."

Wulfe's voice broke in. *"One by one, two by two, the Hardesty witches are traveling through. With a storm of curses, they call from their tomes; they will drink your blood and dine on your bones."*

"Hmm," Marsilia said into the silence that followed. "It sounds remarkably more horrid when you say it, Wulfe."

"It's because I'm scarier to start with," he said.

"Do you need anything more that I can offer?" she asked me.

"Is Stefan okay?"

Stefan grunted an affirmative that managed to sound irritated but not enraged. Pretty impressive communication skills considering I was getting that with the filter of (presumably) a gag and a phone.

"Can I call you if I have more questions?" I asked.

"Of course," she said.

"I appreciate it," I told her, and hung up.

"What does this Frost character have to do with what's going on now?" asked Sherwood, who hadn't been here for that episode.

"I think it's the other way around," I said. "These witches were behind Frost. And now they're screwing with us again."

"The vampire is afraid of them," said Sherwood softly.

"So am I," I said. "I wish I knew where Adam was."

10

~~~

KYLE AND ZACK SHOWED UP ABOUT TWENTY MIN-
utes later, suitcases in hand.

Zack said, "I told Kyle that this didn't sound like a call
for a meeting. This sounded more like a huddle. And hud-
dles sometimes go overnight."

"Warren and Zack have been watching football together
again," said Kyle, kissing my cheek lightly. "It's left Zack
using sports analogies."

"Okay," I said. "I'm not sure how a huddle is different
from a meeting."

"A meeting is boring," said a little girl in passing.

She was about six and carrying a bottle that was probably for the baby I could hear fussing in the living room. The
baby belonged to Luke and Libby, Luke's wife. But the six-
year-old, I thought, might be one of Kelly's. Unusually, for
a werewolf, Kelly had four children under the age of twelve.

"And in a huddle all the guys pat each other's butts," she
finished smugly.

"Makaya," Hannah, Kelly's wife, called out in mock anger. "No 'butts' in public."

The little girl giggled and hurried away.

Kyle and Zack watched her with mixed reactions of longing and amusement. Both of them. But Zack's eyes were sadder.

"I'm not going to pat anyone's butt," I announced.

Makaya's voice said, "Mercy said 'butt,' Mommy. Why can't I say 'butt'?"

"Thanks, Mercy," Hannah said. "I always appreciate it when you help me like that." Presumably to Makaya she said, "Mercy is old. Old and grown-up. Her mommy didn't teach her not to say 'butt' in public—and now she's too old to change. Poor Mercy."

I get no respect.

"A meeting is boring," said Zack. "And nine times out of ten, when Adam calls a meeting, the meeting itself is a punishment for someone being stupid. Peer pressure usually makes sure that person doesn't do the stupid thing again. It's amazingly effective, and I've never seen another Alpha werewolf do it."

"Army training," I said.

"A huddle," he continued, "is what you do when you are in trouble, but you have a plan that might get you out of trouble. But you have to all come together in a safe place, so that the enemy doesn't know what you intend to do."

"Yeah, well," I said, feeling the weight of the world, which had lifted after seeing Kyle on the doorstep, drop back on my shoulders with a thump, "I'm not even sure we have a problem—"

"Witches," called Sherwood from the basement. He'd taken all the boys under fifteen (two of them) downstairs to play video games.

"—an *immediate* problem," I said. Then I got a momentary mental flash of something.

"Mercy?" asked Zack.

I shook my head. "It's nothing. Just a flashback to a dream I had last night. Which is pretty stupid considering that I don't remember what I was dreaming about." I might not remember it consciously, but something about it was trying to wiggle out.

"Was it a Coyote dream?" asked Zack.

I gave a surprised look. "Yes," I said—though I had intended to say no. And it had been. "Oh damn," I said. And I still didn't know what I'd dreamed about.

My phone rang. I pulled it out of my pocket so fast that if it had been a match, my pants would have been on fire. But it wasn't Adam.

I hit the green button. "Uncle Mike?" I said.

"Ruth Gillman has come to us at the pub," Uncle Mike told me gravely. "Best you come, Mercy, and hear what she has to say."

"Put her on the phone," I said.

There was a pause, and I could hear Ruth's agitated voice in the background saying, "I won't, I won't, I won't."

Uncle Mike's voice was dry. "Do you hear that? All she has told us is 'They are all dead. I have to tell Mercy.' In my considerably educated opinion, she has been cursed. If you come, we'll make sure you are safe in our place—but I would bring Adam or someone who can have your back. A lot of somethings about this smells like a trap."

I had a momentary panic attack when he said "they are all dead," but the pack bonds were still in place and healthy. I couldn't tell anything else from them, because the bonds are pretty hit-and-miss for me, even my mate bond.

"Okay," I said, happy to discover that none of the flash of panic came through in my voice. "I'll be right down."

I hung up the phone.

"No," said Sherwood.

"No," said Zack.

I raised an eyebrow at them both. "You aren't the boss of me," I told them. "I am the boss of you."

I turned to Kyle. "We have a clue," I told him. He didn't have a werewolf's senses, so he couldn't be an übereavesdropper.

"I heard," he said, and at my look of surprise, he continued, "Uncle Mike's voice carries."

"You're not the boss of me, either," I said.

He raised his hands. "I'm with you. You need to go talk to her."

I pointed at Sherwood. "I elect you to come with me."

Joel barked insistently.

"I would love to have you with me," I said. "But I can't afford to leave this place undefended. I need you and Zack to keep everyone safe. Kyle." I turned to him. "You are in charge."

Joel's jaw dropped in an approving grin.

"I'm not a werewolf," Kyle said.

"Maybe not, but you are dominant enough to keep everyone in line."

"Mercy?" Libby stood in the kitchen doorway, cradling her baby as he drank from his bottle. "Our men," she said. "They're in trouble?"

I shrugged uncomfortably. "I don't know. I don't like it that they all turned off their phones. That's not like Adam."

"What can I— What can the rest of us do?"

"Stay here," I said. "Stay safe. And if you get a call from your wolves, let me know."

SHERWOOD INSISTED ON DRIVING. I'D HAVE backed him down, but we were taking his car—a four-year-old Toyota that was more likely to make the trip there and back than my Jetta.

I might still have insisted, because I had a policy of never letting any of the wolves get away with macho baloney around me, but he was in a state. I could smell his tension and his fear—he was in a cold sweat, never a good sign around werewolves. Scared werewolves are much more prone to violence. If driving gave him the illusion of control, I could let him have that.

And my Jetta still had only one functional seat.

It wasn't late, so I was surprised at how few cars were at Uncle Mike's—and that the *Closed* sign was lit. With Sherwood standing with his back to me, I knocked on the door.

"Who is't?" hissed Kinsey.

"Mercy and Sherwood," I told him.

The door opened and the hobgoblin, free of the clothing he had to wear when the pub was running, gestured us in. "Come in't, come," he said. "Hurry, do. Don't want to leave the door open on a night like this."

Sherwood brushed past me so that he entered first. I gave Kinsey an apologetic smile as I scooted past.

The pub was empty of customers and mostly empty of workers. There were a handful of fae working at cleaning the rooms and getting them ready for the next day's business.

"Closed early," Kinsey said, leading us with purposeful strides. "If the witches are hunting that one, the master didn't want no one here what couldn't protect themselves."

"Good call," I told him.

"Weren't mine," he said. "But I agree. Here you are, right through that door. Master has her in his office. On through, first door on the left. I'm to stay out here, first line of defense. Keep 'thers safe."

I noted that the hobgoblin, whom I'd always liked but had categorized with the lesser fae, was the one Uncle Mike trusted to keep the bad things out.

Sherwood, again, went through the door first, but this time he held it open for me. It was a graceful procedure, and it looked like he'd done it a time or two. A lot of were-wolves work as guards of one sort or another, but not all of them know how to be a bodyguard.

We didn't need Kinsey's directions to find Uncle Mike and Ruth—all we'd have had to do was follow the sound of her weeping.

"There, there now," said Uncle Mike, looking up as we entered his office. He had Ruth seated in a big leather chair, and he knelt beside it with his arm around her shoulders in a hold that was half-protective and half-restrictive.

The office was large enough to contain a big desk and a wall of filing cabinets and still have ample room for six large mismatched but comfortable-looking chairs. Nearly twice the size of the office where we'd met Senator Campbell, but far more scabby.

"They're all dead," Ruth wept, her hands in front of her face as if she could not bear what she'd seen. It reminded me oddly of the weeping angels from *Doctor Who.* "I have to tell Mercy."

"She was sent with a message," murmured Uncle Mike. "She can't deviate from it without a great deal of effort. I'm a little concerned about what else they've done to her."

He took a better grip on her, then nodded at me.

"I'm here," I told her.

The weeping stopped as she sat up suddenly. She lunged toward me, but Uncle Mike kept her still.

"She's alive," I said, relieved. Her lunge had put her close enough to be certain.

He nodded. "That was our first thought as well, given all the zombies we've had running around the town. Some of them can look very much alive for a while. That reminds me I should have told you that my people took care of a pack of dogs yesterday."

"They are all dead," she told me intently, as if she could not hear Uncle Mike at all.

"They have her under a compulsion," he told me. "I think she's been fighting for all she's worth."

"Who are all dead?" I asked.

Not the pack, I was certain of that much. Ruth's face grew eerily still, and her voice became a monotone that sent off warning signals in my hindbrain. "I was in the study with the senator. Two women, spectacularly beautiful goddesses, walked into the room, with our security team escorting them as if they were knights to their queens."

She gave me a panicked look. The effect of the sudden flash of emotion was a little schizophrenic—as if she were fighting off the hold the witches clearly had over her, only to lose control again.

"The senator asked them who they were, and she, the Ishtar—"

I'd heard that word before. "What is an Ishtar?" I really
wanted to know, but I also wanted to see if she was allowed
to answer questions. Especially a question that Ruth Gillman would not be able to answer.

Had they preloaded the lines they wanted her to say? Or
were they in active control?

She paused midword and breathed in and out a few times.
"The dark goddess," she said, "the goddess of death."

"Hubris," Uncle Mike grumbled. "Why is it that all the
witches carry with them so much hubris?"

"Like a marionette," said Sherwood quietly.

I glanced at him. He thought they were actively controlling her, too. I suppose they could have fed her that information, but it seemed more likely that they were here.
Sherwood's face was tight with something: fear or anger.
Maybe both.

I wondered if Ruth knew that, too. If that had been why
she'd been keeping her eyes covered.

"Ishtar was like Aphrodite," I said. "The goddess of love
and sex and spring, right?"

Ruth started to smile; I could see it try to break out, but
it was gone. I couldn't tell whose smile it was because I
didn't know Ruth well enough.

"Ishtar is the right hand of the coven," she said.

"There are no more covens," Sherwood growled. "Just
make-believe attempts. You don't have witches from thirteen families."

"Ten," she said hotly, as if his words had stung her pride.
"We meant to take one of Elizaveta's. That would have
given us eleven. But none of them was strong enough."

Were they after Elizaveta herself?

Before finding out that she'd been working black magic,
I'd have said that she'd never join with them, especially
after they'd killed her family. But I obviously had not
known Elizaveta as well as I'd thought.

They set things up so that there are many ways for them
to win, Elizaveta had told us. Was one of those possible
wins getting Elizaveta to join them?

After a moment, I spoke, repeating the words Ruth had been reciting when I interrupted her, exactly how she'd been saying them. "The senator asked them who they were, and she, the Ishtar—"

"—and she, the Ishtar, brought the Death and all fell to her power," Ruth said, speaking the first four words at the same time as I had. Those words, I thought, were rote. Something they'd pressed upon her earlier, not something they were actively feeding her. Real people don't use the same exact words each time they say something.

"They died for her glory," Ruth said. "All but the senator and I. They took the senator and left me to make a record. My phone."

She reached for her purse, but Uncle Mike prevented her from touching it. Sherwood reached in and took out her phone, which was lying on top.

"It's not locked," he said.

He tipped it so Uncle Mike and I could see, and went through the photo gallery. Pictures of ten dead bodies, most of whom I didn't know. Spielman was there. The skin around his eye was still bruised. I'd liked Spielman. There were a couple of others who might have been in the meeting I'd attended. None of them were my pack.

Even though the pack bonds were live, I'd half expected to see one of the pack among the dead. The witches terrified me—partially because I really had no good understanding of the limits of their power.

"I suppose they might still be alive," Sherwood said. "If you can think of a reason they'd be acting dead."

"I am . . . I was to drive to your house. The address was programmed into my car," Ruth said, in a completely different voice—her own voice. Then she gasped as if she were having trouble breathing. "I came here instead. Thought the fae could help."

I glanced at Uncle Mike.

He said, "Some of the great ones, maybe, but witchcraft is . . . more like Underhill's magic. It doesn't answer well to the fae."

"Sherwood?" I asked.

Sweat gathered on Ruth's forehead and she gripped Uncle Mike's hands. "Don't let me go," she gasped in a whisper. "Was supposed to attack. There's a knife . . . a knife."

"We took it when you came here," he crooned. "There's no knife now."

I turned to Sherwood, who stood as far from her as he could get, his eyes wild—but not wolfish. It had been the wolf who'd taken down that zombie, I thought. The man didn't want to remember.

I wished Elizaveta were here. Sort of. Wulfe?

If they wanted Elizaveta for their coven, they'd be salivating for Wulfe. I didn't know what witchblood family line he carried—or if he was wizard instead. But he was twisted like a pretzel and he represented a lot of power. On the whole, it was probably good that he wasn't here.

"Sherwood," I said. My voice was quiet, but there was authority in it. Not Adam's, I realized, because the bond between my mate and me felt like it was filled with cold grease—sluggish and reluctant—when I tried to draw on it.

Panicked, I reached for Adam again . . . and our bond was back to being uncommunicative, but healthy. Maybe it had just been that I was smack-dab in the middle of a fog of foul magic.

In any case, I couldn't afford to fret about Adam right now. I put that concern aside. Right now we were dealing with a good woman hexed by witches.

"Mercy, her breathing keeps stopping," Uncle Mike said. "I've already done what we can. We tried the usual salt and circles as soon as we realized she'd been cursed. Had no effect at all. Usually salt and circles work on everything."

"They have her blood," Sherwood said, still with his back against the door. His eyes were trying to go wolf, but he was fighting it. "Blood magic is harder to block."

I didn't need Sherwood Post. I needed—

"Wolf," I said, yanking on the pack bond between him and me.

Sherwood jerked as if that pull had been physical. Then he turned his head toward me and snarled—and this time his eyes were wolf.

"Sherwood," I said clearly. "Fix her." I pointed at Ruth without looking away from his eyes. "Fix her and then we'll go out and hunt some witches."

I didn't know why I said that last. Sherwood certainly had never shown any desire to go out and hunt witches, not even after he'd destroyed the zombie werewolf that had been made from the body of someone he'd obviously known.

He looked at me with golden eyes and growled, "Done."

I was afraid I'd gone too far and he'd begin the change. But I'm not that dominant unless I can pull authority from Adam, and our bond was being stubbornly quiescent.

Sherwood looked at Uncle Mike and rumbled, "I need chalk or a pencil. A candle and a knife."

Uncle Mike went to his desk and opened a drawer from which he gathered a piece of chalk, a pencil, a candle just barely small enough to have fit in a drawer, and a silver knife. He glanced at the knife and put it back.

He handed over everything else to Sherwood, who had left the door to kneel beside Ruth, prosthetic leg stretched out awkwardly. For her part, Ruth was slowly writhing, both hands against her throat, tears sliding out of her eyes.

"Why didn't you give him the knife?" I asked.

"That was the athame the witch gave Ruth to kill you with," Uncle Mike told me. "I don't know how it ended up in my drawer, because that's not where I put it. Under the circumstances, I think that it's probably best not to use it for this."

"I have my cutlass—" I began.

Uncle Mike shook his head. "I have something better than a cutlass, no matter how fine." He pulled a worn pocket-knife out of a pouch on his belt and gave it to Sherwood, who took it with a raised eyebrow.

"My word that for this purpose, it's just a pocketknife. Be careful, wolf, it is sharp."

That seemed to be enough for Sherwood. He took the

chalk and began to draw symbols on Uncle Mike's cement floor.

The leg got in his way again and with a growl he pressed something on the ankle of the prosthetic and pulled it off with so little trouble that I wondered if he'd broken something and would have trouble putting it back on. Especially since he tossed it across the room with frustrated speed. It hit one of the metal file cabinets and left a dent.

His knee seemed to be his own . . . which shouldn't have surprised me. In werewolf form he was missing most of his leg, but a human knee corresponded to the stifle joint, which is farther up the wolf's leg.

The leg dealt with, Sherwood continued to draw. I would have had trouble writing at the speed he moved—and he was drawing things a lot more complicated than a letter from the Latin alphabet. I've never seen a werewolf use their enhanced speed to draw before.

Ruth's breathing was oddly broken. She wouldn't breathe for a minute or two, and then she'd gasp and wheeze for a little bit until she stopped breathing again. While she gasped and wheezed she would flop around like a fish out of water. Her hand hit one of the chalk symbols Sherwood had drawn, scuffing it.

Sherwood caught her arm before she could do it again. He looked at me. "Can you tie her up? I'm drawing a circle."

"No need for bonds, I don't think," said Uncle Mike. The old fae touched Ruth on the shoulder. She quit moving.

"Will that harm your working?" he asked Sherwood. "I put a hold on her arms and legs and back muscles. Bound her a bit to the floor in case. We don't want her moving into your work, but I want her to be able to breathe if she can."

Sherwood looked at Ruth as if he could see something that I couldn't.

"No," said the wolf in Sherwood's human body. "That will be all right. Good."

He didn't say thank you. He was wise enough to know better than to thank a fae, no matter how helpful Uncle Mike had been.

He fixed the symbol Ruth had marred, then went back to work. When his piece of chalk got too small, Sherwood took the pencil—grunting in approval when he saw it was a grease pencil. But he said, "This won't last long and I don't have time to unwrap the damned thing."

"Pencil or chalk?" asked Uncle Mike.

"Pencil if you have a dozen so I don't have to mess with them."

Uncle Mike went back to the drawer and pulled out a handful of pencils—and the silver knife. He frowned at the athame, this time keeping it in his hand. When he got close enough to hand Sherwood the pencils, Ruth's eyes opened, focused on the silver knife.

"Get that away from us," growled Sherwood. "I'll take care of it later."

Every time Ruth quit breathing, I counted the seconds off in my head. I wasn't sure why; I didn't really know how long a person could go without air. But it seemed to me that she had been not breathing a lot longer than earlier episodes.

Sherwood must have been paying attention, too. He quit drawing long enough to put a hand on her forehead.

"Breathe," he said.

She sucked in a breath of air and released it.

"Again," he said.

When she had accomplished that, he went back to drawing.

"Can't do that too often," he muttered—to me, I supposed—but it might have been to himself. "Or I'll disrupt what I'm trying to do here. Still, I suppose this won't do any good if she dies in the meantime."

Ten pencils were discarded the same way his discarded leg had been—as was the chair when it got in his way. The file cabinet acquired another dent—this one bigger than the first. Uncle Mike muttered something that sounded like "Werewolves," but he didn't sound too unhappy about the chair even though it was obviously broken.

Sherwood completed the circle before he had to switch pencils again. Then he lit the candle.

He did it by saying a *word*; I didn't quite catch it, though I was pretty sure it wasn't English. But at the sound of it, there was a pop of magic and the candle wick started to burn.

He held the candle sideways and let the wax drip into a place where the grease made a circle about the size of the base of the candle. When he had enough soft wax on the floor, he set the candle into it, using the wax to create a holder to keep the candle upright.

He took up Uncle Mike's knife and opened it. He frowned at it and cast a wary look at Uncle Mike—who'd moved to the far end of the room, with the silver athame in one hand.

"It's just a knife today," Uncle Mike said. "It will do as you wish." He wiggled the athame in his hand. "This one is not as cooperative. You might want to deal with it quickly, when you're done. It seems to have a taste for one of you—probably Mercy."

"Ruth," said Sherwood, staring at the knife for an instant. "It's supposed to kill Ruth." Again, I had the impression that he could see something I could not. As if the patterns of magic were something his eyes could perceive. It seemed to be more accurate than my scent-and-hair-on-the-back-of-my-neck method.

Sherwood used Uncle Mike's pocketknife to open up a cut on the back of his hand, keeping it open by moving the blade back and forth as he dripped his blood along the edge of the circle all the way around. It was made more difficult because he couldn't use either of his hands to stabilize himself—and the missing leg seemed to put him off-balance.

"This would be easier," he grunted, crawling awkwardly, "if I'd pulled off the liner and the pin with the damned leg."

I got up and put a hand under his elbow to help stabilize him. "Does this help?"

"Yes," he said—then turned his attention to what he was doing.

When he reached the candle again with his blood-drip circle, he dug a little deeper with the knife, pulled it away, and flicked his bleeding hand at Ruth. As the drops of his blood touched her, he said three . . . somethings. They sounded like musical notes more than words, but they were more complex than a single note, as if he could form a chord with his human throat.

For a moment, nothing happened.

That was not quite true. Nothing happened except that the moment he flicked those blood drops on Ruth, the foulness of black magic, or my sense of it, just disappeared. There was plenty of magic, for sure, but only a little of it felt like black magic.

I was eyeing the knife in Uncle Mike's hand, and so I missed the first bit. The little movement that made Uncle Mike stiffen and Sherwood actually relax a little under my hand.

By the time I looked at the circle, Ruth's mouth was already open. The first scream had almost no sound—because she had no air to make a noise. The second scream was even quieter, her whole body shaking with the effort of it. If she could have moved her body with Uncle Mike's magic upon her, I think she would have done so, but all she could do was move her mouth and her rib cage.

My eyes teared up and I dug my fingers into Sherwood's shoulder—because there was nothing, not a darn thing I could do to help her except break the circle (maybe I could do that) and waste all of Sherwood's efforts.

The third scream was silent. Blood gathered in the corners of Ruth's beautiful dark eyes and dribbled out of her mouth, staining her white teeth red.

Sherwood remained as he was, crouched near the circle—ready to intervene if matters didn't go as he thought they should. I let go of him so he could move more quickly if he had to, but he just waited.

"And that's why I hate witchcrafters," said Uncle Mike, his voice a prosaic contrast to the events in the circle. "So much blood in their workings." He sounded vaguely disapproving.

Sherwood raised his head. "And the fae are so gentle."

"No," Uncle Mike agreed. "Mostly we're worse—but not as messy."

As if the circle held the very air inside it as well as the magic, I could not smell the blood—or other things—as matters took their course. Ruth Gillman, elegant and tidy, would not be happy remembering this moment, but hopefully she would be alive.

Ruth's mouth opened wider and blood, bright arterial blood, gushed out, flooding the circle where she lay, unable to move her body. The blood hit the edge of Sherwood's drawings and stopped, as if the chalk and pencil were a raised ledge that it could not cross. Where it touched Sherwood's work, it turned grayish black. Not a color I'd ever seen blood display.

As the liquid began to increase impossibly, I said, quietly, so as not to interrupt things that I might not be able to perceive, "She's going to drown in that if she can't get her head up. She's also going to exsanguinate if she keeps going."

"Patience." Sherwood gave me a quick glance I could not read. I thought maybe he was just making sure I wasn't going to try to rescue her. "And that blood is . . . not all her blood. Well, no, it's her blood but it's reproducing. Cloning, you could say. Though I wouldn't."

"And that makes sense," said Uncle Mike dryly.

"How would you have put it?" asked Sherwood. Sherwood's wolf, I thought, and he put a bit of a growl in his voice.

Uncle Mike smiled slyly. "Magic blood."

Sherwood snorted. "Makes it sound as if it weren't blood at all—or as if you could do something powerful with it." He paused. "But, since it is blood, her blood even, I suppose that's true enough."

They might have been . . . not precisely joking . . . sparring was more like it. But they were both watching Ruth intently.

"She's breathing," I said.

Ruth was still vomiting blood (and everything else she

had eaten or drunk recently), but she was inhaling and exhaling in between spasms.

Sherwood nodded. "This is a nasty bit of work. There's probably a more humane way of breaking this spell, but I don't know it. Maybe if I were in my own space with my own . . ." He shook his head and didn't complete that thought.

He leaned forward, careful not to get too near to the circle. "Poor darling," he said. "Sorry, sorry. It's rough, I know. But you're going to be all right in a moment. I promise that the worst is over."

It was ten or fifteen minutes before the blood and horror subsided. Sherwood, still watching something I couldn't, said, "There now, that's done it."

He snapped his fingers, the candle went out, and the room suddenly bloomed with the smell of everything in the circle, blood and vomit and other things—the sour smell of terror and dissipating black magic underlying everything. Fluids that had been held back by Sherwood's marks slid out over them. But the mess looked to have been reduced to only the nonmagical substances, so it didn't flow very far.

Uncle Mike started over and Sherwood snapped, "Knife. That knife needs to stay away from Ruth."

Uncle Mike gave the knife an . . . intrigued look.

"Hah," he said. "I'd forgotten I had it. What an interesting knife for them to let come into enemy hands."

I glanced at Sherwood. "Is it safe for me to touch her?"

"Maybe," he said. "But she'll not thank you for it. Everything will hurt just now—like being parboiled alive, as I recall. Give her a few minutes."

I'd been reaching for her, but at Sherwood's words, I backed off.

"Ruth needs a shower and clean clothes," I told Uncle Mike. "Is that available here?"

"Of course," he said. "But perhaps Sherwood should deal with the knife first. I need to touch her so she can move again. But I can't get near her with this knife. I don't like the feeling that I should just set this knife down and forget about it."

"Mercy," Sherwood said, "could you get my leg for me, please?"

Happy to have something I could do to help, I fetched the prosthesis for him. He hiked up the leg of his jeans and I saw that he had a spike sticking out of the bottom of the stump of his leg.

He saw my look and smiled with his wolf's eyes.

I was raised by werewolves and I'm mated to one. I'd never seen one smile quite like that. Werewolves just don't do merry, not their wolf part. And the emotion seemed a little out of place with Ruth recovering painfully in a puddle of blood and other substances. But wolves don't always react the way a human might to dire situations.

"The pin isn't coming out of my leg," he told me. "There's a silicone sleeve around the stump that holds the pin."

He took the leg and fitted it on, and got up using only his good leg in a smooth movement that proved he was not human. Someone who was all human would have had a lot more trouble doing that gracefully. Then he put the artificial foot on the ground and stomped with it until there was a sharp click.

"Good," he said. "I was afraid I'd broken it."

He strode over to Uncle Mike and took the knife from him. He looked at it a moment, weighing it in his hand. Then he jammed it point first into Uncle Mike's scarred wooden desk. It sank two inches, more or less, and then he snapped it.

I sucked in a breath as a wave of horrid, filthy magic burst out and left me staggering. I did not fall into Ruth's miserable huddle and the solidifying liquids surrounding her. But it was a near thing.

Judging from the past few days, witchcraft affected me more powerfully than other sorts of magic. Black magic was worse than the other kind. Or maybe I was just getting more sensitive to it.

"Was that wise?" Uncle Mike asked Sherwood with a

raised eyebrow. "You might have blown us to Underhill doing it that way."

"Only way I know of," Sherwood said, tapping his head. "I have to work with the limits of what I've got."

Speaking over his shoulder at Sherwood as he made his way briskly toward Ruth, Uncle Mike said, "If all you needed to do was break the blade, I could have done it at the beginning."

"No," said Sherwood. "I needed to do it. I've got a touch, a link with our enemy, thanks to my work with Ruth—and the witches' work, too. Breaking it that way will have hurt the owner of the athame, almost as much as she hurt Ruth. And if it had tried to blow up in our faces, I could have contained it." He looked at the broken blade on the handle that he still held. "I'm pretty sure, anyway."

RUTH, SCRUBBED AND DRESSED IN FRESH CLOTHES, had not had a lot to add to what she'd already told us. She was frightened, for which none of us blamed her. Uncle Mike assured us—and her—that since Sherwood had broken the witch's hold on her, he and his could keep her safe.

"You did it," Sherwood told her.

"Did what?" The pub was warm enough, but one of Uncle Mike's people had brought Ruth a blanket and she had it wrapped around her as if it were a shield against the dark.

"By coming here," said Uncle Mike. "You put the fox in the henhouse for them. If you had arrived at Mercy's house with that knife, I don't know that anyone could have broken what they tried to do. But you came here and created a weakness in their curse. Sherwood here was able to break the rest."

Uncle Mike looked at Sherwood. "I didn't know you were witchborn."

Sherwood shrugged.

"But they are all dead," Ruth said. "And they have Jake."

"There wasn't anything you could do about that," I said.

"But you held out against them. You won us a chance to find the senator and get him back from them."

I was worried that the witches had Adam and the pack, too. That the pack bonds were strong was good. That I couldn't tell a darned thing from them, except that everyone was healthy, was worrying.

There was still the faint possibility that the president had shown up and all the werewolves had turned off their phones. But that seemed increasingly unlikely.

"Because you held out," Sherwood said—and it was Sherwood again—"we have dealt them a blow, and we have a chance to find them." He held up the broken knife, which he was carrying in a kelly green take-out box from Uncle Mike's.

We left Ruth in the safety of Uncle Mike's hands. As we stepped out into the parking lot, Sherwood held up the box again.

"The trouble being," he said, "I don't know how to use this to find them. May—"

He stopped abruptly and turned in a slow circle.

"It's just me, wolf," said the goblin king, emerging from the shadows along the side of the building.

Larry seemed more tired than he had the last time I'd seen him. He usually looked like a smile was a moment away, if it wasn't already on his face. Not tonight.

"I'm here to give you some information," he said. "In exchange for calling me out to your hunt the other morning."

I had sort of thought the ball was in the other court, but I wasn't about to argue with him.

"Don't go to the senator's house in Pasco until daylight," he said. "And don't let anyone else go, if you can help it. We goblins lost much to the witchcrafting around that place."

"What happened?" I asked.

"I sent three of my best to follow Ruth Gillman after your lunch with her," he said. "One of them was my daughter, who I have had in my heart to be my successor when I quit this duty. She called me to tell me that the witches had set up an immense circle around the house. They set up watching places outside the circle as I directed her."

"That is a very large circle," I said.

He nodded. "The work of days and much power," he agreed. "If they had been working in town where my people patrol, we would have seen it long since. They waited until the witches left with Senator Campbell. They knew that all were dead inside except for Ruth—do not ask me how, because I will not tell you. Our survival depends upon us being aware of things that others try to hide from us. She and her compatriots could feel Ms. Gillman's distress. They thought that the witches had missed one of their targets. She called me and explained all of this. I told her not to go in."

He looked off into the distance. "She made her own decisions, my daughter, from the time she first learned to walk. It was why I chose her to replace me. A leader needs to make her own decisions."

"What happened to her?" I asked.

He sighed. "The other two tell me that she crossed the circle with no trouble. Took another two steps, then turned and looked at them. Said, 'Tell Father I was wrong.' And she died, standing on her feet." He closed his eyes. "But I had to kill her body and we lost four more of my people before we managed to kill them all."

"Them all?" I asked.

"All of the dead rose as reanimates—you call them zombies. With my daughter's fate to warn us, my people crossed the circle and dealt with the dead. I brought them out. But any who cross that circle before daylight without my intervention—and I will not go back there—will suffer the same fate as my daughter."

"I'm sorry," I said.

He made a slashing gesture with his hand. "Not your fault, Mercedes Hauptman. But Uncle Mike told me you are out hunting the witches, and I thought to tell you what we found. The witches are not where Ruth Gillman came from tonight. Doubtless there are clues to be discovered, but they will do you no good until daylight cleanses the land. Do not repeat my daughter's mistake."

I tried to figure out when Uncle Mike would have had time to contact Larry. When Ruth was showering, maybe.

"The senator's residence was the first place I would have gone searching," I told Larry. More carefully I said, "I appreciate your warning."

"We destroyed the bodies," Larry said. "But their wallets are piled by the front door so that their deaths can be made known to their people."

"Good," I said. "Ruth took pictures, so we'll know who they are." That part of this day wasn't going to be my job.

He nodded, turned to leave, and then, with his back to me, said, "You'll be tempted to go to Siebold Adelbertsmiter and his son. You probably know that there is a good chance that the old fae will go with you."

He turned back to me, his features stark. "You could probably ask me, after this night, and I would go with you, too."

"But," I said.

He nodded. "But. It may be that without us you will fail, and with us you will take the day. But the Gray Lords have been quite clear. They will not—*cannot* allow any of us to take part in this battle. They will make sure that if any helps you in direct confrontation with the witches, that fae will die in this day and all days."

"But," Sherwood said in a low voice, "warning us of a trap—that is not direct confrontation."

Larry nodded. He tipped his head toward Uncle Mike's. "And giving shelter is part of the guesting laws, as is protecting an innocent victim."

I looked at Larry. "That's why he couldn't break the spell holding her." Because that had bothered me. Uncle Mike wasn't a Gray Lord, but other fae walked warily around him. That he could not break a witch's spell . . . had made the witches seem a lot more powerful than I had thought they were.

His face became bland. "I don't know what Uncle Mike can or cannot do, Mercedes. All I can tell you is that if he had broken the spell, he would have faced the wrath of the Gray Lords. He asked me if I thought you were clever enough to have a path forward that he did not see."

"Nope," I said. What if we had not had Sherwood? Then I felt a touch of relief. I could have called upon Elizaveta or even, heaven help me, Wulfe. "Not that clever. But I am a coyote and apparently stupid lucky."

Larry did smile then. "And that is exactly what I told him."

11

~~~

I CHECKED MY PHONE ON THE WAY TO SHER-
wood's Toyota and stopped dead. Somehow I'd silenced the
phone, and I'd missed a call from Adam. I tried calling him
back. This time it rang through to his voice mail.

"Adam called you?" Sherwood asked.

I nodded and checked my voice mail. Sure enough there
was a new message from Adam. Two of them. The first
voice mail was from around the time we'd left home to
come to Uncle Mike's.

"Hey, sweetheart," Adam said. "Sorry for being out of
communication all day. POTUS decided he wanted to have
a day at the zoo. Expect pictures of him bravely petting
Warren in tomorrow's papers." His voice was very dry, but
there was a frisson of excitement behind it.

He'd voted for this president, canceling my vote as apparently we'd done all of my life and would do for the foresee-
able future, but Adam didn't really approve of him. Still, he
had a reverence for the office itself that I didn't feel. The
president of the United States had come to visit—and Adam
was thrilled.

My worries for him fell away, and I found myself smiling.

"Anyway, we're all headed home, see you soon." He ended the message.

Sherwood smiled at me. "POTUS," he said. "I called it."

The time stamp on the second message was about five minutes later than the first message. Before I could listen to it, my phone rang again. This time it was my half brother, Gary.

"Kind of busy here," I said.

"I'll call back later," he said. And he hung up.

My half brother had called. And, I remembered abruptly, last night I'd had a dream that I couldn't remember. A dream that apparently involved Coyote.

I called him back.

"I thought—"

"What did you call me for?" I asked.

"It's pretty stupid," he told me.

"Just spit it out," I said.

"Our progenitor called me a few minutes ago and asked me to call you—and see if you'd reached for your dreams."

And that was all it took.

"Son of a bitch," I said.

"He is, I suspect, no one's son," Gary said apologetically. "Created rather than born. What's he done?"

"Interfered," I said.

"For good or ill?"

"I can't tell," I said. "I'll let you know if I survive. I'll call you tomorrow."

"Do you need me to come down?" His voice was serious.

"No," I said. "Yes. But there's no way you could arrive in time. If it helps, your part in this might have saved the day. If the day is saved."

"Good?" he said, a question in his voice.

"I'll tell you tomorrow." I disconnected.

"Mercy?" Sherwood asked.

I held up a finger. I needed to think. To absorb what I remembered.

I knew who and what the Hardesty witches were because I'd spent weeks in the mind of Sherwood's kitten. I knew what they wanted—and Sherwood was on the top of their list. I knew what they could do—and I didn't want any of the wolves within a hundred miles of those witches.

Magda—that was the name of the zombie witch—was a Love Talker, all right. And her power was a lot bigger than Elizaveta had thought. I was pretty sure she would have no trouble controlling a werewolf, because she had taken them before.

"Mercy, are you all right?" Sherwood asked.

"I've been thinking," I told him. "Since the pack is fine—" They were. I had to do this without telling a single lie. Sherwood would know if I lied. "—could you drop me off at the garage?"

He frowned at me. "Sure."

I nodded briskly and got into the passenger seat of the car.

We were on our way when Sherwood said, "Does the reason I'm dropping you off at your shop have something to do with the phone call from your brother?"

I nodded. "Yes. I have some thinking to do—and it's a madhouse at home right now. The shop is quiet."

He smiled. "That it is."

I watched the road ahead of us and asked, "How is your cat doing?"

"I stopped in to check on him after work," he said. "It looks like he's going to make it."

"Good," I said.

Sherwood's lips turned up again. "He purred when I held him."

"Tough cat," I said.

"Yes." He sounded happy.

When he pulled into the dark parking lot, he insisted on coming into the garage with me and sniffing around for intruders. He wasn't happy when he left, but he did leave.

As soon as he turned out of the parking lot, I listened to Adam's second message. I had waited until Sherwood was gone because I didn't think that Coyote would have timed my brother's phone call so precisely without a reason.

"Hey, love," said Adam. "Elizaveta just called. She wants to check something out at her house, and she doesn't want to do it alone. I'm going to go pick her up. Don't worry. Love you."

Yes, I thought, I'd have had trouble convincing Sherwood that I just needed a quiet place to think for a while if he'd heard that message.

I grabbed a set of keys, turned out the light again, and relocked everything up. Then I got into Stefan's bus and headed for Elizaveta's house for some recon. As I traveled I called Stefan's phone and got his voice mail—which I'd expected.

"I stole your bus," I told him. "And I am headed to Elizaveta's to look for Adam. I believe that the Hardesty witches are there, and that they have Adam and Senator Campbell. If I don't call you back in a few hours, would you call Darryl?" Hopefully Marsilia didn't plan on keeping Stefan bound and gagged for long. "Tell him that I think the zombie witch can control werewolves and he should take precautions."

I found a place to park the bus next to a haystack about a half mile away from Elizaveta's. With any luck, it wouldn't draw too much attention. It wasn't exactly a stealth vehicle, but at night it wasn't as noticeable as it was in the daylight. I gave Scooby a pat on his fuzzy head for luck, then stripped to my skin, opened the driver's door, and hopped out.

I shut the door quietly and shifted to coyote. Then I went off to do the thing that coyotes do best—sneak.

There were lights on in Elizaveta's house. I slunk down the edge of the driveway from shadow to shadow, moving as slowly as I could bear. Quick movement catches the eye. If I had been dealing with mere humans, I'd have trotted right along. But I had no idea how well the witches could see in the dark, so I crept.

Elizaveta's driveway was nearly a quarter mile long, and

there was a newish RV parked between the house and the garage. Adam's SUV was parked right in front of the house, as was a Subaru Impreza. I watched the yard from under a raspberry bush. The underbrush had been cleared out and the bush trimmed, so there was plenty of room for me to hide.

I watched for maybe five minutes but saw no movement inside or out—despite the lights in the house.

Maybe they were all in the basement.

That thought had me sliding out of my hiding place. I was halfway out when a sound made me freeze.

A bluish-gray wolf, distinctively marked with darkened feet, muzzle, and tail, walked across the yard. Adam. The deliberate pace of his movement, his pricked ears, and the slow swing of his head told me that he was on patrol.

I stepped out of the shadows and let him see me.

He walked right past me, as if I weren't there.

I am to patrol the grounds and alert them if I come across anything that might threaten them or is unusual.

The thought brushed my mind lightly, as if I were overhearing a conversation that had nothing to do with me. It whispered down our mate bond, and if I had been ten feet farther away, I doubt it would have touched me.

There is nothing threatening or unusual in a coyote running around Finley, he noted. Just for a moment his gold eyes brushed mine, and then he moved on.

But if I were that coyote, I would leave.

And then, as if he could not even think the name, an image floated in my mind's eye: a wolf's face with a red X across it.

Adam was warning me not to let the pack come here.

OF COURSE I DIDN'T LEAVE.

If Adam was here, I could safely assume the senator and Elizaveta were also here. So all I had to do was get a look at their defenses. I had the bare bones of a plan in my head—I didn't like it and I wasn't sure it would work.

I expected my explorations to last longer, even given that I now had to avoid Adam. But after the third zombie in twenty feet, I had all the answer I needed.

I was going to need help.

They had Adam, I thought, trotting back to the bus; I couldn't afford to give them the whole pack. But I had other friends to call upon, which was a good thing. No matter what orders Coyote had given me, I wasn't going to be able to kill those witches all by myself if the witches had an army of zombies to protect them.

I dressed, then pulled out my phone. I had a message from Warren.

Warily I listened to it.

"Mercy, when you get this, call me back."

Nope.

I called Zee instead. I knew, as Larry had told me, that Siebold Adelbertsmiter would help me. I called him, knowing exactly what that help could cost him. But I was hoping that Zee was as formidable as I thought he was—and therefore the Gray Lords would be looking for any excuse not to enforce their death penalty on him.

After I told him who else I was planning to ask for help, I gave Zee the option of staying away. I'm not sure if I would have given him the option had I not been absolutely certain of Zee's response.

"Nein," Zee said. "These witches hurt my son and tried to kill you. The Gray Lords will afterward do as they will. Should we succeed in saving Senator Campbell, the Gray Lords will be quite happy with us, I think."

"You don't think they can ensnare you?" I asked.

"Liebling," he said. "I am not infallible. But witchcraft doesn't work so well on the fae. I have had a talk with Uncle Mike tonight. Uncle Mike informed me that the goblin king was quite clear that I should avoid direct confrontation with the witches."

He'd said very nearly the same thing to me, I thought.

"I take it to mean that as long as I fight the zombies and minions and leave the witches to your"—there was something in his voice I could not read—"other ally, we can be reasonably certain . . ."

"Of what?" I asked when he paused.

"Certain of doing what the goblin king wishes me to do," said Zee. "Since they have just killed his favorite child, I do not think the goblin king would advise us to do anything that would aid them."

I'd kind of thought that the goblin king had been telling me not to ask Zee for help. Interesting that Zee and I had the exact opposite takes on that advice. I decided to believe Zee because it cheered me up and made me feel less guilty.

He continued, "I will not leave you alone to battle them with no one that I trust to have your back. If you are not here in ten minutes to pick me up, I will drive my truck to the witch's house."

And that ended that discussion.

But when I pulled up to Zee's house, it wasn't just Zee who came out. Tad, looking as though he were dressed for a *Lord of the Rings* reunion, carried a long duffel bag that probably contained some of Zee's weapons.

"I know, I know," Tad said, opening the sliding door and setting the bag on the floor. He opened the front passenger door and said, "It's you or me, dog." He picked up Scooby and set him in the two-butt seat that was the middle seat of the bus. To me he acknowledged, "It's a weird shirt, but Dad insisted."

"Is it mithril?" I asked in awe. "You glow in the dark."

Tad looked down at himself and let out a curse. "It's doing it again, Dad."

"I regret the costume-like appearance," Zee said. "It wasn't costume-like when I made it. But the tunic will redirect witchcrafting aimed at him. Some of the time."

He leaned into the bus and tapped the shoulder of the mail-like overcoat that Tad wore. The brightness winked out and it blended with the darkness almost too well.

"It hasn't been out in a good long time," said Zee. "It's a little giddy."

"Giddy," I said.

Zee climbed into the bus, slid the door shut, and then made his way to the far back. It wasn't that he minded sharing a seat with Scooby; it was that Zee always sat so that no one could sit behind him. It was why he had a truck.

"Zee," I said. "Not that I don't love Tad, but I thought it was only going to be you flinging yourself into the hands of fate. The Gray Lords might decide that you are scary enough to leave alone, but Tad isn't."

"The Gray Lords will hold me responsible for Dad's actions anyway," Tad said, belting himself in. "I might as well contribute. Where are we going next?"

"I am not sure," I said, and pulled out my phone.

"You haven't asked yet?" asked Zee.

"Nope," I told him. "I was putting it off until the last minute."

"Mercy," Marsilia answered. "Have you killed them yet?"

"Nope," I told her. "I've lost track. Do you owe me one, or do I owe you?"

WULFE WAS WAITING FOR US WHEN I DROVE UP to the seethe.

He'd been a teenager when he died and he looked it. Tonight he'd dressed in a black hoodie, jeans, and white Converse tennis shoes. He looked like he should be going to a rave or a kegger. He also had both of his hands. Stefan had cut one of them off the last time I'd seen him.

Vampires weren't werewolves—they couldn't just grow them back. I was *pretty* sure they couldn't just grow them back.

He bent down to look in the car to see who was in it. He did an exaggerated double take when he saw Tad's magic garb. Tad huffed indignantly. Satisfied with Tad's reaction, Wulfe opened the sliding door and got in. He belted Scooby in before he belted himself.

The hair on the back of my neck tried to run away. I was really glad that Zee was sitting behind Wulfe to keep watch. If anyone was a match for Wulfe, it was Zee. I was also glad that Scooby was in the seat directly behind me.

"If I'd known we were going medieval, I'd have worn my hair shirt. I'm sure I have it around somewhere." The vampire snapped his fingers. "Damn. I left it at home. It will probably be another half millennium before I get a chance to wear it again. Oh well. These things do tend to come back in fashion."

A lot of the vampires have accents. But Wulfe, today, sounded like any other teenager born and raised in the Tri-Cities. Other than the fact that I would be surprised if there were more than one or two teenagers born and raised here who would even know what a hair shirt was.

He raised his head and sniffed like a dog. "You brought me a present? How kind. Give. Give it to me."

Tad looked at me and I shook my head. "I don't know what he's talking about."

Wulfe made an impatient sound. "You have something that belongs to the witches."

I had grabbed the box with the broken athame when I got out of Sherwood's car. It hadn't been difficult. I'd been carrying it while he drove—and he'd been worried about making sure the garage was safe before he left.

Sherwood's wolf had thought that he could use it to hunt down the witches. I didn't want him anywhere near these witches, so I had taken it when he wasn't looking.

I reached between the front seats, grabbed the take-out box, and held it up.

"Ooooo," Wulfe said, taking it. "Looky here. What naughty children to let this out of their hands. Pity it's broken."

"Why is that?" I asked him.

"Because the witches could have done all sorts of nasty things with that tonight, and I could have watched them. If they really do have an almost completed coven—"

I had given Marsilia a play-by-play of the last day, which had ended about a block from the seethe. I had left nothing out. I didn't know if it had been a mistake to tell her that there was a witch out there who could control werewolves, but she'd told me about Frost, who could control vampires, hadn't she?

Evidently, if he knew about Sherwood's assessment that the witches were running with the power of an almost coven behind them, Wulfe must have been listening the whole time.

"—they could have used it to take over anyone who held this knife. Lots of mischief to be done. I'd say they killed five or six people to make this athame—and that's if they had plenty of practice. They won't be happy that it is broken. It's useless now."

He tossed it back to the front seat and the box spilled the separate pieces onto the floor. Tad bent over and collected them while I put the bus in gear and pulled away from the seethe. Marsilia's home base gave me the creeps.

Not that driving away from the seethe would help much, not when Wulfe was in my car.

"What does it mean?" I asked him. "That there are ten families in their coven. A lot of what I know about the witches comes from Wikipedia; it told me that a coven had thirteen witches."

I could feel him staring at me. I was careful to keep my eyes on the road.

"I get the best spells from Wiki," he said. "Have you read what it says about werewolves? I keep editing the article, but someone—and I think it's Bran Cornick—keeps changing it back."

"Vampire," said Zee. "If you don't answer the question, I will."

"So touchy," said Wulfe, admiration in his tone. But then he said, "Back in the bad old days, a coven of witches was thirteen witches, one from each of thirteen families. If you had a complete coven, then you were limited in power only by your imagination." He sighed. "But, since they are witches, usually that only lasted a few months or a year at a time before someone fought with someone else and the next thing you know, there would be bodies all over the place. Untidy folk, witches."

"Give me an example of what they did," I said.

"Stonehenge," Wulfe said promptly. "The Little Ice Age. A couple of volcanic eruptions. They weren't responsible for the Black Plague itself—but I know that in several instances they used plagues to discipline rulers who worked against them. The Great Plague of London killed a hundred thousand people in eighteen months. I think Bran himself took care of that coven."

"Holy wow," I breathed.

"But they don't have a real coven," said Wulfe. "The best the Hardesty witches managed—with nine different families represented in their coven—was 1816."

Zee grunted.

I had a history degree, but 1816 didn't ring any bells. The War of 1812 ended in 1815. In 1817 James Monroe became president of the United States—and I only knew that because I'd written a paper on him in college.

Wulfe was waiting.

"What happened in 1816?" I asked.

"It was the Year Without a Summer in New England," said Tad.

"I see it isn't true," said Wulfe, "what they say about modern education." He sighed. "Pitiful attempt, really; with a full coven they could have frozen the whole Atlantic seaboard for a couple of years."

Enough of that talk or I was going to pull over and run screaming into the night. I was already scared. We only had two witches to deal with, I reminded myself.

"Elizaveta said she knew when a witch came into her territory," I said, thinking out loud. "Will they know when you get too close?"

"This was my territory a long time before Elizaveta Arkadyevna Vyshnevetskaya came here," Wulfe said, his voice suddenly a purr of power. "So subtly did I lay my hold on the land that she did not, does not even feel it—no more than did the new intruders. They will not know me until I choose."

"I thought the vampires called you the Wizard," Tad said. "Are you a witch or a wizard?"

Wulfe preened. "Yes," he said.

Witches had power over the living—animals, trees, people. Wizards manipulated objects with magic—bending spoons, moving furniture, that kind of thing. Wizards were a lot more rare than witches because witches deliberately bred themselves for power. I didn't know if wizards ever tried it. Maybe they did. But I'd never heard of a wizard family. That he was both . . . and a vampire as well . . .

"Why did they set up at Elizaveta's?" I asked, changing the subject back to the matter at hand. "Isn't that a little obvious?"

"Misery is a thing that seeps into the walls and the floors," Zee said. "A house like Elizaveta's would add power to their spells and protections. Black magic would not be driven from a place where it has taken up residence without a powerful blessing."

"The only place better for their purposes in the Tri-Cities would have been the seethe," said Wulfe. "And they did try that, didn't they? When Frost came up. If Frost had won back in November, we'd have had no way to prevail today. Funny how fate works out."

I glanced into the rearview mirror to see Wulfe smiling, his eyes fixed out the window. Wulfe had been on the wrong side of that fight. Maybe.

He caught me looking and his smile widened until it displayed his delicate fangs. "Go ahead and ask me," he said.

"Whose side were you on?" I asked.

"I don't remember," he lied.

"Why do you have both hands?" I asked.

"Because two is better than one," he said.

He saw me looking at him in the mirror again and blew me a kiss.

"Don't encourage him, Mercy," said Zee. "And you might look where you are going. If you have a wreck before we get there, we might be stuck out in the open when the sun comes up. That would be a shame."

Wulfe laughed, his whole body shaking.

I took Zee's advice then and put my eyes front and center.

"There will be zombies," I said. "I don't know how many or what kind. But they were thick on the ground when I explored about an hour ago."

"Human mostly," said Wulfe. "I went out and peeked last night." I gave him a look of surprise.

"Of course I checked them out," Wulfe said. "A good vampire always knows his enemy's secrets. A few dogs and the like, but mostly human." He paused. "And the ogre."

"Ogre?" asked Tad. "An ogre zombie?"

"It was several hundred years old, I think," Wulfe said. "They had a few very-well-made zombies—made by a different witch." He beamed a smile and I realized I was watching him again. If I wrecked the Mystery Machine, Stefan would be unhappy.

"Such craftsmanship," Wulfe said. "You just don't find zombies like that anymore. Because the lady who made them had an unfortunate accident with one of her pets. The Hardestys have such hope for Magda, you know, because she has the same combination of gifts. But if you ask me, she is far too careless with her workings."

Wulfe sounded like someone gossiping about his neighbors. And he knew more about the witches than I'd thought he did. More than I'd gathered. Hopefully he would be on our side this time.

"I brought one home to examine, to be sure," he said. "It was about two centuries, give or take a year. He was exquisite, not a whiff of rot on him. My mother's coven would have been envious. He could have passed for human, I think, unless you had reason to look very closely—or talk to him. I am positive it was Lieza's work. And I think she was the only one who would have been foolhardy enough to try raising an ogre."

"A zombie ogre," said Tad. "An ogre zombie."

"Do you have a glitch?" asked Wulfe. "Or do you always say the same phrase over and over?"

"They have to be well made not to rot," Zee said. "If they are older, they get smarter. Don't fret, vampire. Tad and I will take care of the zombies. Even the ogre," Zee said. "Once we are done with them, we will aid you with *den Hexen*. The witches."

Wulfe started to bob his head, as if he were listening to drums. Or my heartbeat. The rat.

He bobbed faster as he spoke. "I can deal with one of the witches—that will leave the other to you, Coyote's daughter. Do you know how to kill a witch?"

"Nope," I said, though I was pretty sure that if I could get close enough, my cutlass could do the job. I was really glad I'd started carrying that cutlass wherever I went.

"I wouldn't shoot at them," Wulfe advised. "Witches this old can protect themselves from bullets."

"Noted," I said. I'd pulled the gun from the safe at work, another Sig. It was now in its concealed-carry holster in the small of my back. I'd never regretted having a gun with me in a fight.

"Don't worry, Mercy," said Tad heavily. "Witches die like everyone else."

I gave him a startled glance that he didn't see. I wondered if that was the something he'd learned in college that had seen him return home lacking the indomitable cheer he used to carry with him wherever he went.

"Pretty basic plan," observed Wulfe.

We didn't know enough to make more extensive plans.

"Kill the bad guys," Tad said. "Kill the dead guys again."

"Hey!" said Wulfe with mock affront. "I think I belong to both of those groups."

"Except for our allies," I said. "Are you our ally?"

Wulfe smiled at me and said nothing. I realized I wasn't watching where I was going again. If we all survived, I'd make someone else drive so I didn't have to have Wulfe lurking behind me.

We did work out a better plan, but Tad wasn't wrong

about the basics of it: kill the bad guys, lay the zombies to rest. We did not specify that Wulfe got to pick a witch and I had to take the other one. Whoever had a chance to kill them would do it.

———————

I PARKED THE VAN IN THE SAME PLACE I'D FOUND earlier this evening. Hopefully none of the pack would drive by it and figure out where I'd gone. I had turned off my phone after I picked up Wulfe. No sense making it easy for them to find me.

About halfway to Elizaveta's I'd begun to feel a bit of pull from the pack ties. Adam would have been able to find me—find any of the pack he wanted to locate. But they weren't the Alpha, and the best they could (hopefully) do would be to know that I was terrified out of my mind.

Zee had had another word with the tunic that Tad wore, and Tad became very, very difficult to see. Wulfe gave a soft whistle when he saw it change.

"So that's what that is," he said. "I thought that surcoat was lost in the War of the Roses."

"Someone made it," said Zee. "Someone took it. Someone took it back. It was not lost."

"Hush now, miscreants," I said. "We're hunting witches."

Tad, doubtless hearing the edge of utter terror that I was trying to cover up with humor, ruffled my hair. "We've got your back."

"So do the zombies," said Wulfe in a whisper that sent the hairs on the back of my neck climbing right onto the top of my head.

"Shut up, Wulfe," I said. "I'm scared enough."

"No," Wulfe said, a little sadly or possibly a little smugly, "I don't think you are."

After that optimistic observation, we all lapsed into silence.

We could have approached from the front. Wulfe pointed out that they doubtless would have alarms all around the property. If Elizaveta had really gone over to their side, they might even have access to several circles of her protections. No, I didn't know exactly what that meant, other than it was a bad thing.

But we voted three to one to approach from the rear—which had us traipsing through someone else's property before we marched onto Elizaveta's hayfield. After ten minutes of stumbling through the neighbor's alfalfa field, I was pretty sure that Wulfe had been right, but I wasn't going to tell him that.

Zee finally put a hand under my elbow. The old fae trod through the rough ground as if it were a flat field in daylight. Wulfe and Tad just ghosted through, too. I could have made a better show as a coyote—but that would have meant leaving my weaponry behind.

The first circle, we discovered, was halfway through Elizaveta's neighbor's field.

"Huh," said Wulfe, from somewhere ahead of me.

"Hold up," said Tad.

Zee stopped and I did, too.

Wulfe turned his head, looking at something I couldn't see.

"That's well done," he said. "There's a ward circle here." He swept a hand ahead of him. "Well, not really a circle, more of a square—but that's okay for something like this. Just a warning line. She'd have felt every squirrel or coyote"—he didn't look at me—"that ran across it, but still . . ."

"She?" I asked.

"This is Elizaveta's work," Wulfe said. "What does it say that she has activated it?"

"Not much," said Zee. "We can speculate, of course. Perhaps she has joined forces with them. Or perhaps they found the key to the house protections when they held Elizaveta's family."

"Yeah," said Wulfe with theatrical sadness. "It doesn't tell us much." He scuffed his toe into the ground with exaggerated disappointment. In a five-year-old it would have been cute. In a very scary vampire it was . . . cute.

He bent down and drew a line in the dirt with his finger

about two feet long. "If you will all step over the border right here?"

We did, and he brushed the marks out with his fingers.

Wulfe continued to take point. Ostensibly, this was so that he could keep an eye out for the kinds of things that we could not. Truthfully, there was no way I would have been able to let him trail behind me when I couldn't keep track of where he was. I don't think I was alone in that feeling.

It was Zee who held a hand up the next time. "Witch," he said in a soft murmur, his attention focused ahead of us, "can you keep a battle quiet?"

I felt it, too. The feeling of wrongness that I was beginning to associate with zombies.

Wulfe frowned. "All of the zombies are confined to the yard," he said.

"Evidently not," said Zee. "Witch, keep this quiet if you can. Boy, draw your weapon. Mercy—do not try to shoot or stab this one. Your blade is fine, but it is not one of mine. It will not penetrate an ogre's hide."

Wulfe raised an eyebrow either in mild offense at the gruff order or in mild surprise at the knowledge that the zombie ogre was around, but he closed his eyes and began moving his hands in patterns. His fingers, I noted, were flexible, like a pianist's—even on the hand that I'd *seen* Stefan cut off.

Subtle magic infused the air and the atmosphere attained that odd hollow quality that I associated with the full moon dance. Pack magic sealed the sound on such nights so that only the wolves and their prey could hear the howls of the hunt.

The ogre stepped out of the shadows, shadows that hadn't been there because we were out in an open field where there was nothing but knee-deep alfalfa, carrying an eight-foot-long wooden fence post in one beefy hand. It brought the post smashing down on Wulfe—who took two steps to the side without ceasing his magic-making.

I had never seen an ogre in its real form before. I'd met one at Uncle Mike's, but I'd only ever seen her in her hu-

man guise—tall, slim, and disapproving of the chaos of the
birthday party we'd been celebrating. Tad's fourteenth, as I
recalled.

This ogre was eight feet tall and weighed in at probably
four hundred to five hundred pounds. A stiff ruff of bright
orange hair ringed its neck and then rose up the back of its
head, giving the appearance of a cross between a Mohawk
and the crest of a cockatoo. There were seams in its skin,
tidily stitched up. One ran across its forehead. One looped
its left arm—and as soon as I noted that, I could see that its
left arm was a little longer and the wisps of hair growing on
the forearm were dark brown. Stitches ringed both legs just
below the knee . . . right where Sherwood's leg had been
taken off, I thought with a chill.

That pet who had killed the master-zombie maker that
Wulfe had been so disturbingly impressed with. I wondered
if it had been a werewolf.

Like, presumably, Wulfe's stolen zombie, this one had
no smell of rot. If I hadn't had the past couple of weeks to
get a good taste of what zombies smell like, I wasn't sure
I'd have picked the ogre out as a zombie. And it had used
magic to conceal itself.

Mindful of Zee's assessment of my capabilities, I drew
my cutlass but took up a stance just behind and to the left
of Wulfe.

"Always happy to shield a lady," said Wulfe, a little
breathlessly.

"I figure that when it's occupied smashing you to jelly, I
might get a lucky shot at its eye," I responded. "I don't care
how tough a creature is, I've never seen one shake off a
cutlass in its eye."

"Okay," said Wulfe cheerfully. "Happy to oblige by dis-
tracting the ogre with my grisly remains."

After that first attack, though, the ogre didn't get another
chance at Wulfe. I'd seen Zee fight before. And I'd seen
Tad. But I'd never seen them fight together, armed with
their favorite weapons.

It hurt a little. Somewhere in my head, I had Tad pictured, always, as the bright-eyed, brash, and self-assured little boy who'd run his father's garage by himself for weeks. His mother had just died from cancer and his father, the immortal smith, had tried to drink himself to oblivion. Tad was capable, cheery, confident—and ten years old in my head, until that fight.

He had a pair of hatchets, one in each hand, and a bigger axe strapped to his back. The tunic rippled light so it was difficult to keep track of him, so I mostly saw him in snatches of still movement—midleap six feet in the air throwing one of the hatchets. That hatchet ended up in the ogre's left elbow. The next time I caught a glimpse of him, he was rolling on the ground to get beneath the stroke of that big fence post. He was beautiful and deadly—and decidedly not an innocent, if competent, ten-year-old boy.

If Tad was shadow, then Zee was sunlight. His sword blazed orange and red and hissed as it drew dark lines on the ogre's skin, howled when it slid through flesh and bone. Zee didn't drop his glamour, and it would have been odd for someone who didn't know who and what he was to see an old man moving with such grace and power. He didn't appear to move fast or use any particular effort. He'd step back and the fence post would slide by his face—not by inches but by millimeters. He simply moved his hand and his sword would cut through the ogre's knee joint as if it were cheese, leaving the ogre's severed flesh burning sullenly on both sides of the cut.

It was an amazing, beautiful, fearful dance and it didn't take them a full minute to disable and then, with a smooth, full-bodied swing of the deadly blazing sword, behead the ogre. Zee's sword quit blazing and left us in a darkness that seemed darker than before he'd drawn his weapon.

Wulfe stepped forward and touched the body, pulling out a tuft of the red bristle. He spoke a few words and then planted the hair in the ground.

"She'll not know it's gone for a while," Wulfe said. "My wards kept her from feeling its demise and this will keep its leash from springing back to her. But if she looks for it, she'll know it's gone."

"The ogre clans in Scotland had a young one go missing a few centuries back," murmured Zee. "I'll let them know that we found him and gave him release."

I don't know how anyone else was affected by that fight. Zee seemed, if anything, more somber. Tad's battle alertness precluded me reading anything else off him. And Wulfe, Wulfe was himself. But I felt a little more hopeful at the evidence of my comrades' capabilities. Anyone who could kill a zombie ogre might not be hopeless against a pair of witches, right?

———

ELIZAVETA'S BOUNDARY FENCE WAS MARKED BY a row of poplars thick enough to block her neighbors' observation. It also kept us from having a good view of anything happening near the house.

"There's a fire over there," said Tad softly. "In the backyard, I think."

He was right. The light flickering through the trees had too much movement in it to be coming from a lightbulb.

"Elizaveta had a firepit built in the center of her patio in the backyard," I said. The patio was large, the size of half of a basketball court, which was what its previous owners had used it for. The basketball hoop was still there, but the firepit made future basketball games unlikely.

I could smell a bit of smoke and some burned things that weren't anything I'd scented in a campfire. But there was something wrong. This close, the scent should have been a lot stronger.

"Fire is a good aid to magic of any kind," Zee commented. "Perhaps they are trying to work something now?"

Wulfe closed his eyes and raised a hand—the one that Stefan had cut off—palm out toward Elizaveta's house.

"I don't know what they are doing at the moment," he said. "But they aren't keeping a leash on their dead things.

They've just let them wander inside the circle Elizaveta laid around the place." He tutted. "Careless of them. Wait up a minute."

There was a rush of magic that fluttered by me like a storm of tree leaves. A much more powerful burst of magic than I'd ever felt from him, so I was able to get a better sense of his magic than I had before. It did not smell like black witchcraft . . . or gray witchcraft, either. It smelled clean as the driven snow.

Wulfe was a white witch?

It boggled my mind. I'd seen him torture and kill with my own two eyes. I expected gray. Black magic I'd have noticed, but gray magic doesn't actually smell that different from vampire magic.

As a vampire, he could coax willing cooperation from any human he fed from. I'd seen him do it. I'd seen them beg him to torture them (there are a lot of reasons Wulfe is at the top of my scary monster chart). He didn't need to use black magic if he didn't want to.

I just hadn't expected him not to use dark magic at all. It didn't seem in keeping with the vampire I knew him to be.

"I've sent her creatures to . . . well, not sleep, they don't sleep. But I've made them settle. They won't notice us as we pass. She'll have to call them to her to get them up and moving."

He looked at me thoughtfully. "I could just break her hold. Then she couldn't send them after us, but the circle wouldn't hold them in. They could go on a killing spree and you'd be weeks hunting all of them down. It might be fun."

"A disaster," said Zee. "Keep them in and let Tad and me hunt them. We'll keep them off you."

Wulfe pursed his lips, then nodded. "Okeydokey. We'll leave them be, then. But you should know that some of the zombies are very near the back of Elizaveta's house— probably in the presence of the witches."

In the car, he'd promised that he could quiet the zombies without any of the witches knowing what he'd done. But maybe he hadn't expected them to be so near the witches.

"Will they have felt what you did?" I asked.

"Nah," he said. "But they might notice that the beasties are unresponsive and wake them back up before we're ready for them."

"Okay," I said. "Can you get me across the circle without alerting the witches?"

My part in our plans was that I would scout out whatever the witches were doing, come back, and make a report. Then we'd work out what to do from there.

"Think so," he said. "Maybe. Ish."

I rolled my eyes. "Good to know."

And I stripped down to my skin, dropping weapons to one side and clothing to the other.

"Ni-ice," said Wulfe in a tone that would have made Adam take off his head. "Hey, is that a wolf's paw print or a coyote's below your belly button?"

It was really dark out. If he was seeing my paw-print tattoo, then his night vision was as good as any wolf's. He was a vampire, so I should have expected it.

I am not shy. Shapeshifters—werewolves or coyote shifters like me—get over things like modesty very quickly. But knowing Wulfe was staring at my tattoo made me feel vulnerable. If I were never naked where he could see me again, it would be too soon.

"Yes," I told him.

I shifted into my coyote as quickly as I could.

Wulfe dropped to all fours at the same time. "Follow me," he said, and crawled through the fence and into the trees.

With no choice, I followed him. Just on the other side of the trees, Wulfe put a hand out, with odd deliberation, in front of him, and then did the same with the other hand. Then he straightened his knees until he was in a London Bridge kind of arch.

"You can run over the top of me or under me," he said. "I'm keeping the connection of the spell going—so don't cut me in half or it will sound an alarm."

Unwilling to have him on top of me, I ran over the top

of him. He settled down on the ground without moving his hands. "Remember to come back this way," he said. "I'll be here. Waiting for you." He batted his eyelashes at me and mouthed, *Only you.*

I put Wulfe behind me every which way I could and concentrated on traveling unseen. I didn't make the mistake of running. Quick movement attracts the attention of prey and predator alike. I found a game trail that smelled of coyote and headed, more or less, in the direction I wanted.

Traveling down the trail meant less noise—and I wouldn't be moving grass around. But it would also be a place that traps could be set and patrols run. The zombies were, hopefully, quiescent, but Adam wouldn't be affected. When trying to hide, running right down the road was always the wrong decision. Except that a game trail wasn't exactly a road. Decisions, decisions.

Decisions with Adam's life on the line. And the senator's. It wasn't that I wasn't concerned about him. We were, our pack, obliged legally and ethically to make sure he was safe. I didn't love the senator, however. And I was pretty sure that freeing Adam of the witch's spell—Wulfe had a harrowing suggestion on that—would make the senator safer, too.

I decided to chance it, and took the trail. I passed by a few of the witch's zombies as I skulked toward the house. The first was a squirrel. I don't know that I'd have noticed it except that it was standing motionless on the game trail I was following. Squirrels are seldom motionless for long—and this one wasn't breathing.

There was a boy, about the same age as the Salas boy, the age that Aiden appeared to be. Like the squirrel, he stood absolutely still. As Wulfe had promised, the boy didn't appear to notice me, even though I walked quite close to him.

He didn't smell dead. Like the ogre, there was no sense of rot to him. If he hadn't been caught in Wulfe's spell, I wondered if I'd have realized he was a zombie at all.

Wulfe had indicated that the well-made zombies were old. I hoped this one was old. Hoped that no one in the Tri-

Cities was missing a young boy. It wasn't particularly rational to think that the zombie would be less tragic if the child's death had been a century ago—or yesterday. But rational people wouldn't have been sneaking through the fields behind a house occupied by black witches, either—so there was that.

I counted five more zombies and hoped they were set to watch the path I traveled. Hoped they weren't evenly dispersed, because that would mean there were more zombies than even I'd estimated, based on my earlier run. Maybe too many for the old fae and his son to take care of. I drew even more comfort from the way they'd taken down the ogre zombie.

I kept my eyes away from the fire blazing up in the backyard of Elizaveta's house because I wanted to keep my night vision. Even so, glimpses told me that it climbed into the night sky, five or six feet high, with as much abandoned fury as if there weren't a fire ban on for fear of lighting the dry shrub steppe that surrounded us. Just last week, a fire had burned the west slope of Badger Mountain, taking a manufactured house and two empty barns with it.

The smoke smell had increased tremendously as soon as I'd crossed the ward at the edge of Elizaveta's property. Smoke eventually overwhelmed my sense of smell—and that smoke had more than dry logs in it. Now that I was closer I could pick out various scents, most of which I did not recognize.

Herbs of some sort, I thought, though I couldn't place them beyond that. I knew what lots of herbs smelled like normally, but didn't make a habit of burning them. Other than it wasn't marijuana (because that was almost an incense in college), I didn't know what kinds of herbs they had tossed in the fire.

I also smelled burnt hair and flesh, but I tried not to think about that. The bond between Adam and me was still present. I'd hoped that if I got closer to him, it would . . . do something. Tell me something. But it just sat there—an unresponsive, greasy lump.

The noises from the backyard were oddly muted. Either my hearing was going or they had some magic working to hide what they were doing from eavesdroppers. Likely a human wouldn't have heard a thing. Maybe they wouldn't even have seen the fire.

The trail crossed the edge of the corner of the garden and I left it there to take the rest of the trip on my own.

I chose to go through the garden because a coyote wouldn't stand out among the odd lumps of vegetation the same way it would in the tidy yard. I tried not to think about what the pack had found buried in the garden—I wouldn't have eaten anything grown here on a bet, and coyotes eat pretty much anything.

Elizaveta's garden was huge, filled with flowers, herbs, and vegetables. The sides were edged in grapevines that provided a thick cover for me. Not that anyone staring into that fire stood a chance of seeing a coyote in a garden at night, anyway.

I was making my cautious way through the pumpkin vines when I felt eyes on me. I froze. When that didn't alleviate the feeling, I turned in a slow circle. Nothing.

I looked up.

Just in front of me, where the garden gave way to open lawn, was a scarecrow with a dead crow on its head. The crow peered at me with bright button eyes.

"Mercy," it whispered to me with the voice a cornstalk might have, soft and dry with a bit of rattle.

12

~~~

"MERCY, WHAT ARE YOU DOING IN MY GARDEN?" the bird said, then chuckled, a dry, whispery sound. "Naughty little coyote."

Then it raised its head—the movement engendered by a flash of gray magic—and cried in a loud voice designed to carry into the house, "Coyote, coyote, coyote is here. Coyote, coyote, coyote is here."

I slipped into the dense foliage of the grapevines and froze, hardly daring to breathe.

We'd planned for this, or something like this. Without Wulfe, we knew that I could very well trip one of the protections that Elizaveta or the witches had prepared. I had a couple of things I could do if I triggered them in such a way that my comrades would be otherwise unaware of it.

But the crow's voice would carry well enough for the vampire to hear. Now they would try to sneak into Elizaveta's territory the way I had just done, if they could. Zee's glamour was, he assured us, quite up to hiding their presence unless the witches looked for magic.

I waited for someone, anyone, to hunt for me.

Instead, there was a pop, more of a pressure release than an actual noise. The fire got louder and I heard, for the first time, the witches' voices quite clearly. Another ward had gone down, somewhere between me and the porch.

"Did you hear that, Elizaveta, darlin'?" said Death in a sticky sweet voice. "You have a vermin problem in your garden?"

At the sound of her voice, my soul grew still, grew focused. For the first time since I'd walked into Uncle Mike's, I wasn't afraid.

For weeks, buried in the poor half-grown kitten's head, I had let her hurt us, hurt others, because I was helpless to do anything else. I had had to bear mute witness to the foulness of her actions. Tonight we were going to stop her.

The skin on my muzzle wrinkled and I had to fight back a growl.

"What was that?" asked Magda, the zombie witch, just as the crow sounded off again. She wasn't talking about any sound I'd made—she was talking about the crow-thing, because I hadn't made any noise.

I could feel the animated crow's attention brush by me, but I was out of its area of perception now. It settled back into an inanimate object with a mutter of indignation and a ruffle of its feathers. This wasn't a zombie; there was no semblance of life, no smell of wrongness. It was merely a simulacrum designed to warn intruders off. Elizaveta's work—its voice had sounded like the old witch trying to mimic what a crow might sound like, assuming the crow was Russian, and it smelled like Elizaveta's magic.

Magda made no effort to be quiet or unobtrusive when she came to check it out. She was using her cell phone as a flashlight, but I wasn't worried.

A coyote's fur is every color and blends very well into the shadows. In broad daylight the witch would have had trouble finding me where I lay under the vines. At night, as long as I kept my eyes closed so the light didn't catch the reflection, I was virtually invisible.

Magda marched into the garden as if she owned it.

When both feet were in the worked soil, the crow came to life again.

"Hardesty witch," it said in a soft raspy voice. "You don't belong here. You should go before you meet your doom."

"And who are you to say so?" the witch demanded.

But the crow wasn't really talking to her. "Witch, witch, witch," it cried. "Elizaveta, there is a witch in our garden. Witch, witch, witch."

"It's just an animation," the zombie witch called. She turned around and tramped back out of the garden. "The crow that sits atop the scarecrow is bespelled."

"A scarecrow that is a crow," said Death. Her voice was quiet. I couldn't tell if she was speaking to Magda, who was striding back to the concrete square at the back of the house, or if she was speaking to the other people on the patio.

"It's that scarecrow in the garden," Death said. "That's quite clever; I wonder if it works on skunks."

"I don't have a coyote for my collection," Magda complained. "Why couldn't it freeze the creature when it catches it? What's the use in something that shrieks like that?"

"The whole point of it is to chase the creatures out of the garden," Death said. "I'm sorry about the coyote; it will be miles away by now. If you really want a coyote so badly, we'll set a live trap out tomorrow. Likely the creature will be back."

"If she knows what's good for her, she'll be long gone," said Elizaveta, making it clear that she knew who the coyote the crow had announced was. She sounded awful. Her voice was so hoarse that between the roughness and her Russian accent, I almost didn't understand her. "Pity she didn't come up through the lawn; she could have taken a nip out of you and not one of my little pretties would have warned you." She coughed and spat.

Elizaveta, I thought, relief running through my bloodstream in a wash of hope. *You haven't thrown in with the bad guys in this.*

But my relief came too soon.

"Adam," said Magda, "be a dear. Go find that coyote for me, kill it, and bring it back."

Death snorted. "Really? Don't we have enough to do tonight that you need to make another of those things?"

I didn't hear Magda's reply. I was too busy putting as much distance between me and that porch in as short a time as I could manage.

Adam wouldn't have a choice. I'd seen what that witch had made Elizaveta's family do to each other, and to themselves. They were trained witches and they'd had no chance against Magda.

I was faster than most of the werewolves, I reassured myself. I put my head down and ran for all I was worth.

———————

I DIDN'T MAKE IT A HUNDRED YARDS BEFORE Adam's teeth closed on the back of my neck and bit down. His momentum hit me sideways and we both tumbled to the ground and rolled. His teeth never left my neck.

They didn't close down, either.

I lay limply on the ground, smelling my own blood in the night air. Adam crouched over the top of me. He growled, true anger in his voice, and I could feel the mate bond light up like a bonfire, sizzling flames burning through the muck of Magda's compulsion with the force of Adam's frustrated fury. Relief blossomed over me so strongly I don't think I could have moved if I tried.

Our connection wasn't comfortable, but I didn't care. His rage rolled over me first and his wolf let me know that he was not impressed with my brains or obedience. How dare I risk this, that he might be forced to kill me?

But beneath the rage was terror, so I let him get by with the insults. Relief hit him a few seconds later, as it had me. He let me go and lay down next to me, shivering once. Excess adrenaline, I thought. I felt the buzz, too.

Wulfe appeared a dozen yards off and gave us both a disapproving look. "When I told you that I thought your touch might free him from her hold—given your immunity to their magic—I didn't mean that you should touch your throat to his teeth. That generally doesn't work as well."

Adam rose, head lowered, ears pinned.

I shifted to human and touched his shoulder. "He's on our side this time," I told him. "I think."

"Thanks for that," Wulfe said with a smirk.

I looked at him. "Adam is free. What's the plan now?"

"I don't think the plan needs to change," he said after a moment. "Adam should go back to the witches; they'll think he failed to catch the coyote. As long as you do what she tells you, she'll think you are still in thrall."

"And if she figures it out?" I asked. "I don't want to lose Adam to her again."

His eyebrows rose. "Keep your bond open the way it is now. I don't think she can get him as long as you do." He looked at Adam. "It looks to me like all the players are out on the patio. I heard Elizaveta. Is the senator there, too?"

Adam nodded.

"Go back there and look like nothing is wrong," Wulfe said. "I plan on making an entrance and then killing the witches. Mercy was going to see if she could manage to touch you—because I was pretty sure, given how mate bonds work, that would allow her to lend you her natural talent. Then she was going to go plant herself out of sight, where she would watch for an opportunity to get the senator out of harm's way. And looky, now there are both of you to save the senator, while yours truly bears the brunt of the battle."

He left out the way I was going to help kill the witches. Wulfe was not stupid. Bat-in-the-belfry bizarre, maybe. Psychopathic, certainly. But not stupid.

Adam thought about Wulfe's plan. Then he made a chuffing sound and gave a pointed look all around us. I could smell them, too. He paused, because there was a zombie standing twenty feet away.

She could see us, but she didn't do anything but watch. This one, I was afraid, was someone they had killed here. She was not well made; there was a rotting patch in the center of her right cheek through which I could see her teeth and tongue. She was about Jesse's age.

"Wulfe spelled them to inattentiveness for now," I told Adam. "It won't hold if the witch calls them. But Zee and Tad are out here, too. Their part is to take care of the zombies. They already took care of the ogre."

Adam tilted his head to me, and our mate bond rang with his warning.

"Something worse than the ogre?" I said. "Do you think that Zee will be overmatched?"

He considered that. I felt quite clearly that he wasn't sure—but he decided to trust them.

A piercing whistle carried over the grounds. Adam's muzzle wrinkled and he turned his head, eyes glittering.

"Easy there," I said. "Do you think you can get the wolf to fake obedience?"

The wolf was the one who answered me. How could I doubt that he, who was such a patient hunter, could wait out the witches? He could lie in wait for days if necessary.

Adam had no ego—confidence, but no arrogance. The same was not true of his wolf.

I smiled and kissed his nose, wolf and man with the same caress, then let the change take me to my coyote form.

"I'll go let the others know that we have Adam," Wulfe said. "I'll meet you by the garden."

Back to plan A with improved odds. I felt pretty good about that.

Adam ran back to the witches and I trotted behind him, veering off when we got to the garden. I was careful not to alert the crow, tucking myself under another raspberry bush.

I listened to the witches greet Adam on his return. They came to the conclusion we had expected from them. Then they resumed whatever they were doing that sounded like something wet hitting skin. Sometimes there were hissing sounds, and that was when I smelled burnt flesh.

I caught the scent of something else from that direction—a zombie. The sense of wrongness from this one made me feel vaguely ill, just from the awareness that it was present. As careful as I was to examine the scent, I couldn't put a familiar name to the kind of creature it was. It smelled almost fae, but not. *Like fire magic*, I thought. The hot, bitter scent of Zee's iron-kissed magic was something akin to it, too.

I had waited for maybe fifteen minutes before I decided I needed to see what awaited me on that porch.

I tensed to rise to my feet, when Wulfe's hand came down on my back. I couldn't scent him or see him, but I knew who it was. I don't know how I knew . . . That wasn't quite true. I didn't want to understand how I knew it was Wulfe.

I see ghosts. But I know when a vampire is about, too. My kind used to hunt vampires when they first came to this country. It's why there aren't very many of us—the vampires were better hunters, and there were more of them.

But I knew it was Wulfe, so I didn't yip or do anything to draw the witches' attention back to the garden. My clothes dropped in a pile on the ground next to me, along with my gun and my cutlass.

"Don't try using the gun on the witches," Wulfe breathed into my ear. "It won't work."

His voice in my ear was weird because I couldn't sense him with my normal senses, just with that odd gift I used to find the dead. I didn't like having that connection to him. I didn't want any connection to Wulfe.

I got to my feet and slunk along the ground toward the huge patio where there would have been room for the whole pack to congregate. There was plenty of room for a few witches, a senator, a werewolf, and a . . . I stopped moving because I simply couldn't make myself look away.

Curled up next to Adam, and nearly double his bulk, was . . . a something. It was covered in iridescent white scales about six inches across. I couldn't see its head, only a single silver-and-purple-laced wing—the other presumably on the other side of the dragon.

I put my head back down, and with even more care than before, I moved from one spot of darkness to the next—but it didn't matter. Everyone on that patio was focused on something that wasn't a coyote ghosting in the dark—or a freaking dragon zombie. I could feel their focus with the same hunter's instinct that had kicked in when Elizaveta's crow had detected me. While I was moving, all I cared about—aside from the dragon—was that no one was looking for me.

I didn't look directly at the occupants of the patio until I'd come around to where the firepit wasn't between me and them. Then I took it all in with a single encompassing look, before I let my gaze fall to the side.

I wasn't the only hunter present. I didn't know how good witches are at feeling eyes on them from the darkness. But the dragon was there. I had trusted Wulfe's zombie-sleep spell absolutely until the dragon. But everything I'd ever heard about dragons (aside from the fact that there were no such things) told me that magic wouldn't work on them. But since someone had turned one into a zombie, I was pretty sure that some magic had to work on them. What I didn't know was how well *Wulfe's* magic would work on the one on the patio.

I heard a slithery noise and glanced back over at the patio. The dragon had rolled over and was looking straight at me.

As I looked into its purple eyes, I felt its connection to the witch and through her to all the dead she commanded. Their connection was like spider silk in comparison to the stout chains of our pack's bonds . . . but it was less unlike than I was comfortable with. Later that might bother me.

Right then I was more concerned by how many of them there were. For a moment, caught in our shared gaze, I felt them all—a great weight of misery that stretched across Elizaveta's property. There weren't ten or twenty of them. There were dozens. Hundreds. Some made with great care, others newly made and rotting already.

But they were not my task.

I closed my eyes, breaking our tie. When I opened my eyes again, I watched the dragon, but I did not look at its eyes. I moved cautiously and its gaze did not follow me. I couldn't tell if it was still caught up in Wulfe's spell, or if it was just indifferent to me.

There were other participants that I needed to take note of. Senator Campbell was gagged and tied to a chair, Abbot on the ground beside him. I had forgotten about Tory Abbot, the senator's aide. I watched him, but he had his head down and wasn't moving.

The senator was hurt. I couldn't see anything specific because the flickering firelight hid the tones of his skin and most of him was covered by his clothes. But I could see pain in the hunch of his body.

He saw me. But he didn't know what I was, and he probably assumed that I was another of the zombie witch's creations, her abominations. Maybe, if he'd been paying attention to the witches' conversation, he thought I was just a coyote. A short, sharp scream made him turn his attention away from me, toward the star of tonight's show.

Elizaveta. They had stripped her naked and hung her upside down from the basketball hoop pole next to the house. I don't know how long she'd been there, but the skin on her face was bruised darkly enough that I could see it, even in the poor lighting. Her white hair hung down in an untidy mess. Her arms hung limply, a few inches off the ground, bound together with heavy manacles that looked as though they belonged in a medieval dungeon.

Magda had her hands in front of her mouth, like a child in a candy store who was trying to decide which flavor was best when all of them were wonderful. She swayed a little and hummed. I'd had my eyes shut when she'd joined me in the garden, so this was the first time tonight that I took in her appearance.

She wore a light-colored, silky top with a scoop neck that was just low enough to display the triple strand of pearls that lay over her collarbone. Her slacks were darker, but her mid-heel pumps were the same light color as her top. Pink, I thought. But it might have been lavender. She looked as though she were dressed for a garden party fund-raiser for a high-powered politician. Or posing for a society article in a magazine, maybe titled "What the Well-Put-Together Witch Wears to an Outdoor Torture Session This Year."

In contrast, Death looked like she was dressed for a jewelry heist. She was encased head to toe in black. But this was nothing new. The whole time I'd been with that poor cat in her laboratory, I'd never seen her in any color but black. Tonight she had on a long-sleeved, high-neck tunic top, black jeans, and silver-laced black boots that matched the ones the poppet had worn. The whip in her hand was black and she used it on Elizaveta.

Elizaveta was an old woman, in her early seventies, I thought. She was in good shape for a woman of her age—there were muscles under the thinning, slacking skin. But her age added to the indignity and horror of what they were doing to her.

Unlike the senator, Elizaveta's skin, pale and exposed, displayed the damage they'd been doing. I hated it that somewhere in my head I could look at the welts, burns, and bruises on a naked old woman and think, *They've been taking it easy on her tonight. And they haven't had her up there too long.* Because I knew what it looked like when the witches were really working someone over.

"Again," said Magda. "Please, Ishtar, please. That felt like . . . better than the last witch, better than all the witches here. That felt like—"

"Power," said Death. She hit Elizaveta again and both witches shivered with the aftereffects.

I could think of her as Death because the alternative was Ishtar—essentially calling her a goddess, which I would not do. I had never heard her real name, though I had the impression that she hated it.

"I could do this all night, Elizaveta," crooned Death, working up a rhythm with her whip. "You probably know exactly how wonderful this feels—yes, I had some lovely talks with your people. I almost kept one or two, but in the end decided I could use the power boost more. You have that much of a reputation, which should please you."

She paused, surveying her work. There was a certain satisfaction in her body language. She took pride, I remembered, in the evenness of her lash work.

"I could break you, Elizaveta," she crooned. "I could destroy your flesh and drink down your power."

Magda squeezed herself and shivered. "I like it when you do that, Ishtar. Yummy."

Death gave her a sympathetic smile. "I know, sweetheart. But I was given a task." She started swinging again. This time there was no rhythm in it, no way to plan for the sting.

I knew how that felt.

"I could beat you to death," she said. "We will drink your power and your pain, and my coven would find that acceptable. Particularly when you have given us such interesting toys and spells to take home. I bet you didn't know that your grandson knew where you kept the family spellbook, did you? Stupid of you to leave him alive so long. He died knowing that he'd gotten his revenge."

Robert, I thought, and had an instant, unbidden memory of his featureless, scarred face.

Elizaveta was beginning to pant, though it was more from emotion than from exhaustion. "Or you can surrender. We have ten bloodlines in our coven. Yours would be the eleventh. So close to a full coven. You've felt our power as a victim. Wouldn't you love to feel it as one of us? I offer you power you could only dream about without us."

"I am Elizaveta Arkadyevna Vyshnevetskaya, of house Kikimora. I can trace my bloodline a thousand years. Never would I join your ragtag band of mutts and rejects. I know who you are, Patience Ramsey. There is no house Ramsey. You do not know from where your witchblood comes. It was present in neither your mother's nor in her husband's lineage. Calling yourself Death does not make you a great witch, does not make legitimate your bloodline."

She didn't get it all out at once. But she did pull it off without screams or grunts, and I wasn't sure that I would have managed it if I'd been in her place. By the end of

Elizaveta's little speech, Death—Patience—was trying her best to beat Elizaveta into silence.

I wasn't just waiting around while the witches and Elizaveta had their chat. I used the fire and their preoccupation to slide all the way around the outer edge of the patio. It was really dark tonight; the moon was a bare sliver and there was a storm in the air that was covering the stars. If anyone had been looking, they would have seen me easily. But Elizaveta was giving them enough of a show that no one thought to look.

Except for Adam, who pinned his ears at me. And the dead dragon, which had turned its head in my direction.

I pinned my ears back at Adam. I was good at slinking unseen in plain sight. It was what coyotes do. And I was pretty sure that I wouldn't have drawn the attention of the witches if I jumped up and ran around Adam singing "Love Is a Many-Splendored Thing." They were enjoying themselves so much beating on Elizaveta, they were making this part much easier than it might have been.

As far as the dragon was concerned, I had decided to worry about it when it decided to worry about me.

I came, eventually, one careful pace at a time, to the shadows next to the house, wiggling (carefully) behind a box elder bush. Elizaveta kept her home very neat, and there were no unfortunate dried leaves or weeds to make noise. If we survived, I'd thank her for that. If all went according to plan from here on out, I'd spend the next stage of our battle here, out of the way.

When all hell broke loose, I'd run for my cutlass—especially since I knew that there were a lot of zombies, a lot more than any of us had planned on.

Adam was watching me—and so was the dragon. I wrinkled my nose and showed them both my teeth. I was trying to hide. I couldn't do it if they both were determined to make sure the witches figured out there was something in the bushes.

Look away, I told Adam via our bond.

Adam and the dragon turned their attention to the outer darkness, away from Elizaveta's corner of hell, and away from me. I had the odd thought—I expected a dragon, if I ever met one, to be bigger.

I sighed, put my muzzle on my paws, and settled in to wait. It was Wulfe's show now.

I didn't have to wait long.

Like me, he took advantage of the distraction Elizaveta provided. He stepped onto the concrete without fanfare, and no one—except Campbell, Adam, and . . . Elizaveta—noticed him do it. He just walked up to Death, to Patience, and grabbed her arm midswing.

She jerked, then fought—but he was a vampire. He ignored her and waved a careless hand. The manacles on Elizaveta's ankles and wrists dropped to the ground. Somehow he let go of Death's arm and caught Elizaveta before she hit the ground, too.

I had the uncomfortable thought that he might be faster than most of the werewolves. Maybe faster than me. I counted on my speed to stay safe. I didn't like it that Wulfe was so quick. I would remember that.

He set Elizaveta down on one of the chairs scattered carelessly around the patio, picking one that was several paces outside the action. He took his time, making sure that she was as comfortable as possible—almost as if he were inviting the witches to attack him while they thought he was distracted.

They didn't take him up on it. Patience, rubbing her wrist, had run across the patio until she stood shoulder to shoulder with Magda, where they could touch.

If I'd been Wulfe, I would have been interested in keeping them farther apart.

"Who are you?" Patience asked, her tones wary.

I felt a subtle wash of foul magic.

"Wizard," said Magda. "The Wizard—whatever that means. Wolf and Wizard." Her face twisted unhappily. "He's not a wolf. I don't know why I said that."

"You can call me Wulfe if you want to," said Wulfe with a smile. "Or you can call me Wizard—but not many do that last to my face."

I wondered if he felt the slow build of magic that Death, that Patience, was working. But I needn't have worried.

Wulfe laughed, that horrible boneless laugh, then made a gesture that ended palm out. He used the hand Stefan had cut off again. I wondered if Stefan had cut that one off for a reason.

Patience crumpled around her center, not quite losing her footing, but it looked like a near thing. She screamed, partly out of pain, but I'd wager some of it was anger, too.

"You're a wizard," said Magda indignantly. She reached out to grip Patience's hand. "You used wizard magic to free Elizaveta. You can't be a witch, too."

As soon as she touched the other witch, that one quit screaming. I thought that Wulfe should maybe keep them from touching each other. Instead, Wulfe said, "No?"

He made another gesture with that hand. Patience put a hand, palm up, between them, and this time she didn't scream. But the firelight revealed sweat on her forehead. The tendons of her neck were tense, as if she were making a great effort.

"Babies, help Mama," crooned Magda. The dragon uncurled and lunged—but so did Adam. He grabbed the dragon by the muzzle and held on.

Cutlass. Adam's need reached through our bond.

I bolted out from under the box elder and ran for the garden with every ounce of speed I could muster. I'm pretty sure that the only one who noticed me was Elizaveta, because I ran right in front of her—and because that witch was pretty scarily observant.

A step from the cutlass, I changed back to human. I grabbed the blade and brought it across the throat of the boy zombie I'd passed on my way to the house. I hadn't seen him, just knew that he was running for me. The sharp silver blade snicked through his neck and kept moving as the boy fell.

I felt the force that animated the body break, as if I'd cut through more than flesh and bone. I felt again the likeness to the pack bond—a bare trickle compared to the river of the pack, but both were running water. For a moment, something else lingered where the zombie had fallen. Not a ghost, not a soul, but something tragic and broken. I was pretty sure it was fading, but I couldn't wait around to find out—Adam was fighting a zombie dragon.

I ran.

No one on my side had died yet. Adam was still wrestling with the zombie. His battle was aided by the fact that the zombie was mostly just trying to get to the witches, and fighting Adam only because he was in the way.

Whatever Wulfe was doing—and it made breathing while I was running like breathing underwater—it kept the witches occupied. Magda had had no chance to change her orders to the dragon. I felt like I was overlooking something, but I'd worry about it sometime when Adam wasn't fighting a dragon zombie.

I relied on the bonds between us—mate bond and pack bond—to time my move. I did not slacken my speed as I passed the embattled dragon.

I put my other hand, the one that was not holding the cutlass, on Adam's shoulder. He was braced for it so my weight didn't disturb his balance as I vaulted up and over, out of the way of the half-hearted swipe of wing. Instead, that strike turned a sturdy wooden table into kindling.

Adam twisted his weight suddenly and the dragon's head twisted, too. He released the dragon's muzzle as I slid the cutlass into the soft flesh under the dragon's jaw, up through its snout. Locking the jaws shut with the sword.

I jumped up as the dragon writhed and Adam knocked the creature away from me. The battle was a long way from over, but Adam could fight now, instead of just trying to keep its mouth safely closed. Triumphantly, I dashed across the patio to stop a handbreadth from Elizaveta. Half laughing in exhilaration, I briefly caught Elizaveta's gaze, but her attention slid past me and over my shoulder. The firelight brightened on her face for an instant and I saw her pupils flare.

"She's called them all," she said.

I whirled.

Of course, I thought, the boy zombie I'd killed was no longer settled under Wulfe's thrall. That meant they had been called. All of them, a lot more than a hundred.

I could feel them stirring beneath the tug of Magda's words. Their twisted unnatural state was a sadness that dragged at my heart.

They were running at us—and Elizaveta called out something that sounded like "passion fruit" but equally well could have been something in Russian. Elizaveta could speak English with the precision of a BBC newscaster. But today, her Russian accent was full bore, and that meant I was more than usually likely to misunderstand what she said.

Magic rippled, leaving the air taut with something that felt to my overheated senses like anticipation. A zombie, the first of dozens, made it to the edge of the concrete and ran into an invisible barrier, as did the teeming mass of zombies that followed it. Adam and the dragon had not confined their battle royal to the patio. When Elizaveta had brought up her spell, a warding that followed the edge of the concrete, both Adam and the dragon were on the other side of that barrier.

"They cannot come through my magic," Elizaveta told me.

Adam's back hit the barrier hard, and he used the semi-elastic surface to launch a leap that ended with him atop the dragon, which still had the cutlass stuck through its jaws.

Elizaveta saw what I was watching. "Adam should be able to take care of himself," she said confidently. "He is a splendid beast."

"Elizaveta," I said, whispering furiously, "there are a lot of zombies out there."

She narrowed her eyes at me. "You can do something about that, Coyote's daughter. And I do not know why you are waiting. My barrier will not stop you."

"What—" I started to ask her, but I was interrupted by a commotion followed by the crack of wood.

I looked up to see the senator's chair sliding along the concrete on its side. I couldn't immediately see a cause for it—so it was probably something Wulfe had done. When it had gone over, it'd knocked over a small table where the witches had kept an array of sharp objects.

I jogged over, one eye on Wulfe and the witches. To my shame, Senator Campbell had not been a priority for me, though he was the most vulnerable of us. It was past time to get the senator free of his bonds so at least he could run. Not that running would help him escape the zombies, but maybe he could get out of the way of stray blows not directed at him.

Rather than try to pull the chair upright, I just used a short-bladed knife that had been among the witches' scattered implements. It had no trouble slicing through the ropes Campbell had been tied to the chair with. Once he was freed, I helped the senator lurch to his feet.

With a hand under his elbow, I urged him to the relative safety of the space near Elizaveta. She might even be inclined to help keep him alive. I gave him the knife and he went to work on his gag. As I turned to see what the witches were doing, I got a whiff of fresh blood—a lot of it. We'd left a blood trail behind us. The senator's pant leg was wet with it—and someone had chewed a hole in his leg.

I reviewed that first flash of a glance I'd taken upon my arrival to the tableau on the patio. Abbot had been curled around Senator Campbell's leg. He'd evidently been chewing. I didn't know if he'd been doing it because he was a witch and powering himself up with the senator's pain. Or if he was a zombie now. He hadn't smelled like a witch when I'd met him before—but male witches aren't as powerful as the females. It was possible that Magda's scent had masked his.

I looked for Abbot, but I didn't see him. Maybe he'd ended up on the outside of Elizaveta's circle.

I scanned the darkness, but all I could see were the zombies crowded thickly around us. They were all focused on coming to Magda's aid. As Wulfe had said, the majority of them were humans, but I saw a border collie and a pair of cats.

I glanced over at the witches and was caught in the beauty of their battle. The stench of black magic was so thick that it seemed almost unconnected with the fight between Wulfe and the witches.

I could not see the magic, just felt it on my skin and in my flesh. Some was so vile that I felt as if I would never be able to wash it from my body. Some of it was sharp and sparkly, and it felt the way fireflies look. But that, too, seemed unconnected to their combat. Impossible that such foulness could be a part of the beauty of their dance. When the fight had begun, it had been a thing of gestures, of hands and fingers. Deep into their battle, they moved as if they were doing kata—quick and graceful movements that used their whole bodies.

Wulfe's body had the fluid grace of one of the big cats. Patience's dance consisted of small, efficient movements—precision was her guiding force. Magda—the one I'd have expected grace from—moved instead with jerks and stomps. There was power in her dance, but not elegance.

After a few seconds I began to see the flow of power. I couldn't see the magic that passed between them, but I could infer the path from the connections between the three of them.

I'd seen crime scenes on TV shows where yarn was strung to trace lines of bullet trajectories. If there were enough bullets fired, the string pattern was oddly beautiful, like a freshman art project. The witches' combat reminded me of that.

One of the zombies was big enough it caught my eye and I turned to see that the dragon zombie—a huge wound across its face beginning to scab over as I watched—was dragging its claws against the invisible wall of Elizaveta's working. The cutlass was gone.

Adam's life was bright and whole on the other side of our bond. I could feel the wild joy of battle shiver into my blood. Adam was fine.

"Mercy," Elizaveta said. "You can free them—"

"Vampire," called Magda triumphantly over the top of Elizaveta's voice. "He's a vampire, Ishtar."

"Abbot," purred Death. I mean Patience. Patience is not nearly as scary as Death, right?

The dragon zombie turned its attack to the ground, digging in the dirt at the base of the concrete. Concrete—the kind poured for patios—would not have slowed down a werewolf, and it didn't slow down the dragon, either. For a zombie, this one was smart.

This is wrong, said Coyote's voice in my head, and he didn't mean the way the dragon was burrowing into our zombie-free zone.

There were no words for how beautiful the dragon was— even if it was smaller than I'd expected a dragon to be. The bones of its face were covered by minute scales, each glittering like a gem in the light of the fire. A thousand points of light that blossomed into an iridescent blanket. Delicate, impossibly fragile-looking membranous wings were held out to balance the dragon as it dug. Great purple eyes were fixed on its goal.

I could only imagine what it would have looked like if it had been alive.

This zombie was an abomination.

Wrong.

I raised my hand toward her. Maybe it was by chance, or maybe she had felt me watching her, but she raised her eyes to mine. Hers, not its. There was something looking at me from inside those eyes. Tears gathered in my own eyes at the terrible evil of what had been done to her.

Wood scraped near me and I looked over at the table the dragon had smashed. Abbot crawled out of the shelter he'd found in the broken boards. He was wearing clothing that had once been suitable for meeting the president, but I didn't think there was a dry cleaner in the world who could repair it now. There was blood smeared around his mouth and down the front of his shirt and pants.

"Vampire," he said.

And he gathered power, a black mass of crafting. Witch, I thought, not zombie. He strode forward as if he hadn't just been hiding under a pile of wood, as if he hadn't gnawed into the senator's leg when Campbell was tied and couldn't defend himself. He walked like a warrior wading into a familiar battlefield.

"Wulfe!" I screamed.

Wulfe was too busy with the witches to pay attention. I didn't know what to do. Wulfe had made it quite clear that once he'd engaged in battle, I was to stay away.

Abbot pulled a knife from a pocket, flicked it open, and cut himself. Then in a gesture that reminded me of Sherwood's motion earlier tonight, he flung his own blood at Wulfe's back. I was too far away and it was too dark—the firelight was tricky, full of strong light and shadows—to see if it hit Wulfe.

But it must have. Because when Abbot took all the power he'd gathered and shoved it into his voice, saying, "Vampire," Wulfe froze.

The two witches stopped their dance midmove. I don't know what Magda's face looked like, because I was watching the smile bloom on Patience's face. Death's face. Because patience is a virtue and there was nothing good about the expression on her face.

"Oh, vampire," Magda said. "We haven't had a vampire like you to play with in a long time. Ours used to be fun, but now she only curls up in a corner and cries."

And just at that moment, the dragon's claws broke through the concrete and my attention was forced to a more immediate problem. The zombie ripped a two-foot-square chunk away from the patio and hauled it down.

For a moment I could see a hole, and then it was filled with dragon. She'd misjudged; there wasn't enough room for her to squeeze through. But she'd already proven that Elizaveta's circle only went down to the ground, and that the ground and concrete were no match for her. It would only take a moment for her to widen the hole.

I don't know why I didn't run screaming. But Coyote's voice still rang in my head. Also, after all the sadness I felt in seeing this thing that had once been a dragon, there was no room inside me for anything else—not even healthy emotions like terror or self-preservation.

Touch is important in magic.

I reached down and put my hand on her forehead. She couldn't quite get her shoulders and forelimbs through, but all she would have had to do was twist her head and she could have taken off my arm at the elbow.

A bond lit up between us, bright and clean, a connection both like and unlike the kinds of bonds I was more familiar with. This wasn't pack magic. This was a thing of Coyote, who was the spirit of free agency. Of choice, for good and ill. Of death and dying.

"Go," I told the dragon. I put power into my voice, power that I'd learned from Adam, but I didn't need to borrow from my mate for this. This power came from my father. I whispered, because this was not a power that needed volume. "Go. Be at peace."

"No!" It was Magda's voice, I think. "Stop her!" The dragon went limp beneath my fingers. Her body shrank as if the flesh were nothing without the terrible magic that kept it animate. She no longer filled the hole completely; soon other zombies would break through the opening she had made.

It didn't take long. Something ripped the dragon's desiccating body away and a woman began to slither through. She was smaller than the dragon—there was plenty of room for her.

But I was still caught in that odd headspace where I wasn't afraid of the zombies—I was sad for them. I reached out, but this time I didn't try to touch her skin. This time I reached out for the threads of power that bound this zombie to the witch whose creature she was.

Instead of grasping only her threads, my fingers closed

on dozens of strings. They weren't comfortable to hold, those bonds, too full of that terrible wrongness.

My grip didn't feel firm enough, so I twisted my hands, winding those bonds around my forearms until they were made fast. Then I jerked, giving a tremendous pull that used my whole body.

When all of those bonds were straining and I was pulling with all of my weight, I took a breath. I said softly, with utter conviction, "Go. Be at peace."

It felt so right. I felt as if I were full of light and joy. Of rightness—or at least the opposite of wrongness. I felt clean. And a wide swath of the zombies who had been trying to get onto the patio dropped as if poleaxed.

But there were more zombies. A lot more. I reached out and this time the bonds came eagerly to my hands, as if they were metal and I held a magnet. I took them, and spinning round and round, wrapped my whole body with them. Even as I did so, I felt a few of those threads break in bright, happy sparks—freedom found before I could gift them with it.

Dimly, I heard Tory Abbot say, "Wulfe, stop her." But I was too caught up in the moment to pay much attention to his words.

The bonds let me watch Tad, clad in blackness that made him hard to see, a huge axe in his hands. I felt it hit the zombie whose bonds I held—and my awareness of Tad was gone as the zombie's thread dissolved into fireworks followed by nothingness. If I had wanted to, I felt that I could have tracked Tad from zombie to zombie as he brought them to the final stillness and released the wrongness of their existence.

Zee's path through my zombie-leashes was swifter than his son's. I felt him move like a wave of destruction, his sword singing in joy, and they released zombie after zombie to wherever they would go after their long subjugation.

Adam. Oh, Adam was beautiful in his wrath. He danced with the dead and they fell before him like so many petals in the wind. I was tempted to stop and just watch him.

But I had a job to do.

I think I was a little power drunk. And maybe a bit dizzy.

I raised my hands to the skies and twirled like a top, a naked top. I probably looked a fool. But there was no room for self-analysis in me at that moment. I turned and turned and gathered them all, all the shiny, wispy threads of spider silk and all the zombies. Every last one, every creature bound unwillingly to unnatural life, I held them in my hands, wrapped around my body.

They would have done my bidding more eagerly than they had done the witch's. I knew it, knew I held the power of an unstoppable army in my grasp. They could kill the witches, destroy any threat to me, to my pack, to the people I held dear. I held power in my hands such that had never been available to me before.

But in that moment in time, there was only one thing I wanted from them, one necessity that drove me.

I gave them my order.

"Go," I whispered. "Be at peace."

Wulfe's hand closed ungently on my upper arm at the moment I spoke those words.

Two hundred fourteen . . . thirteen (as one fell beneath Adam's fangs) sparks left their rotting corpses and flew away. Out in the darkness, the corpses dropped, abandoned puppets. Some of them I saw with my eyes; others I just felt.

Wulfe dropped, too, and lay unmoving at my feet.

I sat down abruptly beside him. I felt empty and aching, as though I'd been trampled by a herd of horses. Twice. The euphoria of the moment before was gone, vanished as quickly as it had come.

I didn't know if I'd killed Wulfe when I released the zombies. Rekilled him. Removed him from his vampiric existence. I couldn't decide how I felt about that.

"Passion fruit," said Elizaveta, standing up abruptly from the chair Wulfe had tucked her into. I was almost sure the word really was "passion fruit" this time.

I felt the flutter as her circle fell and the patio was once more open to the night. It was a little easier to see the dead covering the ground, thicker near the patio, but the whole of the yard and beyond was full of bodies. A lot of those were human-zombie bodies.

With the zombies all deanimated, it was easy to pick out Adam, Tad, and Zee—they were the only ones left standing. Tad and Zee were turning in a wary circle, looking for a foe. Adam loped in my direction.

Elizaveta patted my head as she passed me. "Good," she told me. "Now it is my turn."

She walked slowly—no doubt hampered by the damage the witches had inflicted on her—but each step was easy and firm. She walked as if she owned the ground under her feet.

The three witches—Death, Magda, and Abbot—were staring around them, momentarily overwhelmed by the sudden destruction of their army. There was blood dripping from Magda's nose and the ear nearest me.

"Stupid," Elizaveta said in satisfied tones.

Death recovered first. She scowled and opened her mouth.

But before Death could say anything, Elizaveta raised her hand palm up and said, "Tory Abbot, Patience Ramsey, Magda Fischer. Die."

I felt it again, that moment, that instant when everything stopped. To me it felt like a club of darkness that, even not directed at me, tried to freeze the blood in my body.

"Die," said Elizaveta again.

They obeyed Elizaveta, the three Hardesty witches, because there was no possibility for them to do anything else.

They died so fast that there was not even an instant for shock or disbelief. They just dropped dead.

I'd watched Patience use that spell to kill every living thing in Elizaveta's house except for a cat. But Death had not lit up like a blowtorch when she consumed their lives. Elizaveta did. I had felt the magic Patience had harvested from dozens in that house the night Elizaveta's family died. Immortal witches, Coyote had told me. And I'd known then where Death had gotten her immortality.

But I knew for a certainty that that houseful of life had

supplied her with not a tithe of what Elizaveta farmed from the three witches. I felt the filthy magic wash into her and fill her as if she were an empty vessel beneath a water spout. Power lit her from within until I had to bring my arm up and shield my eyes.

My bones ached with the wrongness of that magic. But eventually the tide of filthy black magic faded. I brought my arm down so that I could see.

The first thing I saw wasn't Elizaveta, though. While I hadn't been watching, Adam had shifted all the way back to human. He stood, naked, every muscle in his body clenched like it hurt. His eyes were shut and the muscle in his cheek was twitching. As I watched, he drew in a breath and started to relax.

Elizaveta stood, her hand on his shoulder, beaming at him as if she had done him a favor—instead of pulling him through a full change, wolf to man, in what looked to have been an incredibly painful fashion.

As I watched, she stepped away from him and walked to the bodies of her victims. She knelt beside them and began frisking them like a professional thief. I rolled to my feet and staggered forward.

Elizaveta was on our side, I reminded myself. There was no reason for the anxious terror that filled me at the sight of Elizaveta's tangled white hair darkening to sable, of her slack and bruised dermis being replaced by firm, milky skin without a wrinkle or an age spot.

"I told you they were foolish," Elizaveta said as she set rings, necklaces, and small bits and pieces of cloth, clay, and bone aside. They sparked as she touched them, the magic she was still absorbing bringing them to life. A life that left them as soon as she set them aside.

"Foolish?" Adam said—because of course it was Adam she was speaking to.

She looked up at him and the fickle firelight caught her face and bathed her in a light that was illuminating rather than blinding. The old witch no longer looked like the well-preserved seventy-year-old woman she had been. I'd always thought she would have been stunning when she was young. Beautiful. I was wrong. Her features were still too strong for that. Her nose was still hawkish and her jaw was too long.

But I imagined that if Helen of Troy had been a real person, she might have looked like Elizaveta Arkadyevna. Elizaveta's face could have launched a thousand ships.

She looked away from my mate and down at herself, at skin that was smooth and taut over muscles that would have done credit to a werewolf. She stretched her long and graceful fingers, hands that belonged to a woman in her twenties.

"She used her death-bringing spell in my home," Elizaveta said, giving Abbot's body one last pat-down, taking an amulet out of his pocket.

"I have been looking for that spell ever since I first heard rumors of it—when I was as young as I look right now. And they brought it right to me." Elizaveta stood up.

She nudged Patience with her toe. "Foolish to work secret magic in another witch's stronghold." She gave Adam a flirtatious smile. "I improved it a bit."

He held out his hand. She put her hand in his and he kissed it.

"Is this what it feels like to be a werewolf?" she asked him. "Nothing hurts."

She closed her fingers over his; a beautiful smile lit her face.

"Adam," she said. "I have wanted to do this for years."

She stepped into his space, leaned her beautiful, strong, young, and naked body against his. She was just an inch or two taller than he was, but it didn't matter. Adam was so much wider, more solid, that she looked like a fairy princess to his warrior.

They were beautiful.

She tilted her face to facilitate her kiss, revealing Adam's face to me. Just as her lips touched his, Adam's eyes met mine.

I couldn't read what I saw there. Not then.

Then he closed his eyes. He kissed her. One of his arms

wrapped around her waist. The other one slid down, through her long silky hair, and cupped the back of her head.

He snapped her neck, stepping back so that her body hit the concrete hard instead of cushioning her fall. It didn't matter to her; she was dead. But it said a lot about how Adam felt about her.

He looked at me and waited for my judgment.

I knew that he had liked her. I knew that he thought of her as family, had enjoyed the verbal sparring matches they had sometimes engaged in. Enjoyed dusting off his mother's Russian and flirting with an old woman.

"This is our territory," I said, giving him the words he needed. "We don't allow black magic in our territory."

He closed his eyes and swallowed.

"That's right," he said. When I folded him in my arms, he lifted me against him and buried his face against my neck.

We held each other, surrounded by the dead.

13

~~~

"I CAN ASK THE EARTH TO PUT THEM TO REST," said Zee.

I pulled away from Adam and looked over at the old smith. He stood on the balls of his feet, looking just like he usually did: expression subtly sour as if a scowl were ready to break out at any moment. He looked like a wiry old man who'd done hard physical work his whole life and could outwork any teenager in town—not like a legendary fae who had just faced battle with a foe who had so greatly outnumbered him.

Tad stood just beyond him. And there was an almost existential serenity gathered about his whole body. I had never seen Tad look so at peace with himself.

"They will just dig them up," I said prosaically. "Someone twenty or thirty years from now will decide they want to build a housing development. Stick a backhoe into the ground and—whoopsie."

"A lot of dead people here," said the senator, limping very slowly over to us. "A lot of families who need closure."

"Too many old zombies," Zee said. "They are a feast for the crows."

We must have looked blank—or I did, anyway.

To me, Zee said, "The black-magic users will come to use their bones. I know creatures of the fae who will be drawn to their corpses. I can put them to rest in the ground so that none will find them again."

He looked at the senator. "The goblin king took care of the dead at your brother's house. You won't find the bodies of your people, either. But Uncle Mike tells me that your Ruth has photos, so you can identify them."

"Took care of them?" he said. Then a little less hostilely he said, "The goblin king?"

"He would have treated them with respect," I said, and I was sure I was right. Though what respect meant to a goblin and what it meant to Jake Campbell might not be quite the same thing. "His daughter was among the dead there. She tried to see what was going on and was killed by the witches."

"I see," he said.

"I will need help to lay them all out," said Zee. "Tad and I can do it, but it will take longer and we want to get the bodies out of the way before the neighbors awake, yes?"

"The wolves are on their way," said Adam.

"Did you call them?" I asked.

He shook his head. "But I opened the bonds and they have been looking. They will be here in a few minutes."

The senator had been steadfastly not looking at Adam or me, and now that matters had calmed a bit, I knew why.

"I'll just go get some clothes for us," I said. "And the first-aid kit for your leg, Senator."

I went to the garden first. I gathered up my clothes and put them on, including the concealed-carry holster and my gun—which reminded me that my cutlass was out there in the darkness somewhere. I'd have to go look for it when things calmed down.

I tied my tennis shoes and then took two steps into

Elizaveta's garden. The crow's magic was gone. It was just an inanimate husk tied to a scarecrow now.

I was glad Elizaveta was dead.

I would miss the person I'd thought she was, even though that person was plenty scary. I would miss having her as one of the pieces I counted on to keep the people I loved safe. I worried about the vacuum she left behind. Someone would come, another witch, to take over this territory.

I was still glad that Elizaveta was dead.

I jogged over to Adam's SUV and grabbed the first-aid kit and the spare set of clothes he kept in his gym bag. I started to go, and then turned back and grabbed a wet wipe out of the package he kept in the SUV to clean up messes.

Adam was talking to the senator when I got back.

"—can take you to a hotel, or Uncle Mike's, or you can go wait at my home if you'd like," Adam said.

The senator said, "I think I would like to see this through to the end."

"Okay," Adam said. "If you change your mind, just let me know."

I gave Adam his clothes and watched him dress. When he was finished, he caught the expression on my face.

"What's wrong?" he asked.

I reached up and, very thoroughly, used the wet wipe to clean his mouth. Because I'd had time to analyze what I'd seen in his eyes right before he kissed Elizaveta. It had been horror.

Adam didn't react, just let me finish washing away the stains. Not his stains, but the witch's filthy magic and the results of Elizaveta's choices brought to fruition and set on Adam's plate. I cleaned those things from my mate. He closed his eyes when I was done and rested his face against my hand.

When he opened them again, they were blazing yellow.

"That is mine," I told him sternly. "Be careful what you do with it."

He dropped down on one knee, took my hand, and kissed the palm. "As you wish," he said.

I kissed the top of his head. "I love you, too."

He put his face against my belly and whispered, so softly that only I would hear it.

"Nudge."

I laughed and ruffled his hair. "Work now, play later."

"Promise?" There was humor in the quirk of his lip, but his eyes were serious, almost grim.

————————

"I WILL NOT ASK HER TO CARE FOR THE BLACK-magic users," Zee said, coming up to me where I sat on one of the few unbroken chairs.

I was bone tired and I needed a shower. It took me a moment to figure out that "her" was the earth.

"All right," I said.

"That would be profane," he told me, as if I had argued with him.

I took a breath, girded up my loins (figuratively speaking), and thought about what he'd said. He had a problem. We had a problem. I could figure out problems if they came at me one at a time.

"We need to burn the house," I said. "I don't want whatever witch comes to take over to start with this house. We can put Elizaveta and the Hardesty witches' bodies in there to burn."

"It's not just them," Zee said. "There are black-magic practitioners who were made into reanimates, too. Rivals, maybe."

"There are over two hundred zombies out there," I told him. "I don't know that I could pick out the difference between zombies who were turned into zombies by black magic and zombies who were also black-magic users."

He nodded his head shortly. "I can. I will. We will just use the wolves to move the bodies."

"We buried the ashes of Elizaveta's family in her garden," I told him. "We found the bones of her victims buried there."

He grunted. "The ashes won't be a problem, though it is

good to know that they are there. And I wouldn't recommend anyone eating out of that garden. I think I can take care of that at the same time."

See? Life is about problem-solving. Although I was pretty sure that most people's problems weren't things like what to do with dead witches and two-hundred-plus zombies.

Adam and the others were gathering around the remains of the dragon. Zee started over toward them, and I heaved myself out of the chair and followed.

"It's smaller than I expected a dragon to be," said the senator into the reverent silence. His voice was solemn and the volume was appropriate for a church—or a library.

"I lived for nearly a century in a valley below a dragon's lair," said Zee. "I met her twice. The first time, she came to my workshop in the guise of an old and mute lady. She brought me a flower and while she watched, I built her one like it of gold and gemstones. She took it with her when she left. Five or six years later, she showed up at my doorstep, and I have never seen anything so beautiful. That was the only time I saw her in her natural form." He crouched down and touched the dragon's neck. "She was as large as a school bus nose to tail. This is a baby."

THE PACK CAME AND HELPED ZEE SORT OUT BOD-ies. The senator and I stayed out of the way—and after a very short while, Adam joined us. I think he was afraid I was going to fall out of my chair. But Mary Jo had given me two energy bars and a thermos of hot cocoa. It wasn't as good as what I made, but it was hot and sweet and it helped. The senator had gotten a thermos of coffee and a pair of the same energy bars.

Warren and Darryl had taken it upon themselves to carry the bodies of the witches into Elizaveta's house. They carried the first two bodies in, then spent a while inside the house. I could hear furniture moving—and breaking.

"What are they doing?" the senator asked me. Adam had cleaned and wrapped his leg earlier—and attended to a few other minor injuries. The worst of those were bruises. He'd feel all those wounds tomorrow and the day after that. In a few weeks, he'd be fine, physically at least.

"Making a pyre," Adam said. "To make sure the flames will consume the bodies." He looked at me. "We have both Joel and Aiden coming—I asked Lucia to bring them after we've taken care of the rest of the dead. Aiden doesn't need to see this."

"Aiden?"

"He's a firestarter," said Adam. Which was an answer without being a lie. He had been hanging out with too many politicians.

Darryl and Warren came out and gathered the last of the witches—Elizaveta and Patience. I shivered. I don't think I could have touched either of them.

When they came back, Darryl went to help in the field and Warren headed over to grab the last body on the patio. He bent down to pick up Wulfe—and Wulfe wrapped both of his arms around Warren's shoulders and gave him a hug and a big fat smooch on the cheek.

"Darling boy," said Wulfe. "Where are we going?"

I hadn't killed Wulfe—just made him more dead? Deader? Whatever. Wulfe was okay. I was tired enough to feel happy about that.

"If you don't let go of me," said Warren, still bent over Wulfe. He'd pulled his hands away, but Wulfe dangled from him anyway, held by the vampire's grip on Warren's shoulders. "I will break both of your arms."

Wulfe let him go and dropped back onto the concrete with a thump. He stretched out both arms and legs and made snow angels. Or he would have made snow angels if there had been any snow.

Maybe he wasn't okay.

"Wulfe?" I asked, sliding my chair around so I could see him without giving myself a crick in my neck.

He smiled, a wide, joyful expression—and oddly the fangs didn't rob the smile of its charm. "I am at peace, Mercy," he told me. He closed his eyes and quit moving his body. "Just like you told me. I will never be okay again." He didn't sound unhappy about it.

We watched him for a minute. But he just looked dead again. After a few seconds of that, Warren backed away warily and looked at me.

I shrugged and turned my chair back to its original position. Everyone took their cue from me and ignored the vampire as they gathered the dead.

The senator began to ask questions and I let Adam answer them, closing my eyes until someone put a hand on my knee. I could hear the murmur of Adam's voice, so he wasn't far away, presumably still conversing with the senator. But I was alone on the porch with Sherwood.

He sat on the ground next to my chair—one leg, his prosthetic, up and the other down. As soon as I looked at him, he let his hand fall away from me. My cutlass was on the ground next to him. It was dirty.

Sherwood saw my look and said, "The blade is fine. You just need to clean it."

I'd stabbed a baby dragon with that blade. It had been the right thing to do and I'd do it again. But I didn't know if I could wash that sin off the blade as easily as Sherwood thought I could.

"You got rid of me before you set out to rescue Adam," he said after a minute.

I couldn't tell what he felt about that.

"Of all the things the witches came here looking to do, retaking you would have been their top prize," I told him.

"How do you know that?" he asked. Then he frowned. "And why did your brother's phone call mean that you sent me away?"

"I know some things," I told him. "Not who you were, or how the witches got you. But I learned a little of your story. Do you want me to tell you?"

He drew in a breath and looked away from me, but he nodded.

"I learned a little of this from Wulfe," I told him. I looked over my shoulder, but Wulfe still looked dead.

Sherwood looked at the vampire and called upon pack magic to seal us in our own little soundproof space. I could feel that it was pack magic, but I'd never seen anyone pull that effect off with so little effort. I wasn't surprised that Sherwood had managed.

"Okay, then," I said. "A few centuries back there was a witch. She was, probably, like these two—older than she should be. Her name was Lieza and she was a very good black witch. She was a Love Talker." I could see that Sherwood knew what that was by the way his shoulders tightened. "And she made zombies." I waved my hand out to the night. "Some of those out there are hers—the old ones. The ones who look as though they are alive."

He looked down at his knee.

"Do you want me to stop?"

He shook his head.

"She is somehow connected to the Hardesty witches," I told him. "They revere her, anyway. Our zombie witch"—I tilted my head toward Elizaveta's house, where Magda was waiting—"was hailed as the new Lieza because her powers mirrored the other witch's. Lieza herself grew more daring as she became more powerful. She took a baby dragon and an ogre." I kept my eyes on Sherwood. "And she took two werewolves. One she turned into a zombie. The other she used to power her magic. That one killed her."

He breathed in and out slowly.

"The Hardesty family rushed to Lieza's house, but all they found was her body. Other witches had been there to loot. One of the treasures they had taken was the werewolf."

"Me," he said.

"Yes," I told him. "The Hardestys have made a centuries-long family quest of hunting down all of Lieza's treasures—her zombies, her implements, and you. Some they pay for, some they steal, and some they have gone to war for. And over the years, you, who killed Lieza, have become the most sought-after prize. They almost had you in Seattle, but the werewolves took out that group of witches and you disappeared into the keeping of the Marrok, where they couldn't get to you. But then you came here. They know your name—your current name. They know what you look like. And they know you are pack. The traitor in Bran's pack told them."

"I'm the reason they came," he said.

"No. They had their eyes on Elizaveta—she was the most powerful witch they knew of who wasn't a member of their clan—and they wanted her. Dead or with them."

"Join or die," said Sherwood. I couldn't tell if he'd been quoting Benjamin Franklin or not. Likely not. Joining a coven of witches and joining the American Revolution were, I hoped, two different things.

I nodded at him. "It didn't work out for them in the end, but that was their plan. Along with keeping the government from making a pact with the fae. They were—are still—all about stopping anything that might later be an obstacle to their power."

"How do you know all of this?" he said.

I sighed. "The witches. Wulfe."

He turned to look at me. "That's all the truth, but it isn't all of the truth."

"Coyote dreams," I told him.

"Your father, Coyote?"

I'd quit fighting with everyone about that. In my heart, my father was a rodeo rider named Joe Old Coyote, who had died before I was born. I would never, as my brother Gary did, call him Dad, or any other fatherly appellation. But I'd quit arguing with people about it. Mostly.

"That's the one," I said. "I dreamed one night, and I spent—" Eternity. Years. I swallowed and reminded myself that they were all dead. No kittens would be tortured here again. "I spent a few weeks in the head of your kitten. I am, Coyote tells me, the reason that your kitten survived when everything else died. We overheard things. I learned a lot about them. And when I finally woke up, Coyote made sure I didn't remember it until he wanted me to." I gave him a small smile. "When my brother called."

"I see," he said, when other people would have tried to

take my story apart. *Saved the kitten? I thought you said it was a dream?*

What he asked when he spoke again was "Why did Coyote care about a bunch of witches? Was he taking care of you?"

I laughed, I couldn't help it. "Heaven save me from that. No. I think . . ." I remembered what Coyote had told me. "I think it was the dragon."

"Ah," Sherwood said. "Okay. Is that all?"

"That's all that I know," I told him.

His body relaxed, as if he'd been braced all along for a hit that hadn't happened. He let the pack magic keeping our conversation private slide away before asking, "Should I leave?"

"Why would you do that?" I asked. "I mean, do you want to? Where do you want to go?"

He gave me a look. "There are witches after me."

"And?"

He waved a hand all around us.

"Oh, don't take credit for this," I told him. "This is Elizaveta mostly. And me. If you ever see me start to give a speech again, just step on my toes. Please."

"But they are after me," he said.

"Don't feel too special," I told him. "They—several 'theys'—are after Adam, too." I looked over to where Adam stood near the big fire where the senator was warming his hands. They, whatever "theys" they were, would not touch him. "And I turned the whole pack into a big fat target when I opened my mouth and made us responsible for the Tri-Cities."

"I," said Sherwood dryly, "am more special than you."

"I am more special than everyone," said Wulfe.

I jerked my head around, but he was still lying as if he were dead.

I ALMOST EXPECTED ZEE TO DROP HIS GLAMOUR. But when he pushed us all onto the patio except for the non-black-magic-using dead, he walked out in the middle of the field and stood there. A slightly battered, battle-grubby old man.

We stood in quiet witness, the only sound the rustle of leaves in the wind, as he began working magic.

It began slowly. He raised both hands to chest level, fingers splayed and palms down. After a moment he began tapping his foot on the ground. Zee in his human guise weighs maybe a hundred fifty pounds. I've seen his real form—and he might tip the scales at two hundred, two-ten maybe. But his foot made the earth shake.

"Mutter Erde, deren Schmied ich bin," he said, his voice a rumble that resonated in my bones and made the concrete shake a little harder.

"Is that Elvish?" asked the senator, sounding a little in awe.

"German," murmured Adam.

"He says, 'Mother Earth, whose smith I am,'" translated Sherwood.

Zee repeated himself. *"Mutter Erde, deren Schmied ich bin . . ."*

He tilted his head as if he were listening for a reply. I didn't hear anything, didn't feel anything different, but evidently satisfied, Zee knelt on the ground. His toe was no longer tapping, but that deep, quiet *boom boom boom* continued.

He put both hands on the ground and began to chant, with a driving rhythm that played with the sound of the earth.

> *Öffne Dich, schütt'le Dich, atme und*
> *schließe Dich . . .*
> *Erde, hör'! Erbarme Dich,*
> *Ein tiefes Grab eröffne sich,*
> *um Fleisch, Gebein verforme Dich . . .*
> *und tiefer Friede finde sich . . .*

"Open, shake, breathe, and close," said Sherwood. "Earth, hear me, have mercy. A deep grave shall open, around flesh and bones deform yourself—or re-form yourself. Find a deeper peace."

Zee quit speaking, but the ground rumbled and shuddered beneath us all, rippling and opening . . . A body near
me dropped into the earth, as if the ground beneath it had
turned to air. As I watched, more bodies disappeared, pulled
down into earth.

"Dear God," said the senator, very quietly.

When all of the bodies that I could see were gone—the
dragon had sunk down sometime when I wasn't looking,
though I'd seen the parts of the ogre descend—when only
Zee remained, he spoke again, this time in a voice that was
achingly tender.

> *Eile Dich, leg' sie zur Ruh*
> *und decke sie im Schlafe zu . . .*

"Put them to rest swiftly, and cover them in their sleep,"
murmured Sherwood, in the same tone as Zee had.

Zee stood up and tapped his foot again, this time matching the sound that had never stopped.

The heartbeat of the world, I thought fancifully.

He held up both hands and shouted,

> *Öffne Dich, rütt'le Dich, atme und*
> *schließe Dich!*

On the last syllable he stopped moving his feet. The sound
stopped. And once more, the only noise was the sound of the
leaves in the trees.

All of the dead were gone—and so, I noticed, was the
garden. It was too dark to really see, but I fancied that a
cloud of dust—the ashes of fourteen black witches, Elizaveta's family—blew away on the wind.

"WHAT I DON'T UNDERSTAND," THE SENATOR SAID,
setting his empty cocoa cup on my table, "is why Elizaveta
waited until after they tortured her to kill them."

Wulfe giggled. He'd been alternating laughing with silent tears—and I was beginning to feel sorry for him. Which just felt wrong.

We'd brought him home with us because I wasn't sure he'd have been safe if I just dropped him off at the seethe. Marsilia told me that she'd send Stefan to pick him up, but it might take a while. If Stefan picked him up, Wulfe would be safe.

"She had to wait," Wulfe expounded. "That's how the magic works." He continued less grandly, but there was admiration in his voice. "It's a clever twist on the familiar spell, really. You can kill only people you are connected to if you want to harvest their death magic. She could have taken them as lovers—or tortured them herself. But getting tortured worked—pain and love bind us all together. It's all about the binding together. She didn't love them, but they bound themselves to her when they tortured her. There is a very strong connection between a torturer and the one tortured. Beautiful."

I couldn't tell what part of his speech the last word applied to. The spell, Elizaveta's accomplishment—or the bond between the torturer and her victim.

"She—the other witch—didn't know my people," said the senator in a grim voice.

"That was just killing," Wulfe said airily. "Anyone can kill like that."

"Anyone?" asked Adam, suddenly alert.

"Anyone who spends three days building a circle, and that kind of a circle takes a lot of study. And has the power to wake it—which isn't trivial," said Wulfe. "Okay, not anyone, I guess. Me. Elizaveta could have—but she can't now. Probably the Hardesty witches—they have some more arrows in their quiver." He paused, and said again, "Me. But I won't. Way too much work for too little satisfaction. If I want to kill someone, I prefer up close and personal." He smiled, and the senator scooted his chair a little farther away, even though the table was between them.

"So not that many could work that kind of magic," I said, wanting to be clear.

"Ten, maybe twelve witches alive today," said Wulfe. "I'll let you know if any of them come—" He paused, tilting his head, but I'd heard it, too: booted feet on our porch. I knew the sound of those feet: Stefan. "—knocking." He timed the last word to the sound of the fist on the door.

THE MEETING BETWEEN THE FAE AND THE GOVernment did happen. The pack—as represented by Zack, Sherwood, and me—hosted it at one of the big wineries on Red Mountain. A lot of talking got done, but no one said very much—at least not where I could hear it. Adam told me that the smaller conversation in the boardroom was more interesting. Hopeful, even.

Ruth sent Sherwood and me a thank-you note—and so did her wife. To Uncle Mike she sent a bottle of scotch without the thank-you. He wouldn't have taken it wrong, but that was smarter anyway.

Senator Campbell calls now and again to talk to Adam. He told the families of the people who died at his brother's home that they gave up their lives to protect him from an assassination attempt. The attempt had to be kept secret, but they should know that their kin died heroically, and he was grateful.

I haven't told him that I think he's a walker. I don't see any profit in that for him or for us. I think the witches went to his brother's home to kill him—and blame it on the werewolves in some convoluted fashion that counted upon Ruth doing as she was told. When he didn't die, they decided to take him and see what made him tick. That fits as well as any other scenario.

Sherwood's cat, Pirate, like Medea, has no trouble with the werewolves. Medea runs and hides whenever Sherwood brings him over—which is whenever Sherwood comes over. Since my cat isn't afraid of vampires or werewolves,

I figure she'll quit being afraid of a friendly half-grown cat eventually.

Bran thought, based on our description, that the were-wolf who had been made into a zombie was Abraham Lessing, a London wolf who disappeared a couple of hundred years ago.

And I can't forget about the goblin king's odd and unspecific prediction that we would need to trust him at some future date. That didn't sound ominous at all.

———————

I HAD A NIGHTMARE AND WOKE UP IN A COLD sweat. I rolled out of bed and began pulling on clothes.

"Where are you going?" asked Adam.

"To Elizaveta's," I said tightly. "To make sure."

He didn't ask me what I wanted to make sure of. He just drove me to Elizaveta's and walked out to the ruins with me. There was only a blackened hole where her house had been. The concrete had melted here and there—Aiden had made sure, he'd told me, that the witches would never come back. But sometimes, like tonight, I dreamed a cat's dream and I had to come out and make certain.

I shivered and Adam wrapped his arms around me, letting me look my fill.

"They are dead," Coyote observed casually, hopping out of the hole that had been Elizaveta's basement. Then he did an exaggerated double take at seeing Adam. "Hiya, Adam. Long time no see."

Adam inclined his head warily.

"I brought something for you," Coyote said, digging in the back pocket of his jeans.

He pulled out a scrap of newspaper and held it out to me. I took it cautiously, unfolded it, and saw the president of the United States looking terrified as he touched the head of a disgruntled wolf—Warren.

"People have been leaving these for Warren," I told Coyote. "Under the wiper blades of his truck, tucked into his hat, taped to his mirror."

"I did the one taped to his back," said Coyote, sounding smug. "He never heard me come or go."

"The dragon," I said. "You wanted to release the dragon."

Coyote's face grew somber.

"That's why you sent me after the witches," I said.

Coyote looked at Adam. "Sometimes if you don't kill the bad guys first, they kill you," he said.

Adam's arms tightened around me.

Then Coyote looked at me and his face lit up with a merry smile. "Of course it was the dragon, daughter of mine. Of course it was the dragon. Why else would it be?"

AUTHOR'S NOTE

Here are translations of the spells Zee used in Mercy's garage to break the witch's curse. Michael and Susann Bock's German spells are subtle, using old-style German and rhyme, with a nod to traditional (medieval) versions of authentic spells. It should tell you something to know that when I contact them for help, most of the time I find them going to a medieval faire or coming back from a vampire LARP (live action role-playing) held in an actual freaking castle.

When translating poetry (and spells are poetry), there is always a give-and-take over how much accuracy we should lose to keep the feel of the piece . . .

FIRST SPELL

Water, be my friend,
come and stay by my side.
Flow, wash, bind, grab,
release the curse, take it away,
let go of hand and this place.

SECOND SPELL

Water, be my friend,
come and stay by my side.
Flow, release, bind, grab,
entangle the witchcraft, catch it,
diminish the curse, decay the spell,
take it away, hear me.

Read on for a thrilling excerpt from the next
Mercy Thompson novel

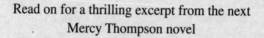

SMOKE BITTEN
BY PATRICIA BRIGGS

Now available from Ace

"ARE YOU OKAY, MERCY?" TAD ASKED ME AS HE disconnected the wiring harness from the headlight of the 2000 Jetta we were working on.

We were replacing a radiator. To do that, we had to take the whole front clip off. It was a rush case; the owner and her three children under five were occupying the office. To speed things up, Tad was taking the left side and I was working on the right.

Like me, he wore grease-stained overalls. Summer still held sway—if only just—so those overalls were stained with sweat, too.

Even his hair showed the effects of working in the heat, sticking out at odd angles. It was also tipped here and there with the same grease that marked the overalls. A smudge of black swooped across his right cheekbone and onto his ear like badly applied war paint. I was pretty sure that if anything, I looked worse than he did.

I'd worked on cars with Tad for more than a decade, nearly half his life. He'd left for an Ivy League education but returned without his degree, and without the cheery optimism that had once been his default. What he had retained was that scary competence that he'd had when I first walked into his father's garage looking for a part to fix my Rabbit and found the elementary-aged Tad ably running the shop.

He was one of the people I most trusted in the world. And I still lied to him.

"Everything's fine," I said.

"Liar," growled Zee's voice from under a '68 Beetle. The little car bounced a bit, like a dog responding to its master. Cars do that sometimes around the iron-kissed fae. Zee said something soft-voiced and calming in German, though I couldn't catch exactly what the words were.

When he started talking to *me* again, he said, "You should not lie to the fae, Mercy. Say instead, 'You are not my friends, I do not trust you with my secrets, so I will not tell you what is wrong.'"

Tad grinned at his father's grumble.

"You are not my friends, I do not trust you with my secrets, so I will not tell you what is wrong," I said deadpan.

"And that, old man," said Tad, grandly setting aside the headlight and starting in on one of the bolts that held the front clip in, "is another lie."

"I love you both," I told them.

"You love me better," said Tad.

"*Most* of the time I love you both," I told him before getting serious. "Something is wrong, but it concerns another person's private issues. If that changes, you'll be the first on my list to talk to."

I would not talk about problems with my mate to someone else—it would be a betrayal.

Tad leaned over, put an arm around me, and kissed the top of my head, which was sweet. But it was 106 degrees outside. Though the new bays in the garage were cooler than the old ones had been, we were all drenched in sweat and the various fluids that were a part of the life of a VW mechanic.

"Yuck," I squawked, batting him away from me. "You are wet and smelly. No kisses. No touches. Ick. Ick."

He laughed and went back to work—and so did I. The laugh felt good. I hadn't been doing a lot of laughing lately.

"There it is again," said Tad, pointing at me with his ratchet. "That sad face. If you change your mind about talking to someone, I'm here. And if necessary, I can kill someone and put the body where no one will find it."

"Drama, drama," grumbled the old fae under the bug. "Always with you there is drama, Mercy. And if you have a body, I can dispose of it in such a way that there would be nothing left to find."

"Hey," I said. "Keep that up and next time I have a horde of zombies to destroy, I won't pick you."

He grunted—either at me or at the bug; it was hard to tell with Zee.

"No one else could have done what I did," he said after a moment. It sounded arrogant, but the fae can't lie, so Zee thought it was true. I did too. "It is good that you have me for a friend to call upon when your drama overwhelms your life, *Liebling*."

And that last was also true. Unlike Tad, Zee wasn't an official employee of the garage he'd sold to me after teaching me how to work on cars and run the business. That didn't mean he was unpaid—just that he came and went on his own terms. Or when I needed him. Zee was dependable like that.

"Hey," said Tad. "Quit chatting, Mercy, and start working. I'm two bolts up on you—and one of those kids just knocked over the garbage can in the office."

I'd heard it too, despite the big door between the office and us. Moreover, just before the garbage can had fallen, I'd heard the tired and overworked mom try to keep her oldest from taking all of the parts stored (for sale) on the shelving units that lined the walls. Tad might be fae, but I was a coyote in my other form—my hearing was better than his.

Despite the possible destruction going on in the office, it

felt good to fix the old car. I didn't know how to fix my marriage. I didn't even know what had gone wrong.

"Ready?" asked Tad.

I caught the crossmember as he pulled the last bolt. A leaking radiator was something I knew how to make right.

BEFORE I'D LEFT WORK, I HAD SHOWERED AND changed to clean clothes and shoes. Even so, I used the kitchen door at home because I didn't want to risk getting anything from the shop on the new carpet.

I'd disemboweled a zombie werewolf on the old carpet, and one of the results of that was that I'd finally discovered a mess that Adam's expert cleaning guru couldn't get out of the white carpet. All of it had been torn up and replaced.

Adam had picked it out because I didn't care beyond "anything but white." His choice, a sandy color, was practical and warm. I liked it.

We'd had to replace the tile in the kitchen a few months earlier. Slowly but surely the house had been changing from the house that Adam's ex-wife, Christy, had decorated into Adam's and my home. If I'd known how much better I'd feel with new carpet, I'd have hunted down a zombie werewolf to disembowel a long time ago.

I toed off my shoes by the back door, glanced farther into the kitchen, and paused. It was like walking into the middle of a scene of a play. I had no idea what was causing all the tension, but I knew I'd interrupted something big.

Darryl drew my eye first—the more dominant wolves tend to do that. He leaned against the counter, his big arms crossed over his chest. He kept his eyes on the ground, his mouth a flat line. Our pack's second carried the blood of warriors of two continents. He had to work to look friendly, and he wasn't working on that right now. Even though he knew I'd come into the house, he didn't look at me. His body held a coiled energy that told me he was ready for a fight.

Auriele, his mate, wore an aura of grim triumph—though

she was seated at the table on the opposite side of the kitchen from Darryl. Not that she was afraid of him. If Darryl was descended from Chinese and African warlords (and he was; his sister, he'd told me once, had done the family history), Auriele could have been a Mayan warrior goddess. I had once seen the two of them fight as a no-holds-barred team against a volcano god, and it had been breathtaking. I liked and respected Auriele.

Auriele's location, which was as far as she could get from Darryl and remain in the kitchen, probably indicated that they were having a disagreement. Interestingly, like Darryl, she didn't look at me, either—though I could feel her attention straining in my direction.

The third and last person in the kitchen was Joel, who was the only pack member besides me who wasn't a werewolf. In his presa Canario form, he sprawled out, as was his habit, and took up most of the free floor space. The strong sunlight streaming through the window brought out the brindle pattern that was usually hidden in the stygian darkness of his coat. His big muzzle rested on his outstretched paws. He glanced at me and then away, without otherwise moving.

No. Not away. I followed his gaze and saw that the door to Adam's soundproof (even to werewolf ears) office was shut.

"What's up?" I asked, looking at Auriele.

Maybe my voice was a little unfriendly, but my stepdaughter Jesse's purse was on the counter and Darryl's unhappiness and Auriele's expression combined told me that something had happened. Probably, given the people involved and my insight into a few things going on in Jesse's life, that something had to do with my nemesis, Adam's ex-wife and Jesse's mother, Christy.

The bane of my existence had returned to Eugene, Oregon, where I'd optimistically thought she might be less of a problem. But Christy had a claim on my husband's protection and a stronger claim on my stepdaughter's affection—she was going to be in my life as long as they were in my life.

Christy's attacks on *me* seldom rated a level above annoyance—she was good, but I'd grown up with Leah, the Marrok's mate, who had been infinitely more dangerous. I would pay a much higher price than dealing with Christy to keep Adam and Jesse. That didn't mean I was going to be happy about her anytime soon. *I* might be able to take her on just fine, but she hurt Adam and Jesse on a regular basis.

Auriele's chin rose, but it was Darryl who spoke. "My wife opened a letter meant for someone else," he said heavily.

"This is your fault," she snapped—and not at Darryl. "*Your* fault. You have Adam, *her* place in the pack, the home that *she* built, and you still won't let Christy have anything."

I might like Auriele, but the reverse was not true, because Christy had a way of making everyone around her hyperprotective of her. Auriele was a dominant wolf, which meant she started out protective anyway. Christy just put all of Auriele's instincts into overdrive.

Still, I couldn't see her opening anyone else's mail because I was Adam's wife instead of Christy. I decided I didn't have enough information to process her accusations.

So I asked, "You opened a letter from Christy? Or for Christy?"

"No," said Darryl, staring at his mate. "She opened a letter for Jesse."

Auriele glanced at the table, and I noticed, for the first time, that on the table in front of Auriele was a stack of mail. On the top of the stack was a white envelope with Washington State University's distinctive cougar logo— and all the pieces clicked.

I pinched my nose. It was a gesture that Bran, the Marrok who ruled all the packs in North America except ours, did so often that it had spread to anyone who associated with him for very long. Since I'd been raised in his pack, it was bound to get to me sooner or later. It didn't help with the frustration, though I felt like it helped me focus. Maybe that's why Bran used it.

"Oh, for the love of Pete," I said. "Jesse told me she was going to call her mom a week ago. Let me guess—she put it off until yesterday or this morning. And Christy called you. You came over, found the letter from WSU on the table—"

"In the mailbox," said Darryl.

I raised my eyebrows, and Auriele's chin elevated a bit more and her shoulders stiffened. Yep, even in her current state of Christy-borne madness, she was a little embarrassed about that one.

"We got here just as the mail carrier left," she said stiffly. "I thought we could take the mail in."

"You found the letter in the mailbox," I corrected myself. "And, given the urgency and trauma that Christy expressed to you about her daughter's change of plans, you had to open it to find proof that dire shenanigans were afoot."

Jesse had been accepted to the University of Oregon in Eugene, where her mom lived. She had also been accepted to the University of Washington in Seattle, where Jesse's boyfriend, Gabriel, was attending school.

Both were good schools, and she'd let her mother think that she'd been debating about which way to go. Adam and I both knew she intended to follow Gabriel—boyfriends outranked parents. I understood why Jesse hadn't wanted to tell her mother—witness the current scene with Auriele—though that had just been putting off the explosion.

But all of Jesse's schooling plans had changed due to recent events. Our pack had acquired some new and very dangerous enemies.

A week ago, Jesse had told me she'd decided to stay in the Tri-Cities and go to Washington State University's local campus (the main campus is in Pullman, a little over a hundred miles away). I'd agreed with her reasons. Jesse was a practical person who made generally good choices when her mother wasn't involved. The only advice I'd given Jesse was that she needed to tell Adam and Christy sooner rather than later.

"Hah," Auriele said with bitter triumph, pointing at me. "I told you it was Mercy's idea."

I opened my mouth to retort, but the door to Adam's office jerked open and Jesse stalked out, her cheeks flushed and her fists clenched. She glanced past me at Auriele and gave her a betrayed look that lasted for a long moment until she took the stairs at a pace that was not quite a run.

I started to go after her and had made it to the foot of the stairs when Adam barreled out of the door of his office. The pause between Jesse's escape and Adam's pursuit told me that he'd tried to let her go but the wolf drove him to pursue her.

I turned so I was blocking the way up the stairs.

"Move," said Adam, his eyes bright yellow. "I will talk to you about this later."

I could feel the push of his dominance, let it wash on by me without effect. I am a coyote shifter, not a werewolf. Adam's Alpha dominance didn't make me want to drop to my belly in instant obedience—it made me want to stick out my tongue or smack him on the nose. A month ago, I might have done that.

Today, I restrained myself to a simple "No."

Adam took in a deep breath and made an effort to control his wolf, which made him gain another inch or so in height and breadth. Under other circumstances, I might have enjoyed a little battle with Adam. I don't mind a fight as long as no one gets hurt.

But Jesse had already been unnecessarily hurt. That made me mad, so I didn't trust myself to poke at Adam. It wasn't, I told myself firmly, that I didn't trust Adam.

"What result do you want?" I asked him in a calm voice. "You might be able to bully her into saying she will do what you want her to do—whatever that is. Is that really the shape you want your relationship with your daughter, who is an adult now, to take?"

"You might consider that I am madder at you than at Jesse," he bit out.

That surprised me for a moment, then I realized that he thought Auriele was right, that I'd done something to influence Jesse's decision without talking to him. Hurt flooded me—he should know me better than that. But I stuffed that hurt down to look at later. Jesse was the important one at the moment.

"You calm down enough that your eyes aren't gold, and I will step out of the way," I told him.

"Fuck me," he growled, then turned and stalked back to his office. He shut the door with a softness that fooled no one about his state of mind.

Adam never swore at me. I stared at the door—thoughtfully, I told myself. I wasn't angry, I decided firmly, because we already had too many angry people here. I wasn't hurt, because that I took care of in private and not in front of enemies. And Auriele apparently saw me as an enemy—I wasn't hurt about that, not at all. Not here where she could see me, anyway.

"You might want to consider," Darryl told his wife in a soft voice, "that Adam told us all that anyone who said a word against his wife, his mate, he would kill."

My stomach dropped to my toes—all the hurt that I was pretending not to feel was suddenly secondary. Yes, he had, hadn't he? Oddly, because that declaration sometimes chafed me like wet wool underwear, I hadn't brought that to bear on the current situation. And he wouldn't go back on his word simply because he was mad at me.

Killing Auriele wouldn't just be stupid; it would break him. *And that, children, is why ultimatums are a bad idea*, said a memory in my head in the Marrok's voice. I think he'd been talking to one of his sons, but it had stuck in my head.

Urgently, I asked Auriele, "Did you say something against me? Or did you just repeat what Christy said?"

She didn't answer, but Darryl did. "I think," he told me, "that he will let us leave rather than fight me. And I won't let him kill my mate without a fight."

Auriele frowned at him. "What? Why? Someone had to tell him what was going on beneath his own nose." From the tone of her voice, it was apparent she didn't think it would be a problem. Darryl glanced at me and then away. He was worried.

"Jesse," I said, then stopped because my voice was a little shaky. Control was one of the things that werewolves respected. When I spoke again, my voice was quieter, a trick I'd learned from Adam because it made people listen.

"Jesse told *me*," I said, "that she'd decided, on her own, to apply to Washington State here in the Tri-Cities. The events of the past few months demonstrated to her that if she goes elsewhere, she will be a weakness for her father's enemies to exploit. I don't know about you, but I don't want Jesse to undergo exploitation by the kinds of monsters who are *our* enemies."

I let that hang in the air for a minute. Saw them think about it.

"Eugene doesn't have a werewolf pack," I said, telling them what they already knew. "Vampires aplenty—but no werewolf pack we could call upon to watch over her. Worse, the vampires are a loosey-goosey bunch of misfits." Frost the vampire had hit Eugene a few years ago and left not much organization behind. "They have no central power, not that I've heard of, who could be negotiated with for Jesse's protection."

"That means that Christy is in danger," said Auriele, her eyes widening. "Why did you make her leave here if you knew Christy is in danger?"

"Christy is an unlikely target," said Darryl before I could. Which was good, because Auriele was more likely to believe him than she would me. "We've discussed this, 'Riele. Adam's ex-wife will not be seen by most powers as a good hostage. Their bond is broken. Most Alphas would not protect a woman with whom they shared a temporary legal arrangement. If Christy had been his mate"—Darryl glanced at me—"it would be a different matter. But if she had been his mate, he would never have let her go in the first place. She is in a very safe position. Attacking her or taking her hostage would net no gains. Hurting her or scaring her might also send Adam and the pack over to teach stray vampires a lesson they will never forget."

Her expression made it clear Auriele didn't want to agree. But they had already, apparently, discussed Christy's living in Eugene. Auriele knew as well as everyone else in the room did that Christy was probably safer away from the pack than she would be living here—unless she physically lived with the pack. But with her in Eugene, Adam's enemies would look closer to home for Adam's vulnerabilities.

When Adam's door opened and my mate stepped out, I ignored him even though his movement didn't sound angry anymore. One mostly unsolvable problem at a time.